THE WIDOW

Rosamund Ridley started her career as a researcher in epidemiology with the Health Education Council. When her eldest child was a few months old, she gave up full-time work to become a part-time Open University tutor. She has written magazine features and fiction for several years, adopting a variety of pseudonyms, and is now a journalist for a local newspaper in Cumbria.

Rosamund Ridley

THE WIDOW BIRD

A·PIATKUS·PAPERBACK

First published in Great Britain in 1986
This edition first published in
Great Britain in 1987 by
Judy Piatkus (Publishers) Ltd of
5 Windmill Street, London W1

British Library Cataloguing in Publication Data

Ridley, Rosamund
The widow bird.
I. Title
823'.914[F] PR6068.I29/

ISBN 0-86188-907-X

Printed and bound in Great Britain by
Biddles Ltd, Guildford and King's Lynn

After David's messy death and tidy burial, Clare did as she was told, and made a new life for herself with the children. She was expected to mourn, and this seemed honest enough, even to herself. Being a social historian, she was well informed in the details of public grief. The Victorian ritual year in black was only the end of a long and carefully-timed tradition. In the weeks that began the year after David's life, Clare made mediaeval calculations: first the octave, then the month-mind, and so on, to the first solemn year-mind. It was, she now discovered, a very human system, pacing the intensity of grief, that begins with the thought: this time yesterday, he was still alive this time last week, last month. It was also an eminently practical system, giving solidity to her changed life. She kept a newspaper from the last day he'd been alive, December 31st, to remind herself of both dimensions, world time, and her own time. For, the moment he died, she became someone else, a widow.

Perversely, she enjoyed the funeral. Having a definite role, if only for a day, is a luxury. As the widow, as the still young and tragic widow, she dressed the part. The cheval glass confirmed that black suited her, far better than bridal white. Knowing this, she already had two perfectly good black dresses. Buying a third was deliberate self indulgence. Women are no longer damned for going hatless into church; all the more reason for choosing black velvet and veiling, no mere wisp, but enough to cover her face. Black dress, black coat, white skin, red hair. Her mother remonstrated when Clare bought black velvet for the now-fatherless Lucy. Clare pointed out that it was an ordinary, off-the-peg child's party dress: Marks and Spencer, age 4, machine washable, and reduced, for January. Daniel's black worsted trousers and white shirt passed without comment. His primary school encouraged uniforms. Clare simply replaced the school burgundy and grey with a plain black tie. She considered explaining to her mother that boys now quite enjoy occasional elegance, but refrained. Instead, she talked carefully about involving the children in the process of mourning, helping them accept the reality of their father's death. Her mother, head of Religious Education in a Catholic college of education, agreed, complimenting her daughter on a sensible decision. For, if Clare behaved well, made sensible decisions and life choices, it was obviously a reflection of the careful upbringing she had received. This was naturally not the time to admit to her mother, who was also a marriage guidance counsellor, that marrying David at all had been the real tragedy. David, safely dead, was no longer the source of all pain, could cause no more trouble. There was nothing, now, to keep secret, like a cancer of some unmentionable organ.

It amused Clare to arrange her husband's funeral in accordance with the rites of Holy Mother Church. In life, the adult David hadn't cared enough about the faith of his fathers to be called an agnostic or atheist. He hadn't examined his conscience, nor had he agonised, publicly or in private about his beliefs. To put it simply and accurately, he had lapsed. But the infant David had been baptised, the child in white polyester silk shorts, later worn for football, had made his First Communion, the uniformed schoolboy had been confirmed. He and Clare had married each other in church, with the solemn nuptial Mass fitting for a Catholic bride and groom. The two children of this marriage had been baptised. That David himself had long since stopped appearing in church, even at Christmas and Easter wasn't grounds for consigning him to civic cremation. As the careful Jesuit chaplain at the university where Clare taught part-time, said, they had no access to David's inmost thoughts. The funeral ceremonies, reception of the body into church, followed, next day, by Requiem Mass, and interment in the Catholic section of the cemetary, were conducted by this priest, Philip Rigby. Clare and her children rarely attended the Catholic parish church. She would explain, to anyone impertinent enough to ask why, that the chaplaincy gave her children a chance to mix with the children of other Catholic staff. Daniel did not attend a Catholic school, ostensibly because the nearest Catholic state school was over six miles away. There was a convent school just up the road, in the heart of their decent suburban village, boys up to seven, girls to eleven. Clare's parents, who were devout, grieved over Daniel, and offered to pay fees. Clare decided to plead her conscience, admit her objection to the continued existence of a private sector in education. It was enough. Jim and Moira didn't agree, but, political creatures themselves, they respected faith, religious and secular. Privately, Clare's objection was to segregation, rather than mere privilege. She might contemplate a scholarship to Winchester or Eton for her son, but never Ampleforth or Stonyhurst. But David, not caring one way or the other, said, if they want to throw their money away, was there any harm in sending Lucy to the convent since, in any case, Daniel was now over the age of reason.

David and his younger brother had always been at different schools. First, the catchment area for his primary school had been arbitrarily altered. Too timid to do battle with the indifferent authorities, his mother had taken one son to the main road, and handed him over to the lollypop man, before turning right, to walk another mile to a different school with five-year old Alan. David's father, a television engineer, did battle with anyone, whenever he felt like it, but, as he didn't consider the children his business, this arrangement lasted all their childhood. David went to one school, Alan, and in her turn Bridget, going somewhere else. David, the alien, was systematically bullied by other children, but he had no friends or parents around to notice. The hostility intensified when, at twelve, he won a county scholarship to a minor public school. Possibly, this separate schooling accounted for the strange distance between David and every other member of his family.

Standing in her pew, with her two exquisite children, Clare corrected herself. The distance wasn't simply between David and the rest. All five were entirely separate, merely people who had lived in the same house for a certain number of years, lodgers, not intimates. She could see Alan and his wife, and realised that they were strangers, whose names she happened to know. Alan, Julia, a card at Christmas, stiff, expensive, overprinted with their address in Weybridge; a card for Lucy's birth, not coyly pink with a cradle and sentimental verse, but a Chinese watercolour, blank, for special messages. Congratulations, Alan, Julia. Clare remembered that Alan was in business with three contemporaries from the University of Bristol, selling computer time. She wasn't entirely sure what this involved, but, she was entirely satisfied about Julia's as yet unannounced pregnancy. Brittle, flat chested Julia must be wearing a 36B bra, and her belly was beginning to swell. She had, too, Clare saw, that interesting butterfly-shaped pigmentation called the 'mask of pregnancy' which intrigues otherwise bored ante-natal staff.

Bridget, third child, only daughter of Leonard and Betty Carradus stood in a row otherwise filled by Clare's own family. At a funeral, the mourners stand united in their grief, not ushered to opposing sides, as in the divorce court. The last time Clare and Bridget had been in a church together was for Lucy's baptism, and before that, for Alan and Julia's wedding. Bridget was a sturdy girl, five foot nine, with coarse, waist-length dark hair; at twenty-four still a postgraduate student, working on Romano-British iconography. Clare, with no particular reason to be ashamed of her own degrees, knew that she deferred instinctively to Bridget, scholar, with her predictable First in Greats. Bridget towered over the small Kelly women. She had dressed in her best *sub fusc*, dramatically black and white to mourn for her dead brother. In Christian churches, she took care to behave correctly, though refusing, honourably, to make the sign of the cross. Bridget had become a Buddhist, quietly, shortly after Mods, but David, her brother, was being buried as a Catholic. So be it.

Eternal rest grant unto him, O Lord
and let perpetual light shine upon him . . .

Daniel knew the words, had learned them by heart, and now spoke them solemnly while gazing at his father's coffin. Last night, he had read the square silver inscription; his father's name, date of birth, date of death. Thirty one, nearly thirty two. It sounded quite old, but the Grandads were both seventy, more than twice as old. On the coffin, just below this inscription, there was a little bunch of violets and Christmas roses, 'with love to Daddy from Daniel and Lucy'. He had written that himself, in black and purple felt-tip, ornamenting the message with a pattern of purple ribbons. Lucy, just four, had done well to sign her own wobbly name. It was interesting how clever Lucy was. She could read easy books, but she wasn't ready for prayer book words. Anyway, the flimsy dog-eared funeral mass sheets were boring, without any pictures. Lucy was starting to misbehave, drumming her feet, and noisily counting wreaths on the altar steps. Daniel looked up, carefully, to see whether his mother was crying. Hard to tell, with the veil, like a beekeeper's, covering her face. Probably not. She cried by herself, in her bedroom, with the door locked, which was what he did himself, except his door had no lock. Daniel felt for Clare's hand and held it tight.

Alan was reading the bidding prayers, a stranger, with some of David's face; the same eyes, the same seductive cleft chin, the family nose. A different mouth. Ten years ago, Clare thought she wanted the red curves of David's mouth, full of promise, sex, love, generosity. Now, knowing better, she would choose an Alan, whose mouth was narrow and controlled, like her own father's. Alan was giving nothing away, staring past the black congregation, reading in a voice stripped, cleansed of accent, of any links with the past. Our brother David received in baptism the seeds of eternal life. May he enjoy the company of the saints forever. Then the response, with sounds of unsuppressed tears, Lord, graciously hear us. Alan could have said, my brother David, and ought to know, better than anyone, whether David believed in eternal life, or company of saints. Not knowing Alan at all, Clare didn't know whether he had remained a Catholic. Living so many years with a man who had dropped religion as one drops an unwanted subject at school, she found the faithless normal. Believers were weak-minded, or women, or both. There were exceptions: her father, both brothers, especially, conspicuously, Richard, last-born sacrifice of Holy Mother Church, the family priest. There was the Pope and all the purple hierarchies but she hadn't lived day to day with them, sharing a bed, giving birth to their children.

Clare wondered now about the absence of her brothers and sister, though there seemed little enough reason for them to come. Alive, David had ignored their existence. Bernard, the eldest, a pathologist, could not leave his London hospital, might, at this moment, be examining the body of some other victim. His Polish wife, Anna, had written the gently pious letter that came with the Mass card, so very sorry, and so very sorry, too, that she would be in court, wearing her J.P. hat. Anna and Bernard were with her in spirit. Naturally. Ruth's absence was no real mystery. She gave nothing away, ever, unless she wanted to, and certainly not her prayers or her time. Better that she should stay away; Ruth would know how little Clare had to mourn. The sisters met rarely now, and wrote only about essentials. As for Richard, who had left father and mother entirely, he was needed in the parish where he was playing curate, and called 'Father'.

David's mother, Betty, nee O'Connell, born in Galway, might be taken for a Kelly. Her black coat was twenty years old, unconsciously the height of fashion, her black mantilla had been inherited from her own mother, bought from the piety in Tuam Cathedral. Betty had given his generous-seeming mouth, but none of her own simplicity or devotion. She made no effort to control her tears, raw, salted furrows down her cheeks, her nose childishly red from days of weeping for her first-born son.

The mass was almost over, Clare noted with interest Alan and Julia both receiving communion. So Julia had become a Catholic. Nothing had been said; perhaps it was in tribute to the coming child.Clare found it incomprehensible. She could not imagine choosing to become a Catholic, nor, herself, choosing any faith.

All that remained to be done now was the business of burying David, husband, son, brother, friend, father. David would have said the burying was the only necessary part. At the graveside Daniel and Lucy solemnly dropped their handful of earth each. Betty still wept openly, comforted by Alan and Bridget, Leonard and Julia looking on, embarrassed, impotent. Cremation would have been easier. The gravediggers were demanding a bonus for breaking the iron ground. Two days of thaw had eased the task, but now it was freezing hard again. Clare, shivering, wanted familiar winter jeans and sweaters, indoor warmth, playing with the Christmas toys. She had, with polite sympathy, kept one secret. Moreover, the press, chasing too many blizzard dramas, as well as the New Year births and local M.B.E.s, had left her in peace.

David hadn't been alone when his car left the road. Clare knew the girl slightly, enough to recognise what was left of her face, front seat passenger, no seat belt. She had been small and slight, with red hair, in short David's type. Off-duty from nursing, she was a better than average amateur cellist, on her way to perform, with David, at a New Year house party. Clare remembered now to pray for her, and the unborn child, the third innocent victim of the accident. The autopsy had revealed that David hadn't been drinking; he, and the girl, and the child she carried died because of an unseen, snow-covered fallen branch. Verdict: Accident. The coroner was satisfied, the solicitors and insurance companies had been informed, and now, David was more than half buried. Soon, the piled wreaths would mark the fresh grave, before they too were covered with fresh snow.

The first night alone. She lay in the double bed once shared with David, weary, too alert, half listening to the World Service, trying to remember lost days. New Year's Day, it had been, two hours into January 1st, when the police, meaning one grey-faced nineteen-year-old, had arrived. 'Tomorrow, the morning, will be soon enough, Madam,' he had said, afraid, sick at the thought of her grief. She had thanked him politely, offered coffee, a mince pie, Christmas cake, sat by the fire with him, watching the snow melt on blue-black serge, asking questions, not believing at all, and so, quite in control. After he left, she had dressed again, passing the night easily enough, reading something familiar, the complete Sherlock Holmes stories, all construction and events, without emotion. She had read the same stories, giving birth to Lucy, in this house. At ten past seven, she had telephoned her parents, asking for her father, when her mother answered. He was summoned to the downstairs phone, from the kitchen, where he had been making tea. 'David was killed in a car crash, late last night. No other vehicle involved, apparently he skidded, may have hit something buried by the new snow.' She heard Jim Kelly's murmured, instinctive prayer . . . 'God rest him . . .' and remembered that she hadn't thought of David all night, certainly hadn't prayed for him. The plots of *The Speckled Band* and *The Five Orange Pips* were sharp in her mind.

She reconstructed a day: Her parents, with less than fifty miles to travel, arrived before lunch, carrying neat suitcases, and small gifts for the children, as if this were the ordinary New Year visit. Last year, when they had come the whole family had gone to a pantomime, in the town theatre. Daniel asked about Aladdin, this year's show, before they had even unpacked, just as Lucy, puzzled, came down to report that Daddy wasn't in his bed. Bed was the place she expected to find him, holiday lazy, after his party. David, alive and well, was perfectly capable of spending the entire day in bed, reading, eating, living like an invalid and enjoying himself. Clare appealed to her mother for help. How many ways to say, Daddy is dead? How much should be spared? Daddy's car crashed in the snow, she told the children at last. Then the grandmother took command, cradling a silent Lucy. Moira, who had given up classroom teaching fifteen years ago, hadn't absorbed the idea that the modern child of four is too young to understand death, or know grief. Daniel said nothing, holding his grandfather's hand tightly. Seventy, and seven, they returned to their game of chess. Clare heard her son say, 'perpetual check', saw her father nod, the remaining pieces swept off the board, reassembled, for another game. After lunch, they all built a snowman, in snow which was precisely the right condition for sculpture. Clare excelled at this, though she never modelled in clay. The children, friendly, without discretion, invited the child next door to join them, and accepted, as they always did, that this wouldn't be allowed. The immediate neighbours kept themselves to themselves, for reasons of their own.

January 2nd, 3rd, 4th, 5th. Then Twelfth Night. Every year, her parents had the same argument. Count, starting on

December 25th, and January 6th is the thirteenth day. 'Twelfth Night is the fifth', Moira insisted, as usual. 'It is the sixth', Jim repeated, not entirely confident, because Moira was the professional. He had been a watchmaker, still did the occasional repair for friends and family. Clare, appealed to, produced her Pepys Diary, pedantically checking every year.

'Twelfe Daye, or Night, every single year, except 1667.'

'What happened then?'

'A mighty dull sermon, after which he enjoyed himself mightily at table.'

'So it is the sixth.'

Moira said: 'Then the counting must begin on the 26th', as if they were the infants she had once taught.

Clare replaced the volume of Pepys, given, for Christmas or a birthday, like a pearl, until the series was complete. Every volume was inscribed, 'C, from D.' Love, no love, no David. Pepys' diary was complete now, the index bought for her last birthday. David's last Christmas presents had been, coming from him, curiously personal. The first to be unwrapped was a small watercolour of a child, softly falling asleep, cradling her own doll-child. The artist had recorded very little, only tumbled hair, the curve of a flushed cheek, one arm, one small hand; only a sleeping child. The second was utterly different. Only David could have chosen it for her; a woman, old in body, her face unseen, a picture stark in colour and emotion, the white cottage lit by cloud-hidden sun. She was opening the door of her empty house, had set down her wicker basket, still carried kindling. Clare, on Christmas morning, studied the two prints, academic, wondering. She tried to fathom David's choice. Contrasts? Two female subjects, young and old, both alone, only one lonely. The sleeping child would soon be cuddled, the old woman not be touched again before death. Curiously, or not curiously, the colours of the second were dark echoes of the first, dun, grey, red and black, after soft pink and whites. Raking memory, she located the original, in an Edinburgh museum, the year they married.

'Me, after you die.'

'Never. Even if I die first, there will be children.'

'Children grow up and go away.'

She remembered no more. The two prints, already framed, had taken their place around the house.

'Clare!'

How often had that happened? She had pressed every day like this, drifting thoughts veiling reality, as if mind and body barely touched. Deliberately, she had sat straighter in her chair, made herself see the everyday room, still gaudy for Christmas, the tree, the children, her parents, anxious, concerned, pathetically protective.

Moira was uneasy with intimacy.

'Why not have an early night? You haven't been sleeping. I'll bring you some supper. Or maybe just a milky drink?'

Clare had smiled, aware of Moira's difficulty.

'Not Horlicks! Do you know what we used to do, me and Ruth? We would make a row, bounce on our beds, anything. And then pour it out of the window. It froze, one night, and you thought a child had been sick.'

Jim, silent conspirator, smiled, revealed himself.

'I knew. I didn't give you away. Terrible stuff. But your mother said it would do you good.'

Moira couldn't scold a little girl. She had no naughty children now. There was clever Ruth, turning out a book and more, every year. And now Clare was a widow. She couldn't find her way to Clare, never had, never would, not now.

'Milky drinks', she said, sure of her ground now, speaking in her working day voice, 'It's a medical fact, there's something in milk that encourages sleep.'

Jim stood up, flexing a cramped leg.

'Then why not give the children just that? They never minded milk.'

Clare was smiling still, waiting, ready to shatter another illusion.

'The cats. All the cats, years of cats. They drank it. We hated milk. So do my children. They never drink it.'

'But a child must have milk.'

'The only milk they wanted was mine.'

Moira would hear no more. Details, no more than details, but Clare was denying precious truths. She preferred to keep to the memory of her children, not to know the men and women, yet Clare, in her grief, could hardly be left alone.

There were forms to be signed, letters to be written, instructions for the undertakers. The inquest was a formality; the police were satisfied. It was an accident, in the snow, pure and simple. Clare wrote, herself, to David's parents, to Betty really, imagining herself with Daniel dead, and belonging, anyway, to another woman. Her parents knew, now, about the passenger. Longer concealment would have been difficult; she needed them as allies. Even so, she gave nothing away. The girl was known to her, simply another musician. They could believe that or not as they chose. As to why David had gone without her, on New Year's Eve, the answer was simple enough. Baby sitters were hard to come by, on such a night, all the likeliest people heading for parties, or giving them. So David had gone, with his flute, giving a lift to this girl and her 'cello.

'In any case,' she added, almost too defensively, 'Lucy had been ill, with tonsillitis.'

Jim managed to object.

'I wouldn't have done it. Not to your mother, not with one of you ill. But there, it's up to you, families do these things differently.'

Clare, writing out a shopping list, reflected on this. It was true. Her father, even in the 'fifties, before the new fashion in fathering, had been the one to stand in the lavatory with a sweating, vomiting child, or sitting, afterwards, gently talking, gently bringing sleep. He had paced the streets at two in the morning, pushing a screaming baby, he had dabbed calomine on chickenpox, sat with them through the red misery of measles. Illness made him angry, but gentle too, angry with whatever unseen agent made his child suffer, but with the sufferer, more tender than any woman. If his own stomach heaved at the sight and smell of vomit, the more he felt for the sick child. Moira was not an unnatural mother, only efficient. She encouraged all talents. Jim would have made a good nurse, she said, without disparagement or intended insult. Jim accepted mess, emotional, physical, dealt with either or both, and had enough love left to cherish the victim. Moira simply acknowledged his superiority in this, anonymously citing him as an example, in her lectures on marriage. She loved her children no less, was sorry, of course, when they were ill. But, she reasoned, sensibly enough, that they would soon be well, and/or happy again. She spoke, with professional assurance, of the resilience of childhood, her way of accommodating the fact that a child has no choice. Moira was of most use when her intelligent children were well, ordering their lives, planning their futures.

The weather, this first week, was January unsettled: showers, and longer periods of snow. An anti-cyclone would bring, not heat, but glassy frost, new treachery on the roads. But the trains were still running, there was a station in the town. Clare tried to calculate which mourners might come by train, which friends cared enough about David to come to this funeral, and gave up. They had a freezer; any surplus would do for the family. If only Queen Gertrude had owned a freezer, she could have bought in fresh for the wedding, and not upset her son so much. Clare, social historian, re-examined that remark in historical context. Funeral baked meats; Hamlet's remark was classic male chauvinism, double standard, no more, no less. No one had ever called St Thomas More a lecher, and he too had remarried within a month. Someone else, in the too empty bed; it was natural enough to want that. If only her parents were not staying, she would have a child in with her.

They were allowed to do everything, before the funeral. They gave her the tranquillisers, prescribed so she would sleep, eat, behave more or less normally. Rejecting help would have been too unkind. In death, they could at last accept the ungracious stranger as their son-in-law. Dead, David gathered virtues. Cards were arriving now, by every post, and by hand, since the notice in the local paper. Clare hadn't seen the point, but Moira was adamant.

'In a community, people like to know. It's important, being part of the community.'

Better not to argue. Moira had lived, all her life, in the same half mile, in a city village. The only, unintended break had been two years at college in Devon. Unintended, because her Liverpool training college had been blitzed and evacuated. Moira had taught for twenty-five years, in the same Manchester school she had attended as a child; being head of department in a college was the pinnacle of her career. She could have reached higher, but would not move. It was easy enough to see why. In another place, Moira Kelly would be unknown, only a woman, fifty or sixty. Clare considered her own gypsy life since seventeen, Sussex, Oxford, Exeter—where Daniel had been born. Then the move up here, her own, lucky, part-time work. David had explained, pompously, that the move was that they should expect, three years, four years, gaining experience. The firm paid what it cost to move. Correction: The firm paid the financial cost. Which was one more reason for gratitude; Clare need not think again about the crude chaos of their divorce, planned for the spring. David had just been promoted, and they were, naturally, expected to move, David Carradus, Esq.' his wife, his children, all strangers again. In Manchester, they all had a fixed identity, a record, Moira Kelly's daughter, grandchildren, known.

So the notice had been inserted. 'On January 1st, the result of an accident, David Charles Carradus, in his thirty-second year, husband of Clare, father of Daniel and Lucy, elder son of Leonard and Elizabeth . . .'

And evidently, Moira had been right. People did want to know, did, inexplicably, read these notices, had him now, could talk in post office and pub about the tragedy. Flowers arrived, cards black with grief, messages in verse for David's nasty snigger. Clare made the first, small step towards her new life; never again would she hear that irritating, nearly effeminate giggle. Then the new widow had to push this thought away, and open more cards. In the paper, she had, invited donations to any charity, none specified. This was a gesture towards the real David. He had not been a giving man, fumbling for the smallest coin that would rid him of doorstep collectors. He was learned on the subject of mismanaged charities, misguided giving, the folly of sponsorship schemes, the futility of most cancer research. She would not lie in his name about a favourite charity.

The family had invaded the nuclear family house. For the last night, before the funeral, Clare and her children had to camp in Lucy's room, the children sharing a bed, their mother, in a sleeping bag, sleepless. Bridget had Daniel's room. The two sets of parents had a double bed, and the sofa, which converted into another double bed. Clare let them sort out the details for themselves. There was no point, certainly now now, in telling any of them how long it was since she and David had really shared a bed. In the morning, she found that Len and Betty had used the sofa, ostensibly because Moira's old back trouble required a firmer base.

The funeral morning began with the pleasant business of any family ritual. It was rather like Lucy's christening, only then there had been fog, not snow. The first crisis came early. Overnight, the snow had returned, and, being off the main road, they were snowed in. The council was short of grit. It was, as Leonard said, just as well the body hadn't been brought home. He managed to say 'the body' as if he had known David only slightly. If necessary, they would have to walk to the church. The cemetery, being on a main road, should be accessible. Leonard busied himself, happily enough, working out what he called 'contingency plans', including an arrangement which left Moira at home, with her grandchildren, as the least important members of the family party. He explained this reasoning with all the dignity of the Earl Marshal. He and Betty would attend, as bereaved parents, Bridget, as sister, Clare, as widow, and Jim, because he was now restored to his former position as her next of kin. This position he shared equally with Daniel, but until the former's decease, or the latter's coming of age, Jim would be the natural choice. Clare, buttering bridge rolls with the other women, asked if this meant that she should change all records, even her kidney and eye donor cards, and the answer was yes. Bridget, asking for trouble, wanted to know; why Jim and not Moira. Leonard didn't bother to answer. He had borrowed black polish and a brush from Jim. The two men, exact contemporaries, shared their generations's reverence of good shoe leather and a high polish. But had taken upon themselves the duty of shining their families' black shoes.

Bridget was doorkeeper. Callers began to arrive before eight, wading through the snow, booted, muffled, some asking, despite information in the paper, when the service would begin, where it would be. Most came with wreaths, or great sheafs of cellophaned cut flowers. Clare, the widow, bride-like centre of attention, would emerge to thank the givers of mimosa, irises, daffodils, and the scentless roses and carnations florists sell in winter at great price. She showed herself to them, Mrs David Carradus, young widow in black, and gave thanks. Afterwards, as often as not, the callers would agree to take the flowers up to the service themselves, to save the family trouble and car space.

About nine-thirty, the council did send round a gritting team. The yellow machine arrived, dredging muddy red salt along their Christmas card road, and Moira was formally re-admitted to the funeral party. She had never liked Len, nor, for that matter, his elder son. The children were told to go upstairs, to be washed and dressed. Clare wanted a minute or two alone with them; locked in the bathroom, they could at least be together.

Daniel had tried to tie his tie without help, failed, and now held up his head for Clare. She found an unseen feature of David. The Kelly neck was thin, potentially scraggy, with worn, hanging skin, like a tortoise. Carradus genes produced a neck with statuesque solidity, the Adam's apple not prominent, because it was so well supported. Perhaps, even if styles changed, it would be worth hoarding David's good shirts, especially his dress shirts, for his son. Clare studied the child, looking hard for other evidence of his father, found nothing definite. But a third child might have been in David's image; it was simply the kaleidoscope genes, making patterns. She recalled a time, late in protected childhood, when she had been quite unable to tell one black face from another, or one baby. Daniel suddenly held her close, his head crushing soft breasts.

'I'll look after you. Don't cry. Please don't cry!'

Lucy was ready, black and white, except for her hair, flossy from last night's washing, uncombed. She roared, horribly, as Clare tried to untangle the fine matted hair that had been lain on all night. They were all three reflected in the large Edwardian mirror David had fixed up on the bathroom wall; his successful effort to make eight by nine look spacious. The widow with her children. Clare remembered, from somewhere, a portrait photograph of a little German, plump, very clean and bald, with two close-cropped sons, in long shorts and sandals. They had no beauty, and nowhere near enough love. Both facts were equally apparent in the photograph. The bathroom mirror was, as yet, less revealing. Clare, Daniel, and Lucy were dressed for an occasion; even Daniel's black tie a mark of celebration, as much as mourning. The children were expecting a party, had seen food, glasses, both rooms made ready for guests. Downstairs again, Daniel ate crisps, then peanuts, before being caught.

'Why are we having a party?'

'It isn't really a party. It's because Daddy has gone to Heaven.'

'A Heaven party?'

Clare agreed. She remembered the phrase, to remind herself how the children had reacted to their father's death. Lucy danced round, holding her black velvet skirt, singing; a Heaven party, a Heaven party. It was only a week, and they were used to longer absences. They had not been close to their father; one way and another, they hadn't been given the chance.

She comforted herself with this thought because, with the morning post, she had received a long letter from someone who signed herself Ellen Kenyon (Mrs), Enrolling Member, Mother's Union, St John the Baptist's. Clare had seen, in magazines, popular weeklies, letters signed like this, but didn't, herself, know the kind of women who would insist on their title, public wives. Ellen Kenyon (Mrs) had been widowed herself, with three children, aged ten, seven and three, some thirty years ago. She would be praying, as would all the Mothers Union, for Clare and her little family. The children could only have happy memories of their Father. She must tell them that their Father had gone to join their Father in Heaven. Clare tried to think of David as Father, with or without the capital, and could not. 'Cherish the memory of their Father by praying nightly together.' She imagined, accurately, as it turned out, the late Mr Kenyon, framed in silver, probably on the piano, and the young Kenyons, praying for him. As a Catholic, she wasn't sure of her ground, but had thought the Church of England didn't encourage prayers for the dead. Mrs Kenyon concluded with a promise to visit soon, if Clare had no objection. Or, perhaps, they would all like to come for tea?

The road was clear, the funeral car waiting. Clare led her children to the car. It was designed to seat eight; there was room for all the family. Driving to the church, the idea of celebration, some happy ritual, was reinforced. David had only been in the way, last time, at Lucy's christening, assuming that he need do nothing, arriving downstairs expecting Sunday breakfast as usual. Today, all the adults, even Leonard, had been decently occupied. Now, they all looked superb, like the Royal Family on Remembrance Sunday. The two men, heads of families, deserved equal honours; Leonard, tall and distinguished, Jim small and commanding. Black did well for the women, Moira, who had grown stout, frail Betty, lovely Clare. Bridget, elegant in a tailored suit and black velour hat might be a winter wedding guest. Clare found this comforting, on her way to David's funeral.

Lying in bed now, really alone, she dared to think of what might have been. There had been so little time left. They had agreed, at last, the situation could no longer be endured. She counted up how long it was, since she had last slept in this bed. Six months, no, more than that. It had been in June, when David was away for a fortnight, 'don't ask where, you might not like the answer'. She had enjoyed the room for ten days, putting the new sheets on, the new duvet cover, bought in the sales with her own money. She'd covered the worn patch of carpet with a rug, three years old, unused, bought after she had been banned from this room. The rug was a present from Jim and Moira, or rather, Clare had bought it in Marks and Spencer, with a Christmas gift voucher. She liked to use such presents to buy things for the home, at least semi-permanent. The rug was inoffensive, a very passable substitute for the kind that cost three times as much in Heal's. It was also useful, cosmetic and practical, hiding that worn patch. Young marrieds should be warned to think twice about cheap bedroom carpet, think, at any rate, of the long bedroom pacing nights of babyhood. Hence the worn patch, almost a hole, after only a year.

David had banned the rug. It had been as simple as that. Roll it up, he'd said 'Or else, there will be no sex.' Clare, for a time, had tried subterfuge, putting the rug down when he left for work, taking it up before his return. The colours were exactly what was needed to bring the room's colours into focus. Also, as a woman with a threadbare carpet, she felt demoralised and down at heel, utterly unlike the woman in the black velvet robe (Jim and Moira again) who had been clever enough to choose something necessary with such flair. She had been caught out, the day David had come home early, and found her, lying on their bed, breastfeeding the two month old Lucy, and listening to Story Time on the radio. That was, of course, the end of the rug. That, though neither quite realised it at the time, was also the end of their sex life.

'If the rug goes, then so do I.'

David had rolled it up, put it out of her reach, in the loft. Underneath, the carpet's scalp was exposed, crumbled foam below, a hint of floorboards. Since then, she had slept in Lucy's room, at first in a camp bed, by the cot, later, in a bunk.

The arrangement worked well enough, most of the time. If Daniel was ill, she moved across the landing into his room for the night. Moving in with Lucy was not so very uncommon. For the first year, she was suckling the child, who would never accept a bottle. Her breasts burst with milk, especially in the early morning. David found this disgusting, even though Clare was careful to wash her nightdress and the sheets, daily, if needs be, to check the cheesy smell of motherhood. David's objections didn't extend to his own body fluids. He masturbated, which was fair enough; he also left the semen soaked tissues in the bed, for her to clear away. Clare, sucked by her baby, did not, at least at first, crave mere sex. She still wanted David. Many years earlier, Moira, loathing it, had explained to her daughters that once a family is complete, the mother and father no longer need to do anything that might lead to the birth of another child. Ten years old, seeing them kiss, she had waited for a fifth baby. A year later, enlightened at school, she wondered why Jim and Moira didn't get themselves separate beds, now they didn't need room for doing that any more. Moira, suspecting that her amateur efforts had not been entirely successful, bought books to leave around for her daughters, and was profoundly grateful that she could leave the boys to Jim.

Until Daniel was almost five, he had taken the situation for granted. At playgroup, at school, he discovered that it was bizarre, barely credible. Men and women, especially if they were married, liked to be in bed together. He tackled Clare, one day when she was defrosting the fridge, wearing a bikini, because the temperature was close on 90.

'Why don't you go in bed with Daddy?'

'Because I don't.'

'But why not?'

'Because Daddy doesn't like me to.'

Daniel, naked, asked these innocent questions with an erect penis, saw his mother's concealed tears, kissed her, and didn't ask again.

Four years, then, all but a couple of weeks. Clare lay, enjoying the smell, prosperous, self assured, of the filler in new cloth, new bedding. She'd bought them simply in the course of housewifely duty. It was theoretically, given constant fine weather, or a good tumble drier, possible to get by with just one set of bedding. At best, though, it was an awkward business, stripping the bed, before breakfast, grappling with the washed and dried cover at night. David, who took Betty as his model, pointed out that she had managed, draping bedding around the fire, all day, on clothes horses. Clare had bought the tumble drier with her own earnings; David charged her a portion of the electricity bill for using it, even to dry nappies, because Betty had managed without such an extravagance. David was barely credible; what madness had induced her to marry him?

So she had stored it all away, new duvet covers, valances, pillowcases, buried in a trunk with old student files. The very first thing she had done, January 1st, was to climb shakily up into the loft for her rug, and then deck every bed in new finery, admired by Jim and Moira, who had bred their daughter in their own wasteful and careless habits. One fresh cover was kept for the glory of this first night alone. Clare fell suddenly asleep, which she had not expected to do, and didn't wake, even when Lucy, unused to being alone, crept in beside her, or even when Daniel joined them, on the other side. They slept well, through the bitterest night in twenty years.

Daniel had a diary, three inches by two, red, issued free by his school, the kind of diary that allows one scant sentence. Not intimidated, then, by too much space, he had kept it more or less regularly since New Year's Day. 'Friday, January 8th. I'—crossed out, 'We went to Daddy's . . .'

'How do I spell "funeral"?'

Clare spelled it out for him, her voice drowned in the grim jangle, BBC evening news.

'Tell me again. I didn't hear.'

Clare put down her magazine, forced herself to get up, cross the room, sit down with Daniel at the table.

'F . . . U . . . N . . .'.

'That spells "fun".'

So it did. In adult life, using the word, she never spelled it out like this.

'Funeral', wrote Daniel, in black felt tip. There was just enough room to add, without help, 'Then we had a party'. Clare, honourably, tried not to read any more, but Daniel put the diary into her hand.

'Read it! I've put something in nearly every day of this year.'

At seven, he was young enough to glory in a new year, chase time. His birthday was December 6th, but it pleased him to say, now, 'This year I will be eight, next year nine, the year after, ten.' Clare allowed herself to read eight days of Daniel's New Year. He had missed, yesterday. Every entry was a different colour, red, blue, purple, barely legible yellow. 'January 1st. It is snowy. Grandad and Grandma came and made a snowman. January 2nd. We went to the Sales and had hot dogs. January 3rd. We went to Aladdin'.

Clare handed it back to him, saying, seriously.

'You've done very well. I never keep a diary.'

'Why not?'

She told him. David, who knew the story, had, long ago,

sympathised. Thirteen, passionate, she had been give a five-year diary, blue leather, gold tooling, had kept it, all the way to June, with thirteen-year-old energy and indiscretion. On July 2nd, writing, with convent piety, 'This is the anniversary of my First Communion.', she saw one line, added to the previous day's entry, necessary secret love: 'Thrilling! Sensational! I couldn't put this book down', Ruth's writing, of course. The diary had not been used again, nor had Ruth ever been forgiven. Nor would she be, Clare added, to herself.

Daniel put his pens away, carefully replacing the caps. He wasn't by nature a tidy child, but the pencil box, a Christmas present from Alan and Julia was still something of a novelty, being the kind with a magical sliding lid. Clare had coveted this kind of box; she had coveted such things all her childhood. They were still, tribal items of distinction, still immeasurably superior to the mundane zipped pouch, or hinged box. Even now, she couldn't work out where the folded wood hid itself. She envied her son for owning such a thing; on the other hand, she was also glad that he was privileged, unlike the child she had been, singularly ill-equipped. The box had arrived stocked impressively with pencils, rubbers, sharpeners, and a wooden ruler. Daniel had dismissed the lead pencils, graded HH to BB, replacing them with his beloved, messy, modern, neon bright felt pens. 'Dear Uncle Alan, and Aunt Julia, thank you for the box, it is very nice and Mum likes it.'

Good children from good homes wrote thank-you letters. Clare had discovered this social grace only in thick magazines, and books about the kind of children who went to boarding schools. Maybe it was, simply, a matter of convenience, propinquity. Clare's own present-giving kin had lived in the same city village, the most distant, bold emigrants, only two bus journeys away. Presents were delivered by hand, thanks were verbal. Move up the social ladder, migrate, become distant, and presents are consigned to the post, for postal thanks. Even now, a phone-call was not really good enough. For Daniel, this was the first year of such letters. He still wanted Father Christmas, still believed, at least three quarters of the time. His Great Western Railway trainset and stocking had been delivered by reindeer, like Lucy's vulgar doll's pram, but other presents, like the pencil box, now kept their gift tags, so the donors could be thanked. The thank-you letters had been written on January 2nd, to give the child an occupation. Moira had not approved. Four children, she had, but so far only these two grandchildren. Daniel and Lucy must stay young, her babies, must believe in Father Christmas, in the tooth fairy, in Baby Jesus, newborn each Christmas Day. Clare should thank people by letter, herself, and let the children have their childhood, bounty from an unseen, barely credible stranger.

She touched her son's hand lightly.

'You're a good boy, Daniel.'

Why say that, seducing the child, back to clinging babyhood, her son, centre of their private universe. He leaned against her, a tall child, lean rather than thin. He had cried, openly, just once, on January 2nd, the day of the shopping trip. The tears had come suddenly, riding in a lift. Enclosed, they were more conspicuous, the fellow passengers embarrassed. Clare had allowed her mother to organise this expedition, for the children, for herself. Her father had driven them all into town, and then arranged a later meeting place. His job was that of finding out, from the police, the registrar, the coroner, the lawyers, exactly what remained to be done; how soon they could arrange the funeral. Clare, taken to buy socks, thermal vests and pants, school shirts, all unseasonably reduced, was not considered capable. She imagined Jim Kelly, small, courteous, gravely determined to do the right thing, addressing these various officials, showing them the evidence he had already. My daughter's husband, killed in a road accident, January 1st. How do we proceed? What do we do now? And, in character, he knew most of it already, had arrived, with the Consumer's Association handbook, bought two years ago, when Gran Sheridan died, on loan, since, to one widowed Sheridan aunt, passed on around the neighbours, and now home again.

Daniel hadn't explained his tears, not in the lift. They had been spared that. The fellow passengers kindly ignored his distress, except for one bone thin woman in aged furs, who patted his head: 'Poor little boy, the heat, the excitement, all the rich food, far too much, I feel it myself.' She gave him a lilac sugared almond, and they parted, well before Daniel could reach the nut, and spit it out, disgusted. Lucy had been given one too, palest pink, sucked it briefly, transferred it to Clare's pocket. Lucy's dislike of sweets was distinctly up market, something to be encouraged. 'No thank-you, she doesn't like sweets.' But it wasn't a virtue, merely instinct, a matter of tastebuds. Lucy, at six months had spat out strained apricots and rice, had helped herself to kallia yekhanee from David's plate. Her first solid food had been a radish, gnawed with two teeth. Lucy did not like sweets, and Lucy had not cried. According to the text books, she was simply unable to conceptualise death.

Now alone with her children, Clare cherished the details of those recent family days, only two extra people, but seeming more. Jim and Moira brought with them the extended family, mass cards, brief messages, from half remembered cousins, aunts, schoolfriends. Setting the table for a meal she called supper, Clare behaved as her mother would, making a ritual out of necessity. She took out the everyday cloth, wipe-clean William Morris, to match the curtains that matched the loose covers on the auction sale scroll sofa; all too expensive to change, now she no longer liked the pattern. Moira had twenty or more cloths, linen, lace, breakfast seersucker, spread for heavy adult meals with Jim. In the days of four children, assorted ages and sexes, there had been no cloth, only a series of mats, imperfectly wiped after meals, faintly malodorous. The William Morris cloth argued comfortably with the children's trays. Moira suspected, correctly, that the cloth was a concession, because of the grandparents, that, alone, they ate only from trays, as if in a canteen. But Moira gloated over the nursery preciousness of these trays, bought on a Lakeland holiday, the year Lucy was born; Flopsy Bunnies, for Lucy, bad Peter and Benjamin for Daniel. This picture was nearly worn away, but still wanted, one of Daniel's household gods. Clare was busy, now, setting out Peter Rabbit bowls, mugs, an egg-cup each, Lucy had Mrs Tiggy-winkle on hers. The meal itself was to be a deliberate nursery menu, bread cut into soldiers, soft boiled eggs, an iced bun each, a small mug of milk.

She had decided to bath them first, and then serve this meal to children at their best, sweet-smelling, in pyjamas, night dress, dressing gowns. Six o'clock; it could be six, seven, eight hours before she would sleep. The time had to be re-shaped, filled with things to do, however unnecessary. At six o'clock Daddy comes home. That was what it said in Lucy's little reading book, telling the time, a time to get up, a time to eat breakfast, a time to shop, a time to play, a time to feed the cat, a time to welcome home the Daddy who claimed his children at the end of every day.

She denied herself the local news programme, going upstairs to run their bath, idly wondering when they should be separated. Leave them to decide for themselves? The brother and sister sex play, curious, less than innocent, took place no matter what. Only the week before Christmas, she had found Daniel with a magazine, an ordinary glossy, fascinated, erect, wide dilated pupils, staring at an advertisement for bath essence. David, consulted, had laughed, offering a detail from his own remembered childhood. Too poor, too shy, maybe even then, too mean for anything else, he and a ten-year-old friend had bought *Woman's Own*, agony, adverts, and veiled mysterious female complaints. They had offered each other such details, over the years, defining and redefining what they were; the twenty hidden years before meeting. Well, there would be no more of that; she had the end of the story now.

Reaching for Christmas bubble bath, Clare was ready to pour it in, then stopped, just in time, to call Lucy. The bubbles could foam in meringue peaks, but if Lucy hadn't put the mixture in herself, there would be tears. And there had been enough tears. She called again, and this time heard Lucy, clomping up the stairs, her mother's boots thigh high. She shrieked:

'Let me do it! You never let me!'

Then Daniel came, hard behind his sister. His turn. She knew, she must know, it was his turn. The diarist knew exactly what privilege had been allowed, and when, jealousy notching every non-quota smile, embrace, kiss. Chocolate must be broken exactly, apples, bananas, oranges, divided, callipered by his firstborn eyes. Clare, commercial mother, loving, gentle, living for her children, as she must, held out the bottle.

'Both have a turn.'

This week, it was Snoopy. Christmas Day, they opened Paddington. New Year's Day, they'd started on the Tardis, which arrived in a cardboard box with all six incarnations of Dr Who.

'Like God, isn't he?'

'God?'

'Only, he's six people, not just three.' Pass. Jim, more successful than Moira in seeing his children as adults, confided.

'Answer even a quarter of their questions and you'll go mad. The little beggars take nothing for granted.'

Daniel squirted a jet of green liquid, the precise shade of their current lavatory cleaner. Lucy added her share, slow, maddening, dribbling down the white bath. Daniel was already attacking the water with a loofah; David's loofah, no-one else had ever used the thing. Clare wondered, lazily, why the foam was only white, when the water had turned grass green. Maybe David would have been able to explain, maybe it was something to do with the shape of bubbles, refraction making rainbow shimmers, rather than mere green. She had panicked, momentarily, but now saw the lavatory cleaner in its usual place, on top of the cistern, where it should not be. She composed a letter to someone, somewhere, maybe a woman's magazine. 'Dear Editor, Why don't architects include built-in, eye-level, lockable cupboards in bathrooms?' Once, even in Betty's care, Bridget had drunk bleach, burning her mouth and throat.

Clare began to speak, heard herself say, 'David, remember . . .'. And then remembered that there would be no answer.

The children had climbed into their brief igloo, and could not see her. She stood on the lavatory seat, trying to judge whether Lucy could reach so high, and decided that the ancient cistern, clanking at ceiling height, was safe enough. David had said:

'This museum piece will come out, of course. The whole lot. Another five hundred on the mortgage should do it.'

'But it's beautiful!'

David's blessed inertia won the day; four years, and the too-short bath still pawed at quarry tiles with lion's feet, the brass taps still had to be done with Brasso, every week. Clare, losing that small battle, had her victory whenever visitors admired, coveted, begged for the supplier's name.

They were old enough, really, to bath themselves, her children, who had been babies for so many lonely days. Seven years since freedom, seven summers and winters of Mothercare catalogues, broken nights, nappies, vomit, first smiles, injections, bricks and worse on the floor, Lego in the hoover, sitting up all night marking. She and Daniel had seen a Blue Peter team grow old; the years were transforming at least one child into a friend, lifelong. She knelt down beside them, on the bathmat, to wash faces, ready for the ritual howl. Lucy obliged. Contorted, her face looked old and ugly. Once, she had photographed Lucy like this, one gesture to the dark side of childhood. On her wall, in the shared bathroom, Clare had hung a photograph, black and white, eloquent, a girl, maybe five or six years old, in a city street. The dress, dark, waisted, puff sleeves, said the late 1950s, Clare's own time. The buildings said Engles, de Toqueville, Dickens. There were no cars. The child clutched her elbow, her face a mask of agony, pathetic and hideous. The photograph had a title; 'Hurt Girl'. Clare had tried to explain to David why she kept and displayed this ugliness.

'She could be me. She could be Lucy. Don't you remember feeling like that, as if the world had become just pain?'

But David couldn't. He was interested, trying to locate pain in his neat curriculum vitae, but there was none on record. His teeth were excellent, no extractions, only two small fillings. No cuts had ever been stitched, he had broken no bones, never suffered from migraine. Once, in their nine years of marriage, he had needed a doctor, for an infected insect bite. Likewise, he had been spared grief, and too early death. Both his grandmothers and one grandfather were still alive, no close relative, or friend of his own generation had died. Together, they considered Clare's record, as if completing an insurance questionnaire. Broken leg, broken collar bone, right hand crushed with multiple fractures, in three separate accidents. Stitches, without number, for various cuts. Concussion, falling down a spiral staircase in Caernarvon Castle, 1969, after the Investiture. A torn ligament, climbing, all four wisdom teeth impacted, three miscarriages in succession, and finally, childbirth. Giving birth, she had settled for pain, familiar, bearable. The family record wasn't good either, one grandfather and one grandmother killed in road accidents, the other grandfather gassed, in October, 1918. At ten, she had seen a schoolfriend thrown from the top of a fairground wheel. Then, a year later, her brother Bernard, twenty, hero, shaven and lifeless in intensive care. Some of him had recovered, and the law had awarded him compensation of a sort for the rest. He was a good pathologist, might have been a better surgeon.

David was pleased with his own painless family. But the record had been redressed. They had cut the steering wheel out of his chest, picked the windscreen out of his pulped face, carried his severed leg to hospital with the rest of him. Death instantaneous, they'd said, surely a lie. Nothing human is so quick. He had died in one minute of purest agony. His kidneys had survived, intact, and she had given them away.

Clare ended bathtime in her usual way, pulling the plug, reaching for the shower knob. The children, laughing, scrambled over the side, rolled themselves into togas, saris, huge bathtowels she had fetched for them. She offered Lucy talcum powder, something from an aunt, safe, what she could expect now, being no-one's mate. Lucy, who liked such things, agreed, and Daniel dredged her thickly, tickling as she rubbed it into every crevice. Time to stop them? Clare joined in, yelled and ducked as Daniel tried to powder her hair, april violet.

The game had come to an end. No-one else would restore order, pick up and dry wet towels, clean the bath, wipe the washbasin, replace the empty lavatory roll. Clare did all these things, even helped Lucy to put on her nightdress. There was no need to hurry, nothing else she might be doing. At least, when Daniel had been made to stop hooting down the empty cardboard tube, put it in the pedal-bin, they were ready to go downstairs. Again, without good reason, Clare carried Lucy, holding the scented child close, as David might. She took Daniel's hand, so he wouldn't feel left out. The evening belonged to the three of them, supper, television, maybe a story, bed. And then sleep.

The curtains had not been drawn. Indigo and moonlit, the sky was on the ebb, lightening, as it would for another hour, before real sunrise. The house faced south. David had said, a house should always be facing south. Len had told him this. The Carradus house hadn't been their own, but Len had been careful to choose one with a southerly aspect, from those offered to him by the council. Their house, built above Parker Morris standards, in the confident mid-fifties, was more luxurious than most on private estates. Having three children, they had been given a four-bedroomed house, on three floors. The Kellys had only an Edwardian bay villa, three bedrooms, shared by two adults, two girls, two boys. They might have bought something better, when Moira's teaching career turned out successful, but the idea of moving was offensive. Jim and Moira remembered the moonlight flits of poverty, which had never disgraced their own families. The respectable did not move house. Furthermore, they did not see the need. Jim, with two brothers and a war widow mother, had grown up in a two-bedroomed house, with a tin bath, Moira, with both parents alive, had fared little better.

Middlewood, stone semi, three beds, two recep., kitchen, bathroom, garage, mature garden, southerly aspect. Offers of? Clare thought, lying in bed, staring through the indigo window, this is David's house. He chose it. She had accepted his pronouncement that a house ought to face south, without question. David, after failing his D. Phil., had trained as an accountant and this new status gave him authority. Much later, she thought of asking for an explanation. The answer was sun. A house facing south catches the best sun. One that looks to the north gets no direct sun until late afternoon, in summer, and little indeed in a British winter. Therefore, a house should face south. Clare thought, now, but I don't like sun. I exclude it, draw blinds and curtains, except at night, when the sky has the stars and moon in it. The sun was her enemy, burning fair dry skin, making lines, exposing dust. And, anyway, if a house faces south, then the back must be north. Answer that, David, why couldn't we buy the house I wanted? You could have gone into another room for your precious sun.

Still in bed, she considered moving. Lucy's round head lay heavily, flattening one breast. The child's face was creased with sleep, lightly beaded with sweat, sweet-smelling. Clare held both her children close, enjoying her burden, the weight of them. They were entirely hers, now, said the law. Widow, only surviving parent, she had sole custody, sole parental rights. In time, especially if she went on seeing little of David's parents, there would be no-one to remember whether or not they looked like their father. Time would tell, of course. She would know in the end, no men could be more unalike than Jim and Len. But without David, more or less present, as his model of manhood, would Daniel remain his father's son? Jim had no memory of his own father, only of buying soup for him, too late, because the train took his father away, before they were served. The camera said that Jim was his mother's child, entirely. In old age, his face was Gran Kelly's; no difference of sex, as in the newborn.

She left the bed slowly, seeing the children nestle together male and female. Motherly, she covered them again, and thought about getting dressed. In her marriage, clothes had become only putting back what had been discarded at night, or finding something clean. David was indifferent to what she wore, except the cost of it. He admired nothing, set her a miserly target for the year, made her include the details, a bra, tights, shoe repairs. Lies were the only answer; the automatic dependent female halving of every price tag, even though she had always worked, paid her way. After a year or two, she had two sets of clothes, for David, and for the world outside.

Yesterday's cold black dress would not do. Now it was nearly dawn, she could see the ice fronds, thickly waving across the glass. There was a radiator, but years of David had hardened them all too frigid bedrooms. That was a lie too: accustomed, yes, hardened, never. Cold ate into her, a knife in the back, cruel, vicious. The children held each other closer, not allowing the cold any space to get in. Today, she could end all that, end the sick shivering, and only by turning on a radiator, paying whatever it might cost. No-one else would see the bill. She remembered the first visit to his home, pretending to be ill, so she might go to bed, with a hot water bottle. Poor David, so cold, all his life, counting the cost, afraid of what it might be; poor David. Because he was no longer here, to condemn, she didn't dress after all, but put on the black velvet dressing gown, pausing, at the door, to study her face in the dressing table mirror, lace framing her pale widow's face.

Moonlight on snow was deceptive. It wasn't quite six-thirty, earlier than she had thought. The kitchen wireless, 1930s bakelite, warmed up, meandering slowly into life and the shipping forecast, Saturday morning, indulgently half an hour later than a weekday. She filled the kettle as David liked it done, measured to cover the element, no more. Yesterday's milk, hoarded for this morning cup of coffee would see her through until the milkman came. She used instant coffee, and a mug, in a style she had wanted for a dinner service. In a cupboard, there was one small plate, one bowl, an egg cup. David favoured thin china, even with a sickly design of forget-me-nots and roses, gilt edged. Betty had bought their china, seconds, from the town market, when she came to stay.

Farming programme, fatstock prices; did the Archers' scriptwriters get up for this? Early morning was her own time, had been, all the married years. Time to wash, dress, see her own morning face in the mirror. Also, she disliked the exposure of sleep, did not want David to see her helpless. Once, on a school trip, a classmate had fallen asleep in a train, her mouth hanging open. They had filled her mouth with paper, and she had choked, almost to death. The first morning, David had laughed, describing the flushed cheeks, the foetal curve of her body, the way her breasts lay flat, being so small. So, from the first week of marriage, she had been up first, dressed, for this solitary cup of coffee, yesterday's paper, time with herself. Events, circumstances, had shaped this free time. She had used it variously for extra work, writing her thesis, reports, marking essays. In the days of working full time, she had to be out of the house by seven thirty. When

Daniel was born, she had still been working, rushing with him to the university crèche, before hurrying on to her own department. Then, for so long, she had had the children's company, feeding them, changing nappies, stripping wet beds. She dealt with the evil buckets, admiring the ruthless hygienic Swedes, who used only the disposable nappies David condemned, because they were extravagant. So she would get up at six, in time to have a hot wash done, and out on the line, before David woke at eight, expecting breakfast. She had read, recently, an article praising morning sex; a pity to waste the fine morning erection. Yes, well, but there are other things to do, catch trains, feed babies, make breakfast. And if David really wanted morning sex, he seemed to manage well enough on his own.

The snow was causing problems with early lambing. Weary farmers were interviewed. Clare conserved her sympathy for the sheep and their dead lambs. January lambing was sheer commercial greed; she had learned that the week before. No, it must have been longer than that, ten days at least, because she had been talking to David.

'It's simply a matter of getting the spring market.'

'Why?'

'Why? Why?' He had mimicked her voice, not so very much lighter than his own. 'You ask questions like a child; what would you do with no-one here? Look, they simply want to compete with the import market. All very well in the south, I suppose, but this hill farm subsidy . . . we pay in the end.'

'But the land must be farmed. There's the amenity value . . .'

'Forestry. It would pay better to grow our own timber and import cheap meat. Anyway, I thought you were a vegetarian? Or was that another of your fads.'

She could see him, half drunk cup of coffee, toast, with two bites out of it, the empty eggshell, almost ready to leave for work. The egg had been free range. David, though not a vegetarian, shared some of her scruples. He bought the family eggs from a farm, or one of many farms. Work often took him to small scale farms, fringe land, sub-rural. He was thinking of taking more exams, even changing his hated job, going to estate management. And he was, sometimes, quite willing to talk to his wife like this, liberal, educated people, casually interested in one thing and another.

After farming, there was news, more farming, God, programme news, and the weather. She drank a second cup of coffee, black, because there was now no milk at all, already conscious of being a woman in a dressing gown, when the day had already begun. Yesterday's paper was, naturally, deep in snow stories. Someone with a long lens had contrived some pictures of a small child, said to be Prince William of Wales, playing in the snow. It would not do for Lucy, looking, as it did, unacceptably like any other child of either sex. She read on, trying to account for the gaps in her history of the world, and remembered that she hadn't read a paper yet this year, busy with other things. But nothing much had happened, no revolutions, it was too hot, or too cold for that, in either hemisphere. In the north, and in Scotland, the frost had held all over Christmas. Rydal Water, Grasmere, and parts of Windermere were bearing. Someone had captioned a photograph of skaters in moonlight; Frost at Midnight, finding some use at last for the second in English which had prefaced journalism.

She lived in hope of the woman's page, saving it for last, like the best crisp in the bag, as Daniel would say. But this was Len's *Daily Telegraph*, offering only London sales, and recipes for a winter luncheon, with due credit given to Lady Jekyll, D.B.E. Was it possible to care enough about food to pack Potage à L'Ecossaisse in a wide-necked flask? She read the instructions for stuffed salmon rolls, so much indiscriminate aspic, Worcester sauce, gherkins, and woman-time. As a wife she had learned to be a useful cook, not ever quite good enough. David had said; 'I couldn't invite my boss to dinner, not yet, why not go on a course?' Betty's standards were exacting. David grew up accustomed to a choice of three puddings, a well-tended cheese board, iced water, clean napkins at every meal, never folded, never replaced in a ring. Betty had married late, and disappointingly. Her father had been a country rector in Essex, Constable country. Her mother, still living, in a nursing home somewhere, had money. Betty had taken for granted, a pony, a governess, the large rectory, peaches in the conservatory, and napkins, crumpled and abandoned, after every meal. She couldn't quite meet those standards, married to Len, but she managed the napkins. She had, wilfully, married beneath her station, and must take the consequences. At first, it hadn't been so very bad. Newly married, Len had rented a Victorian flat. But when the lease expired, they had two children, and a baby girl, and were eligible for council housing. Len could perfectly well afford to buy, but he informed Betty that the subsidised council housing was better value for money. And Betty, of course, had no say in the matter. She could wait for him to die, that was all.

Clare folded the *Daily Telegraph*. Len and Betty had left early, yesterday, accepting Bridget's suggestion of a shared taxi. Bridget was due back in Oxford, for a dinner, at least, she gave that excuse. Len wanted to get his wife home. All the kindness didn't help, seemed to make her worse; no point in dragging things out. He stressed the importance of getting home, as if home were more than an empty council house in Croydon. In his eagerness to be gone, the paper had been accidentally left behind. Clare felt almost guilty, reading it, as if she ought to send payment. But there must be more to Len? Something, surely, to account for Betty's extraordinarily bad marriage, she who had been born to so much?

Upstairs, Daniel was awake, lying, as it happened, in the exact spot where he had been born; not in this house, but in the bed itself. Lucy could go one better, the bed and room comprising her exact birthplace. She owed it to posterity, Bridget said, to become famous. So did Daniel. Otherwise, the makers of blue plaques would go out of business. Clare was particularly proud of Daniel, firstborn, delivered at home the year hospital confinements topped 99 per cent. Accidentally-on-purpose, that had been. They had questioned her dates. Clare, who had miscarried the previous baby in the sixteenth week, knew precisely when she had become pregnant, but was ruled out of court by the consultant and the ultrasound. The day he was born, she was told there was at least a month to go. Dismissing labour as a false alarm, and no more painful than a miscarriage, she had delivered Daniel at midnight, and only ten minutes after David had brought the midwife. Lucy's birth was more decorous, organised at home because Clare had managed all right the first time.

Daniel's birth bed, Lucy's exact birthplace. So easily then, they had returned to their roots, their origin, and at this moment, seemed happy enough, until one, or the other, and more likely both, kicked. Clare, hearing the noise, worried about the neighbours (the party walls were too thin), came up to referee.

'She kicked me!'

'He did it first!'

'Liar. You rotten stinking liar!'

Daniel had a handful of Lucy's hair; one ill-timed jerk and she would suffer. She screamed, loud and shrill, in anticipation of this pain. Next door, someone banged, rapid, angry, allowing no doubt that it might be accidental.

Daniel turned to his sister.

'Now look what you've done! That old cow will be nag, nag, nag. Anyway, I can hear them, much louder than us.'

Clare listened, and decided not to hear. She did not love her neighbours; they were nothing, let them make their own hell. The children noticed nothing, still absorbed in their own intricate squabbles. She handed her son clean pants, socks, vest.

'I had a clean vest yesterday, for the fun. What's that word for burying?'

'Funeral.'

'Well, I had a clean one for it, yesterday.'

'All right, then. Get dressed quickly, it's cold.'

'Then why aren't you dressed? Why are you still wearing that?'

Why indeed? She had to dress with the children now, childlike, as if this were a dormitory. A black, lambswool sweater, trimmed with lace, one of Ruth's rare, generous cast-offs. Black trousers.

'You haven't put your necklace on.' Daniel held it out, insistent, because it was his own Christmas present, a polished pebble, rose quartz, on a cheap steel chain. She let him fasten the clasp, while she zipped up Lucy's dress, yesterday's black velvet.

So it was an ordinary Saturday morning. Every Saturday is

the day after someone's funeral, many funerals, nothing is more certain than death. David was dead. His children were hungry, loudly deciding on loud cereals. Snap! Crackle! Pop! Crunch! But no sizzle, no spitting fat. All week, there'd been Jim's breakfast, two rashers, one egg, one slice of fried bread. He said 'rasher' not bacon, always. Clare had an idea that this was an Irish legacy, but neither she nor Jim had ever been across the sea to Ireland, and Jim, despite his name, despite his faith, managed to be anti-Irish. Clare suddenly, hopelessly, wanted him back, here, irascible, loving, Daddy. Not yesterday, not that again, but somewhere around the 3rd and 4th, when they had been comfortable together. Perhaps that was just another illusion, because Moira had been there too, vigilant.

She dawdled, setting the table with Beatrix Potter again, seeing her children, man and woman, still spooning up their Rice Krispies to find Peter Rabbit. The milk was late, understandably, with so many farms still cut off. She thought about mixing up some powder, but then, the real stuff might arrive any minute. She wouldn't call them to the table yet, engrossed as they were in an Open University programme, the pre-school child, sharing a learning experience with his supermarket mother. They had seen it several times before, but hadn't stopped complaining: 'you never do this, you don't do it *right*.' If Jim were still here, she might say something like this;

'No Mummies really talk like that. It's a joke. They made this programme on April Fool's Day. All children whine, all Mummies are cross and in a hurry. That's the real way to do shopping.'

Jim, in the first years of retirement, had worked for his Open University degree, honours, a two-two, making him equal to Ruth and Richard, decently close enough to Bernard and Clare. Moira was alone now, in having no degree. The two younger children hadn't cared; it wasn't that Bernard and Clare were intrinsically brighter.

Doorbell, or rather, buzzer. That was David's work, the last, rare job he had done on this house. Three years, they'd spent, loathing the fussy suburban chimes. The buzzer had been bought two, maybe three years ago. The first year, Clare bought, and fitted by herself, a black lion's head door-knocker, but callers still pressed the button, ding-dong, someone calling. Two weeks before the last Christmas, David had made the change. He had also, taking a further two hours, with the door open, and fog invading, worked with blue hands, fitting the mortice lock bought the week they moved in. Clare remembered, physically, holding his numb hands in hers, sharing her own warmth. The date, December 12th, was easy to locate, touching David being such a rare thing. The buzzer sounded again.

She paid the milkman, wondering why it was so much, what had they been doing? Happy New Year, said the bottle caps, still. Two were frozen solid, wearing their caps high, like tall schoolboys. The third was laced, with ice.

'Three going to be enough?'

She looked at him, puzzled.

'Yes . . . yes, they've all gone home now. We've had people staying.'

The milkman, in the manner of milkmen, knew that, and knew why, but he persisted. And it was hardly the weather for doorstep salesmanship. Clare tucked a bottle under each arm, held the third by its neck, wondered when it would be decent to close the door.

'No more Sunday deliveries, see, from this week, see. Sure three's enough?'

Not sure at all, Clare said, to be rid of him, Yes, thank you. The milkman wore fingerless gloves. He held her hand briefly.

'Very sorry to hear about Mr Carradus. Very sorry indeed.'

She thanked him, for the milk, for being sorry, and went in to feed her children. Soon after nine, the snow, as promised, began to fall again, and the house became their quiet igloo. The day had no form, no obligations. They expected no visitors, the children could not play outside. She did the only thing possible, becoming, deliberately, a child herself, a motherly girl, not a mother. The role was familiar. Bernard, three years older, and male, and not expected to look after the little ones. Very occasionally, he would agree to take Clare out on her own, but never a trail of little children. Sister, mother, Clare, sitting on the sofa, playing cats-cradles, watching Champion, the Wonder Horse, thinking with her term-time ahead, reflected that this type of motherly small girl must be a dying species, if not extinct. Two-point-something children, two years apart, with the occasional accidental third didn't offer her enough scope. She belonged, herself, to the end of a generation, with families of five and six still common enough, ruled over, in streets and playgrounds by the essential child-mother. Clare had been thinking for some time about an oral history project, investigating this little mother figure, before memory faded. Oral history was coming on well, more human, more accessible than the starkly quantitative analysis in vogue for the past decade. And even the laziest students enjoyed playing with cassette recorders, asking impertinent, calculated questions. Once interested, they could be coaxed into serious work, defining their topic of interest, locating a sample, contacting, gossiping, all in the name of learning. They would discover, of course, that the process was by no means as simple as it looked, but by then they would be getting enough reward to see them through. Clare, mother of small children, deliberately risked treating her students like children, pacing them with carefully-timed rewards.

Champion, the Wonder Horse hadn't changed. She told Daniel, who was sitting on her knee, about watching the identical programme with Ruth and Richard, a lifetime ago. Daniel interviewed her. How old was she, then? And Ruth? And Uncle Richard? He wanted these memories, his own history. David did not remember childhood. The two boys and their sister had rarely played together; being at different schools, they had no mutual friends. As boys, as Betty's children, they were never expected to be surrogate parents, and Bridget, properly close to her mother, had played in gardens, with girls of her own age. David dismissed the past. It was over, and therefore of little importance. He applied this measure to everything; thus, his love for Clare, being finished, done with, was forgotten. He lived for the present, only occasionally for the foreseeable future. Almost as if he had known it wouldn't be for long.

Ruth and Richard, children of the past, were Daniel's nearest link with the past. Richard, appointed godfather, had made nonsense of the young male's alleged disinterest in small children, Daniel, at three, four, five, six, had known Richard's Oxford, fed the Cherwell ducks, fallen out of a punt, watched Richard captain his college's First Eleven, cheered Oxford, jeered Cambridge from Hammersmith Bridge. Even Lucy, female, and a baby, had been tolerated. A reward for the elder sister, child-mother? Probably not. The simple, somewhat extraordinary explanation was that Richard delighted in these children. Besides, as a priest, his sister's children were all he would ever have. Ruth was a mystery. She contrived a living, no-one quite knew where, from her two favourite occupations, cooking, and writing. It seemed likely that she still lived in London; no-one was quite sure, except Moira, who accepted the address Ruth had given.

Clare tried leaving the children, to retreat upstairs and get this idea of hers down on paper for her professor. She slid Daniel down onto the floor, eased her cramped legs, made her escape. They didn't follow her up for nearly half an hour. When they invaded, Clare came back to her other role, Little mother, playing with her children, all she had. She let the weekend pass like this, bartering with them for pieces of time to herself. The snow, when it stopped, had made one more new world, a clean sheet spread over last week's shabbiness, and they played, all three, making snowmen, coming in afterwards to sit on the floor and eat buttered toast. On Monday morning, the new term began; another way of life.

'I am someone else today,' she told the stranger's face in her mirror. Monday morning, time for today, new term, discipline, the working world and another name. University and school terms began the same day; no lazy gap letting her drift for a week or more, making up a life out of mere motherhood. The alarm was switched off, the children chased out of bed, into clothes, down to breakfast, back upstairs to brush teeth.

She scavenged five minutes to do things to her face, add more colours to the shadows around her eyes, brush her hair into careful disorder. Today she dressed as career mother, winter colours, high brown boots polished by Jim, without reproof. They might be ready for the watchful camera, the three of them, the children snug in Aran knitwear, Betty's Christmas presents. At the door, Clare transferred Lucy's wellingtons to the right feet.

'But I like them the other way!'

That was the explanation then. David had said 'It must be random, you simply don't count the times she gets it right.' Wrong, David, she prefers them on the wrong feet. I said it was every time, and you wouldn't believe me.

Time was short, especially as she had no car. Her own beloved Riley 1.5 had failed its M.O.T. last September; not worth the repairs, said David and the garage. All the wet and cold autumn, she had depended, uneasily, on goodwill, on friends, even occasionally, on David; usually, the bus. David's Volvo, which he called the family car, fuelled with mileage-allowance petrol, had been a write-off. Find time, make time to get the insurance claim honoured. 'But madam, this was your husband's car; how can you need it, not living his life? The day before the funeral, she hadn't been ready for battle. But today, as someone else, she was quite equal to it all. Burying David was done, finished. There were, still, the hospital, the insurers, solicitors, all in the day's work. She had one class today eleven to twelve, an oasis in this wasteland David had made. One blissful hour with the untroubled young; there was that to savour.

At the front door, the children began to bicker, loudly. Clare felt her throat constrict, tears threatening; so much to be done, so little left of her own, even the babies grown into these battling children. Slap them into submission? She drew her hand back, not quickly enough. Daniel had seen, flinching instinctively. Clare saw pain, and was ashamed, because in the unloving recent past, she had hit him, more than once, too often.

Timetable for the day: Eight-thirty, walk Daniel to school, kiss goodbye before reaching the corner of school lane, the place for furtive kisses. At seven, the boys were in conflict, scorning kisses, hungry for their mothers' lips. Eight-fifty, leave Daniel, walk briskly to the top of school lane, left, and up to the main road. There had been no more snow, and the gritters had been out at dawn. Nine-fifteen, walking up to the next stop, fare stage, she could catch the bus up to the university, and settle Lucy in the crèche. There would even be an hour of her own. And now, there was no time at all. The children, aware of haste and tension, played up in the accepted way, grizzling, complaining, Daniel, half-way to school, announced a stomach ache. Lucy, more subtle, had left an essential doll at home. Daniel had been consistent in his love, inseparable from a creature knitted by Bridget, called 'Panda', because it was black and white. Lucy, capricious, transferred her affections daily. There was no way of knowing which toy had become briefly precious.

Daniel looked pale, had eaten little breakfast, but he was not feverish. Clare did a quick re-cap. Not measles, mumps, whooping-cough, chicken pox, diphtheria or german measles, which had all been accounted for, one way and another. Holding his hand, she talked about yesterday's garden snowman, the igloo they would build if more snow fell, what they might have for supper, whether it was 'Blue Peter' tonight. They were walking in procession with the other schoolward mothers and children Clare heard the silence around them; whispers, quickly hushed; No, don't look now, she's right behind us, with poor little Daniel. She was invisible, an intrusion, seen, not quite ignored or spoken too. The words crackled in frosted air; women, displeased that there had been no warning.

At the school gate, Daniel let go, whispered, 'bye, Mum', and ran to join his friends. Clare waited, not yet dismissed. The headmaster was approaching; no escape from that, for either of them.

'Mrs Carradus, I'm so very, very sorry.'

She found something to say, just as meaningless.

'Daniel seems to be taking it quite well. But he's been complaining of tummy-ache!'

What rubbish she was talking: how was the child supposed to take death, well or badly? He could hardly say, I don't like this, let's have him back now. The child, in a tantrum, had said: 'I wish you were dead, Mummy', but never the same threat for Daddy.

The headmaster, edged one step away from her; she was free.

'If he really isn't well, I'll be at the university until about twelve-thirty. After that, I have to be in town.'

The school bell said it was time for mothers to go. One or two managed, at last, to speak, say something, that would make her less terrifying. Clare faked wan smiles, hurried Lucy along. Another half hour and she would be out of this mother's life, however briefly.

At the crèche, ignoring Lucy's tears, she handed the child over with a kiss, hurried away from anything they might say. In the library, everything was easy. She worked steadily, making notes, filling in cards. She asked to use the microfiche reader, to identify new publications, not yet in the main catalogue. It was easy to call this work. As a student, she had wasted long days like this, time filling. Now, she used it as a device for changing gear, mother into woman, fifteen minutes only. Part timers were good value for money. She worked hard, but it would be easy enough to sack her, no redundancy to pay. All the more reason to sell Pakenham the idea of an Oral History course, which was why she was compiling this bibliography.

Clare had a system. It had served her well for the past nine years. Moira, re-organising her department had found over five thousand filing cards, pink and white, in imperial sizes. The Education Committee had voted to use all metric sizes. The details of this transaction might not bear too much scrutiny, especially for someone in Moira's position, but the cards had kept Clare supplied through postgraduate research. Open University, and now this job. She had an eclectic intelli-ence, coupled with a photographic memory, but, as teachers and tutor had complained, not enough order and self discipline. They would not complain now; her brain was in good house wife order.

The system was, in equal parts, complex and simple. She was a compulsive reader, browser, academic Autolycus, too readily interested in everything. The system worked by forcing her to fill in a file card for every stray article and book she read. It had to be a habit, to control an inborn defect, just as a diabetic injects insulin; an essential chore. By recording everything, Clare could elevate casual reading to the status of research. It mattered little to this system whether she had read a particular book in the Anderson Room, or Duke Humphrey, in the Public Record Office, or, in her Devon wife days, in the mobile library van. It worked, and that was enough. She used a handbag diary to note down stray ideas, like her irreverent coupling of Gertrude (cf Hamlet, Act I, scene ii) and Sir Thomas More, who had, in 1511, done the same; remarried within a month, that is; she conceded that Dame Alice, More's second wife was no murderess. Students would relish such details, and in the history department they agreed that women had a natural flair for the trivia of historical sociology. She was thinking of shaping all this ephemera into a computer programme, another idea Pakenham might buy. Last term, she had persuaded him to order microfilms of the Victorian census returns, for her course on urban settlement.

Ten-fifty. Time to gather up books and cards, walk through the library maze, have her bag inspected, and scramble across the obstacle course to the Faculty of Social Science, where the architects, silencing debate, had housed the historians. The obstacle course was a partly natural rock and cobble formation, re-designed at regular intervals, an extreme solution to unwanted parking on campus. Members of the University mountaineering club, who now had to travel to Wales, the Lakes or Derbyshire for their sport, argued that larger boulders should be brought in; a couple from Stonehenge would be ideal. To prove themselves serious, they had voted a sum from club funds, as a token contribution. The idea was not without attraction; these days, there were summer tourists, as well as the dwindling conference trade.

Dr Kelly, who had never, except socially, taken her husband's name, walked up the too-steep steps of her workplace, showed her pass to the porter, and took the lift up to the fourth floor. Tutorial, 11–12, Urban Migration, 1841–1881. She had, miraculously, prepared this in the first idle week of Christmas vacation, setting a good example. As she told her students, 'it's not a good idea to leave things to the last minute. You never know what might happen'. In fact, none of them, nervous first years, referred to David's death. They had heard, but were too polite, maybe too young to mention it. Either way, she was grateful.

Later, over a cup of S.C.R. coffee, she sought out Pakenham. All around them, sherry was being drunk, with the greed of the first day of term. Pakenham was a traditional Methodist, uneasy with alcohol, which he was sometimes obliged to drink, or else give offence, Clare disliked sherry, and the S.C.R. coffee was, curiously, very good.

'Er . . . Dr Kelly . . . Clare . . .'

She accepted the momentary pause, the avuncular pat on the shoulder. Widows, she had discovered, are patted, even by men who would never touch another's wife. Pakenham, with two other historians, the Vice-Chancellor and his wife, and a handful of students, had been at the funeral, but had not presumed to come back to the house afterwards.

She accepted, for a second time, brown-eyed condolence. That was another thing, the lightly-averted social glance gave way to eye contact.

'Thank-you.'

With that over, she had, at best, ten minutes to plant the idea, and leave it to mature. The next departmental meeting would be on Friday. By mid-term, if not sooner, Senate would be asked to approve projected changes for the new academic year. It was, now, a delicate matter of flirtation and academic hard sell. Clare's strategy was old fashioned because no other method worked the Pakenham. An idea must be his own, and a matter for congratulation. It was little enough to ask, and he had few other pleasures in life, nor, come to that, much life at all beyond the department. His own special field was the German economy, 1870–1914, not popular with students, especially as Pakenham demanded fluent German.

Pakenham, being a bachelor in the old maid style, could make the job his whole life. Deeming it his business to keep up to date in every field of history taught in his department, he even read abstracts of papers in Chinese and Japanese, disconcerting the International Relations group, who had ambitions for a chair of their own. Although he lived a stone's throw from the library, in a professorial, detached house, he subscribed to most historical journals. He terrorised young lecturers by cornering them at lunch, forcing a discussion on books published only that week. But he wasn't deliberately cruel, merely ignorant of any other subject. Life was simple for him, being nothing more than the study of history. He wasn't conspicuously successful even in this, knew that, at forty nine he would never progress from this chair at a campus university. The only way, now, to enhance his own status was to be jealous of standards, to hone and perfect the department, if that were possible. His interest in Clare was purely academic: anyone who suspected otherwise didn't understand Pakenham.

Clare thought about a second cup of coffee, then remembered that her time was short. Pakenham pulled his own chair marginally closer to the fire, and to Clare's. This was a good sign. She came straight to the point.

'I'm not really happy, Prof, with the way things are going.'

Pause, allow time for them both to speculate about this unhappiness. She waited, carefully, for Pakenham's cue. Twelve minutes to go. The bus down to town left from outside the student's union at twelve thirty-two. And she had to collect Lucy . . .

She had been right. The professor, soft and heavy in middle-age, moved largely.

'This quantification business, isn't it? All very well, but it's getting rather out of hand. It's historians we need, not Senior Wranglers. I've taken a look at some of the stuff your friends are turning out. Need to be a Senior Wrangler to make head or tail of it.'

Clare murmured, the kind of noise that means polite assent. Pakenham was a Oxford man, from the days when Oxford had belonged decently to men. She translated the unspoken message; you and I know, these students of ours are not Oxbridge material, schoolteachers, social workers, local government. We mustn't expect too much.

Ten minutes left. Pakenham's reading, covering as it did the special subjects of eight full-time and one part-time lecturer, was extensive but not profound. It was safe, now, to take over. They had given each other enough cues.

'All these exercises on Ravenstein's laws of migration', she said, 'All these figures, observed and expected distributions, ratios, hypothetico-deductive method. . . . It's very clever, very thorough, but is it history?' She left the definition of 'History' to him. Pakenham gave his unchanging views on this subject annually, to the first year students. Once, at a party, he had confided to Clare his difficulty in passing School Certificate maths. A whole year of cramming, it had taken, before he managed to matriculate. Exactly why he had later inflicted Economics on himself was not explained. He had, still, a decent scholar's distrust of something that called itself History amidst a litter of capital Sigmas, Chi-square tests, and skewed distributions.

Clare managed a casual glance towards the window. It was snowing again which made her next move even easier.

'I do agree, Prof. They could do these things so much better in Maths. Look at the snow.'

They both looked at the same snow, Clare thinking, would there be enough for a garden igloo, Pakenham, pleased with himself, for fitting snowchains.

'Did you hear that old fellow on the radio this morning, talking about the 1929 winter?'

Pakenham nodded. This was better. He was always a little uneasy with Clare, not because she was a woman; there were two others in the department, but because her work was so obscure. Difficult. And yet, it was supposed to be the new thing, cliometrics, all this forming hypotheses, measuring, testing. How the devil were you supposed to quantify the hunger pangs of Manchester urchins in the 1840's, or measure the spiritual anguish of Protestants and Catholics in all that Tudor upheaval? Or they'd have you assaying the purity of a Golden Age. He was safe, now, could relax into a conversation with this pretty woman. People seemed to think he could talk of nothing but history.

'1947, that was my winter. Before your time, of course.'

Clare smiled. It wasn't so very long before her time. Jim and Moira had married in a blizzard. She told him the old story of their wedding breakfast, frozen pipes in the parish hall, melting snow in the tea urn, and the guests bringing their own sugar. They had been given, not as a joke, an old pram, and used it, lined with sacking, to fetch coal dust from the depot, all the bitter winter. And they had managed not to have Bernard for another two years, despite going to bed to keep warm, despite being good Catholics. She told Pakenham her own winter's tale, from 1963.

'The budgie died, on Boxing Day, 1962. And the ground was already too hard to dig. My brother buried him in the snow, and we found the body on March 23rd when the thaw came, absolutely fresh. Bernard fed him to the cat. No . . . seriously, I want to talk to you about oral history. The voice of the past. Living memory is the fragile history of ordinary people. And there's really no other record of their lives; not from that viewpoint. All we know now is interpretation and the middle-class gloss.'

Five minutes. Pakenham was suspicious of 'pop' history, clever young men turning history into entertainment in peak viewing time. No-one had ever invited him to present a series, or even a single late night programme. He let Clare talk, suspicious, all the while, of the soft option.

It was an interesting idea. He's often thought this, especially when watching Dr Who, alone, in his big empty house. What would a historian give for a Tardis, crossing the dimension of time, even just for a chat, dinner, coming home safely? Simply going back would remove so much idle speculation. All the unresolved mysteries could be solved, if the right people could be rounded up, asked a few blunt questions. On the other hand, it would spoil so many useful pot-boilers, like the Princes in the Tower, and the death of Napoleon. And in his own field, even time travel would probably confuse matters still further. The essays he'd set for the Christmas vacation . . .

One minute. Clare stood up.

'So you think there's some value in it, Prof? The basis of a real discipline, not just entertainment?'

She knew, and so must he, that many perfectly respectable universities already taught oral history; she wasn't suggesting anything outrageous. And it was time to go. The snow was falling heavily now, ready to block more roads, close the schools, kill more lambs and generally make life memorable, a winter for the history books, stories for Clio's gossip column.

Pakenham brought out his diary, cleared his throat, embarrassed.

'Err, I know life is . . . must be . . . rather difficult . . . things to be done. But we must talk again. Thursday afternoon, after lunch, at my house?'

Clare, knowing they would be safe, offered him her cards.

'Ideas for the bibliography, if we decide to start a course.' That was dangerous, perhaps better unsaid, but, no matter, it was done now.

The legal business all took less time than she'd expected. Solicitors, insurers, hospital social workers know death is routine, all in a day's work. David, careful, meticulous David had agreed to make a will, when they bought their first house. So had she; still lovers, they had left almost everything to each other. The flute was bequeathed to Bridget. He had also, at twenty-four, self-important, left £1,000, inherited from his grandfather, to fund a prize, at his old college, the money to be used to visit the Salzburg Festival.

'One day, I'm going to take you to Austria.'

'Why?'

'Because you must come to Salzburg.'

And now, the clever, unknown students would go, at David's expense. He hadn't bothered to make a fresh will, when the children were born. They had an endowment policy each, for their eighteenth birthdays, that was all. Clare agreed, readily, to draw up a new will; she believed in death now.

The car insurance was up to date. The police escort, and the inquest verdict simplified matters: David hadn't been drinking, there was no evidence of negligence; brakes, steering and tyres were all in good order, and anyway, the car was hardly five months old, bought for the new registration. She listened, learned, signed, made new appointments. She was comforted by one small, significant detail. The mortgage protection policy was up to date, paid by her, with her own earnings. David had said this was only reasonable; Clare would benefit if he died, therefore she should pay. There was no easy conversational way of finding out whether most, or any other husbands shared this view.

No matter; this time the insurance gamble had paid off. Lost, one husband, gained, one mortgage. It was no great sum, only their original loan, taken out in the late seventies. Since then, moving north, they had been able to trade up merely using their profit from the Exeter sale. And you could see why, said David, nastily, when they came up house hunting. It was company policy to move staff around, gaining experience. David, with one blatant failure behind him was in no position to object. This job, as Len liked reminding him, was the second chance; he must make the most of it. Poor David, who had known so much glory, scholarships to public school, and then Oxford, my eldest boy, the physicist, come to this. Poor David, who had never settled here, looking ahead, in hope, to the next move, knowing full well that Clare would say: you go, I'm staying here, this suits me. Now David was dead, accidentally, the insurers were ready to pay up. It had all been arranged, protection for the widow and her children.

'I wouldn't move anywhere, you know. I mean, not just anywhere. Not Manchester, or Birmingham, nowhere like that. There's the children to think of.'

'And what about me? What about my job? Don't I matter?' Then the jeering note in his voice, not looking at her.

'Oh, yes, of course. I tell them, sorry, we can't move, my wife has a part-time job. Wonderful.'

The people she saw, all afternoon, were professionally kind, finding sweets for Lucy, beautiful Victorian lavatories in the solicitors chambers, a cup of tea from the hospital social worker, who told her that, after all, there would be no charge for treating David's passenger, who had lived for half an hour. The insurance firm found Lucy a comic, and two chocolate novelties, from the staff Christmas tree, unluckily left standing; didn't they know about Twelfth Night? Clare was labelled, Widow, recent, handle with care. Lucy was a poor little thing, poor lamb; at the hospital, poor wee hen. After all this kindness, it was a shock to emerge into the cold, silent, hurrying crowds, their Christmas smiles worn out. Feeling rich, because of the insurance, Clare took a taxi from town to Daniel's school, asked him to wait, and took her family home. She gave a generous tip, because he hadn't exercised his right to charge more for extra passengers. He was a local man, knew what had happened, knew what she was.

Daniel, man of the house, closed the door, Lucy, who had enjoyed herself hugely all day, told Daniel about the sweets, the comic, the Christmas novelty, and he, a child again, wailed; it's not fair. Clare produced from her handbag the second foil-wrapped Father Christmas. She became her other self again, only Clare, their mother.

In the night, Daniel came trembling and crying to her bed. She accepted him, cold and frightened as he was, waiting patiently until he could speak.

'Make them stop! I don't like it. I'm scared.'

The snow had stopped hours ago. Outside there was only silence. It wasn't the time for cats; that would be February. A bad dream then? She held him close.

'It's alright, darling. You're safe.' But he clung to her, still crying.

'Can't you hear them?'

Then she did hear. She had the outside wall, with Lucy. Daniel's room and the bathroom having the party wall. Lucy came now, bewildered.

'They're fighting.'

Clare, in bed, safely with her children, listened. A child cried, a high shrill of terror, unbearably sad. The blows—blows, not banging; she had not been deceived, the other time, came hard, flesh pounding flesh, a woman's tears, ugly words, a low scream of pure agony.

'It's all right. You're safe. Go to sleep.'

She remembered the title of a book. *Scream quietly, or the neighbours will hear*. The woman screamed once more, then there was silence. Clare fell asleep, thinking, no one helped me; I was crying, all the time, no one came. And this is none of my business.

Daniel built an igloo. The dome fell in, three times. Clare, tired of marking plagiarised first year essays, came out to help.

'Those wretched students, they copy things word for word; do they seriously think I can't recognise Hobsbawm and Asa Briggs? If they'd acknowledge things, I wouldn't mind so much, but there's no bibliography, nothing.' Her son nodded sympathetically. Copying was discouraged at school, though it seemed a good way of getting things right. And you were supposed to copy dictionaries. Even so, he had come to understand this academic inconsistency at an early age. He had, from time to time, met Clare's students, wondering which couldn't spell, which couldn't write a sentence, never answered the question at all. He was always polite to them though. After all, his own teacher couldn't spell. Daniel knew more about grown ups than most of his friends ever would, and it was Clare's fault.

'Never mind the wretched students now. Tell me how I finish this thing.' Clare stood inside the igloo, which looked like an egg with the top spooned off. Daniel had his father's dogged persistence. Merely pressing together a snow wall wasn't good enough. He had shaped snow bricks, more or less rectangular, recruiting schoolfriends to help. The friends, tired and hungry, with red stiff hands, had gone home, but Daniel was determined to finish the job. The year had been all snow, so far, but, being seven now, he knew this might not last, must be enjoyed, because tomorrow might be too late. He explained this to Clare.

'*Carpe diem.*'

She remembered with irritation, that he was Daniel, and wouldn't understand; contrived a translation.

'But that's lots of words. You only said two before.'

She offered another, somewhat better version, and told him that the original would do; people would know what he meant, added, for no good reason; Horace. 'A roman poet. You can read his poems when you know some Latin.'

Suggest no difficulties, that was her policy with Daniel. Given the idea that knowing Latin would simply take time, he would contrive to learn Latin, if he still wanted to, in or out of school. He had a greedy brain, like Richard's.

'I know, we could make a flat roof.'

Clare agreed, and together, they contrived a roof of sorts, from bean poles, laid crossways, for joists, then a skin of polythene sheeting, a thatch of old pea-sticks, then a crust of snow, patted and shaped almost into a dome. By the time they had finished, it was quite dark.

'When's Lucy coming home?'

They were crouched inside the igloo, a white womb.

'Soon. When the party's over. Cressida's Daddy will bring her.'

'It's not fair! Why wasn't I invited?'

'She's Lucy's friend. They didn't want big boys at the party.'

'They wanted me last year; I remember.'

Clare was crawling out, cold, tired of being a child.

'Last year was last year. You're older now.'

Daniel seemed satisfied, even though it was no explanation. And at their gate, little girls, party girls, danced in the snow, twirled party frocks, patted balloons on strings, blew squeakers. They moved in formation, chanted the words of a rhyme no-one would every teach him. He needed no other explanation. They were girls, he was a boy. The birthday child, Cressida, was five, bossy, important, a girl born to rule in the streets, claim an end wall for bouncing balls, skirt in her knickers, born to take small brothers and sister to pee behind a bush or down a grid, to fetch chips, laundry, a quarter of tea. She had the voice for it, nothing to do with accent, the knowing, female look, born a woman. All wasted. She was the second child of two in a completed family, boy, girl. Her father a Civil Servant, had arranged his vasectomy the day she was born.

Clare thanked Cressida's Daddy. It was too dark to see whether he was actually wearing his vasectomy tie. She helped him to re-load the van with small girls. Lucy had a balloon, a prize, which was a Matchbox model of a tractor shovel, authentically ugly and yellow. She had too a slice of cake for Daniel, and a small tube of Smarties. The balloon bore the message; Happy Birthday Cressida, 5 Today!

On the doorstep, Lucy stopped, groaned, heaved, and was sick, several times. Daniel stood by, interested.

'Red sick. Is that jelly, Lucy?'

Lucy wailed, was sick again, and clung to her mother. The vomit had splashed all over her good wool coat, onto Clare, and copiously down the party dress. Another whimper was followed by long painful retching. Lucy produced one more mouthful of vomit and collapsed.

'Get out of my way!'

Clare pushed Daniel roughly aside, carrying Lucy. In the hall, on the carpet, Lucy vomited again. Clare hissed obscenities, fought the rising bile in her own throat. Under the beeches, May sunlight dappling his arms, close around her, she told David: No. I can't. You see, I couldn't ever have children, because they're sick. And I can't bear people being sick.' Then he had laughed.

'Our children won't be sick. Marry me?'

Well, David, where are you now? Lucy's heaving her guts out, Daniel's tired and hungry, after building an igloo till the stars came out. Bugger you, David. She was crying a little herself now. It was true, what she had told David. She was afraid of sickness, could remember, in nasty detail, the last time she had been sick herself, the cry of misery, like Lucy's, the whole body given up to heaving and foulness. In the cold hard corner of her mind that had schemed in the S.C.R., she stored a message: No more parties, not at this price. If this is the price, I'm not paying again.

Daniel had remembered Jim's parting words. He was the man of the house. He came, now, staggering, with a bucket of water, sloshed it over the step, and went back for more. Clare had no time to be grateful. Lucy couldn't walk, not now. She was a heavy, foul-smelling burden, to be carried upstairs, stripped, sponged clean. Half way through this procedure, she began to retch and moan again. Clare made her kneel by the bath, her little damp head over the side, as if sea-sick. The last retching produced only bile, tinged with blood. At last, the child was still. Clare washed her small hot hands and face, covered her with a towel. Daniel, stolid beloved Daniel was still washing the step, shovelling dirty snow onto the front lawn. She could hear the swish of a brush.

Clare stripped off her own clothes, thick with vomit, walked, naked through the house, to the washing machine. She knew what to do now, no longer the squeamish girl laughing under May beeches. Rinse cycle, to get the worst of the mess off. Time to sort out programmes later. At the sink, she washed her hands again, splashed her face with cold water. She felt sick herself now, but she knew this nausea; only her sorrow for the child who had suffered.

Lucy, scented with lavender, dressed in an old nightgown, was carried to bed. She whispered, weakly.

'I'm sorry, Mummy', and slept. Clare left a bucket at her bedside, though there could surely be nothing left inside by now. Downstairs again, she took a bowl, J-cloths, floral disinfectant, and cleared up the mess on the hall carpet. Daniel had already cleaned up the worst of it. Ready to flop, she remembered Lucy's coat, sponged it clean, recalled the useful hint that soda water was good for evil smells. She was grateful for left-over Christmas soda. Then, finally, she remembered why it was that there was left over soda, whisky no one would drink. When she collapsed, at last, onto the sofa, Daniel whispered,

'I'm hungry. You didn't give me any supper.'

She made him cheese on toast, and fell asleep, in her dressing gown, woke, on the sofa, with Daniel, at half past five. They took each other up to bed, for the rest of the night.

Morning was Friday. The day still had, undeserved, its festive air, and for no good reason. It was weekends she'd come to dread, the enforced retreat into real life. Lucy woke early, hungry, but Clare would allow no breakfast, only orange juice; teach her not to be so greedy. Daniel ate bread and Marmite, six slices, because, once more, there was no milk, and he rejected powder. He ate quickly, in front of Lucy, talking with his mouth full, gently nagging Clare to have at least a cup of coffee.

'You need something, on a day like this.' So she obeyed.

The day was all freezing fog, nothing else existed. There was no sun to light the hoar frost. After the scuffle to be out, there was time, after all, to pause, wonder at the lovely unnatural flowers the frost had made. Lucy held one in her bare warm hand.

'I didn't know God made flowers out of ice.'

Clare, before motherhood, hadn't believed that children would really say such things.

'David, you know what Lucy said today? . . . Children must have a First Cause; they want us to be omniscient, and when they find us out, they go on looking.'

Don't kid yourself, she sneered, checking that the keys were in her bag before locking the door; don't kid yourself, the real David stopped listening, how many years ago? So don't make friends with this ghost. The children slid down the path. Next door, someone had put salt down, had piled snow on either side of the path, dark scar across so much white. And, next door, an arm, in a cord housecoat, came round the door, only to take in the milk.

Five days, now, a school week, so they were used to her, used to the children. All three really looked normal. Some even spoke to her of other things, the school pantomime, performed by the P.T.A. and their children. Clare remembered Moira's unveiled distaste for the P.T.A., her pitying tolerance for 'the mothers', which was, partly, why she wasn't taking part. Even so, she had been flattered, two years ago, when they tried to recruit her. They were sweet, gentle women, or very deceitful. They were worried, now, not about the weather, or sudden death, but about something that should be in their grasp; costumes. All the easy promises had come to nothing.

'If it's just a question of straight sewing, cutting out, I can run up a few. But my machine doesn't do tricks.'

'Tricks?'

Stupid of her, that wasn't the way to talk to these nice women. Thick, David would call them, slow on the uptake. Clare corrected herself.

'I mean, it only does straight stitch. It's very old, you see.'

The woman she was talking to couldn't be more than four feet nine. Clare was used to feeling small, even frail, married to David, and working in a place full of men, but this woman was only bones, her face caved in like an octogenarian. She had no teeth in, and so lisped.

'You really can thew, then? Put in thipth, and all?'

Clare nodded. She thought of saying, my father taught me, even showed me how to set out a pattern. Better not. There was too much explanation involved, why it should be Jim, and not Moira. Moira knew that a needle has one end sharper than the other. She could, just, sew on buttons, crooked, and had survived her daughters' drooping hems with the help of a staple gun. When she remembered to tell Jim about these crises, he would sit by the window, patiently making his children's clothes fit to be seen. He had taught all four of them to hem, seam, fit a zip, exactly as he had taught them to mend a fuse, change a washer, or a flat tyre.

'Nithe to be clever!'

Clare said, truthfully, that there was very little to it. She supposed, correctly, that the woman didn't mean whatever she did at the university. Working at the university meant cleaning, or washing up, refectory plates, or laboratory glassware. She could place this woman now, mother of three small, thin children, who lived in the house on the edge of the council estate. Attached to her skinniness was evidence of a fourth child. Clare, taken in hand by this thin and toothless mother, was presented to the pantomime producer and the Chairman of the P.T.A. Daniel lingered, mildly curious about this new departure. Clare got rid of him easily enough; all the other women were surreptitiously kissing children, handling over lunch boxes, late dinner money.

'Mithith Carraduth can make cothtumeth.'

Clare, in a vile temper, angry with herself, snapped,

'Clare. Actually, I'm not called Carradus. My name's Kelly.'

'Kelly? but . . .'

The circle around her grew. Daniel heard the school bell, reluctantly left to join his classmates. Clare was his own property now. He resented her sudden notoreity. A school gate mother should be seen, not heard, should dress like the ladies who read the news, should never, ever kiss or slap in public. And lavish praise for a bad painting or clumsy model was worse than indifference. Daniel had heard the word pantomime early in Clare's conversation with Wayne Dixon's mum. It could've been worse. John McBride's mum was Cinderella, and ended up kissing Emma Wilson's mum. Stupid, women kissing women. Yesterday, there'd been a fight, because Wayne said his mum said Emma's mum had bad breath. Emma had bit him, which was only fair. But just making costumes might be safe enough. She might even let him have a go, turning the handle. When Daniel, an obedient boy, fell into line, he remembered that there had been no kiss, too busy yacking with Mrs Sterne, looks like a worm.

'Just Kelly', Clare repeated.

'But you are married, aren't you? I mean, the kids are Carradus, aren't they?'

Then, falling silent, they seemed to remember that Clare, if she had been, was no longer married. It was her turn to be kind, rescue them from this embarrassment she had caused, make light of it, laugh at herself.

'It was all Women's Lib when we got married, no wearing a ring, no taking his name, nothing. I gave in about the ring; pity, David said, it'd save a bit of money if more woman had that idea. But I've always been Kelly, except at home. And there's not much point changing now, is there? As for the kids—well, why shouldn't they have my name? They're mine as much as his.'

Someone, interested, chipped in,

'There's the Queen. The family have her name, not his'

Someone else, insistent, said,

'But your two are Carradus, aren't they?'

Clare, desperate, smiled and agreed, yes, they were, added that it was an awful name to have, no-one could spell it. They were on her side now. She had conceded nothing, reminded them that David was dead. Add female chauvinism, patriotic allusions, and she couldn't lose. It was wonderful what you could do with words.

'Where are these costumes then?'

The three or four women, all trying to claim her at once, told her how to buy, if not actually make friends. She remembered the ten o'clock tutorial, and another session with Pakenham.

'Yes, well, could someone bring the material round? I've no car at the moment. Come on, Lucy.'

A voice, the voice of a woman with nothing to do but the breakfast dishes, tried to call her back, but Clare was gone.

Lazy little sods, she thought, at twenty past ten, when her three competing campus lords still hadn't turned up. This term, Urquart, the Registrar was investigating attendance. Nothing was actually compulsory; it wasn't the students who were being watched like delinquent fourth formers. Clare, and she wasn't alone in this, suspected that it was the staff who were on trial. The Bolognese pattern, as Fraser said, knowing perfectly well that this remark would mystify anyone outside the history department; come to that, would mystify everyone except Clare and the other mediaevalist. Fraser had been promoted to Reader, a year ago, and knew perfectly well that he was the compromise candidate. The only other mediaevalist was still on minimum salary, an under-sized, over-clever young man, with a starred first and far too many prizes. He had already published two books, at twenty-six, and his third paper had just been accepted by the English Historical Review.

Clare understood all too well this reference to the student-orientated organisation of the University of Bologna, in its early days. Fraser dismissed her as a mine of useless information, an open cast mine, without depth. She had published nothing serious; indeed, what she taught could scarcely be defined as history at all. He discounted, absolutely, her contributions to Open University texts. Nevertheless, he did all this benignly, because he liked to have women about, especially pretty ones.

Any minute now, and Urquart's minion would be arriving to collect the attendance figures. Kelly, part-timer, students voting with their feet to have the course scrapped. It was so bloody unfair. At their age, she too had regarded a ten o'clock start as dawn. There had been rumours of nine o'clock lectures, but these she had never investigated. And now . . . children to get up, fed, out of school, nine forty-five, she had hared up to the photo-copier, to collect copies of notes she'd made for this tutorial. Wednesday, she'd sat up all night, writing, drawing, simplier and yet simplier diagrams, ten distribution tables, pages of explanation, to save the lazy little beggars the trouble of actually consulting books, or, God forbid, actually using any original data. Sitting in her high-backed, staff issue black leather armchair, breathing in fumes of Gauloise and the women's various scents, she remembered the way Open University students would creep up her path at midnight, delivering work on time, no matter if they'd been working shifts or the baby was teething. This lot. . . . The teak veneered, slightly warped sixties door creaked open. Adams, Powell and Jones, apprentice Welsh wizards, and respectively next year's Union President, next year's President of Debates, and the newly appointed editor of the campus newspaper.

'Taliesin, Aneurin and Owain Glyndwr. Bore da, gentlemen.' They sat down.

'Sorry Clare. We've been in the press room all night. There was a major policy statement to get out in today's issue. Taliesin, Aneurin, Glyndwr? Which of us is which?'

The spokesman was Garwy Jones, writer, seducer, christened in the rising nationalism of the 1960's. Another few years, Clare thought, sadly, and they could be my sons.

'Work it out for yourselves; later. Pass them copies of the notes, somebody. Ieuan, why do you think statistical measures are appropriate when we're analysing and describing this type of data?'

She got the expected blank look, and set about explaining, once more, the rationale for the use of quantitative methods as a tool, within the scientific methodology of the new interdisciplinary approach to history as a social science. Urquart's minion, only a small secretary, came in, unseen or heard, and collected the attendance slip; almost a full house, and the absentee had 'flu, badly enough to be in sick bay.

Garwy offered Clare a peppermint.

'For your throat. Do you really understand all those long words?'

Bells rang everywhere, uncivilised, electric. Clare had to resist Garwy, resist black hair, blue eyes, a mouth like David's, lean young body. Gross moral turpitude, it was, and a sacking matter, if a member of staff corrupted the innocent young. But that supposed innocent girls, lecherous men. And it wouldn't be adultery, not now. She made her voice very crisp, tutorial.

'Essays, please, from all of you. Take down the title: "The analyses are unnecessarily elaborate, and constitute a justification for the jibe that quantitative methods describe the obvious." Discuss, with specific examples. Two thousand words, two weeks from today.'

They let her go, she let them go, closing the teak door on the room where they were staff and students. At the bottom of the stairs, she felt Garwy touch her arm.

'Clare . . . about your husband. We were all so sorry.' Then he was gone, after slipping an envelope into her hand. A Mass card, signed by Rigby. The Holy Sacrifice of the Mass will be offered for the repose of the soul of David Carradus, and a card for herself, signed by every student she taught. It occurred to her, hurrying up for crèche duty, that not one member of staff had done this, linked two unmentionables, his death, her faith, such as it was.

Abigail had the doll stuffed into her tights, under her jumper.

'I'm having a baby. Quite soon, actually.'

She was crouching in readiness, surrounded by three or four midwives, both sexes. Clare wondered whether the crouching posture was instinctive, or the result of too much exposure to the Guardian women's page. Anyway, it seemed that a little more education could do no harm. She removed the doll, and replaced it head downwards.

'That's the way a baby lies when it's ready to be born. Hardly any come feet-first. It's much better if they're like this.'

A small boy, who wore a badge, Cat lovers against the Bomb, approved this arrangement.

'So they can see where they've landed.'

Definitely time to start organising lunch. Clare rounded them up; preparation for a meal, is a lesson in life, a social skill, civilise the creatures, as best we can. On a kinder day, she would have turned them outside for an hour, but the snow was back, and meant business.

At half past one, they had a police message. The A52,

between the town and the University had been closed to all traffic. A bus and a lorry were stuck, half way up and down Constitution Hill. Those on campus were advised not to attempt to leave. Clare, who had been buttoning Lucy's coat said nothing, thought a great deal, and began to unbutton.

'You thought something rude.'

'Very rude. I've had enough of snow.'

Lucy didn't at all object to staying in the crèche. She planned to spend the afternoon finding out how a television works, from a postgraduate Communications student. The crèche wasn't over stocked; most of the afternoon children wouldn't be coming. Lucy could safely monopolise him. Clare had to find a phone, make arrangements for Daniel.

All three phones were in use. She went downstairs, to the Union concourse, found two out of order, one occupied, and beat Garwy to the fourth. The school secretary put her straight through to Woodburn, concerned, controlled Woodburn with 198 children to get home that night, or, failing that, to feed and shelter in a place designed only for learning. Hope advised her to wait and see; if it came to the worst, Daniel wouldn't be the only one in school for the night.

Garwy made his own brief call, caught up with Clare.

'So you're stranded?'

'Yes.'

'Lunch?'

'I never eat lunch.'

'Only drink it? No? Coffee? With Schnapps?'

Clare accepted gravely.

'Nothing I'd enjoy more.'

'Nothing?'

Then, possibly, Garwy remembered that he was speaking to his tutor, newly widowed tutor. He held the heavy plate door open for her, leading the way, then took her arm, to stagger, blinded, chilled, battered, through the whipping snow, under low branches, down the dark path to his rooms in the Stables. For Gawry, quite at random, had been awarded rooms in the University's one concession to wealth and privilege, the old stable block of the great Hall. The loose boxes had been converted into student bedsitters, and the groom's lodgings into a flat, intended for some junior member of staff, acting as warden. There were fewer young staff, these days, and for no extra rent, the accommodation office computer had given Garwy this flat, with its own bathroom and separate kitchen, with miniature fridge and Baby Belling cooker. In return for this luxury, rare now, even at Oxbridge, he had only to mow the lawn outside, or sweep the yard moderately clear of leaves, according to season.

Separate rooms, then, so there was no inevitablity about the bed. Clare's own cramped student room had grieved Moira, probably Jim too, though in those days, he hadn't been able to put this distress into words. Moira had been coyly explicit. 'At Mount Carmel, if we entertained men, we had to leave the door open, wide open. And that was sharing rooms. I don't like this, dear.'

Garwy helped her off with her snowladen coat, offered a towel, wiped her wet face, rubbed her hair. Already, too much touching. She did this for her children, though they were perfectly capable of removing their own clothes, drying their own hair. She followed, wordless, where he led, allowed herself to lie down.

'We'll have the coffee afterwards.'

'Afterwards?'

Removing her bra, he paused, felt in his pocket.

'One of these, or are you on the pill?'

Clare removed her own knickers, already craving, already wanting, shameless, not Garwy, but any man, anything.

He had drawn the curtains, shutting out snow and cold. They were tawny velvet, a good investment, twenty years ago. Coming in, he had switched on a dim light, so they were ready now, in a room like an autumn beechwood.

'No pill, but we don't need that thing either. My period finished yesterday.'

'Your crazy religion.'

'Absolutely not. The chances of getting pregnant today mean we needn't worry.'

'I'll take your word for it, then. Shouldn't you be resisting temptation? He stroked her breasts, caressing, soft as a baby's exploring hand. Clare had her eyes closed.

'Domine, da mihi castitatem . . .'

Garwy silenced her.

'Bloody pedantic rubbish you talk, Clare. Admit it?' He was covering her now, young body, not quite so young body.

'How old are you?'

'Nineteen. Twenty, soon. I know you're thirty, so you needn't bother lying.'

He had her face now, naked, scrubbed dry with a university towel.

'No wrinkles, though. Not bad at all. Ready? Only, no more talking. I don't like women who talk.'

'I won't talk.'

They progressed greedily. Clare had been such a coward, afraid of the pill, afraid of pregnancy, afraid of abortion, because she would know it was murder. David had been her only lover, and then only for a couple of months, before marriage. She had nothing to go by, only David's efforts.

At half past two. Garwy rested, lay beside her, one white arm around her, his hand cupping one small breast.

'When must you go?'

'Half past three. And I must phone the school again. Lucy might. . . .'

'Never mind Lucy.'

He pulled her across, practised. Remember, no, better forget David's clumsiness.

'You do the work this time. Lazy, you women are.'

Then they lay side by side again, content. Garwy remarked, with interest, as if in a tutorial,

'It's true then. I've always wondered. Women do peak at around thirty, and men in the late teens. So this is perfection. Agreed?'

'I'm an old woman. A mother.'

He kissed her, possibly for the first time. It didn't seem to matter.

'You're doing well. Twenty-five. And that's not flattery. I don't believe in flattering women. You look hardly twenty-five, and feel . . . mmmm.

'Every rich day of thirty. More?'

Then he saw her tears.

'Clare! . . . I forgot.'

She pitied the boy's confusion, fear, had to explain, before he grieved too much.

'You think this is because David is dead? I wouldn't cry for David. He stopped loving me years ago. Besides, we hadn't . . .'

She stopped, wondering what word there could be, what the young said now.

'Not since Lucy was born. Before that, even. Nearly five years.'

Garwy stared at her.

'Honestly?'

'Honestly.'

'And no-one else?'

She laughed, pulled him close, kissed, before being kissed.

'With two children to keep me well behaved?'

'Then you must make up for lost time.'

She bathed in silence, dressed in silence, followed Garwy into the kitchen, watched while he made coffee, poured out the promised Schnapps, then said, casually.

'You must think I'm a right slut. Tramp, whatever word you use these days.'

'Sugar?'

'Sugar. Two spoons, I need it.'

He handed her the mug.

'I think you're very, very good. You must come again. I mean, we must do this again.'

Clare finished her coffee, found, to her surprise, that it was still quite easy to face him; how long since she had looked at David, afterwards? Be careful, this could be dangerous, at least, let him think it was only a game.

'Is that an invitation?'

'An order. You, we, are the perfect experience. You came so many times I stopped counting.'

She had the right tone now, mocking, too easily giving everything away.

'That began after I had Daniel. I used to be a slow starter. Now . . .'

He began to kiss her again, a child's kisses, not measured. Just once more. . . .

She pushed him away, reproving a child.

'No. You're forgetting; children to collect, motherly duties to be done.'

'I'll ring you.'

She went straight to the crèche, for Lucy. No-one asked where she had been. The postgraduate and his girl had gone, no-one on duty knew how long she'd been away. Besides, no one was going anywhere in a hurry. Three hours of busy snowfall had given a six inch cover up here in the hills. Seven hundred feet above sea-level, said the prospectus, panoramic views. Now that the air was still and clear, the Arctic landscape would grace any newsreel. In the crèche, someone had switched on a radio, tuned to the local station. M6 blocked, of course. M62, naturally. Even their own Constitution Hill rated a mention. Lifting gear had been used to remove a lorry jack-knifed on the hill for three hours. The road was now passable with care, but all buses had been called back to the depot.

'We'll get home somehow.'

Lucy protested.

'It's not fair! I want to stay here! Chrissie's going to let us stay the night, you and me in her flat, and have orange juice for breakfast.'

'Other wellington . . .'

Sulking, Lucy stuck out her foot.

'Chrissie said we could stay, and have a sleeping bag.'

Clare wedged the boot over Lucy's stiff instep, pointing out, reasonably, that they had orange juice at home, even, if she insisted, a sleeping bag. And what about Daniel?

Lucy felt cheated.

'Daniel's staying in his school. Chrissie told me. He'll like that, you know he will. And now we're going home, just like ordinary.'

She began to wail. Clare thought, without love, how ugly the child's face looked, red, turning purple, the features squashed and distorted. She had been a textbook nightmare baby, three months' screaming colic, then early teething. And now such a lovely child, the face already a woman's, like a Velasquez. She had no infant chubbiness. Clare envied especially her daughter's legs, graceful, even covered with thick tights, stuffed into boots. Specifically she envied the ankles, thoroughbred, below perfectly rounded calves; the whole a surprising legacy from David. Her own legs were spindly, better hidden.

Chrissie Hallam, a psychology lecturer, observing in the crèche, and, incidentally, doing her rota duty, came over to Clare.

'If you'd rather not chance it, my offer still stands. Did Lucy tell you?'

Chrissie, having as yet no children of her own, accepted children as she found them. Lucy, who was precocious and clever, she treated exactly like an adult, or at least, like a student.

'Thanks, yes, she did. But there's Daniel, stuck in school.'

'But they'll cope, somehow, won't they? Why spoil his fun?'

'Because he isn't having any. Five leftover bottles of milk from break, and half a packet of staff room biscuits. And yes, the infants have asked for a repeat miracle. Miracles are off today. It's a C of E school, and they're strong on Bible stories.'

'Sweets, crisps?'

'The head closed down the tuck shop, last year, because of teeth.' Chrissie reflected on this.

'But even so, wouldn't being hungry simply become part of the total experience? Kids don't know the sensation of hunger, they're deprived of it in our culture. Is it really fair to cheat Daniel just because you want the security of a night at home?'

Clare winced, because Chrissie has often teased her about this, no matter how barren the life with David, she wouldn't leave, in love with the safe routine of unhappy marriage, putting her own children to bed, washing the dishes. But a mere child psychologist couldn't be allowed the upper hand.

'Hunger, though. You're forgetting; children can cope with just about anything else, not that. They really do eat to live. You can trek them across the Kalihari desert, or coax them up Snowdon at two, but *only* if there's food, plenty of it, preferably every half hour. Woodburn's cursing himself now. He could shiver this out happily with a gross or two of crisps and

Mars bars.' She thought of adding, 'and I'm not the slave of routine you take me for. I spent this afternoon in bed with the campus stud, Garwy Jones, no less.' But Lucy and assorted staff children were listening. Clare thought she probably would tell, soon, and tell Chrissie, for a variety of reasons, her unappeased Catholic conscience foremost. She didn't need to worry about any disclosure from Garwy. A new bed mate for that young man scarcely rated as news; besides, the press was his to censor. And he had enjoyed himself too much to risk losing the new toy so soon.

While Lucy was safely distracted, accepting crisps from a student helper, Chrissie announced news of her own.

'I'm thinking of getting pregnant.' Not 'I'm pregnant' or 'I might be pregnant', but mere contemplation. Clare wondered how to react. Chrissie helped by explaining.

'I'm not getting any younger. Gynaecologically, that is. I'm thirty two, nearly thirty three. My fertility will be dropping, and I can't afford to waste time trying to conceive. And, career-wise, this is a good time to have one.'

Clare nodded.

'I read the same article. The only other time is the July or August after 'A' levels. David was up with someone who arrived at Oxford in the October, complete with wife and three-month-old kid. Or rather, they both arrived, at the same college. And they both got Firsts, and had two more while working for their D.Phils. Now they run a wildlife reserve in Cornwall, and moonlight for the B.B.C. The first kid just won a scholarship to Winchester.'

Chrissie nodded.

'It happens. It happens. You get two people who just operate much better as a unit. Maybe it's that last growing up stage together. Eighteen, nineteen, twenty, a lot happens. Mentally, I mean. No . . . emotionally.' Chrissie's pronouncements were often like this, superficial, but delivered slowly, in the mid-Atlantic accent she had cultivated as a student in the late sixties. She intended to sound profound, as if she had found the human behaviour equivalent to the First Law of Thermo–Dynamics. She spoke as if in capitals. Clare would ridicule Chrissie behind her back, and then hate herself, because she didn't know, didn't expect to know, ever again, anyone more loving, uncritically giving.

Impatient now, Lucy tugged at her mother's coat sleeve.

'Stop that talking. I want to go home. And you want Daniel too. His school is buried in snow, did you know?'

She had been engrossed, watching the television afternoon news, before Playschool, helicopters dropping food for sheep and humans, wise virgin motorists with spades digging out their cars, the foolish sitting tight, behind misted windscreens, an igloo, far more magnificent than Daniel's, an interview with a travelling salesman who had, snowed up on the moor, dressed in his stock of ladies' tights.

'Come on!' Imperious, Lucy could look, and sound, very like her grandmother.

Chrissie laughed.

'Looks like you have to go!'

'A few minutes ago she was begging to stay the night.'

But go they must, because there was a lift offered, because Woodburn had sounded desperate, because, after this day's work, Clare longed for routine, Friday night, Crackerjack, shampooing the children's hair, ironing to Any Questions? Daniel had had enough excitement already, with snow two feet deep around the school, and a real snowplough to dig them out. She took Lucy's hand, leading her out to find the offered lift. The cold, even at the door, stung her face, electric, making her eyes water.

Their driver was James Lewis, lecturer in French, thin, fair hair already receding, jacket buttons sewn on with three different colours of thread. Unmarried. Clare thought this, rather than 'single'. She knew hm only from the S.C.R., occasionally the chapel. The lift had been found for her by one of the Vice Chancellor's secretaries, using the Tannoy and internal telephones to get as many people as possible off campus for the weekend.

The snow was coming down again, not very hard, thin crystals, like sherbet. People were walking from labs and lecture halls to residence blocks, heads bent down. The crystals, chased by an east wind, stung and cut. Lewis accelerated.

'We don't want to be marooned after all, do we?'

Clare relished the embracing 'we', thinking of how she

might have struggled home, on foot, like as not carrying a tired child, waiting for a precious taxi. They passed the university entrance, crest and motto floating in a featherbed.

'Thank ye Godde.' Lucy, reading, because she had never noticed this before asked,

'Do we thank Him for snow too?'

Lewis, who enjoyed answering questions, obliged.

'Benedicite omnia opera Domini, Laudate et superexaltate eum in secula. Of course we should. No one else provides snow.'

Lucy considered this.

'We can't buy it in shops, can we? Only things people make?'

At the main road bus stop, shrouded figures tried to thumb lifts. Lewis slowed, then thought of trying to fit snow covered bodies around Lucy, and gathered speed.

'Besides, I don't want too much weight in her. The floor's a bit dodgy at the back.'

Clare, grateful, dependant again, turned to him, smiling woman.

'I haven't told you where we live.'

'But we're neighbours. I pass your corner every day. I live in the next huddle of houses on that road.'

'Bradford village?'

'I wouldn't call it a village. No pub, no shop.'

'I've never seen you.'

The car began to skid. Lewis handled it expertly, observed, when he could talk again,

'I've seen you once or twice, but then, you were with the family. Families tend not to see out.' He said this without self-pity, simply as an observed fact.

They had reached the crossroads, skirting the town, read, through a snow veil, Middlewood 2, Motorway 3. Down here, the road was urban, well-gritted, a dark slash across white. They passed another sad queue, but Lewis pointed to an approaching bus, back on the road. Clare thought, passing the four-deep queue, that they must look like a family, father, mother, daughter; normal. In the back, Lucy had fallen asleep, despite the cold. Lewis, relaxing now, switched on the radio, music for the homeward bound and all of you in the drifts. The d.j. in his warm studio enjoyed the drama of five blocked motorways, no trains in the Western region, the hands of Big Ben frozen. If you ever do get home, folks, stay there, that's my advice. Let's all play squirrels and bears this winter. And you know the best way to keep warm, don't you? The music made her feel young, and then very much older, because it was all so long ago; will you still need me? She wished Lucy would wake up.

Lewis swore, then apologised quaintly to Clare. 'Look at that . . .'

Ahead, the snake of tail lights wasn't moving. A neon policeman was positioning a road sign. Accident. The headlights of cars passing on the right were complacent, safely lighting their own way home. Lewis opened his door, and the cold came in to find them. One smug passing car hailed them:

'Three miles of this. Another of those bloody containers, stuck at Bradford Bridge. The police think it could be morning before they get the bugger shifted.' Lewis asked, as Jim would,

'Anyone hurt?'

'God knows why, no.' Then he was gone, well out of it.

Clare said, boldly,

'Would you take a chance? We could try the back lanes.'

Lewis shook his head.

'Bound to be blocked. The gritters wouldn't go up there.'

Clare explained.

'But the snow doesn't drift, that side, not with an east wind. That lane only gets a dusting. And if I'm wrong, we can always come down again.'

'No harm in trying.'

He moved out slowly, making the U-turn very precise; the policeman, in his orange and white coat, was watching them. Clare was worrying about Daniel now. Lewis pointed out that Daniel was better off than the three of them. At worst he might be hungry.

The lane was, as she hoped, swept bare of snow, which had climbed in fantastic drifts, up trees and telegraph posts.

'I must be getting old. I don't want to be snowed in anywhere. All I want is to be at home, with the children.'

Carefully, she added, 'Will anyone be worried? I mean, were you expected any particular time?'

'I live alone.' And it was another statement of fact.

Lucy, awake again, broke the snow silence.

'We used to have a Daddy, but he went to Heaven. Are you a Daddy?'

Turning his head, Lewis smiled at the child.

'Hello, Miss. We're nearly home now. No, I'm not anybody's Daddy.'

'Good, then we can borrow you.'

Clare wriggled round, reached for one of Lucy's hands.

'Is she warm enough?'

She released the child; why should he care?

'As toast.'

Now they even sounded like a family, mother and father talking about their shared daughter. They were coming down into Middlewood now, ribbon development country, street lights strung out between the necklace of semis.

'Left, here, for the school.'

Time to thank him now, say goodbye, quite sure that they would meet again. She wanted more, in love with the human comfort of a man beside her. He stopped a little way from the school gate. It was quite dark now, the open door shining yellow light across the clean white of the playground. Many children had been collected already, but the fine powder snow had covered the trail of footprints, large and small. Lewis helped her out, tipped the front seat forward to release Lucy.

'You go in for him, then I'll run you home.'

She said, truthfully, that it would be easier to walk; he wouldn't get the car down School Lane.

'If you're sure?'

'Quite sure. You've been very kind.' She thought of the cottage, where no-one would be waiting, invited him back for supper; held her breath, willing him to refuse.

He managed it very well.

'I'd love to, but some other time. Or maybe you and the kids come round to me?'

Leave it at that, then. They were both too tired for any other answer.

''Bye then, Clare.'

Did she now have to say, self-conscious, 'night, James, thanks again? But she'd left it too late to say anything; he was gone.

Chrissie was right. Daniel did not want to be rescued, objected to being rescued. Iron rations had just been produced, squares of chocolate, bought from the pub slot machine, ferried in by the vicar, on a toboggan, and biscuits, slightly soft, kept for nourishing the faithful after Holy Communion. There was also the promise of coffee, made with the five small bottles of milk and the staffroom Nescafe. Nothing else, because all the shops had closed at lunchtime, to give staff a chance to get home.

Daniel, surprisingly, hugged her, kissed his sister. Dawdle now, and he might get both the coffee, and be home in time for Laurel and Hardy after all. It was a matter of timing.

'Mr Woodburn said you were stuck up at the university. Then we had a message from a policeman, because the road to town is blocked by a lorry. So why arc you here?'

'I came in a car, along the back lanes.'

'All by yourself?'

'No, of course not. One of the men I work with brought us home.'

'A nice man? Do we know him?'

'He lives near here.'

There were other children, looking for their own snowfast parents. Clare explained to Woodburn that she had risked the back lanes; the road was indeed blocked. She offered to return, once her own children were safely home, with food for the hungry. She didn't say funeral leftovers.

Woodburn, reflecting on this episode later, thought he had handled things very well. Forty-odd children still, poor little Mrs Carradus, and the promise of crisps, peanuts, mince-pies, half an Edam cheese. Frozen stuff, too, if they had somewhere to thaw it out. And offering to deliver it herself. He had nearly said, not in your condition, stopped in time, managed the far more suitable 'with the children on their own.' The food would be collected by sledge. And in gratitude, she was allowed to take Lucy home on the big vicarage sledge.

On the doorstep, she forced white fingers round her key, willed numb hands to move again. Daniel stowed the sledge upright, began to roll a snowball around the front garden.

'Daniel! Come and help!'

He didn't, and she yelled, loud and angry, until he came at last. The lock was high up on the door, and she had to lift him. Three times he tried and failed, whimpering with frustration. She thought of trying the house next door, their other half. Zweifamilienhaus, the German's called semis, didn't they? No car must mean the man wasn't at home; how many wouldn't get home tonight?

'Let me try again. I think I know how to wiggle it now.'

The key clicked, and she put him down. Pleased, he pushed the door open and groped for the light switch. Before closing the door, Clare looked out on Middlewood, still, huddled. The snow was giving up at last; the sky clearing. She held her children close, wanting to share the moment with them. Lucy began to cry.

'I'm hungry. It's not fair, Daniel had chocolate.'

Nothing is fair, Clare told her children, but they didn't believe her; for one thing, they had all this world of snow. She took them upstairs to a hot bath, Mrs Carradus, with her little ones. Downstairs again, in the kitchen, sorting out the food, she reflected on migration, ending, re-shaping, changing. Three does, and then does not make a family; the ingredients must be right.

Family or not, they weren't left in isolation. Woodburn turned up himself, ten minutes later, for the food. Mrs Kenyon rang, to find out how Clare was managing, 'in this wicked weather'. They talked about the sleigh ride home, singing Jingle Bells, and Daniel's triumph with the key, about blocked roads, and the difficulty for old folk, getting about. Mrs Kenyon added, robustly,

'We all have our own turn at being old or young. People forget they once build snowmen.' Clare, weather permitting, accepted an invitation to tea, Sunday, or the week after.

While they were watching a police series, any police series, crime for family viewing, with Lucy asleep between them, the phone rang again. This time it was Lewis. She corrected herself. James.

'You got home safely then.'

Clare told him they were all fine, told him about the sleigh ride, which they would have missed, which would become a legend, longer, colder, deeper, in memory. She told him what they were doing, wondered what else to say, what else could be said. Telephones, Chrissie said, allowed no cues, no body language. They also flattened out individual voice patterns, distorted inflexion. She enthused about video phones, about which she had written a paper, after a working holiday in the States. But Chrissie was ugly, with no looks to care about, no matter if she had just got out of the bath. Chrissie's face was always much the same, broad, rosy-cheeked, freckled.

'Interesting, that, don't you think, what Lucy said?'

'Lucy?'

'About the snow. One cannot buy the works of God in a shop. Man intervenes, and charges for his labour.'

She let the conversation drift on like this. He didn't seem to be troubled about the telephone bill, but then, it was only a local call. And a bachelor would hardly starve on a lecturer's pay. She tried to see his cottage. Dilapidated, unloved? Scruffy. Dishes dirty, windows filmed with dirt? Spinster prim, and a quiet friend to share it with? He'd only denied marriage, nothing else, and James Lewis didn't seem hard enough for a life in his own company. Finally, he came to the point, suggested that they go for a drink, not tonight, of course. She explained why not, and they said goodnight, agreed to watch the same Friday horror film. Clare, at thirteen, had tried and failed to see it at the local cinema, with schoolfriends. The rest were let in, only Clare turned away at the door. The Kelly's, Moira's children, were too well known. That had been the trouble, all the time.

Five minutes before it started, the phone rang again. Garwy. She knew, immediately. Well, he had better be quick. She'd waited a lifetime and more to see this film.

'Clare?'

'Of course.'

'I just wanted to hear you. You are there? I can't see you.'

'Are you drunk or something?'

'Impossible. I spent the whole evening trying to understand that crap you handed out this morning. Tell me you made it all up?'

'I'm off duty.'

'So you're not my tutor at night? I'll remember that. But I really don't understand it.'

'Then see me next week. Look, I don't want to be rude, but I'm getting frozen out here by the door.'

She could hear the late night news ending, then a commercial.

'Monday?'

'Monday.'

Clare hung up, guilty; convent school catechism: we sin by thought, word, deed and omission. Time to watch The Pit and the Pendulum.

Clare was writing to Ruth, or rather, typing, because the machine came between them, guarding both from too much exposure or disclosure. Ruth had to be told about David's death and funeral. Skiing in Austria or Switzerland, she might have been summoned home, skiing at Aviemore or thereabouts, she had managed to be inaccessible. Ruth heard nothing until she came home, met her sister-in-law Anna by chance, in Oxford Street. For this crisis, Ruth offered her current address, and even a telephone number, on a scrap of paper evidently torn from the debris of her latest book. Clare had once tried to visit her sister, in the days when research meant emerging from the Chancery Lane tube station, spending eight hours in the P.R.O., punctuated by one break for machine coffee, and returning home at night. Stranded by a train strike, she sought out Ruth, but Ruth had moved on, with no forwarding address. Clare, grudging the money for a hotel, spent the night at the station. She rang David's college, because their flat wasn't on the phone. Evidently the message had got through, evidently David had made contingency plans. In the morning, the ticket collectors allowed passengers through on yesterday's tickets. Clare arrived home from the dawn train, the one normally used by theatre-goers who had progressed to night clubs, and the travelling young, loaded high like old-fashioned hay wains, come to see if Oxford was still there. It was, and so was David's partner for the night. Clare had apologised, left them to it, drunk a cup of coffee in the kitchen, and then spent two hours walking round the Parks, feeding the ducks with all the bread in the house.

This information eventually came Ruth's way. Despite the diary incident, there was really no-one else, not even Chrissie, who could be told. Ruth had unique qualifications; total immunity to David, total recall of their shared childhood, and primitive kin loyalty to her sister. It was, incidentally, this gift of memory which made Ruth's books such an uncanny success. Bernard, as a pathologist, wanted this memory of hers tested, wanted his young sister to offer herself for investigation. Ask her what she had been doing on the 27th of July, 1966, she would describe the day in forensic detail, the morning expedition, shopping with Clare on Cheetham Hill Road, buying bread from the Jewish bakers, and picking off the caraway seeds on the way home, seeing a dead ginger cat at the kerbside near the Northern Hospital, stopping to catch elephant hawk moth caterpillars on the rose-bay willow herb. Richard had been at the caterpillar age. They had eaten only half frozen strawberry jelly for lunch, because the day was heavily humid, and Moira at the sales, not there to insist on a proper meal. All afternoon, they had lolled on the grass, eating sherbet dips, and eavesdropping on Bernard's new record; The Kinks, Lazing on a Summer Afternoon. Ruth could type out, fluently, the jeering torments of little girls, heard in a playground twenty years ago. She knew exactly how to leave the adult world. The critics were fascinated; not so Ruth's family and friends. It was them she had exposed.

Forewarned then, Clare still wrote to Ruth:

February 1st, month-mind. Thirty-one days since that unreal policeman came at one in the morning. I have behaved quite well in the circumstances. You missed the funeral, of course. Daniel pointed out that the first syllable is 'fun'. Requiem Mass for an unbeliever; I wonder if it counts? I wonder if any of us count? At vulnerable times, I admire, or do I mean envy, those men and women who can stand under a starry sky and find it proof that there is no God. It has quite the opposite effect on me. Bernard says he was once transfixed with the beauty of a slide he had to study, first year histology. It was merely the parotid gland of a rat, and—he says—of such appalling beauty, he couldn't leave it, as one may be haunted by just one picture in a gallery. At our age, at my age, it's probably too late to change. I will sin, I do sin, but that doesn't let me off. I used to think it did.

Remember the baby books? You sent them by the crate load, imperfect copies, when you were working for that publisher. They were all different, all the same, with their chapters on 'getting into a routine'. I wasn't having any, not then. Mine weren't routine babies. It's true, though, they do reshape your life. Not the six-ten-two thing; if that were all, it would soon be over. It's nothing so straightforward as a change in routine it's . . . do you remember the chrysalids? . . . how we tried to transfer one 'butterfly soup' into another species. I found out, only this week, reading a mag. in the library, they really can do it. We had the right idea, only, not the equipment. How old were we . . . seven and ten? Well, that's what's happened to me, whoever I used to be. I broke down, and now I'm something quite different. That is, I was . . .

It's happening again. I'm not David's wife now, not anybody's woman. So where do I, we, go from here? The children are changing too—the relationship is different already.

Perhaps you might come and stay sometime. (A safe suggestion . . . Ruth liked her family at a distance.)

Daniel says, please write a ghost book next.

C.

Pakenham's note was in Clare's pigeon hole, in the Social Sciences building.

Cofferidge is, in principle, keen on the idea. There's a good deal of suspicion, though. You know how he feels about gimmicks. Can you spare half an hour?

She rang him on the internal phone, even though he was no more than two floors away. The possibility of an afternoon with Garwy had occurred to her. In dank February, there was so little else to do.

The 'phone was answered immediately.

'I'm free now, if you care to come up.'

She could, through the misted glass wall, see Garwy, taking the short cut from the Union to the Stables, alone.

'I'll meet you in my room then.'

Pakenham's department room, like an end terraced house, demonstrated his status as, at best, primus inter pares. In some departments the professor enjoyed a suite of rooms, definitely separate from more lowly colleagues. Pakenham had been allotted only 30% more space than the other historians, only a teak veneered desk with an imitation leather top—a bad marriage, that, two low armchairs, one black padded swivel chair, university issue curtains, twenty years old, and floor to ceiling crudely metal shelves. On the cork pinboard, there was a functional, ugly year planner, marked out with coloured blobs, denoting his staff, plotting their teaching hours. Clare was fuschia. There were very few fuschia blobs, Clare, as a part-timer, having the shortest teaching hours, one less than Pakenham himself. She found him in this retreat, behind the desk, not exactly smiling, ill at ease.

'I can give you twenty minutes. Sorry, but it's Senate this afternoon.'

This she knew perfectly well. On this afternoon's Senate meeting depended not just the Oral History idea, but, very likely, her future at the university.

'Now, I don't deny you pull your weight, Dr Kelly, (He did, on other occasions, select 'Clare', but not with a desk between them). The sad fact is that we can't really afford part-timers.'

Clare did her best to indicate sympathy, understanding, pleading, tried not to show desperation.

'Time-tabling', Pakenham gabbled, 'National Insurance . . . all that sort of thing.'

She stared past him at the yucca tree, the Swiss cheese plant, the still-flowering Christmas cactus, and the vine that was efficiently climbing past bound volumes of the English Historical Review. In one corner of the room stood a carboy garden. On the window ledge stood a pot containing four bonsai trees. On the desk itself, there was a dying cyclamen. All but this last were University issue, and status markers. In Pakenham's room, the plants were serviced, dead leaves removed, dull ones polished with leaf shine, sickly plants fed Baby Bio, and the over-enthusiastic pruned; all part of the cleaning service. Clare shared a room and one spider plant with a part-timer from Politics, who was Belgian, reputed to be an expert on the Common Agricultural Policy. She could hear Pakenham timing the silence.

He picked up the thick file she had given him a week ago, the result of five sleepless nights, and five evenings during which the children had been scrappily fed on toast and cups of milk, delivered between shouts of 'Go away!' and 'Shut up!' She'd had all the usual interruptions; marking the second year's essays justifying—or not, as the case might be, the use of quantitative methods in historical research, unblocking the washing machine pump, which contained one sock and Lucy's doll's knickers, and watching an episode of this winter's blockbuster serial. There had also been someone collecting for the Blind, a pair of Jehovah's witnesses, and intermittent children playing knock and run.

Pakenham made a show of thumbing through this file, neatly typed as it was, bound in a patent file which gave A4 sheets the dignity of a book. The bibliography alone took up fifteen pages.

Throat-clearing, foot tapping. He must say something soon. Clare was sweating now; her throat constricted, palms wet, stomach churning. She had worked against the clock, thinking, this will not happen. Even opening Pakenham's note had been sheer terror, cliff-edge panic. Her name had been typed; she was quite ready to see Cofferidge's signature, polite regrets, and then the packing; exit Dr C.P.M. Kelly. With some obvious reservations, life after David had gone on much as before up to now, give or take blizzards, the day to day crises of childhood. The job defined her: Dr Kelly—Historical Demography and Quantitative Analysis. Lucy's world centred on the crèche. Daniel played chess with campus sons.

She repeated, in her head, like a mantra, like the Rosary; they can't take this away. She was on the point of praying; any words would do . . . remember, O most loving Virgin Mary . . .

'It's very impressive, Clare,' Pakenham said at last. 'It should carry a lot of weight. Well researched, well documented. Even well costed.'

She nodded, prompting him. From Pakenham, this rated as dizzying praise. The costing might be slightly out of date, and anyway, all she had done was quote a figure for equipping students with pocket cassette recorders. The friend she had phoned actually gave two prices, the bulk order contract price, and current chain store, which was cheaper.

Pakenham closed the file, and made a better attempt at a reassuring smile. Even so, there must be no preferential treatment; the job would have to be advertised. He tried to think of something else to say, failed, and fell back on the device which always stood him well in tutorials. Encouraged, now, Clare outlined the programme she proposed. It was all down there, in neat typescript, but she wanted to convince herself all over again.

'First, they must master basic methodology. And before they're let loose on real people, they're given an introductory course in interview technique. That's where we'll want to liase with Sociology. And then they have to identify a topic of interest. I've suggested a few possibilities, like 'Attitudes to the 1926 strike', taking three groups, railway workers, miners, and non-employed females, matched for age and class.

Pakenham was tempted to send her along to Senate and argue the case herself. Instead, he said, cautiously.

'Er . . . I may be mistaken but was that you . . .' (coming furtively away from the Stables, said Clare's conscience) 'talking on Peak Radio? Carradus? That was your married name wasn't it? They said 'Dr Clare Carradus', and I felt sure it must be you.'

Moonlighting? Was he going to object? No use worrying now. Besides, they had only bought her part-time, not body and soul.

'They had me down as Carradus, because the producer is

one of David's old Oxford friends. He remembered my D.Phil., and said, well, we must have that in; still impresses the listeners. It was fixed up last autumn, before . . . Nicely judged, that pause; enough to remind Pakenham that she was a poor widow-woman. When in doubt, play for sympathy.

'I couldn't ask him to call me Kelly, not then. It would have seemed . . .' She appeared lost for words. Pakenham, uneasy, found one, offered it as if they were sharing a crossword.

'Disloyal?'

He changed the subject quickly; messy human relations must not interfere with serious work.

'I've never heard you on radio before.'

'I've never been on radio before. Except for one phone-in when Daniel was a baby and I was bored.'

'Really? Well, you surprise me. You were very good.' 'Little Women', wasn't it?

'Little Mothers', Clare corrected. 'He left the choice of subject up to me. So I wrote to the local paper, three weeks ago, asking for women who remembered looking after strings of little ones. I'd this image in my mind of a girl, ten or eleven, mothering all the younger ones. By that time, you see, with five or more pregnancies, and a poor diet, the mothers would be worn out, and the burden would shift more and more to this eldest girl. I even knew more or less what she would look like, unkempt hair, holes in her stockings. Very much a child, of course, physically. Eleven year olds in the 'twenties were a long way from puberty, especially in that class.'

Pakenham blushed, and Clare remembered his innocence.

'Well, it was very interesting. Authentic social history. Local, too. You should have put that in your report, giving talks on local history.

'Only one programme.'

'They might ask you back. You really made it sound . . . interesting.'

Well, he'd handed her that one; time for cards on the table.

'They have.'

'Well . . .' He lowered his voice, conspiratorial, almost sly. 'We must make the most of this. Peak Radio again?'

Clare smiled. Waking alone, only with her children, she

had told nobody the news, hadn't mentioned it to Ruth.

'No. Radio 4. Very simple, of course. The First War, General Strike, the Abdication, Declaration of War, V.E. day, and the Coronation.' Presented by Clare Kelly. I insisted on that. Daft name, Carradus. No-one can spell it. And it's not mine anyway. If anyone remembers me from Peak Radio the B.B.C. can always explain.'

Pakenham was impressed, almost enough to make no secret of it. Of course, all this energy, all this work must be a kind of therapy for her. Compensation? At all events, she'd given him plenty to report to Senate.

'I don't suppose you could spare me that letter from the B.B.C., could you? I mean, there must be a letter? Something I could show to Coff . . . to the Vice-Chancellor?'

He paused, look very carefully at the red and blue pseudo Persian rug; a new arrival, every effort was being made to bring Sixties decor up to date.

'I think you should know . . . the post . . . if we get it, will be advertised next week. Nationally, of course.'

Clare's hand shook. Don't give anything away, don't let them see quite how desperate you are.

Pakenham went on, evenly,

'We expect you to apply, of course, that's understood. I shouldn't say this, but we'd . . . I mean, I, would like to appoint you. If we can make an appointment at all. I really would like that letter. If the V.C. knew about the B.B.C. . . .'

She shivered, violently.

'Are you all right? Not going down with this flu?'

Imagine him, alone, ill, aching in bed, heaving in the bathroom; not for us the comfort of someone else, even if they only say; 'oh, come on, it's only a cold.' Anyway, all Pakenham would worry about would be the students, untaught.

She reassured him.

'Actually, the V.C. knows already. I had to consult him. The Registrar had to know. They both seemed quite pleased, really.'

Pakenham sighed.

'I wish you weren't so secretive, Clare. Still, I suppose

there's no harm done. They say Desert Island Discs began with a six week run.'

'The Archers got thirteen.'

'Really? Well, you never know. Now, I must be off. You might as well pick up an application form from the Registrar's office. Get the best referees you can. I'll be one, of course.'

Not a flicker. Clare, ready to go, met his eyes. One brown, one green. She'd never noticed before. Pakenham was on his way out too, picking up her file. He flicked through it once more, page after page of tables, prototype interviews, analyses, quantified, categorised; a page explaining correlation coefficients.

'Cofferidge was worried about anything gimmicky. Lack of academic rigour, that kind of thing. This can't do any harm.'

She remembered, almost too late, the snowdrops for Moira, for tomorrow, Candlemas Day. This had begun in childhood, Jim, buying snowdrops from Manchester barrow boys, on his way home from work; one ivy leaf, twenty or so drooping white heads, strangled together with a rubber band. Then, in Devon, when Daniel was a baby, she had filled the long days with walking, down empty lanes, only with her baby. On such a walk, late in January, she had stopped to feed him. Under the hedge, madonna of the ditch, she had seen them, white against the dirty melting snow, and had picked them, for no particular reason. But at home, feeding the baby again, she saw the date, picked out in red, on the tri-lingual, expensive calendar that had arrived, bent, in the Christmas post. February 2nd, Candlemas. Feast of the Purification of the Virgin Mary—origin of the six week post natal check? Candlemas. A little convent girl lighted candles at a shrine, choir-boys' voices, singing the last Britten carol; Wolkum, Candlemas . . .

The baby—she had still been trying to think of him as 'Daniel', was no longer hungry, wanted to be amused. She had tucked him under one arm, to let his watch as she washed the flowers. Then—every detail of this was in proof condition, the snowdrops had been packed, wrapped in film, in a box that had held cotton wool buds, for Grandma. Grandma was, and was not Moira. Opening this package at breakfast, on the second of February, Moira cried and said, inexplicably, 'I have my daughter back', as if she had only one daughter, as if she and Clare had been cruelly separated. To Clare, she wrote: For the snowdrops, thank-you. Nothing I have received has ever given me more pleasure. It was clear that this note had taken some time to compose; even its final form, the position of 'ever' had been changed.

There were snowdrops in the woods, near the lake. Clare walked along the shore path, with Lucy, maternally holding her hand for as long as it might be allowed.

'Why are we going down here?'

Clare explained.

'But why does Grandma want snowdrops? She's got crocuses, I saw them before Christmas.'

'They will be dead by now.'

Lucy persisted, in the way a young child will, mercilessly demanding an explanation. Adults could not be allowed to indulge in strange whims. The winter jasmine was in flower in hedges around the Senate House lawns. Lucy considered this superior. Clare explained that it was garden, not to be touched. Snowdrops grew wild, abundantly, and could be picked.

'Like dandelions?'

On the lake, ducks cruised about, hungry, hopeful. Students were usually good for a few crusts. They would need energy soon, for mating. How had Anas platyrhynchos survived, before the days of stale cake? And did they now die of duckish diseases of civilisation? Somebody should write a paper for Bird Life; someone probably had.

Lucy complained that they had brought no food, scolding.

'You stupid mummy, you never remember, ever, anything.'

Garwy had either followed them, unseen, or had taken the other path, quite by chance. At any rate, he had come provided. Lucy ran over to him.

'Can I have some of your bread, man?'

He handed over two crusts, slightly mouldy.

'Do they eat the green bits?'

'They've never refused yet.'

'Mummy cuts them off, then toasts the rest. She says it's only penicillin and no harm.'

Clare had to join them; wondering, would Lucy, wise child, place Garwy?

'That happened once, before they were born, when we were just married and very poor. David never forgot, and the children certainly won't. But it was either that or no breakfast.'

'Remind me to bring my own loaf, if I ever have breakfast with you. Sometimes, I buy those scraps of cheese and bacon they sell off cheap in the grocer's, if you get there early enough.'

'Do you? Do you really?'

Clare was delighted, taken back to her own poverty. And she knew so little, shared so little of his life.

'I used to do that, and then make a flan, call it a quiche, spend all the money I'd saved on booze and invite friends to supper.'

'No quiches now. I put them under the grill, on toast, soaked in butter, meaning marge.'

She had a picture of him now, preparing food, eating it, melted butter dribbling a little on his chin. And then washing up?

'I once spent a weekend with nothing to eat but a tin of Marvel.'

Lucy tossed bread. The ducks came to eat. Garwy bent down, offering a soft biscuit to the only white duck.

'This one is either too well-mannered to fight with the rest, or rather poorly. I always feed him like this.'

Clare laughed, to shut out a memory.

'He's full of low cunning, that's all. Someone I once knew did just that with a white duck on the Cam.'

'Your husband?'

'No. And he was at Oxford' . . . and I never knew him?

'Same thing. And you?'

'I thought I told you. Sussex. Then research at Oxford.'

'Valhalla at last.'

'Definitely not. I had a place at Edinburgh, but David was at Oxford.'

'So now you can go to Edinburgh.'

The food was gone, the ducks not satisfied. Clare had once seen ducks refuse food, ornamental ducks, on an ornamental pond, in a Bath park, in the tourist season, but never since. She remembered the snow drops. Lucy explained to Garwy, as if embarrassed, as if it were only some adult nonsense of Moira's. Garwy said, politely,

'Mind if I join you?'

He picked Lucy up, carrying her on his shoulders. A month ago, on New Year's Eve, David had done that, taking the children on their annual search for the man with as many noses as there are days in the year. Lucy tweaked at his hair. Clare followed them, but she picked no snowdrops; it was all done by Garwy and Lucy.

'Three o'clock. We must go.'

'Must you?'

She explained about having no car still, about bus times, about meeting Daniel. And, today, there were the snowdrops to be posted. Garwy was holding them, carrying Lucy.

'It's hard to imagine you at home, with children.'

Lucy objected.

'Silly! She's my mummy and Daniel's too.'

'She's my teacher.'

Lucy was squirming, begging to be put down.

'Are you a student?'

'Sometimes.'

They had reached the Senate House, and a busy signpost. Clare could see the bus waiting. Garwy handed over the snowdrops.

'I hope your mother likes them.'

'She expects them. They're essential, like pancakes on Shrove Tuesday. Like catching that bus.'

Clare took Lucy's hand, and ran, swinging up onto the platform just before the doors closed.

Daniel grumbled about being taken up to the post-office after school, when he wanted to watch cartoons.

'Leave me in the house. Lock me in.'

'No.'

'I'll be alright. I wouldn't let anyone in.'

Clare knew that other women would leave a seven-year-old, not merely in the house, but in charge of younger children. Ten minutes, nothing much could happen, only the house completely gutted. Daniel looked mulish. Ask next door to keep an eye on him? Only two days ago, Lucy had come in crying, because she had asked the next-door child to play, climbing over the fence. The result had been slaps, and the child scurrying back into her house.

'No . . . you'll have to come. You know we send Grandma snowdrops for Candlemas.'

'Will she send me money? Like last year?'

Clare winced. Nasty, greedy brat, out for all he could get. As for her own motives . . . better not look too deep. At least Daniel was simply, childlike. Walking up to the post office, she couldn't get rid of this thought. Better admit it then. Like dandelions? Lucy had said. And there it was, the supreme childish gesture; Mummy, this is for you, worthless, but see, it's from me. Perversely then, she bought a card too, expensive best wishes, and appeased her children with crisps from the corner shop.

'You must publish', Pakenham said, over S.C.R. coffee, congratulating her a week later on Senate's approval for the new course. The bitter weather had returned dutifully after a sunny Candlemas Day. Someone, as usual, identified a Buchan cold spell. Clare had her own contribution.

'I know Valentine's Day comes in this one. My brother arrived in a blizzard; dead heat with the midwife.'

Pakenham repeated, gently,

'Really, Clare, you must publish. It's going to cause some difficulty, that. The broadcasting will help but . . .'

They were attracting too much attention. He put down his own not quite finished coffee, deliberately steered her over to a leaking Chesterfield in the farthest corner.

'Everything I think of seems banal, or obvious, or even just plain boring.'

Pakenham sighed.

'That isn't the point. Your teaching's good, I'd say very good. You seem to have the knack of extracting good work from the most unexpected students, but it's no earthly use telling the Selection Committee that. They need evidence.'

'And well-taught students isn't evidence?'

'Not enough. This is a university, remember, not a school.' He was beginning to sound tetchy, driven as he was to repeating remarks made by an otherwise silent Roman Britain specialist, whose contributions enlivened Antiquity, the Numismatic Chronicle and, on the subject of amendments to the Creed at the Council of Rimini, the Downside Review.

More kindly, he added:

'Perhaps you're too critical: Self-critical, I mean. There's no reason why your work shouldn't be accepted. On the other hand, it doesn't do to be too worried about rejection. The worst they can do is turn your stuff down.' He added, lamely,

'They don't bite.'

Clare, who had been come in shivering, after two hours teaching in a room with no heating and ill-fitting windows, went to fetch another cup of coffee, added a measure of brandy, donated by the visiting rep for a Lancashire brewers, who wanted to get the Union order. Brandy, just to face Pakenham?

'Actually, I've just sent a paper to Local Population Studies. Differential rates of re-marriage, widows and widowers. I've been thinking about it for some time. There's literary allusions too . . . it's not all head-counting. For instance, no-one called Thomas More frail, or stewed in corruption . . . at any rate, not that kind.'

Pakenham looked startled.

'Gertrude. According to Hamlet, she re-married within a month. Very rude he was about it too, if I remember my A-level Eng. Lit. correctly. Well, so did Thomas More, and the dates aren't all that different. About twenty-five per cent of all sixteenth century marriages were the second for bride or groom, sometimes both. What I'd like to do . . .' she was becoming more confident. '. . . is a complete family reconstitution study. You know, whether widowers with young children actually married more quickly than any other category. Like More, of course.'

'And when will you do this work?'

The brandy, despite its origins, had taken effect. She wanted to laugh in his solemn face.

'I told you, the paper's written. I collected some of the data last year, and I've just written it up.'

Pakenham was peevish;

'Didn't you think of getting an opinion?'

'Whose? No-one else really touches this field, not here. And I've written up my Peak Radio broadcast for Word of Mouth. You know, the new oral history magazine. That's been accepted. I had the letter on Monday.'

She was suddenly afraid, startled by the pure venom in his expression. One more miscalculation like that could be fatal.

'I'm sorry, Prof. I really should have told you. The truth is . . .' It was going to be alright. The look of venom had gone; she must have been mistaken. And he couldn't be callous enough to disbelieve. Continue, then:

'I still haven't taken all this in. Some days, I wake up, wondering where he is.' Maybe that was going too far, but it had worked, because Pakenham was patting her arm, mercifully lost for words. And, again mercifully, he had a third year seminar, crying out for him.

Leaving the S.C.R., Clare swayed, faint, from hunger, from brandy, terrified. 'I'd like to appoint you.' It wasn't enough. It wasn't by any means enough. She wanted so little, only her job, just as it was, secure. The law and its allies were sorting out her finances with their usual haste. Paying off the mortgage could shift, now, to paying a child minder. Four and a half months more widow's allowance. If only David had skidded so disastrously in the course of duty, they would be almost rich; especially if he'd waited until the April promotion. It was sheer bad luck that David had finally stopped loving her when he'd at last reached a salary level good enough to finance decent insurance. As it was. . . . She tried to add up all their pieces of income, could not. And, quite apart from all this, quite apart from the undertaker's letter, reminding her about David's headstone, Lucy would be at school in September. Being a wife and mother might be a kind of occupation, being only a part-time mother definitely not. Several of the campus wives, with second children of Lucy's age or thereabouts, and no chance of a job, had contrived third pregnancies. Clare thought, nastily, there's a nice project for someone. It would have to be retrospective, and therefore of doubtful validity, demanding of these women why they had embarked on a late third child. Worth a feature in Woman's Own, anyway. 'Where did you come from, baby dear? Out of the dole queue, into here.' Throw in a few pregnant school leavers, and it might do for New Society. The woman she knew had various excuses, worries about the pill, at their age—none over thirty-two, sheath failure, cap failure, coil fell out. She tried to calculate the probability of all this failure in her own small circle, and stopped, stopped because of the memory, etched in acid: David's third child that would never be born.

Lewis had her by the arm, steadied her towards the only sitting equipment around; a hooded hall chair. He pushed her head down, attempted a few buttons, felt her pulse. Clare let the world swing round, back, up and down again, shut her eyes, then tried again. This time, things kept fairly still; at least, the only moving parts seemed to be Cofferidge and assorted professors and readers from the faculty of Science. Clare knew only one of these by name, and only because he was a devout Catholic.

'Thanks, James. I'm alright now. It's been a tiring week.'

Lewis was muttering figures, trying to remember a St John's Ambulance first-aid course he had once begun.

'Your pulse is weak. And you feel thin.'

He had an arm on her shoulder, touching bones. A woman would be busy with all the stock questions; are you looking after yourself, shall I call for a doctor, see you home, discreetly asking . . . could you be? But James, for a long time now, had been concerned only with the writing of two books; one being a vital re-examination of L'Affaire Dreyfus, the other a biography of Baudelaire. He had a title for the latter: 'Perceptions of a New Reality', also two imperfectly-typed chapters, and some two hundred more pages in heavily corrected longhand. He had begun both almost ten years earlier, soon after completing his London Ph.D.

'I expect you need a holiday', he said at last. 'A good night's sleep, anyway. Could I run you home?'

'No, thanks all the same. Lucy enjoys her afternoons in the crèche. She's busy on some great project too. I mustn't interrupt. There's only afternoon TV at home. Besides, I want to work in the library.'

Lewis let her go. She seemed well enough, and he was

hungry, eager for refectory lunch, even though he'd breakfasted on muesli porridge and scrambled eggs. Designed to be thin, he was growing a white floppy stomach, all bread and beer, food for a labouring peasant, not a lecturer in French. But he was glad she'd called him James.

Garwy found her by the lake. This second winter, there had been only one dusting of snow, like the mean dredge of icing powder that covers shop-bought sponges. The frost crusted everywhere with sugar crystals, crunched underfoot, the blossom was like a cookery page fantasy, in a glossy magazine. She explained this to him, sucking the crystals from a spray of jasmine.

'I know what you mean. One day I'll give dinner parties with a display of frosted fruit no-one dares touch. And afterwards, it will all be mine.'

'Greedy brat.'

She took his hand, walked completely round the lake with him, back along the path on opposite shore. There was no sign at all of the ducks.

'Maybe they're frozen, under the ice. Hibernating, like frogs. The way people thought swallows did.'

'Idiot. I'd be scared, believing the things they did. Homonunculi, for instance. When van Leuwenhoek discovered the microscope, people drew pictures of sperm as little men, little human creatures, to grow inside the woman. The reality is bad enough, heaven knows.'

'That's why real time-travel would be so unbearable. All the hopelessness of knowing you're right, they're wrong.'

'The future would be even worse, finding that we were wrong after all. Or would it? Which would you choose?'

'Pass.'

'I'd find all the pain unbearable. So much unnecessary death.' Garwy, thinking of David, let her go on.

'I must tell you something. When Daniel was about a year old, I wanted another child. It wasn't easy, because David didn't want me. Even when I did get pregnant, I had a bloody miscarriage. I'd made friends, more or less, with a woman who had a son Daniel's age. She was pregnant, and I hated her. You won't understand this, but I hated that creature inside her. Afterwards, when it was born, I went on hating, saying it was beautiful.'

'Was it beautiful?'

She stared across the lake, across time.

'Yes, it was. Babies are hardly ever beautiful but this one was. Anyway, I kept seeing them. We were supposed to be friends; women always say 'friends', as if we were all Quakers. Then, one night, about midnight, she rang me. The baby, Flora, had died. Cot-death. She was telling me first, wanted me with her. Her husband had taken the baby's body to Sheffield. The local hospital were just messing about, and he knew that if it was a virus, the pathologist has to see the body quickly. They're unstable, you see, there's often no trace. And they wanted to know. Now you know what I'm like.'

'But you went to her, didn't you?'

'Of course. I didn't hate her any more. And quite soon, we were both pregnant again. She was the only one who knew it was my last chance.'

Garwy said, gently.

'I was the first born after my mother's baby died. She never did forget, not with four other children. She told me once, about going to his cot, telling my father, Geraint is dead. Five months old, he was. But you didn't kill that baby.'

'Oh yes, I did.'

They had come to the dark place, under joining yews. This time in February, the birds had eaten nearly all the coral fruit. A squirrel silvered across the path, sat quivering, tail arched, exactly as a squirrel should be. He held an acorn, like a carved squirrel, a picture. Then he was gone, no more than movement overhead.

'Dying babies, demographic crises, I thought it was all in a day's work for you.'

'Only on paper.'

In silence, they walked up to the Stables. On this kind of day, chill drifting fog, it would be easy to believe the world was dead.

'Everyone disappears. I see them walk into the mist, and then they're gone.'

Under the brick arch, someone had propped a bicycle,

though this wasn't a cyclists' University.

'So he's still around.'

'Who?'

'The solitary cyclist. A man without a name. Fifties hair cut, but I think that's an accident; his barber never changed. Baggy grey flannel. National Health eyes. Shirts three inches too short. Some people would make that look deliberate, but I've seen him in the basement, washing grey woollen socks in Lux flakes.'

'What's he reading?'

'English and Education, of course.'

'You're very cruel.'

This time, she was following, up the stone staircase. Pinned to his door, there was a note. He took out the drawing pin, and replaced it before opening the envelope, read it in front of her.

'Excuse me. I must make a phone call.'

'Must you?'

'I must. Will you wait?'

He unlocked the door with a key worn, childlike, around his neck, and left her. Clare, abandoned, had no scruples. She assumed, correctly, that the note was from a woman, that Garwy was doing his best to avoid complications; or confrontations, come to that.

She stood by the window, gazing out across dead land, bare trees, bare ruined choirs . . . the land grey with a scurf of old snow and frost. Autumn's leaves had long since lost all colour and beauty. The lake didn't move, the only colour, artificial, alien, came from rhododendrons and winter jasmine. There were a few huddled bodies, walking very close to the buildings. The senate house clock said twenty to two. She switched on Garwy's radio, which was tuned to the Third, pressed buttons, found the news headlines, lay down on his bed for lunchtime at The Bull, only, it was evening in Ambridge, and snowing too. Clare found the imperturbable Archers comforting. Sudden death, illegitimate babies, the summer fête, and dogs worrying sheep; it was all so tranquil, a story for cooking supper, frying Sunday bacon and eggs.

Hungry, she hunted for food, found ginger biscuits, a new packet. She felt happily sinful stealing from him, like Lucy, snitching chocolate fingers. Her stomach growled, reminding her of no breakfast, and a bad-tempered scurry around the house, chasing lost shoes, lost tie, her own bag of still-unmarked essays. Nibbling ginger biscuits, she listened to dinner at Brookfield, tried to imagine life with grumpy short-fused Phil Archer. Lying on Garwy's bed, she smelt man, nothing unclean, merely different, not woman. She tried to remember marriage, and before, sharing bed and room with David. The idea seemed more than strange, on the other hand, was it better to think of the next fifty years alone? To be married was to be normal; look now quickly the divorced rush to do it all again. The habit of being a half is hard to break, even if the first search for platonic completion ended in failure.

Woman's Hour. If Garwy didn't come back soon, he would find her gone. No doubt he would find some other way to fill the time. Her programme was, as usual, busy with expected duties. Three o'clock, collect Lucy, catch the five-past bus, collect Daniel from school. Then motherhood, all the way to bedtime. They deserved that much, today. She'd been neglecting them, raging from her typewriter, go away, leave me alone. On the radio, a voice was saying, good afternoon, promising one hour, all your own. In Daniel's babyhood, the first winter, she had used this time for ironing, sewing on buttons, starching David's office shirts. Woman's Hour had changed, conscience-stricken. She switched off, felt under his pillow for the flat lump of a book, found John Donne. Naturally. She held it lightly, to see where it fell open. The Sunne Rising. Love all alike, no season knowe nor do young men change very much, not in one short decade. Footsteps on the stairs warned her to close it.

'Sorry, Clare. I'm a bastard, aren't I?'

Lying on his bed, she said, easily, 'Are you?'

'Leaving you alone so long.'

'Doesn't matter. I was tired. It's peaceful here. Did you manage to put her off?'

'Yes . . . I mean, no . . . it wasn't a woman.'

'Rotten liar.'

He was sitting down now, on the bed, stroking her legs in smooth black stockings.

'Alright, so I put her off. I see so little of you. Did you expect me to be faithful?'

'Of course not.'

Time to undress; there was so little time. Off with all the winter black, that covered winter white. Passive, Clare allowed whatever he wanted, until definition stopped.

Afterwards, lying very still beside him, she thought, nothing like this, never before, not once in all those years of marriage was I so close to David. She pulled the boy closer, cradling his head. She hadn't noticed, before, the new, narrow moustache.

'I must go soon.'

'No. Please stay.'

She sat up. 'Essays to mark, children to feed, and I have to ring the undertakers, about David's headstone.'

'What will it say?'

Clare told him.

'David Charles Carradus, husband of Clare, father of Daniel and Lucy, elder son of Leonard and Elizabeth Carradus. Then his dates, and R.I.P. Black letters on white Carrara marble.'

'No verse? No Beloved? No weeping angels?'

'They charge by the letter. And he didn't love me.'

She was shivering, trying to dress. Garwy took her in his arms again.

'You don't look well.'

'I told you, I'm tired.'

'Then stay. Rest here longer. Surely someone can look after the children?'

Clare pushed his arms away.

'No. There isn't anyone. No-one I would trust.'

'Grandparents, neighbours?'

'So I can stay here? And besides, I wouldn't leave them, not for you or anyone.'

Garwy was silent. Clare thought; this is the real gulf, not sex, or age, or status. It is simply that I have children and he has not, and there can be no bridge, no understanding. She finished dressing, began to comb her hair.

'No!'

'No?'

'Not like that. You look better with your hair all tangled, the way I left it.'

'As if I've just got out of bed?' She combed lightly, ran her fingers through it again, laughing.

'That's better. You looked so weak and sad before.'

He kissed her, touched her forehead lightly, fastened the top button of her coat.

'Haven't you got a scarf?'

Easy to laugh at him now. 'No, Nanny, must I wear one, and a vest?'

'I'd like to be a Nanny. Maybe a children's nurse.'

Clare was laughing still, until she saw that he was quite serious. Then she was gone, running down the stairs, across the courtyard, past a frozen fountain, and up more stairs, into the crèche Chrissie was on duty. Lucy had made something, something she whisked out of sight.

'Secret.'

'They all have secrets,' Chrissie explained. 'Did you know it was Valentine's Day tomorrow.'

'Roses are red, violets are blue, nobody loves me, please will you? No, I'd forgotten. Chrissic, break it to me, since when did the likes of Garwy Jones nurse ambitions to empty bedpans? In my day, the Garwy Jones types were all writing novels, applying to the B.B.C. and lining up for postgraduate scholarships to do a D.Phil on the mediaeval love lyric.'

Chrissie smiled, ready to ask, why Garwy Jones, what do you want to tell me. Instead, she hissed in Clare's ear.

'News. I'm in pod. October.'

Clare hurried Lucy down, raced for the bus. Chrissie could open a book now, guess the father, the result to be judged according to whom the resulting infant best resembled. Chrissie, even now, was not slim. In the SCR, one sherry-ridden lunch time, she'd confessed that the whole project stemmed from a conversation with a visiting professor of psychology, who had asked, conversationally, 'and when is your baby due?' He'd recovered very well, explaining that she moved like a pregnant woman, had the aura of motherhood. Clare added nine months to Chrissie's bulk, and told her brain to change the subject. Last week, she had bled; the first time since David's death. Pregnancy was out of the question; even so, she had found this widowed bleeding unbearably sad.

'Can we have chips tonight, Mum? Can we? Anyway, you promised.'

Lucy joined in, chanting, 'chips, chips, chips', two-tone, like a siren. Putting down her still-unread Guardian Clare, devoted mother, tried to remember that morning. Had she promised? 'At breakfast,' the children told her, allies, two against one. Clare thought of several good reasons why they shouldn't have chips, and gave in. If Daniel were older, or even her husband, she could be priggish about cholesterol . . . only, wasn't that all blown up now? If Lucy was older, she could threaten spots. Unlikely. Lucy, with her perfect legs, didn't look the kind to get spots. Daniel, with a sidelong glance at his sister, sneaked up and planted a kiss.

'Chips, please?'

Garwy, Daniel, she was a slave to young men.

'Yes, but I'm not making them. Put your coats on. We'll go to the chippy.'

'Chippy?'

'Chip-shop.' . . . David's finicky ghost wouldn't like this; imagine Betty Carradus's grandchildren, taking home chips in paper. Rest in peace, David, it can't hurt now. The children danced around the room, whooping, cheering, singing an instant idiot song about chips, which proved how rare the treat was. Satisfied, David?

'I said, put your coats on.'

'But "Blue Peter" hasn't finished.'

'Come *on*.'

Outside, the sky was navy and eau de nil, the evening rush hour on the main road already past its peak. Even so, they were ten minutes trying to cross the road. Lucy danced on the spot, swung around the white bollard.

'When will we have a car again?'

'When the insurance people pay up.'

'Daddy shouldn't of broken our car.'

'Shouldn't *have*!'

Taking them both by the hand, Clare thought of a diary entry: six weeks, Daniel's first mention of his father. And then all he thinks of is the blasted car. Or was this the only way he could cope, regret for a machine, that could soon be replaced?

At the chip shop, they stood in a queue that began on the pavement. In the ten minutes of waiting, twilight became real darkness. Lucy asked for a pickled egg, pale, floating like a bloated cave-fish. Daniel wanted a sausage in batter.

'The eggs are poisoned. Craig in my class told me.'

Clare ordered two lots of chips, two sausages, refused wooden forks.

'But we want to eat them now.'

'You're not eating on the way home.'

An old woman, toothless, stood at the counter eating battered cod, with her fingers, with superb dignity. Time to explain, listen, kids, it's fine to eat anywhere you like, I just want to get home, because it's dark, and I'm alone in the world?

No explanations then. The cars had all gone, as if a tap had turned off the flowing traffic. Daniel walked backwards across the road. Clare aimed a whack at his bottom and missed.

'Run, run, as fast as you can. . . . You can't catch me, I'm the gingerbread man!' He was gone, darting ahead of them, past the chemist's, the bank, the bakers, the two rival pubs, side by side. The Fox and Hounds had degenerated into a much advertised road house, serving steaks, with frilly chips and limp salad. It had been bought, a year ago, by a national chain. Next door, Middlewood drank in the White Lion, signboard unpainted in forty years, a coal fire blazing most nights of the year, the floor still flagged because no-one had ever thought of changing it. Above the fire hung a loyal Coronation portrait of George V and Queen Mary. The White Lion had sold real ale without knowing it; Sam Carson reasoning that pipes generally delivered one of two things, petrol and water. His customers weren't likely to fancy either. He didn't mind if the College lot drank in his pub, so long as they didn't upset regulars.

Passing the 'Lion', Clare hesitated, knew exactly what she wanted to do; walk in, order a drink, sit by that living fire, become one with them. And it was out of the question. Outside, she had hungry children who must be fed, bathed, read stories. Besides, Sam Carson wouldn't serve a woman alone, never had, never would. Besides, Sam Carson would know about the abandoned fatherless children.

Daniel was shouting.

'Come *on*! Our chips will get cold. And you don't like beer.'

Further down the road, Lucy was running back to find them, calling, excited.

'There's someone at our door!'

Clare cursed, not silently, wondering who was catching her like this, feeding her children on chips out of paper. Ten to one it would be Ellen Kenyon, (Mrs). And there were essays, still unmarked, an interview schedule to work on for the B.B.C. Whoever it was, she would contrive to be ruthless, send them away, if necessary feign an attack of grief, if that didn't work, she would simply be rude.

But the intruder was a child, sitting on their doorstep, coatless and shivering. She was wearing wellingtons, and had been crying. Daniel and Lucy stared, then Daniel carefully slid the parcel of chips from under Clare's arm, opened it, offered one to the child.

'It's Emma. Emma from next door.'

Emma ate several chips, very fast. Daniel and Lucy sat down beside her, settling into the chips. Passers-by, if they noticed, politely ignored this dark picnic. After much steady eating, punctuated by the echoes of sobs, Emma, who must be about Lucy's age, decided to explain.

'My Mummy won't wake up. She went to bed crying, and now she won't wake up.'

Clare picked the child up, felt the thin cold body. Pretending to be calm, she asked,

'When did Mummy go to sleep?'

The child was dressed only in a nightdress, last year's Marks and Spencer, pretty, the sort of thing Betty would buy for Lucy.

'Yesterday, she went to sleep. She wouldn't wake up and give me any breakfast.'

Clare tried to think, and failed. Don't panic, said the St John's Ambulance course; if the patient is unconscious, take command of the situation. Send for help, give first aid, don't panic. Yesterday? But children of this age had no sense of time. Balls to that; if they were late home Lucy knew exactly how many seconds of a cartoon show they'd missed.

Selfless was the exact word for this, self being entirely absent. Much later, Clare tried to order the events, remembered unlocking her own door, telling Daniel to dial 999, then running to the house next door, leaving all the children.

Clear the airways, feel for a pulse, any signs of breathing. Then the vileness of breathing life into cold flesh, the mouth so foul, the tongue pressing wetly against her own. Release. Another breath, and another. And on, without thought. Five minutes, and her hands were claws, cramped, agonising, pins and needles. She located a word. Hyperventilation, giving birth to Lucy, panting too hard, the midwife said. Take a deep breath, and give it away, heart pounding too hard for hearing the other. No more, please, because I can't bear it. The cramps were worse now, had shifted across the pain threshold. Another breath, surely the last, wet lips slopping together, warm flesh against cold.

Remembering birth, she thought, what if I give up now, will she live or die anyway? The woman didn't want life, why intrude on death? Clare still knelt astride the body, stopped thinking again, gave one more breath.

Disgusted, indifferent, she held the retching creature, watched the flood of vomit, and then bile, mucus, covering the bedside rug, her hands, clothes. When the last spasms was over, she propped her neighbour up on pillows, went to the bathroom to fetch a facecloth, towel, even cologne. Instinct said, clear the nasty mess away, sense made her go downstairs into the kitchen in search of a jam-jar, something that would hold a specimen for the path lab. After that, she carried the rug, folded, into the bathroom, rinsed it clean. She remembered a missed detail: keep the patient warm, cover with blankets. It was all done, and well done by the time the ambulance arrived. Next day, the papers weren't fair to Daniel. He had the intelligence to ask for an ambulance when the 999 call was answered. They gave Clare all the credit, in one paragraph, bottom of the front page, which was where the story landed.

The drink machine was out of order. It ate their money, and jerked out an empty beaker, which bounced onto the floor and split. Daniel, thirsty, pleaded for more money, but Clare refused.

'That was all I had.'

She took them to the ladies and let them drink from the fountain. The water was warm, and over-chlorinated. She washed the children's faces, still greasy from chips, glad to find clean towels. After that, Daniel and Lucy were presentable enough. The child Emma was a different matter, her hair matted and uncombed for days, knickers stinking of dried urine. Afraid to go upstairs, to a dead mother?

There was a rocking horse in one corner of the waiting room, and a skip full of tattered comics. Daniel rummaged through them, looking for 'Spiderman'. The small girls sat on the horse together. Clare found a magazine for herself. She turned the pages, but couldn't read. The words lay there, making no sense.

'Mrs Kelly?'

'I'm the medical social worker. I wonder if we could have a talk about Mrs Sinclair.'

Clare glanced at the children. Lucy and Emma were squabbling, the horse wasn't big enough for two. They seemed happy enough, didn't need her. Daniel was beyond her, lying on his stomach, happily engrossed in the kind of comic she would never buy.

'A nurse will come to look after them.'

Clare sat down in the room that was only a section of something bigger, the ceiling pathetically high, like the nun's cell she had once slept in, as a pilgrim in France. She felt a childish impulse to swing on the long flex, escape through the high barred window. But aren't I the heroine, this time?

'I gather that you broke in to Mrs Sinclair's house and found her unconscious. You'd already sent for the ambulance. Can you tell me why?'

Clare stifled hostility; the woman was merely asking reasonable questions.

'The little girl turned up at my house in her nightdress, though it was only about six. She said her Mummy wouldn't wake up.'

No longer sullen, she added, very low, suddenly afraid.

'Is she still alive?'

Better not to ask, like the times she'd asked, will I lose this baby; a question better unanswered. But the paid comforter was smiling, touching her gently.

'I'm sorry, dear. I should have told you straight away. Mrs Sinclair is comfortable. She regained consciousness, and is sleeping. I expect they'll let you see her tomorrow.'

Clare said, abruptly, 'I don't know her very well. Not at all really, though she lives next door.'

The next questions were routine enough. How long had she known the Sinclairs? When did she last remember seeing Mr Sinclair? Did she know of any relatives who might be contacted? Did she know where the husband worked?

The tears were a mistake, miscalculation; she had determined to remain in control, cool, professional, a passing Samaritan who had done what needed to be done and would now like to get on with her own journey.

'I'm sorry, I'm making a fool of myself . . .'

Therer was a box of tissues on the table, ready for adult tears. Across the desk, this neat composed little woman who was accustomed to emotion, trained to deal with all the mess efficiently. Clare gave up, let the tears flow, because it was less painful. Afterwards, she felt better, tired, her face stick with salt, but healed. She could trust herself again.

'There's something you should know. I had to go into the kitchen, and there doesn't seem to be much food in the house. A tin of tomatoes, some damp cornflakes, and the remains of a bottle of squash. The little girl—Emma—says she had a biscuit this morning.' Then she added, knowing it was a confession.

'Look, I didn't even know their name.'

'But you were neighbours?'

'Not friends.'

'A quarrel?'

'No. Nothing like that. Merely no contact.'

No comment. The woman stood up, ending the interview, closing her notebook.

'You've been a great help, Mrs Kelly. I expect you'd like to get home now with those children.'

'And Emma?'

She hadn't intended that at all. Don't get involved, David and Len told their wives, don't be anything except what we want.

'If you could have her for the night, that would solve one problem. By the way, Mrs Sinclair's name is Jo . . . or Josephine.'

Assent set the system in action. Clare found herself impressed with the efficiency of it all. They brought her a form to sign. Title? Delete Mr, Mrs, Miss. Dr Kelly?

Address, telephone number; day, evening. A social worker would call tomorrow. In the meantime, Emma could be discharged with Clare. They dealt smoothly, too, with a small practical difficulty.

'I'm afraid I've left my handbag at home. If I could borrow money for a taxi? . . .'

They found her a ward sister, going off duty, whoh would pass the house anyway. The whole episode had taken less than three hours; one life among many lost and saved. Clare defined her own weary elation. It was precisely that of giving birth.

When the children were all asleep, Clare slipped out into the night, even now careful to walk all the way round to the other door. Sinclair territory had been carefully staked; no trespassing, you are only my neighbour. She opened the door with the Sinclair woman's key, wandered around the house, like a prospective buyer. The child was a careful secret; there was no sign of her anywhere, only cold neatness, as if they had all left long ago.

Upstairs, in Emma's room, there was a kidney dressing table, skirted prettily with lace. The bedspread matched the curtains, was echoed softly by the wallpaper. One white cushion deliberately off centre on the seat of a child-sized rocking chair, two more in the window seat. The toys sat like dead things on a gamekeeper's gibbet, all in a row. On the bed, she found something more familiar, an elephant, home-made out of curling furry cloth, with a red and gold braided saddle. He had one flat leg, and his tail was missing. He was also very far from clean, and much sucked about the trunk. Clare picked it up, and then remembered why she had come. Behind white louvred doors, every shelf was labelled, and lined with wallpaper. The shelves held what the labels said, and nothing else: socks, slips, knickers. She collected a blue pinafore dress, a kilt, a blouse, an Aran sweater, two slips, tights, knickers and vests. Betty had kept house like this, when David was a child, and did it still, for Len.

Back in her own house, Clare looked down at the tear-stained small face, and gently folded the child's hands around her elephant. In her sleep, Emma sucked at him, content.

Two till three, they said, and then seven till eight. So it would have to be faced at two. Clare decided to arrive late, and leave early, having the good excuse of children to be fetched. Emma had given no trouble, happily sharing the double bed with Lucy. The child had asked, once, about her mother, and seemed to believe what she was told. She joined Lucy in the university crèche, ate voraciously, with no fads, and could, it turned out, read quite as well as Lucy. For no good reason, Clare had assumed her neighbour would speak with a local accent. If so, she had not passed it on to the child.

Outside the hospital, Clare had to buy flowers. She never bought flowers for the house, another legacy from David. Len had never condoned such extravagance. When Daniel was born, her colleagues had clubbed together and sent orchids and lilies, enough to fill her room, but they had been delivered to the wrong address, and didn't reach her until they were dead. Entering the shop, she wondered whether chocolates would have been a better choice, but it was too late, she had been seen. There is no decent way of leaving a florist's empty-handed, so she stood there, meekly, being equipped for visiting time. Evidently it gave the thin grey woman pleasure to hear that the sick friend had been close to death. Clare paid up, and followed the flower-bearing crowd.

The Sinclair woman had been left in a side ward. She was dressed conspicuously in hospital winceyette. Clare, suddenly guilty, knew that a better neighbour, a more natural woman, would have thought to bring in frills from home, proof that the patient was not merely hospital property. She held out the flowers, half-grudging the loss of them.

'Thank-you.'

Emma's voice, clear, standard English, but northern, rather than from the south. Moira, who still classified, would say, an educated voice. Moira liked to feel herself apart from her neighbours—not better—but undeniably different. Perhaps that explained why she would never move into a better superb, become merely ordinary.

Jo Sinclair smiled. It was, especially in the circumstances, a brave smile, conveyed by cool grey eyes, firm, pale lips, in a face of painful intelligence, hung with fine blonde hair.

'They say you saved my life. I suppose I ought to thank you. How's Emma?'

Clare, ill at ease, forgot restraint, all the carefully rehearsed speeches she had practised on the bus, lashed out,

'No thanks to you, she's fine. No thanks to you, well-fed, dressed, playing with other children. No thanks to you, she seems unharmed, but God only knows what she went through last night. If you must go in for bloody stupid attention seeking, at least keep the kid out of it.'

Jo said, still calm, only her eyes downcast,

'I needed that. They've all been so bloody kind . . . as if I were half-witted.' She was allowing herself to cry now, convulsive sobs, making it necessary for anyone human standing close to touch, offer comfort. When the tears were over, she buried her face in the flowers, getting pollen on her nose.

'Flowers for me . . . you're crazy. Why the hell did you bring me flowers?'

Clare laughed. 'Dutch courage? Everyone on the bus had flowers. I couldn't face coming in without any, so I bought these at the gate.'

Jo held them out.

'You take them home. I don't deserve them. And I am grateful. I wanted to die, when I did it, but now I'd rather be alive after all.'

'Your husband . . .'

'Since coming round, I've discovered he's not worth dying for after all.'

Clare divided the flowers, wrapped her own share in paper.

'There . . . half each. Look, I must go now. The girls are up on campus.'

'You teach there, don't you?'

'Part-time, yes.'

'I used to teach. Oh, nothing so high-powered as you. Juniors.'

'Would you like me to bring Emma, tomorrow?'

'If it's not too much trouble. . . . Is she really alright?'

'Absolutely fine, I promise. I'll bring her tomorrow.'

Then Clare, who disliked kissing women so much that she took care to stand between men, for the kiss of peace at Mass, who never kissed mother or sister, bent down and kissed Jo Sinclair.

At the bus stop, she had to wait a quarter of an hour. There had been no need to rush; it was only her pathetic fear of hospitals, all hospitals, and this hospital in particular, where they had shown her what was left of David.

Quarter past seven. Chrissie was on thc phonc, groaning.

Daft place to have the phone, David said, when they moved in. Clare had to reach past marmalade, cornflakes and honey. In the last furtive year of their marriage, he must have used call boxes.

At the end of the line, there was a painful retching noise, and the clatter of a falling receiver. Clare smiled to herself smugly, and put the phone down. The kettle had just boiled. Coffee, strong, with a dash of milk, one and a half sugars and cheerful catastrophe on Radio 4. Five, ten minutes, maybe, before the first child would wake. A time for peace that made all the difference to her day. Quite extraordinary, this difference between waking and being woken by one, two, or three children. Back to two again after today, and a whole new world beginning. The insurance claim had been settled. Teach all morning, and in the afternoon, wait at home for the car. And then, either collect Jo, or wait here for her. The hospital would confirm at eleven.

The phone rang again . . . Chrissie, of course.

'Sorry about that, Clare.'

'So you should be. My morning peace is sacred.'

'Why in God's name didn't you tell me?'

'You wanted to get pregnant, didn't you?'

Another groan, more retching. Exasperated, Clare abandoned her coffee. How often had puking infants put her off food? She called down the phone . . .

'Chrissie! Shut up. Or at least get off the 'phone. You've ruined my breakfast as it is. How long have you been sick?'

Groan. 'Since I woke up. Two hours . . . all my life . . .'

'Then stop. Nothing more to come up. It's just a reflex by now. Don't move, breathe deeply. Imagine you're in front of a class. Count to ten . . . twenty . . . thirty . . . Do as you're told. . . .'

She waited. Any minute now, someone would pad in, barefoot, dressed gloriously, blouses inside out, shirt tail hanging, hobbled in one knicker leg . . .

Chrissie came back, a little tearful, but sounding better.

'Thanks, Clare.'

'Now eat something. Biscuit . . . toast . . . suck a sweet.'

'All the same, I wish you'd warned me.'

'Why? You wanted a kid. Anyway, not everyone is sick. I wasn't. I felt rough, but I never actually puked. Are you teaching this morning?'

'No. Nothing till two. Tutorial on memory with the third years.'

'Back to bed, then. Don't try to read. Listen to the wireless. By the way, you never did tell me. . . . Or is that an indecent question?'

'Jon Ellis.'

'But . . .'

'So he is. So am I. I wanted a kid and he obliged.'

She hung up. Clare reflected on this. A paper on the hereditary nature of homosexuality? A cohort study of children born to homosexual parents? She thought idly about selecting a sample. Gay News? New Society? Discreet adverts in The Guardian? She could almost see Pakenham's distressed face. Don't be frivolous, Clare. People might not understand. But I can only be frivolous . . . either that or tears without end.

Emma and Lucy had surprised her, hand in hand, dressed. Only their socks were inside out. And there was another small problem. Lucy whispered in her mother's ear.

'We wet the bed'.

Upstairs, Clare stripped the bed they had shared. She took the little girls to the bathroom, washed their bottoms.

'But we're dressed. We didn't need a wash.'

Clare explained, dispassionately, that dried urine smells unpleasant, and offered talcum powder. The washing machine and tumble drier were in the bathroom; take your choice, damp steamy bathroom or damp steamy kitchen.

David had said, better aggregate the damp. He had hovered over the plumber, supervising, had argued about paying cash, insisted on a receipt, in the end made the man drop his asking price. They expect it, he'd said afterwards. Clare tried to imagine herself haggling like that, knew she would not, knew that, women alone, she would pay up, shut up, pay over the odds. One pink double sheet, one duvet cover, two slightly damp nightdresses. Clare shook in the powder, dialled, switched on her slave.

She went to Daniel. His pyjamas might as well go in with the next load. Would that be finished in time to chuck the lot in the tumble drier? Or would she come home to a machine full of wet clothes, beds to be made up, her mother's work undone?

Clare held her son, letting him wake in her arms, flushed, soft skin beaded with sweat. She kissed him, saw blue eyes open. That was all passports wanted to know, in this age of wigs and dyes. Colour of eyes/Couleur des yeux. David had changed his mind, last renewal, to grey. At eighteen, he had thought they were green. He had fathered only blue-eyed children. Yesterday, Garwy had brought out a book on wild flowers, looking for the exact colour of her eyes, holding the book up to her face.

'Chicory.'

'Not very poetic.'

'My love is like a blue, blue. . . . No, I suppose not. Accurate though. You should like that. And listen . . . it's not such a bad thing. . . .'

She had taken the book from him, reading for herself. A typical companion of man, *Cichorium intibus*, a medical and edible herb, a deeply-rooted pioneer plant, the dried roots a coffee substitute, the fresh leaves eaten in salads.

'Wouldn't you rather be useful?'

'A "typical companion of man"? Well, so are nettles.'

Daniel, asked, 'Is it morning?'

Clare showed him her watch.

'Nearly ten to eight. Come on, dress. The girls are up already.'

'It sounds funny, that, doesn't it? Saying "the girls".'

'I expect Emma will go home today when Mrs Sinclair comes out of hospital.'

Daniel had already pulled off his pyjamas. She thought past the years from this hard, manly little body to the baby who had been Daniel. These days she was always putting thoughts into words, talking to Daniel, because there was no David.

'It was me, still. I just looked like a baby then. And I'll still be me when I'm bigger . . . when I turn into a man.'

'Don't turn too quickly. . . .'

'Do you feel different from when you were a little girl?'

'No. Not now.'

And that was true enough. Pregnancy, childbirth, suckling, that had been ageing. Now the children were older, she actually felt younger, restored to her own body. Healed. Even her breasts, small and shrivelled after weaning had become quite firm again, small, but firm. She tied Daniel's tie.

'Friday, goody, no tie for two days. Is it true Emma's mum committed suicide?'

Clare stiffened, remembered that this was a child, not her equal.

'Where did you hear that?'

'At school. She committed suicide because Emma's Dad's run off. Where did he go?'

The door was closed. That was something. God knows what the girls would be up to in the bathroom.

'He has run off, hasn't he? Like ours?'

They were both standing, tall Daniel almost at Clare's shoulder. The child hung his head, wouldn't meet her eye.

Sly, the nuns would say, and bold if you dared to look up. Let it pass, hold him close.

'Daniel . . . this is the truth. Understand?'

He nodded.

'First, your Daddy hasn't run away. He died. He was killed in a car crash, and we all went to his funeral, remember? We haven't been back to his grave because it wasn't ready. We'll go on Sunday with Mrs Kenyon, and take flowers for Daddy.'

Daniel whispered, still not looking up,

'I know, but at school, they said he's just run off, or else he's in the nick. Could you write a letter to my teacher so she can tell the others?'

'I did write. I'll write again, or I'll come to school.'

'Is Emma's Dad dead?'

'I don't think so. Some Daddy's do go away. Perhaps he's just gone away to work somewhere else. Lots of men do that, if they get a new job. The family have to wait behind until they sell the house.'

'But it doesn't say "House For Sale". I think he has run off, don't you?'

The truth, then, nothing but the truth. Children deserve better than the lies adults tell.

'Yes, I think he has . . . but I don't know for certain.'

'Emma does. She says her Dad used to hit her Mum, and then her Mum would cry. I said we used to hear her, and we did, didn't we?'

Clare heard the wireless downstairs, pip, pip, pip. Eight o'clock. Daniel hadn't finished.

'Did she commit suicide? Paul Cleary said 'did herself in', but that's really suicide, isn't it? How do you spell it?'

Hold him close, Clare thought, let him believe me. . . .

'She was very sad, and took some pills to make her go to sleep, so she couldn't be unhappy.'

'But you can have bad dreams.'

Clare said, firmly,

'And now she's better, and coming home.' As if they had been talking about something else entirely. She led him downstairs. The bathroom, when they passed it, was empty. Only the washing machine, sloshing about its business, made any sound. There was a little talc spilled on the carpet, but no more than she she might have spilled herself.

In the dining room, Emma and Lucy were busy eating cornflakes. There was a glistening of sugar near the bowl, two small damp patches where they had spilled milk . . . not bad, not bad at all. Lucy had almost finished.

'An egg, please.'

'Sorry, no eggs. Not till I go shopping.'

'Bacon?'

'No bacon.'

'You are a stupid Mummy. Bad as Emma's. That's what she says all the time, no, there's nothing in the house. Is it because you haven't any money?'

'No. I just forgot.'

Emma looked up, managing, even with a milk moustache, to look solemn.

'My Mummy hasn't any money, for real. Daddy took it all when he went away.

Clare, ashamed, shook out cornflakes for Daniel.

'I'm sorry. I just forgot to go shopping this week. I've been busy, doing my work, going to see Emma's Mummy.'

'You should of remembered . . .', Lucy appealed to the others, '. . . shouldn't she? They nodded, deprived, accusing. And they were quite right. She should have remembered, gone dutifully to the supermarket, pushed her cart around in step with the music, loading it with all the food they told her to buy. They wanted to go on living, and she was still their food supply.

'If the man comes early with my new car, then we'll fetch Mrs Sinclair, and all go to Sainsbury's. And if she comes later, we'll go after tea.' Friday night, queues, the till ringing up ahead, sixty-five, seventy . . . dear God, where do they put it all. Two months ago, she had been a wife, doing wifely things, making out lists, planning the week's menu every Sunday so she would not bore David. After the death of her little Riley, she had humped it all home, somehow, on the bus. Shopping bored David. Since his death, she had lost the habit. Shopping was merely something else to be done, not routine.

Clearing the table, she tried to think what was routine now, Long, long hours, three times a week, in the library, almost at Pakenham's bidding . . . reading, writing, you simply must publish, Clare. Tuesday was her crèche duty. Friday . . . Friday was newly sacred, for Garwy; his only free afternoon, all the time she could spare. All the time she wanted to spare? And so she had run out of eggs, bacon, the necessities of life.

Lately, her classes were better attended. The prospect of her radio series? Hardly. The university already had its share of staff leading a sweet double life, a philosopher wit ready to answer any questions, a lecturer in politics had starred in his own show, last General Election. The criminologists had worked on two documentaries, and an Egyptian physicist had been a runner up for the Booker prize. More likely all the extra energy she had put into work this term was really paying off. Link that with her new widowhood, and you would get people like Pakenham trying to bring back donnish celibacy. She could see Garwy at the back, and didn't need to pretend to indifference. He existed, but as a student, no more, brighter than average, good for an upper second if he didn't work. Was this the way the men felt, picking out their prettiest girls? She passed his essay down with the rest, A−, scattered with terse comments, good, not quite good enough.

Then she made them all move up, bring their chairs closer, refused, herself, to stand at the podium, even though Pakenham had this down as a lecture. The subject was family structure, step-parenting, the re-marriage of men and women with existing children. Agreeably topical, anyway. She began jauntily, suggesting that divorce had to be devised to cope with the falling death rate. If they thought at all of her circumstances, that was their problem. One crisp sentence to dismiss the subject. . . . 'Today, marriages are very rarely ended by the death of one partner before both reach the sixties and may have been married more than forty years.' The Registrar General's figures were printed for them on the sheets she had handed out at the door. Now for the seventeenth and eighteenth centuries . . . one child in four being an orphan or having a step-parent before the age of fifteen. She waited for some response, finally extracting from a pale blonde the suggestion that children had never liked re-marriage, hence the wicked step-mother myth. Clare fixed herself on this girl, challenging.

'And why step-mother? What about the wicked step-father? He would exist, wouldn't he?'

'Claudius?'

Clare was delighted. She had them now, enjoying her observations about Sir Thomas More. Five minutes playtime, Onan—with sniggers and blushes; Naomi, determined to get Ruth remarried to a man with a decent income. Then she got them down to work, taking notes, thinking. At the end of their hour, she drew their attention to the lengthy reading list they'd been given, and asked, waiting for no answer, 'I wonder if the children really care which it is, death or divorce.'

'Clare, you really don't look well.'

James had taken her bag, was leading her down the corridor, along the semi-basement tunnel that lead to the refectory.

'But I'm not staying for lunch. There's Lucy to collect from the crèche, then I'm off home to wait for my car.'

'And eat? You've lost weight, and it doesn't suit you.'

She was in David's arms, warm and laughing . . . 'I like cuddly women'.

'I'm not hungry. These days I'm just not hungry.'

'Did you know, that's not a symptom of depression after all. That's the latest theory . . . not eating actually causes depression. I read it somewhere this week.'

'I'll have a cup of coffee.'

'Caffeine . . . No good for you at all.'

'I like coffee. James . . . has anyone ever told you how boring you are?'

He stopped, detached himself.

'Frequently . . . my ex-wife . . .'

'I'm sorry.'

'No you're not. . . . At least, you still think I'm boring, don't you.'

No answer to that. The doorway wasn't wide enough for two. James dropped back.

'After you.'

She allowed the courtesy, went in first, hearing the jangle of knives and forks, young voices, greedily queuing for early lunch. Poor students, housed, fed, subsidised, given work.

Hardly fair to turn them loose at the end. Last autumn, one of Daniel's gerbils had escaped, or rather, had been let out by Lucy. Daniel cried, Lucy sulked, Clare thought of the helpless, useless creature, dying unseen, becoming a bad smell. In the end she had found it, a skin full of bones, glad to be caged again.

'I really am sorry for saying that. . . .'

'Forget it. I am boring.'

'No. You must let me explain. It wasn't you at all. It's the way everyone treats me now. . . . Like glass. . . . No, like an invalid. Even the students. They had a lecture this morning, mortality rates and family structure. There was no way I could talk about widows without that look. . . . You know—poor Clare. They didn't get any tears.'

'No?'

'Pas devant. . . .'

James found a place at the far end of high table, where they could see the lake.

'I'll get your coffee. White?'

'Dark brown.'

He returned, carrying a tray which he stacked beside his chair.

'I refuse to behave as if we're in Woolies. You don't mind if I eat?'

Clare saw a triangle of blue cheese, two rolls, two frilled pats of butter, an apple, a wrapped chocolate biscuit.

'That's for you.'

'Thanks.'

The chocolate woke her stomach up.

'Perhaps I am hungry. I'll make myself something at home.'

'Promise?'

'Perhaps. There's a lot to do. I told you about the woman next door, didn't I?'

'The suicide?'

'Sssh. . . . It's not official. I had to tell Pakenham why I cancelled Tuesday morning's class. He was dreadfully . . . earnest. After all I've been through . . .'

James laughed.

'Bit of excitement for the old woman.'

He flinched. 'Figure of speech. Doesn't mean . . .'

'Precisely. You'd better change the subject.'

'Chrissie Hallam's pregnant.'

'Since she rang me in the middle of her morning-sickness, I know that already. Any more news?'

James was looking almost sly, a naughty boy, betraying a secret.

'I bet you don't know who the father is.'

'Jon Ellis.'

Resigned, James tore open a roll, and buttered it. He ate the cheese with his fingers.

'That's the one thing I can't stand about Chrissie. She tells you it's all hush-hush, only for nearest dearest friends, and the next thing you know it's all over campus.'

'You told me.'

'That's different. You don't gossip . . . poor Clare, pure Clare. You come and go and make no trouble.'

Clare ate the last crumbs of her biscuit, drained the coffee, suddenly hungry, too proud to ask for the untouched second roll. She thought of saying, 'guess what, James, today's tragedy is that I miss my afternoon with Garwy Jones'. She studied James's funny, earnest little boy's face, wondered who could possibly cut his hair like that. Only the collar of his shirt seemed to have been ironed. Little boy lost . . . Time for a mental kick . . . James should have no trouble finding a maternal type, if that was what he wanted. Time to go.

'Thanks. I must go now, collect Lucy and Emma, and wait in all afternoon for my car. Nearly two months, and I finally get it. How's that for instant action?' Then she was gone, before James had time to think, two months since. . . .

Lucy had her nose pressed against the misted window. Emma was drawing finger pictures. The washing machine had taken its time. They had come home soaked in the unkind rain of February's end. Across the road, the brook that ran past the White Lion had overflowed onto the road. There was an evil smell, and they had been forced to wade home, through water almost a foot deep, hand in hand. She could have carried one child, but which? The Sinclair woman had trusted her with Emma.

'Yuck. Stinky-poo! Smells like poo and wee.'

Emma was about right. The sewage farm was in the next valley, but this brook flowed past a pig farm. Lucy, with an elder brother, disdained baby-talk.

'Shitty pissy water. Pigs' and cows' shit and piss.'

She began to sing a lavatory version of 'This Old Man'. Clare thought, sadly, this is my baby, my little girl, my sweet innocent child.

In the house, she ran a bath, found them dry clothes. Two of Emma's outfits were in the wash, clean now, but wet. No point in going back to the Sinclair's, not in the rain. She could borrow something for Lucy's. In four days of non-stop eating, Emma had gained flesh. Properly fed, she would be a chunkier child than Lucy.

When the girls were dressed, she sent them down to watch television, then peeled off her own wet jeans, wet shirt, bra, knickers. Lying in the bath, listening to all their wet clothes being made clean, she began thinking about Jo, trying to imagine her life. Two children were just about company for each other, even, a little, for their adult keeper. They fought, laughed, played. They brought home friends, and the mothers of their friends. They formed the first link in a chain of something more than friendship; more useful anyway. Whatever else . . . and the description had angered her once . . . she had an identity in Middlewood: Daniel's mum, Mrs Carradus, who made the costumes for the panto. She hadn't told Pakenham that extra-curricular reason for her weariness, hour after hour, stitch, stitch, stitch, but in domestic comfort, and for nothing at all. Jo Sinclair had all the time in the world to do such things. And so. . . . At the hospital, Clare had overheard a young houseman saying, crossly, 'I blame the G.P's of course. . . . How else would these wretched women get their pills? . . . Five, ten, twenty, a handful . . . Clare's throat would gag and close up on one aspirin. How desperate had Jo been? Because someone she called, bleakly, my husband, had gone away at last and left her in peace? Clare remembered, with shame, the nights of thumping and crying long before David's death. So what did you do? Ring the doorbell at one in the morning? . . . Excuse me, will you please bash your wife quietly . . . we can't get to sleep.

'Mummy! . . . Aunty Clare! . . .' (damn . . . Jo's doing, that . . . she must learn to call me Clare.)

'Come on, quick. . . . There's a man at the door to see you.'

The car. Hell . . . and she'd just been about to wash her hair, sticky from the rain. Soak in the bath, shampoo under the shower, sybaritic best of both worlds. She pulled the plug, called . . . let him in, say I'm coming . . . towelled herself dry with a bathsheet still soggy from the girls, and put on her black dressing gown. At two o'clock . . . David, are you turning in your grave . . . it's me, woman in a dressing gown.

'Come *on*, Mummy!'

Keep him waiting while she dressed? Two little girls, alone with a strange man? Besides, he might go away with her precious car, wet walk to school to fetch Daniel, wet weekend ahead. Damn you, David, I'm decent enough. She was not quite dry, and the robe clung to wet skin.

'You!'

Garwy was on the sofa, with Lucy on his knee. Clare had ten seconds silence, standing there, naked under black velvet. So? . . . he had seen her properly naked often enough. Only the place was new. Garwy was not embarrassed . . . keep him in his place, student visiting a staff house.

'How come you weren't soaked? We had to paddle. . . .'

Garwy, bouncing Lucy . . . ride-a-cock-horse, explained.

'Came by car, following the diversions. The main road's under water now. Invitation for you . . . sorry it's such short notice.'

'Party?'

Emma and Lucy made a grab for the envelope.

'Can we come?'

'It's for your mum. For Clare.'

He passed it to her over their heads.

'I meant to give it to you on Monday. You don't seem to have been around, and then you were off like a shot this morning.'

Emma explained the situation.

'My mummy was nearly dead, and Aunty Clare got her alive. She's in host . . . I can't say it.'

'Hostipul?' Lucy offered . . .

'Hos—where we went in an ambulance. And I came to live here.'

Live? After four days? Clare wondered about the child's concept of time, remembering with peculiarly intense pain, her own months in hospital at the age of four . . . for ever and a day. She opened the stiff envelope neatly, with the thumbnail kept sharp for biscuit packets. In another life, she too had indulged in such paper, discreetly good.

'St David's Day?'

'A bit late, I know. Tomorrow . . . Hell Fire rooms. You'll come?'

Clare sat down, primly holding her dressing gown close. The invitation was bi-lingual, a dragon, with a daffodil behind his ear, munching a leek.

'Your date let you down?'

Not a flicker.

'I didn't invite anyone else. You just haven't been around to ask.'

'There's the phone.'

She was carefully cruel now, wickedly enjoying his discomfort. Emma had him pinned down now, sniffing after-shave . . .

'You smell nice. Why are you wearing a necklace?'

'Because I want to.'

'Why do you have whiskers and not a beard?'

'Because I don't like beards.'

Lucy joined in, climbing up beside Emma. 'My daddy used to have a beard. There's a picture. Would you like to see?'

She had the album, flipped through coloured squares of memory, censored and selected.

'There's my daddy, a long time ago. Before there was any Daniel or me.' Clare snapped the album shut.

'That's enough. . . . Scram! When the man does come with my car, I want you two ready to leave the house.'

'Isn't this him?'

'No!'

Garwy had picked up the album, studied the wedding group, his face naked of all expression.

'Sorry. I'm disturbing you. . . .'

Clare propped the invitation on the piano.

'That's what pianos are for. Visiting kids playing chopsticks, photos in silver frames, and invitations. I'd love to come. The only problem is getting a sitter at short notice.'

'You mean . . . you'll come, with me?'

'Why not?'

He reached for her hand.

'Clare. . . .'

One, two, three, four. . . . She detached his fingers.

'Not now.'

'All this week . . . I haven't even seen you.'

'Saved by the bell. This, I hope, is my car.'

She went to the door, found the expected man, and car, with forms for her to sign.

'Mrs Carradus? Could you sign here please?'

Clare signed, thinking, I will not sign in this name again. It doesn't belong to me. I'm not David Carradus' wife. She signed in five places, and offered the man coffee.

'Thanks, missis, but I'd rather get straight on the road. Dirty weather, this, not for hanging about.' He left, delivery plates tucked under his arm.

Garwy was at the door.

'I'd better be off. That's a beast of an essay you set this week.'

'Sooner you get to work the better then. Where did you park?'

'Park what?'

'I thought you came by car?'

'Lift . . . that fellow Lewis.'

Clare looked at her watch. Half past two. If they could avoid the flooding, there was more than enough time to take Garwy back to campus and be home to fetch Daniel. . . . And why the hell hadn't James offered her a lift?

'Come on. I'll run you back. . . . Don't argue—just give me five minutes to get dressed.'

The car smelt of newness. It had been David's car, really, five months old when he crashed it, the car he'd driven round all day on August 1st. First, First, First. He should have chosen another day to die. Two months precisely between this life and the other. She put the children in the back, fastened their belts: special instructions, fit child seats. Garwy was clipping his seat belt. Much good that had done David, as the car crumpled.

The sobs choked her, thick as vomit. David . . .

Garwy held her close, waited politely until she could speak at last.

'I'm sorry. I'm so sorry. In front of you . . . and the children. . . .'

Lucy was free, reaching over to stroke her mother's hair. 'Poor Mummy.'

The car had come supplied with a box of tissues. In the glove compartment, there was one of those round, expensive chemist-shop boxes of sweets. Garwy mopped her tears, handed each child a sweet.

'Better?'

Clare began to say, yes, of course, I'm fine, and stopped herself.

'Of course not. I manage to forget . . . most of the time. Sorry.'

She added, briskly,

'I'm afraid there isn't time to go up to campus now. Not until we've fetched Daniel. Can you hang on?'

Thc rain was coming down in rods. She was safe enough. He was almost bound to stay.

'If you're sure that's alright.'

Outside the school, wet mother hens waited under a corrugated roof that had been a bike shed. Cycling to school was no longer encouraged. All good mothers had cars, or lived ncar the school. And they arrived on time, to talk in favoured cliques, to hang back, shy, uncertain, if they didn't sit on the P.T.A. committee and/or live next door to each other. Clare cherished a particular hatred for an advertisement which ran in the kind of magazine that gathers in waiting rooms . . . lacquered young women in furs, meeting little boys in caps. She parked at the top of School Lane. Damn. Only ten-past. Daniel wasn't due out until quarter past. On Fridays, they were often late—but not often enough to bank on it.

'I'll look after the kids, if you want to go down to fetch him.'

Unspoken words spoke like thoughts . . . don't park any nearer, the women will see, will want to know . . . who was that . . . did you see?

'Would you? The headmaster doesn't like us to park closer. It stops the staff making a quick getaway. The official reason is danger to small children.'

'Leave them to me. I promise not to drive away. I'll tell them a story.'

'Sweets.' Lucy was reaching for them. 'We need more sweets. And anyway they were free, weren't they, like the hankies for when you cried, Mummy.'

Clare left them, lover, daughter, stray child, in the shiny new car that came free with two tins of glucose travel sweets, one box of Kleenex, and one dead husband. The rain chilled several degrees, mixed in a few hailstones. She scurried to the bicycle shed, into the only space left. God . . . no . . . Jenny Taylor . . . P.T.A. secretary . . . the woman who had organised costume making.

'Mrs Carradus . . . Clare . . . It *is* Clare, isn't it? *Just* the person I wanted to see. You never gave us a chance, did you? . . . All that work . . . and not a word.'

Clare felt the rain dribbling nastily down inside her coat.

'It's been rather difficult . . .' Hell—what was the woman on about? She'd made the blasted costumes, hadn't she? Fur-fabric bear suits, as ordered, zips sewn in by hand . . . what more did they want? Hand-stirred bowls of porridge?

Jenny Taylor was nattily dressed in scarlet salopettes, under a white quilted jacket, topped with a yellow sou'wester. She had announced herself as an ex-gym mistress, 'and determined to stay ex, thank-you'. Clare wondered why. All that beefy energy would surely go to waste anywhere else. The scarlet salopettes were tucked into royal blue boots, like elephants' feet. She tugged Clare closer, head prefect with a first-former. Three inches taller.

'We heard, dear. . . . No . . . not a *word* . . . and I do *so* admire you. The secret is safe, if that's what you want. But you're very, very, brave. And after all you've been through yourself. . . .'

Very clever, Clare thought. Not a word . . . implying that she knows the whole story. Then we hold an inquest, and I feed her the details. She said:

'I've been busy all week . . . planning a new course.'

'Oh, but. . . .'

Clare had turned away, making a show of looking for Daniel.

'Nearly twenty-five past. They did ought to. . . .'

The women agreed with each other, talked about their children, about the floods, about the bad smell from the brook, the promise of more rain . . . and, in whispers, about Jo Sinclair. Clare knew, with absolute certainty, that nothing had been said. Middlewood had nothing to go on. Correction: Middlewood had the arrival and departure of one ambulance, the fact that Clare had taken in Mrs Sinclair's child, and the absence of Mr Sinclair. Middlewood said, too, that Mr Sinclair had been free with his fists. And that it was nice, wasn't it, for two young women, in such trouble, to live next door, handy for each other. Next week, they would find something else to talk about.

Daniel came running headlong, anorak like Batman's cape. 'Did it come?'

Daniel had marked this day on the calendar, boldly, 'we get our car.'

'Yes.'

'Race you up the lane. . . .'

'Mrs Carradus. . . .'

Damn that name. Clare stopped, hauled back by the Taylor woman's voice.

'There you go again . . . always in such a rush.'

'I'm taking a student back up to the university.' Someone was bound to spot Garwy. Better, then, to let Jenny Taylor spread the news. . . . Mrs Carradus is giving extra coaching. Clare moved impatiently. Daniel had already reached the car.

'Dear girl, you simply didn't give us a chance to thank you for those *super* costumes. And why in heaven's name didn't you tell us you had no ticket. We could have fixed it up easily. Dear, never be afraid to ask. So many good people round here, only too pleased to help. . . .'

Clare behaved herself. She might, one day, need their help. Also, it suited her now to play the grateful widow.

'Mrs Kenyon wrote to me. The children and I are going to see . . . David's grave, on Sunday, now the headstone's ready. She's invited us for tea.'

'Wonderful woman. Absolutely wonderful. You won't go wrong, dear, with Mrs Kenyon on your side. Now, I can see you're in a hurry. Can I give you a lift?'

Did the woman hear anything but her own voice? Clare pointed to the Volvo.

'Thank you, but I'm back on the road. The insurance settled up.'

Daniel grumbled, 'You could go much faster.'

'So I could. But not on wet slippery roads, and not when I'm running it in.'

Garwy explained. He earned his fare back to campus answering that, and a dozen other questions.

'And are there really red dragons in Wales?'

'Of course.'

When he was dropped at the Student's Union, the children wailed. Clare locked them in, and went to ring the hospital. No explanation, no apology. She asked the switchboard for Jo's ward, informed the sister that she would collect Mrs Sinclair within the next half hour, or, if they preferred, wait in for her next morning. They would like her collected? Very well then. . . .

Jo didn't speak, until they were near the ring-road. She looked a bad colour, but how were you supposed to look, four days after an overdose? The hospital had taken their time, checking every item of clothing, her rings, her appointments at Clare House.

'Clare House?'

'The psychiatric unit, Mrs Sinclair. Much nicer, don't you think? And easier to say.'

At the ring-road, Jo began to speak, very softly, as if someone might hear,

'I am. . . . He knew, exactly. If you read that poem, and you haven't been there yourself, it means nothing . . . like giving the fifth form Lear.'

Clare said, eyes thankfully on the road ahead,

'Or Donne, to kids who've never loved or mourned. I once marked twenty identical soulful essays on the subject of public and private grief, apt quotations pre-selected. Ended up pitying the poetry. By the way, they don't call the funny farm after John Clare. It was some local business man called

Alfred. Though I suppose he could be a relative. Look, I don't really fancy driving all the way home and then back into town to shop. Can you all bear to come with me?'

The children, squabbling happily, had no choice.

'Push me in a trolley!'

'And me!'

'One Mummy each pushing silly baby girls!'

Sneering, Daniel suddenly looked like David. Clare could not take it, turned away.

At the car-park, Jo was ready with money before Clare could reach for her bag. The man had come to Jo's side, the wife's side, of course. Lucy shrieked with excitement,

'Right to the top, Mummy.'

Easy enough to please them, but these places were sinister, like the tower with an evil creature lurking, and no way down. Once, she had been cornered, second floor from the top, a November night, weeks before Daniel's birth. That, she thought, had saved her, letting the man see her swollen belly; woman with child, not fair game. The half light was frightening still, concrete pillars, stalagmites, stalactites, wicked glinting eyes of cars, the reek of dribbed petrol and oil.

At the top, hand in hand, the children danced in rooftop puddles, ran to the balustrade, to look down on a town without landmarks, with nothing fit for even the most hopeful of guidebooks. It had been a market town since the days of King John, boasted a mosaic plaque in the shopping precinct, but even the parish church was only Victorian, mock-Pugin, Sainsbury's was directly opposite, and there was an organised trolley run from this car-park to the precinct, staffed by boys and old men. Jo pulled away, away from the narrow ledge; held the child too tight.

'You're hurting! Let go!'

Emma darted away, not seeing her mother's white face. They had reached the lift. Jo pressed the button.

'Out of Order', read Daniel. 'It would be.'

They walked down, holding the rail all the way, for there were no lights. Jo must be tiny, barely five foot. Clare felt lumpish and heavy beside her.

David, splendidly six-foot five, had once been so protective, fascinated by her own smallness. He'd tried to put this fascination into words.

'It's hard to imagine, being grown up, and no bigger than I was at ten. Do you feel like a child?'

Clare, lying, said, no, this is me, this is how big I am, and for a woman she wasn't really small.

Jo was whispering something.

'I'm alright for money. There was a social worker. . . . They're sorting out my claim with the D.H.S.S.'

The rest was wordless, don't look, don't see, there is so little, only enough for bargain basement food, enough to keep us alive. Clare held Daniel's hand firmly.

'No running about. Mrs Sinclair and I will have our own trolleys, and we'll all meet outside.'

Clare watched Jo and Emma turn left, Emma, who had spent merely four days in their house, and Jo, the stranger. She lifted Lucy up to sit in the trolley, and caught the smell of new leather on her hands. But the car was no better than the one Sinclair had driven. David was dead. Greater love hath no man than to lay down the insurance policies, the widow's benefit, the right to mourn. Jo, merely abandoned, had the D.H.S.S.; 'Can you stay alive on this?' 'No'. 'Too bad, it just shows what a lousy manager you are.' Widows and orphans did quite nicely, thank-you. Reaching for emergency milk, Clare wondered whether Ellen Kenyon had written, would write, all kindness, to Jo Sinclair.

Daniel fetched heavily-advertised orange squash.

'Not that one.'

Lucy was singing the jingle. When they were younger, Clare had resorted to the sherry bottle trick, decanting the own-brand into a posh bottle. Time for a lesson in life.

'Fifteen pence difference, Daniel. That means fifteen pence to spend on things we want.'

'Crisps?'

'If you like. If we can save enough money by getting cheaper things . . . this marmalade, see, not the other . . .'

'But you never get cheap coffee. You say it tastes yuck!'

David, Jo, Chrissie, someone, come shopping with me, laugh, say, 'hoist with my own petard'. Clare, shopping with all the family she had, decided to laugh, and ask her children which own-brands did, and did not taste 'yuck'. Baked beans, chutney, sardines, peanut butter . . . Cornflakes?

'No. Get the ones with a bird on.'

Lucy giggled. 'Snap, Crackle, Pop. I want Rice Krispies anyway. You promised.'

'What kind of yoghourt?'

'Peach. Only if it's peach. And Lucy only likes strawberry. Don't you know that?'

Coffee, sugar, sultanas and cherries to make her birthday cake, beware the Ides of March. Loo-paper, lavatory cleaner, new scourers, paper bun cases, black shoe polish, a bottle for tomorrow's party? Did one still take bottles? Would she really go? Anyway, they were now as far as they could be from the drinks.

'Stay here with the trolley. Lucy—you're not to get out.'

'You've forgotten the crisps.'

She returned, carrying two packets, two bottles, one for the party, one simply to have something in the house again. Two months since the ritual evening drink with David. The machine gave her a printed list of everything, but there was no David now to check every item, every penny. 'One bill in ten is wrong, you know.'

'Life's too short to check a grocery list. And half the mistakes go our way.'

'That isn't the point. Do you mean you'd keep the wrong change?'

Yes, David . . . to cancel out the times I paid too much. Understand?

Outside, the children clamoured for crisps.

'When we get to the car.'

Jo said:

'If you bring the car down, I'll wait here with the kids. No point in all trudging up, with the lift out of order.'

Clare, climbing too-steep steps with shopping husbands, looked down at each landing, saw Jo with other women, other children. Friday night, family shopping night. If Jo had not been here, how would she have managed? Left the trolley, risked losing everything? The children, and risk them running away, or worse, in the dark? Or heaving the loaded trolley to the top, with Daniel whimpering as he tried to help? Jo evidently had her uses, and, as a bonus, she would never be unfaithful.

It was Emma who cried when they reached home. 'I don't want to go back to my house. I like Lucy's best.'

Jo was already opening her own front door. The garden, on her side of the privet hedge, was neat as needlepoint, crocuses bright on the cropped lawn, daffodils in bud in painted tubs. Clare had left cutting the grass too late, last autumn, the roses needed pruning, there was muddy lego, and a rusting toy car in the flower bed. But they each had their sturdy Edwardian semi-detached, a roof over respectability, and a door, for locking out strangers. One cold, empty house, where Jo had decided to die.

'Jo, I'm so sorry, keeping you out all this time. I should've lit the fire . . . put the heating on or something.'

'A waste, if we're not there. Gas fire, gas water heating. We'll be fine.'

'But you shouldn't be coming back to a cold house. . . .'

Clare knew that, that was Moira, another generation's atavistic fear of a cold house, that had no woman at home to keep the fire burning. Daniel carried boxes of groceries to the doorstep, asked, cheerfully,

'Have you got slugs in your house? We have. They crawl all over the kitchen. Mum trod on one last week in bare feet, and it stuck like super-glue.'

Jo giggled weakly.

'Do you? Honestly?'

'Black ones, yellow ones.'

'Fat ones, smelly ones.'

The women were laughing, together, apart, relieved.

'Horrible!'

'I thought it was just our house. Did you ever see that programme, David Bellamy, stuck in slug slime?'

'Wood-lice, spiders, a rat, once—blame the pig-farm. Silver-fish, crickets.'

'I don't count crickets.'

'The fact is, these houses are so hopelessly damp. I'm sure there's wet rot in the floorboards. David was always going to lay a concrete floor. He said that the week we moved in and found there was earth below the floorboards.'

The children, sitting in a row on the wet doorstep ate crisps, played 'Ten green bottles' with tins and packets.

'At least have supper with us?'

'Jo, before you go . . . say no if you can't manage it. . . .'

They had bathed Emma and Lucy together, let the children eat supper cross-legged on the floor, watching television. Clare, lazy cook, had made piles of buttered toast and crumpets. Jo, licking warm butter from her chin confessed,

'I gave Mike a three-course meal, every night. Cloth, glasses, flowers on the table, little wife ready and waiting. He never rang, never warned me he would be late. I never knew what to do, eat with Emma or wait.'

'You can wait for ever.'

'You and David. . . .'

Their eyes met, nothing to give away. Clare remembered that she was decently widowed. Who knew any different. Only Garwy and Garwy didn't count.

'Could you really manage? I shouldn't be asking you, so soon after. . . .'

Jo cradled Emma, who had fallen asleep.

'The rain's stopped. If you just drape the coat over her, I can manage. What time do you think you'll be back?'

Clare had a woman to exploit now, wait for me, be here in case I need you. Well, why not.

'Could you stay the night? I mean, sleep in our house? It would save you the bother of checking up on my two all evening.'

Jo, suddenly decisive, made her offer.

'Let them come to me. You've had Emma all this week. I owe you that.'

The door chain was fixed. She had carried two sleeping children up to bed, and now lay on the sofa, exhausted. The room, lit only by a standard lamp, did not look too disastrous; toast-crumbs and gritty unwashed plates all in shadow. She switched the television back on, half-watching a vampire film. Predictable, terrifying, safe. Tomorrow, she would have too much freedom. Jo had made it even easier. No children in the house, no husband, she would be hideously free.

Lucy was watching her mother dress. Clare had tried on, and rejected a long black velvet skirt, then black taffeta.

'What shall I wear, Lucy?'

Lucy explored the wardrobe, four-year-old confidante, confident, woman to woman.

'This.'

'This' was also black, bought long before widowhood, almost, not quite the little cliché. Long, close sleeves, tiny waist, nothing to it, nothing to her.

'Eye shadow, Mummy. You can't go to a party without eye shadow.'

The phone rang when Clare was half-way through her eyes.

'About tomorrow, dear. You're still coming?'

Clare told Mrs Ellen Kenyon about the Saturday morning call, grave assurance that David's headstone was, that very minute, on its way to the cemetary. Only, there had been a slight mistake in the lettering. Clare kept this part to herself. Beloved Husband. If it was written in stone, so be it.

'Then we'll meet tomorrow dear, just as we arranged.' And then came the questions about Jo. So wonderful that Clare had been able to act so promptly.

Clare gave nothing back, told the Kenyon woman only what she must know already, that she had looked after Emma, that Jo was home and well enough. Tomorrow, then, they would see the grave together.

She hung up, went back upstairs to finish the other eye, brushed her hair. The black dress had a neckline just low enough for her grandmother's amethyst pendant, only heirloom from a family that failed in everything material. She had married Jim's father, Liverpool Irish, merchant seaman, and brought up the three boys alone after his ship went down in 1917. A sepia photograph, May 4th, 1914 was the only record of this family; Gran Kelly, who had been beautiful, on her wedding day.

She pulled on a fur jacket, musquash, 'forties, complete with brown cord frogging, padded shoulders, and the Utility mark, from an Oxford jumble-sale, ten years ago. The children had packed a case, pyjamas, nightdress, clean socks, a tiny present for Jo. Time to kiss goodbye, wish a nice time all round, hope for good behaviour, fear the worst. Clare waved again from the car, and left them.

The Hell-Fire rooms were not quite authentic, but good enough, really dens of iniquity, really eighteenth century. It was, anyway, the nearest this university could get to ancient decadence. Perhaps parties had changed? She tried to recall the last time with David, not counting suburban dinners here, or in Exeter. Leaving the Oxford flat? Someone had gone to sleep in the bath, tucked up in towels. Their own bed had been claimed, two men from David's college. She and David had spent the night washing up instead. Memorable, anyway, which is a lot to ask of a party. This one was difficult, having no centre. Yesterday, Clare had been unaware of the Mabinogi, the University Welsh Society. Why not choose a Welsh university? She put this question to James, the only familiar face.

'Don't ask me. I took the only job going. And you're not allowed to ask questions. You're an alien.'

He held out a bowl of black slime, drifted away. The slime tasted of wet salt. In another room, there were black ties and mail-order glitter, hard-drinking scientists and their sharp wives, speaking Welsh. They stopped, as the Welsh do, when they saw Clare. James padded up behind, introduced her. Clare begged a glass of Perrier water, and ate a few crisps. Gwyrnos Lloyd-Evans, a tiny physicist, came over, leading an even smaller man.

'Garaman Hassan . . .'

'Croeso . . . Duo Mawr, woman, don't look so scared. I found out something last week—the computer here thought I was foreign.'

'No?'

'Foreign as Cleo-patra Laine, I am. Devil of a job I had getting these boys to take my subscription . . .'

There were tables sparsely dotted with plates of food, bowls of crisps, lumps of cheese, butter, roughly cut French loaves. Nobody had been trying very hard. As people arrived, the lights grew dimmer. One room was all mattresses, under red light, one couple, all alone, better left that way. However, when she glanced in later, the mattresses were full.

'Fill your glass?'

'No, thank-you.'

It was easier now, drifting in and out of conversations. They had drunk enough to be singing. And how dared they, drunken louts, achieve eight-part harmony?

Easier, and so very much harder. The adolescent feeling of every eye staring had gone. The party was well established now, and an old-fashioned affair after all, drink, sex, bawdy and beautiful songs, according to mood. She saw Cofferidge, paying a duty visit of half an hour to show willing. James had his hand on her shoulder. Why bother resisting? Let him kiss. There was no sign of Garwy. James held her closer, stroking her small breasts, whispering softly in Welsh. She felt her nipples stand up.

'Translate.'

'Better not.'

He was kissing her still, seriously, the kisses tasting quite pleasantly of mead, honey-sweet, like the thick muscatel Moira always bought at Christmas.

'Clare . . .'

'No. Not in there. . . .'

She was sorry for him now. Poor old James . . . if it meant so much to him, why not? She had so very little to lose, this time. She might try an old trick, used since David stopped loving her, and still wanted occasional sex. Give the body another face. It is, when you think about it, such a ridiculous business. Now he was leading her out, one hand firmly on her buttocks. On Monday they would be colleagues again . . . quite safe. And Sunday was for something else entirely. So?

'Clare . . .'

'That's the fourth time. . . . Cat got your tongue?'

'I don't know what to say.'

'Then say nothing, or tell me where we're going.'

'I don't know.'

Two cars, two houses, too early, and too much choice. If they drove back in convoy now, where would they go? His place? Evidently not. She was being led into the dark S.C.R. James steered her towards an oak settle. The heavy door was still half-open, the Hell-Fire rooms audible.

'I was married. I told you, didn't I?'

'Yes.'

'She met someone else.'

No comment.

'I don't suppose you'd understand that, being unloved?'

Down the corridor, they were singing again, Cwm Rhondda. Clare felt alien, alienated, allowing herself to be kissed. Angry, too. It was pity making her angry. There was nothing really wrong with James, not even bad breath. Yesterday, the flood diversion had taken her past his cottage, setting for an idyll. It should be quite easy to let James fall in love, ask her to marry him. Or even do the asking herself. Over James' shoulder, she saw Garwy pass, on his way to the party.

'No . . . not here . . .'

'Let's go home . . .'

'Not tonight . . .'

'Please, Clare. . . . Please.'

Without the second 'please', she might have given in, spent the night with him, driven home in the guilty dawn. If he loved her, even thought of love, that would be too cruel. She detached herself, grazing his hand with her engagement ring.

'Too soon . . . you do understand . . .?'

Garwy found her in the corridor, coming out of the ladies.

'I saw you with Lewis. Don't bother lying.'

'So? You weren't here.'

'He's gone. I just saw his car. Why didn't you go off home with him.'

'I didn't want to.'

He kissed her, until she wrenched her head away.

Don't bruise me. The children . . .'

'Did he give you a good time?'

'Gangway!'

Someone was carried out between them, vomiting into a bucket.

'Let's get out of here!'

Clare followed him, then made for her car.

'May I explain?'

He stared ahead, sullen. In thin moonlight, she saw his lip tremble.

'Nothing happened. You'd better believe me.'

'I've been writing that bloody essay.'

Out on the main road, Garwy asked.

'Where are we going?'

'My house, if that's alright with you. And if you don't mind being taken home before breakfast.'

Clare bathed, lay in soft water, trying to remember the beginning with David, wanting so much. Had they been in love? But Garwy had been quite explicit; no love, no promises.

He stripped, stood naked by the bed, not very tall, not even very much of a man, slight, almost androgynous.

'I've never slept in a double bed before.'

'Make the most of it.'

She grappled with him, pulling him close, feeling his hard young body. James was, at most, thirty-five, probably less, but he was growing soft, slack-bellied. Make the most of this, because it won't last. Nothing that makes me so happy can be all bad.

They slept a little, woke often, like restless children. At dawn they woke again. She kissed him on the cheek. David, in his last years, had, hard stubble of a man, black and purple stippling his face. Garwy's skin was still soft, without the thin moustache would be almost feminine.

'Morning.'

'Coffee?'

'Later.'

Lying still, Clare thought, I need nothing else, now. The tenderness was new, and totally unexpected. A free gift. He was stroking her breasts, which were quite flat, lying as she was.

'They used to be better. Before the children.'

'What's it like, having a child? Giving birth?'

'I can't tell you.'

'I'll never know.'

'You're a man. It wouldn't be any use. I have children, and I'm their mother. That's all.'

'And you love them?'

'I love them. I like the finality of it. Whatever else, they are my children.'

She dropped him at the university gates, reversed, drove away without a backward glance. Passing a newsagent's, she stopped to buy the papers. They were selling off children's annuals, fifty pence. She bought three. Guilty conscience? But why feel guilty? And then, at the Catholic church, she stopped, parked, walked in for seven o'clock Mass. She knelt in the back pew. No need to be any nearer. In the candlelit darkness, she could see and hear well enough. And if everything was known, nothing need be said. She began, not to pray, but to argue: I tried being good, and where did that get me? Besides, I did one good thing last night, refusing Lewis.

She could see all the congregation; two men—shift workers? A girl of thirteen or so, carrying her pack of newspapers. Then women, only one young, a nurse, the rest everywhere from middle age to the eighties. Nearest was a round little woman, all in black, her skirt caught up accidentally, showing fat white legs, black suspenders, black woollen stocking. She was saying her rosary, in Polish. If she went up to the communion rail like that, everyone would see. Clare was ready to touch her on the shoulder, then realised that they were at the Consecration. She prayed herself now, because it cut out thoughts. She watched them all go up, take the host, return, heads bowed. The Polish woman's skirt fell into place as she stood up. There had been no need to worry about something so trivial. Fifteen of them, and then herself, deliberately outcast. If she went up now, no-one would know any better; there was no outward sign of sin. She wasn't branded, nor marked in any way. She tried to feel sorry. Act of Contrition. Repeat these words, and, with a firm purpose of amendment, resolve to sin no more. O, my God, I am very sorry that I have sinned against thee, and by the help of Thy Grace, I will not sin again, Amen. The words meant exactly nothing. A child had once learned them by heart, repeated them every week in Confession, so the woman knew they could not be true.

Jo, from her Sunday Times supplement said,

'I didn't ask. Was it a good party?'

Clare, reading reviews of programmes she hadn't seen, described it.

'I'm too old for parties. Or out of practice. Perhaps they were always like that.'

There was a crash overhead, laughter, a wild yell. Jo looked alarmed.

'That's Emma. I'd better go up.'

'I wouldn't. They won't want you. The crash was someone leaping off the top bunk. The yell is more or less obligatory. They drape the bunks with bath-towels and make a cave. They hide food so they can eat up there. They are nothing to do with us until they come down hungry. Or until it's time for Mrs Kenyon. The mess will be diabolical, but what else would you have them do? Watch the box?'

'Morning Service, improve your golf, and something called Econometrics by the Open University.'

'Precisely. More coffee?'

'If you're having some. Thanks.'

The papers had been stirred and swopped around. Jo was reading an Observer fashion report.

'I just don't believe people pay this for clothes.'

'Of course they do, or why make them. Black or white?'

'White, if there's enough milk. Perhaps the clothes are made just to be reported? To be worn by models and photographed. Job-creation, and publicity for the off-the peg lines. If I had a dress that cost so much, I'd never dare wear it.'

'I'd wear it every day to get my money's worth. Let's have a look.'

Clare frowned. Now and then the paper printed letters of complaint; how dare they flaunt clothes for the rich and then profess to weep for the poor? Cue for a feature on how to survive on S.S. money, cue for letters about lentils, potato pie, and nearly-new shops. At least one about vicar's wives, at least one from a vicar's wife. Like Mrs Greville? The Greville daughters were sent to the village school, but their classmates knew about the ponies, the house in Scotland, the heated pool. Schoolgate mothers could see for themselves that Mrs Greville had never bought her clothes for 10p at a jumble-sale. Jumble-sale helpers with daughters fought over the vicarage donations.

'I think we're out of date. At least, my sister spends this much quite often.'

'Rich?'

'No. It's not something we go in for in our family. There's a knack, and none of us seem to have it.'

'Mike used to say, anyone could be rich, if only they'd a mind to it. Put in enough hours, swing enough deals, go where the money is.'

'That's it. It can't be laziness. I mean, my parents both put in hours of voluntary work. Dad's at it full-time, since he retired. Bernard has half the alphabet after his name. The only hope for us now is little brother Richard.'

'What's he planning?'

'Ordination. That means he can't even marry money, like our lovely Mrs Greville.'

'There's always the Vatican coffers.'

Agreeable silence. No hurry about this, no demands. So far, it was only a sketch, outlines, you, me, our children, our past. Memories offered slowly, adding definition. Clare tried to think back to last Sunday. What had been done? Low-lying mist, day-long drizzle. She had taken the children up to campus, to Mass in the chaplaincy. Rigby giving his clever congregation their due. They had lingered afterwards in the bar. She had bought crisps, orange squash. No car, so they had accepted a lift home, eight packed into a car meant for four.

'Can we go to Katy's house?'

'Another time.'

'You always say that. It's boring, just us.'

'Sunday is the worst day.'

Clare still had the fashion page, heavy silk, hand-washable: don't tell me to consider the lilies.

Jo went on, too late now for going back.

'Last week, do you know what I did, last Sunday? Like all the Sundays, these past weeks. I got Emma up, dressed her, fed her, switched on the box. She was desperate enough for electromagnets and de-schooling society by then. Half-past eleven, it was, before I even gave the child breakfast. I put more food out for her on a tray, like a cat. Biscuits, cheese, orange, milk. Then I took six tranquillisers. . . .'

'I thought. . . .'

'No, listen. Monday was different. Monday was the only time I really tried. I'm telling you about every Sunday. Food out for Emma, and a handful of tranquillisers for me. I save them up, you see. Managed without for a day or two, and then binged. Travel sick pills, codeine, anti-histamine . . . anything to knock me out. With any luck, I'd just doze off, on the sofa, let the day drift away. I'd wake up about seven or eight, get her washed for bed, and then sleep again. It was the only way. Sunday is the end of the world.'

Clare was silent. My neighbour can live next door in her own sweet private hell. Zweifamilienhaus for strangers.

Jo was picking up scattered paper, sports news, business news, how to do everything right. Clare remembered Mrs Kenyon.

'Would you come with us? To the cemetery?'

Jo didn't even hesitate.

'We'll come. But do they know? Will they understand?'

'They came to his funeral. As for understanding, I'm not sure that I do. He has no right to be dead.'

Jo had folded every section of paper neatly, lining up the sheets. It looked as if they had never been opened. David has teased, in the beginning, about the way Clare mangled a paper, then complained, then said nothing at all.

'I used to think about it. Mike dying, I mean. I could walk back from town, pushing the buggy, carrying bags, even crying. Once someone stopped to ask what was the matter, and I said, my husband is dead, killed outright in a car crash, on his way home from work. It was alright, she was just staying with friends. She was very kind, but I don't think it got round.'

'People are kind. I was thinking of Emma. Will she understand, that David is dead, and her daddy isn't?'

'Why worry? I don't understand, so why should she? Why should they? And you have to go there, don't you?'

'Mine like graveyards. Daniel can read the stones now. He loves to walk round, finding children's graves. In Manchester, last year, I found him crying at the grave of a five-year-old, who died in 1875, and I said, look, "he's been dead more than a hundred years." But he was only *five* . . . it's still sad. He made me promise, don't let Lucy die.'

'You shouldn't have done that.'

'No? . . . No, I suppose not.'

Daniel came in, carrying Emma, piggy-back.

'We're starving! Emma's so weak and hungry she can't walk. And Lucy's dead of starvation already.'

Clare said,

'I'll clear up the bedrooms if you make a start on lunch. They'd better not have much. Ellen Kenyon—Mrs has invited us to tea.'

'You'll say that to her face, if you don't watch out.'

'So? I was in the bank on Thursday, getting my new account sorted out. You know I told you we had three, mine, his, ours? I wanted just one account, in my name. First, I couldn't get the man to understand that I wanted my name . . . Kelly—not Carradus. As if keeping David's name would bring him back. . . . Then we had five tedious minutes explaining, no, I don't want Mrs, or Miss. He came over unctious, let's keep the little woman happy, and offered me "Ms".'

'I can see him . . . twenty-eight, going on forty-five, little pot belly, waistcoat, watch chain, oiled hair. . . .'

'Near enough. "Well, Madam, what would you like us to call you?" I said, "Dr." One up to him, "Naturally, Madam. Your new cheque books can be stamped Dr C.P.M. Kelly." So there was no need for all that. I should've walked in, said I wanted the account in that name, signed their forms, and walked out. but I was crying.'

'Why?'

'God knows . . . no, of course I know. Lucy was with me. I went in as David's widow. I think I wanted to make a scene. Come on, I feel strong enough to face upstairs now.'

'About lunch. What shall I give them?'

Clare was already half-way upstairs.

'Look in the fridge. Lucy will want to finish the rabbit jelly she made yesterday. Mine aren't fussy. Anything you like.'

Daniel's room wasn't so very bad. Pull the den apart, re-arrange floor cushions, shake duvet, box bricks, scoop up

Lego, cram dressing-up clothes back into the old trunk. Ten minutes swearing quietly, two minutes growl from the Hoover, and it would be neatly destroyed, a male version of Emma's room. She stood in the doorway, heard only the softest breathing. She crept away, called from the landing,

'Lunch in five minutes.'

David used to make what he called 'tours of inspection', fingers along bookshelves, opening drawers, holding glasses up to the light. There was no original malice in this. Len had always done it. Keeping up standards, it was called, and Betty knew what to expect. Only last year, in December, Clare had raced the clock, prodding potatoes, picking up toys, making a house for grown-ups again. Hearing the car was the signal to run up and down stairs, wiping the bannisters clean, drying them, welcome home, husband, here is your wife, your house, your children, clean and sweet, playing with one toy each. The meal is ready, has been ready, will be ready, whenever you want it. We are all waiting. Well, there was no more David, petulant, saying, have you seen the state of Daniel's room? He's not a baby now Clare. Then Lucy's welcome.

'Where's my girl? Where's my lovely darling girl?'

Soft face, lifted to kiss his bristles, Daddy's five-minute-girl. Lucy's photo was on his desk at work. They had seen it, the day she took the children to town for Father Christmas, called in on Daddy, his happy family.

'By the way, I'll be late back.'

'How late?'

'Very.'

'Do you want supper?'

'No.'

So what was there, really, to be missed, except an idea?

Jo had opened a packet of cheese squares, toasted three slices of bread, softly toasted the cheese. Clare found her painting ketchup smiles below Marmite eyes. Wedding-present ramekins had been filled with sliced banana and raisins. The whole a set-piece from a woman's magazine.

'More than they deserve. No, I'm just lazy. Years and years of thankless meals. Now I only feed them.'

'This is compensation, for Emma. Your two might as well have the same.'

'What about you?'
'I never eat lunch. Anyway, it's your food.'
'Idiot.'
'I can't go on eating your food, drinking your coffee.'
Clare called the children down to eat.
'And if you're not down by the time I count three, I'll spank you down the stairs.'
One, two, two and a half, two and three quarters.
They came.

Lucy had found her own name, tracing the black letters with one small finger. One small, *grubby* finger. Mrs Kenyon was bound to see that. Daniel's hands too were fringed with urchin nails. If she tried to use a nailbrush they screamed and wriggled and fought. She resorted to soaking them clean, like heavily soiled clothes, lifting them out of the bath pink and crumpled, nails like pretty shells. This week, with Emma, there had been less time, and so, grubby nails. The only thing to do was cut them off. There were nail-clippers in her handbag . . . how, when, could it be done?
'Hide and Seek!,' called Daniel. . . . 'You and Emma hide. But I'm only counting to twenty.'
One, two. . . . The little girls squealed and ran. Daniel slowed down, decided to make his century, twenty-one, a hundred.
They were the only children in the cemetery. Clare had asked for nothing, taking what was given, a dark plot on the eastern side, already in shadow. All the bare hillside was sprigged white, a Laura Ashley landscape. The newest dead were nearly all up there, coffin lengths of banked flowers, dying wreaths. Chance had brought David to a real graveyard, yew trees, heavy black poplars, ranks of Victorian monuments. There had been a chapel here, stained glass pieta, grotto with crusted candles, wheezy harmonium, chipped plaster statue of St Joseph, patron of the dying. Here the faithful had met, on August Bank Holiday, to pray for the faithful departed. Now the chapel was gone, decayed beyond what anyone was prepared to pay, deconsecrated, demolished, the site cleared to take more graves. They had said, when she went in with Jim to buy this plot, was it a Catholic

grave they wanted, reduced rates, on the old chapel?

Ellen Kenyon stood now between Jo and Clare. From her handbag, she brought out a bible, gold leaf all but worn away, leather binding crumbling at the corners. Clare thought: I will never wear out a Bible, nor will I ever stand and mourn with a stranger. Mrs Kenyon made the sign of the cross, said the Catholic prayer for the dead.

'Eternal rest grant unto him, O Lord
And let perpetual light shine upon him
May he rest in peace.'

The younger women muttered, 'Amen'.

Then Mrs Kenyon was reading, but as if she had no need of the book: to everything there is a season, and a time to every purpose under Heaven. Clare let her eyes close, leaving time and place. A time to weep, and a time to laugh, a time to mourn, and a time to dance. She saw herself sitting beside David . . . somewhere, years ago. They had come to hear the German Requiem, soon after her third miscarriage. The choir sang: they that sow in tears shall come again rejoicing. And it was true. She opened her eyes again, saw Daniel backing away, then leaping high over polished pink granite, stone brawn.

Ellen had nearly finished now, holding her prayer-book for them to read. Nunc Dimittis. David again, in New College chapel, Purcell's setting, then walking back in the red-gold evening, up Catte Street, into David's college. She gave that memory a date, October, soon after their marriage, and they were walking home, up Parks Road, past Keble, across St Giles, up to their flat above a shop in Little Clarendon Street, the streets briefly quiet because people were eating. They had passed four young women, still, so early in the term, dressed in the clothes they had bought with their mothers. Then climbing the stairs, tripping over a milk-bottle that bounced, unbroken, down to the next landing.

'One day we'll have our own house, with a garden, and you'll put the bottles out at night.'

'Why me? Why not you?'

Jo had her by the arm. Mrs Kenyon called the children.

Clare remembered her camera, a picture for Betty.
'Daniel, Lucy, over here by the grave.'
They pulled faces. Daniel had one finger on the end of his nose. Lucy, giggling, put up two fingers. Emma, excluded, sat down on the next grave.
'Stop that. I want a picture for Granny.'
Click, on solemn faces.
'Are you quite alright, dear?'
Mrs Kenyon had taken over from Jo, had not missed the flickers of pain, the hint of tears. It was no more than she had expected. The rites of passage had been duly observed, to the last act. One husband, married until death, buried, commemorated. What else can you do with a corpse? Pickle it, like Jeremy Bentham's? Clare giggled, remembering a ghost story she had read, with a mummified body kept in the case of a grandfather clock.
'Sorry. I was just remembering something.'
Daniel had won a race, first past the Angel of Death, Michael with his flaming marble sword, guarding the cemetery gates. Lucy groaned, began to whine and cry. Jo tried to apologise.
'They're tired. You see, it was so difficult, getting them to settle last night.'
'Last night?'
'I was baby-sitting for Clare. There was a . . . supper . . . at the university. For St David's day.'
'How very kind.' Mrs Kenyon patted Jo's arm, turned to Clare.
'And how brave and sensible of you to go, my dear. The first time on one's own is so very difficult. Perhaps waiting that full year did help, but I'm not so sure. There's so little we *can* do except go on living.'
'It's so much a Victorian thing, that mourning. If you look at the old marriage registers, you find people remarrying pretty promptly.'
They had reached the car. Clare didn't recognise it yet. The rear window 'Running-In' sticker made it as alien as a house with the 'For Sale' sign still up. She unlocked the doors, let them all settle down.
'So good of you to come for me.'

'It seemed silly, using two cars. And I need to get used to this one.'

'Mrs Kenyon . . .'

'I would be so glad if you could call me "Ellen".'

Clare tried to find words that were not too cruel; nothing will bridge the years, make you Ellen, and me Clare, friends.

'But I like to say "Mrs Kenyon". You know what I like best about Wimbledon? It's not the tennis, or even the wickedness of watching T.V. in the afternoon. It's the lovely formality, the way they call all the women "Mrs" or "Miss.'

'Then I'm behind the times. I thought all you young people used first names.'

'We used to, a long time ago.'

'Speak for yourself!' Jo, in the back, with the children, thought Clare was going too far.

'We're not middle-aged yet. Not even half-way through.'

'Old enough.'

Ellen Kenyon was putting on her gloves, could see her own house, where she had lived for longer than these women had lived at all.

'You are all very young.'

Tea was a success because the children knew the limits, what was expected, allowed. They ate, sitting in low chairs, around a little table, from miniature Willow pattern plates, drank from matching tiny cups.

'A coffee service, really,' Mrs Kenyon explained. 'My children always used it, then the grandchildren. I keep it for any little visitors.'

The little visitors ate obediently, bread and butter, *then* biscuits, or a slice of cake. Jo and Clare, sitting at the adult table, glanced furtively, watching for sleight of hand with crusts, or talking with a full mouth. The children were Victorian angels, eating what was put before them.

Clare very nearly said, 'I never drink tea', then caught sight of her obedient children. She managed to pour her own, not more than half a cup.

When the children had finished, they were taken to the playroom, introduced to a doll's house, a dapple-grey horse, with flaring nostrils and tossing silver mane, a fort, a grinning nigger, hand cupped, ready to eat pennies. Mrs Kenyon signalled that the children could be left. Jo hung back, staying with them. She had been invited by stealth, yes, we would still like to come, but there is my neighbour, I can't leave her, think of what might happen.

'You too, Mrs Sinclair.'

'Jo. It's quite alright . . . I'll keep an eye on them.'

'I think they will do very well on their own.'

Lucy had found a cradle, bog oak, Elizabethan in style, but the carved date was 1900, 'Let them all come' the accepting welcome around its sides. The doll was bisque, ivory pale, dressed in gossamer silks and lace. The children played mothers and fathers. Clare, from the hall, heard her son, participant father.

'I don't change nappies. Stinky-poo!'

'Come on, dears. They're quite happy without us.'

Photographs of smiling faces, happy couples, one, two, three. Grandchildren, not on her knee, everywhere, out of reach, Aberdeen, Cambridge, Bristol. Clare had a chance to say,

'Really? My sister Ruth was at Bristol. Ruth Kelly.'

'Now that *is* a familiar name.'

'She writes. Very well, I think. So do the critics, which is more to the point.'

Five minutes, then, to talk about Ruth, and the Kenyon son who had, after all as a postgraduate, overlapped with her, even lived in the same patch of Clifton. Princess Victoria Street, seedy elegance, still struggling back to prosperity. The Suspension Bridge, the strange impulse Ellen and Clare had felt . . . what would happen if . . . and the murky Avon slime there at the bottom. Are you afraid of spiders, do you prefer cats or dogs. They had stood together at a graveside, and had to try for common ground. Ellen Kenyon was saying,

'The one thing no-one will admit, with all this talk of one-parent families, is the way one craves comfort, even just the presence of someone else. Not merely sex, though that is part of the loss. One simply misses human company, waking in the same bed, kissing the children goodnight, together, putting out the milk bottles. Arguing over things in the paper.'

The younger women were silent, for their own reasons.

'Am I saying too much? I'm afraid it's a habit one gets into. So many years, when there's no one around to share the joke, take your part, count to ten, or a hundred, when a child is driving you insane.'

Clare had noted the shift of pronoun, one, you. Ellen was not at all the woman she had invented, laughed at. Nor was she Jenny Taylor's fiction. So it lasted this long, the indecent animal craving for someone else? She had to say something, for Ellen's sake.

'Most of the time, I just don't believe it.'

Jo was plaiting and unplaiting one long strand of hair that fell past her shoulders. It was the same style she had worn ten years ago; don't change, because that signifies a changing world, time can stand still for you, wife, mother.

David's mother, marrying in 1948, had worn her hair for the next twenty years in that heavy page-boy bob. Then her sister had driven her up to London, returned with a revised edition of Betty.

'Bridget cried. Alan and I wouldn't speak to her. Dad asked whether she'd sold it. She should've stayed the way she was.'

'You mean, your mother had no right to change?'

'Yes. No . . . no right at all.'

The plaiting had left ripples. Clare tried to imagine this hair shorter, wavy, the face less thin, but if the unknown Sinclair ever returned, would he too resent change?

'Your husbands are dead. There's some security in that. I don't know where I am. I can't start to make my own life.'

'But that's the mistake you all make. Your life *should not* depend on a husband. On any man. On any other person at all.'

Ellen became gentler.

'Don't look so shocked, dears. I'm not denying marriage, only the sin of living only through a man. That wickedly bad theology of Milton's.'

'He for God only, she for God in him?'

'Not a very admirable character. Not one's model husband. Of course, the second chapter of Genesis suited his book. The first is so much finer. In the image of God created he him; male and female created he them. But people like the fairy story about spare ribs. And they make their God a man.'

Lucy came in, wailing, a deep, baying noise, all her own, almost the noise she had made as a screaming baby, so many sleepless nights.

'It's my go . . . my go . . . and they won't let me.'

She buried her face in Clare's skirt, wetting and crumpling it. Jo fetched Emma, they searched for coats, hats, gloves. Looking for Daniel, Clare found him still in the nursery, tidying everything away, with Mrs Kenyon standing by.

'Daniel, say sorry to Mrs Kenyon for fighting.'

'But it wasn't her go. We had one go each, and this time it was me sharing with Emma. That's why she was screaming. Horrible old screamer she is.'

Ellen said,

'I don't allow two people on my horse, my Dapple-Grey. He's very old, and he can carry only one child. When you come again, you must remember that.'

He turned away, shoulders hunched.

'I didn't know. I'm sorry.'

It was over. She let them go. Sunday had grown dark, and they had got through it well enough.

'But people can't be planned, Clare.'

They were in Chrissie's flat, overlooking the lake, high above black lace trees. There was, already, the lightest gauze of colour, too faint, yet, to be called green, against the wine red and purple of alder catkins, balsam poplars. Chrissie's hands were never still, pleating and gathering a length of linen. The pattern book was on the coffee table between them. Clare picked it up, studied the open page: an Elizabethan christening robe, smocked, embroidered, with matching bonnet. The flat was only a box, above and below other boxes, but Chrissie had lined her own box, bright as a bower-bird's nest. Even the rug at their feet was her creation, rags and sacking, poverty transfigured. All the hectic dying colours of autumn, Chrissie had brought together, and called 'October'. The rug was her window view, re-formed. She had been very precise in her preparations, taking many photographs exactly when the sun set over the lake, coding the colour spectrographically, consulting interior decorators, to find the exact match, in any fabric. She had mixed velvets, satins, cottons, wools, to make the crispness and damp of autumn woods, begging or buying anything of the right colour for her scheme. The lake's solitary swan was shaped out of his own feathers. There were, really, two swans, and many ducks, but, as Chrissie said, reality can only be taken so far. Clare thought of her grandmother's rag rugs, made out of old flannel trousers, worn-out dresses handed down from Moira to the aunts, even old bed-ticking. The dominant colour of those rugs had been a muddy grey.

'What do I do, while you're making things like this?'

Chrissie whipped a row of feather-stitch across fine gathers.

'I've been waiting to do this. Pleating and marking out is so tedious. I suppose you do other things. Look after your children.'

'Not very creative.'

Chrissie smiled sweetly, re-threaded her needle.

'Surely, having children is the most creative thing a woman can do?'

'You sound like the men. Anyone can get pregnant. Most people, anyway.'

Chrissie agreed, placid, fecund.

'Yes, it seems to have worked out right for me. Didn't take so long either. Just as well I was never invited to sleep around. How did the rest of you manage?'

Clare, her hands idle, making nothing, was embarrassed. It was unfair, this way Chrissie had of setting herself apart, as if size made her, not virginal, but sexless. She thought, ridiculously, 'maybe it's vegetative; there is so much of Chrissie that she must divide herself, and didn't need a man.'

'I don't know. How should I know? I was always scared. Once, I spent the night in a man's bed after a party, and the next week I was three days late. Scared rigid, jumping downstairs ten at a time, scalding baths, couldn't afford gin because it was end of term. I thought he might've done it while I was asleep.'

Chrissie giggled.
'As if you could sleep through that!'
'Yes, but I didn't know . . .'
'Oh, but surely . . .'
Clare flushed. Until this pregnancy, Chrissie had been the safest person for any talk about sex, because she supposed herself entirely tolerant. She loved women, but could never produce a lover. The pregnant Chrissie had become strangely prurient.
'I knew the mechanics. The principle, if you like. I couldn't imagine the reality.'
She wanted the subject to change. The idea of Chrissie in bed was disturbing. Maybe not in bed? What arrangement had she come to? The Jon Ellis story seemed unconvincing.
Chrissie picked up a thread, pierced fine cloth, took them safely back to the conversation that had gone adrift.
'You were saying, about this Kenyon woman and her double standards?'
'She had me neatly labelled. Tragic widow, like the deserving poor. My dear children, lucky little things, have two Fathers in Heaven. Then there's Jo . . .'
'The woman next door?'
'She didn't say all this while we were there, she has that much decency, I suppose, but it's all been said now, over the phone. Jo evidently drove her husband away. If she were a good wife, the kind a man expects, then he would come home to her. So she should wait now, keep everything shining and ready, welcome the bastard if he ever does show up. The Kenyon woman even segregates the children. She called in the other evening, and found Emma staying for tea. Warned me off . . . "I wouldn't make a habit of this, dear. Things are . . . well, different, aren't they. It can be very confusing for children."'
'Emma and Lucy had been having a scrap, and the Kenyon creature tried to make out it was all Emma's doing. She's disturbed, you see. Bound to be, with her father deserting. Bloody hypocritical rubbish. Jo's on her own, I'm on my own, the kids have no Daddy coming home at night, but I'm in the clear. It wasn't my fault, you see, but the Will of God.'
Chrissie held up the robe, examined her work, then folded it.

'That's my stint for today. I'm going to make you a cup of coffee. And something to eat. You're not looking after yourself.'

'Coffee would be lovely. Nothing to eat, though. I couldn't.'

'The interview? But you must keep your strength up.'

'I would be sick. Maybe I shouldn't risk the coffee.'

'I'm still sick, mornings. How much longer will it be?'

'I told you before, there's no fixed time. It's supposed to improve in the fourth month, when the placenta's fully operational. I refuse to believe you've done all this in the past five weeks. You were working on the rug half the time.'

'Good, isn't it? Perhaps I'll make one for each season, maybe use them as wall hangings. No, I started the robe months ago. Last summer, when I first thought about having a child. Well, not first thought . . . I always wanted one. When I realised it was now or never.'

'People have had kids in their fifties.'

'For me, though. Look at it from the kid's point of view. I earn enough to give it a decent home. I'm still fairly young. If I'd waited, I might've been too committed, career wise, to slot in a kid. Then there's the risk of handicap . . .'

'Are you having the test?'

'Amniocentesis? No. No point. I wouldn't want an abortion.'

'But . . .'

'You Catholics think you've cornered the market in eccentric morality. Aborting this kid for a technical fault would be morally indefensible. I chose to become pregnant.'

'You mean, you chose to allow the possibility.'

'Nit-picking. More precisely than most, I asked for it. Besides, I want my nine months worth.'

'Giving birth, no matter what?'

'The whole thing. Swelling up, feeling it move, all the creative agony. I've lived too much like a man.'

Clare glanced around the created room, lovely with all that Chrissie had made. Chrissie deliberately followed the glance.

'Yes, but, any man could do all this, if he wanted. There's nothing supremely female about the things I do with my hands. Feminine, maybe, but not necessarily female.'

'So you must have a child?'

'Yes. I couldn't bear the idea that I might be barren, or that I might lose it. I don't think you can imagine it.'

Clare thought of gyny wards, on-duty regret, sympathy, tests, the emptiness of being no longer pregnant, while complacent women swelled.

Chrissie saw the thoughts.

'I'm sorry. Once women have children, one forgets that they were not always mothers. Like Pat Murphy, all those months in bed, and Caesars every time. I can't imagine her without children, and look how much it costs. Sinister, isn't it, that it should be so easy for me?'

Coffee dripped through the filter. Chrissie poured on more boiling water, until the jug was full, then fixed it on its stand, over the candle.

'You've lost weight.'

'Milk? . . . I was wondering if anyone would notice before I start to blow up. Would you believe, I've lost a stone. All these years, all my life, trying to shift the fat, and see. . . .'

She held the loose dress taut.

'You never know, I might end up looking like a real woman.'

They drank the coffee. It tasted, subtly, of filter-paper. Clare prefered the posh instant she drank at home. From the window, she could see Garwy, centre of a group of young men, campus lords, manipulators, bound to succeed.

'Beautiful, aren't they?'

Chrissie stood by the window.

'I see what you mean. That one in the middle . . . the Donatello . . . the arrogance of him. I don't usually want men, but that one could be a pleasure.'

Thinner, pregnant, was Chrissie becoming a normal, craven woman?

'Maybe he would oblige. If one asked. You teach him, don't you?'

'Three of them.'

'Which?'

Clare pointed. 'Adams . . . and Powell and Jones.'

'Jammy. Do you find yourself doing that, these days? Lusting after beautiful young men?'

Clare put down her cup. Garwy and the rest were out of sight now, gone up to his room. Well, she had waited long enough.

'I do more than eye them up. The Donatello. . . . Every bit as good as he looks I promise.'

'More coffee?'

Clare swore, quietly.

'I said, more coffee? If you've finished, I'd like to wash up.'

'Is that all you can say? I've just told you I'm screwing a student.'

Chrissie gathered up cups, coffee jug, sugar bowl.

'Well, I'm hardly in a position to cast stones, am I? I take it this is recent.'

'This term.'

'There you are then . . . not even adultery. Hey . . . Clare . . . sweetheart. . . . You're serious, aren't you? You really mean it?'

'I mean it.'

Clare looked up. Chrissie's pale brown eyes oozed comfort, like warm fudge.

'Tell me to mind my own bloody business but . . .'

'Strictly rationed of course. Friday afternoons. The only time we're both free.'

'And my crèche duty. . . .'

'Precisely. Afternoon in bed, collect kids, feed, wash, read bedtime stories spend the evening marking. Is it so very depraved? You don't look at . . . say, James Lewis and think, well, he's not married, where's he getting it, will it interfere with his work?'

'No, but . . .'

'But Lewis isn't a woman with two small kids? Vive la difference . . .'

'You will be careful?'

Clare was inspecting herself in a mirror borrowed from Lucy, the Lilac Fairy, blossoming in her tree. Her face looked back, not dramatically older than ten years ago, only sharper.

'Too late now, isn't it? I must be mad, telling you. Come tomorrow it'll be all over campus, and I can forget about the job. Everyone I meet tells me you're pregnant.'

'That was deliberate. I really did tell you first. Then I tried to think of one good reason for keeping it dark. And there wasn't one, so I told everybody.'

'Well, I'll just have to take my chance . . . Oh, for crying out loud, Chrissie . . . don't look so sanctimonious. This is the only thing keeping me sane. I won't give him up.'

She held up the mirror again, combed her hair, applied lip-gloss. She was pale, but no more so than usual.

'Ten to two. Time I went.'

'Shall I come over with you?'

'Take me to the school gate? No . . . thanks all the same. I'll be alright. Either they appoint me or they don't.'

'So much at stake. . . .'

'I'll survive. . . .'

She left by the back stairs, practical and unswept concrete, sprayed somewhere by a tom-cat. On the bottom flight, she passed Ellis, supposed father of Chrissie's child.

'Off to that interview?'

'Yes.'

'Chrissie told me. . . . Well, best of luck.'

Clare pushed through the heavy plate-glass doors, saw Ellis's thin figure climbing up, co-opted father. Well, why not? Chrissie was right; she was wasted without motherhood, all that understanding patience,those clever creating hands, wasted, because men were stupid enough to fuss about her bulk. Not all men though. Shopping in town the other day, she had seen a thin, gipsy-dark boy walking with billows of woman. Daniel and Lucy had stared, impressed, but the couple were oblivious. Perhaps Ellis and Chrissie would marry? They had, after all, the classic motive; nothing so banal as being in love.

Cofferidge, Pakenham, and Fraser must have been studying interview strategy. Fraser sat on one side thoughout, micro-cassette moving, soundless.

'You have no objection, Dr Kelly? It's more efficient than bringing a secretary along. The choice is now between you and four other candidates.'

Clare answered all the expected questions, fielded the unexpected, made them define their terms, made an answer to fit. When it was her turn, she risked an aggressive line. How much freedom would she have to devise new courses.

Unprepared, they fell silent, then listened to her proposals. The interview progressed. Near the end, she felt a weariness like the last stage of labour. No going back now. Fraser, who had, until this point remained aloof, now turned pebble lenses on her.

'Dr Kelly, I'm afraid we must consider your personal circumstances . . .'

Natural pause. She should have used it, but her prepared defence might be seen as over-reaction. Better to let Fraser do his best.

'We have to consider all these things. A demanding job . . . responsibility for those two children. . . .'

Clare scrapped her prepared speech, said, crisply,

'If appointed, I will employ a neighbour, a qualified teacher with only one child of her own. Now . . . going back to the matter of linking with the Maths department for basic statistics. . . .'

Driving Lucy home, Clare stopped to buy herself a woman's magazine, happy birthday from me to me. Last year, there had been David's ritual card.

'I suppose you want me to buy you a card.'

'I don't suppose anything. Don't bother, if you don't want to.'

Here we go again. If I don't buy a card, you sulk for days. If I do, it won't be your style, and I get your nasty clever remarks.'

'I couldn't care less whether you send me a card or not. Most women I know get a present too.'

'Why on earth should I get you a present?'

'Why indeed?'

And then they had discovered that he would be away for her birthday, for a conference in Cambridge. There are telephones in Cambridge, and post-offices. The florists do Interflora. The week of her parents' silver wedding, she had paid for flowers with part of her first ever grant cheque. No David, in those days, to say, flowers die, why not get something useful? No David now, or she would not be driving this car.

'Happy Birthday to you, Squashed tomatoes and stew!'

Lucy collapsed, giggling.

'Daniel taught me that. Are you very old?'

'Ninety-two.'

'That's a story. You're thirty. I know. I asked Uncle Richard, when we saw him at Grandma's. And he said, twenty-nine. So now you're thirty.'

Clare remembered, birthdays are achievement, I should be pleased. A good age, nothing to be scared of. Womanhood at last.

'Who's coming to the party?'

'What party?'

Red lights. Clare pulled up. They were bound to be late now, lights against them all the way.

'But there has to be a party! Cake, and jelly, and presents . . .'

'Not for me.'

Lucy began to cry.

'But I wanted to get a present! I didn't know, until Daniel telled me.'

'Told.' Hey, Lucy, are you listening? Today is the Ides of March, my birthday. The fifteenth. . . .'

The child was not interested, and didn't hear. She was crying, inexplicably deprived. Clare kept her tears inside. Ridiculous, of course, to care now. Jim and Moira's card would arrive late, as usual, because they were mean about postage. Yet Moira would ring tonight, talk for half an hour. The card itself would be expensive, for a dear daughter. Two dear daughters they had, two sons, never a birthday forgotten. David's family ignored commercial sentiment, did not, as Len put it, celebrate to order. The birthday child was allowed to choose the evening menu, that was all. Betty kept a box of charity cards in a kitchen drawer, which she posted without consulting Len. A card from Betty, then, second post? Undeserved. She hadn't written to Betty once, all these weeks. Imagine making up a life around meals on time for Len, eking out the shopping, day by day, so there would be something to do. In two months though, there would be Julia's child. If it was a boy, they would be brave not to call it David. Perhaps Betty was happy enough in her own way, knitting for Julia's child, finding ways to her own few minutes of pleasure each day.

'The lights, Mummy!'

Clare started, only just in time. She remembered now. It was like this all the way back, single-line traffic, emergency lights, delays of up to an hour. The local radio had described it all in loving detail at breakfast, a new sewage scheme.

'We won't be home in a minute, will we?'

'No.'

'Daniel will cry.'

'No he won't.'

'Yes he will. You know he will.'

Daniel would indeed cry. 'You didn't come. I waited and waited and you didn't come. All the mummies, but not you.' It had happened once before, when a lorry had shed its load at the crossroads, bucketing through a bridge and fifteen feet down the bank into the river. She had raced down to the school, found Daniel gone, then home, to find that sad, hunched figure on the doorstep.

'Another Mummy brought me home.'

'Perhaps Jo will get him.'

'Perhaps.'

They edged forward, but it was only the movement that comes when someone ahead sneaks out, makes a U-turn, goes to find another way home. She switched on the radio, found the repeat of something she had heard last night, while baking the secret cake she had crept down to ice at five a.m. Pink sugar rose, shiny gold message, both three years old. One dozen iced buns, dotted with silver cachous that they would crunch horribly. Furtive arrangements with Jo, and the heavy warning—don't give me anything, understand? They had exchanged birthdays without intent; one Hallowe'en, the other Ides of March.

'Green again. Hooray!'

Clare snapped at the child, suddenly incensed by the ritual cheer. Tonight, she would cringe as they sang 'Happy Birthday.' And where had they learned that? Other people's houses. Remember, if you can, a happy birthday. Childhood parties all had that grim heartiness, the exhausted tears, grieving for a day that was supposed to be perfect. Far better to agree with Humpty Dumpty, enjoy the un-birthdays. As for the excuse, this is just for the children, that was Moira's excuse for Christmas now. We do all these things because our children expect it and must not be disappointed.

'I'm bored. I want to go home.'

'So am I. So do I.'

'Then why don't we? Why don't you tell them all to hurry up?'

'No point. Men are digging up the road, and we can only use one side. You know where Daniel's friend Paul lives?'

'In that big house?'

'Yes. Well, from back up there, all the way to Paul's, they're digging up this road, to put down new pipes. So there's only room for one-way traffic.'

'I didn't know that.'

Clare was tired of talking, so much hard work, explaining one simple everyday disruption. Driving alone, or with anyone safely adult, they need say nothing, only curse a little, switch on the radio. At least she would have been spared this need to explain. Nor would a homecoming father be sick with guilt about his child, out of school, abandoned, without so much as a latchkey. In the mirror, she saw, not her own eyes, but Daniel's. I waited and waited, and you didn't come.

The second emergency lights flashed up to green. Ten past four. Black looks from Hope, from the Woodburn woman, Daniel's teacher. (His security depends so much on you now, Mrs Carradus.) More tears from Daniel. Better, then, do what she could for her other child.

'But what are the pipes for? You haven't told me.'

Clare gave in. Might as well be thorough. Lucy listened, enthralled.

'Say it again. . . .'

'Cholera.'

'And they all died?'

'Lots of them, anyway. And now the pipes they put down are worn out.'

'Will we get cholera?'

'Not if we have new pipes, no.'

They were out of it at last, in the High Street, passing pushchair mothers, busy with after-school shopping. Past the pubs, left, up to the house, and after all, no Daniel crying on the doorstep.

'I guessed you might be late. The roadworks are news, did you know? Anyway, I went to school, and brought him home.'

At ten past six, the phone rang. Jo had stayed for the birthday tea, bringing her own card, with love from Jo and Emma, and, no, please take it, a lead-heavy parcel, two bound volumes of Punch, from the twenties.

'Only from the junk-shop.'

They were reading them now, while the children watched television. Clare said,

'That will be Grandma. You get it, Daniel.'

Lucy followed him, shrieking.

'My turn. You always talk to her.'

'I came first . . .'

'First the worst, second the best. . . .'

The 'phone clattered to the floor. Lucy came back, aggrieved.

'It isn't Grandma. It's a man.'

She sent them back to television, resented Moira, for never being there when she was wanted.

'Sorry about that. I was expecting a call from my mother, so I let them answer.'

'Pakenham here. Is this a bad time?'

'I didn't recognise your voice.'

'People tell me I sound different on the phone. I thought I'd better let you know.'

Clare felt the sweat break out. The clichés were entirely accurate. Hot and cold, stomach churning, in agony, on tenterhooks.

'Spotted the date on your forms. We're making the appointment. You'll hear officially in a day or two. Happy Birthday, by the way . . . I couldn't persuade them to bring it forward a term. You start October 1st. Still, that gives you plenty of time to get on with your work, doesn't it.'

She focussed on the row of winter clothes, her musquash jacket Jo's shabby duffle coat. Daniel's nasty fur-trimmed parka, the little girls' quilted anoraks. Clumsy heaps of shoes and wellies, her bag, just where she'd dumped it, essays to be marked, a packet of soap powder, her magazine.

'Thanks for ringing.'

'I take it you will accept?'

Clare thanked him, replaced the receiver. Immediately, it began to ring again. Jim.

'I told your mother we only need wait. Happy birthday. All well?'

'Very well. We've got friends in for tea.' (Your little girl had a birthday party, Daddy, everything's fine, guest of honour is my suicidal neighbour.) She had told them nothing about Jo. Moira was bound to say, protecting her own, 'don't get involved, you've been through so much'.

'Dad, guess what . . . my professor just rang. I've got the job.'

She heard Jim calling for Moira, could see, lovingly, the hallway, gilt mirrors, framed photographs of the Kelly children, twin watercolours of the Lake District, daffodils in a cut glass vase before an olive-wood statute of the Virgin Mary. '. . . never hears a word I say, watching that thing.'

Moira came at last.

'Daddy just told me. Congratulations, darling. We've been praying.'

Of course, that was the explanation, no credit, only an answer to prayer, twist God's arm, just for me, after all, I've asked nicely. Moira was a mystery; calmly objective in her work, more than open-minded about religious education, brightly multi-cultural, an earnest student of man's religious quest. Then, there she would be, down at church, on her knees making a Novena.

'So the prayers worked? Which brand do you use? It isn't fair to keep a secret like that.'

'Don't be silly, Clare. You know perfectly well what I mean.'

Clare called the children back.

'It is Grandma now.'

'And Grandad?'

'Of course.'

Two more minutes of family life, have you been good for Mummy on her birthday? A complicated account, from Daniel, of the card he had made, forgotten, finally brought home tonight. Downcast silence from Lucy.

'Bye then, Mum. Thanks for ringing.'

Emma hovered, greedy-eyed, near the cake, more than half of it left.

'Could she have just one more piece, Jo, to take home? We'll only get bored with it.'

Emma said,

'There's only bread and butter in our house. And cornflakes. There isn't any money to buy things.'

'Emma!'

Clare cut the cake into two wedges, wrapped one in a left-over Christmas napkin.

'Always Christmas in this house. With their birthdays in December, there's nothing else in the shops.'

Jo was bustling Emma out, gathering up stray toys, fastening her anorak, even for the journey next door. She took the cake, held Emma's hand cruelly tight, and was gone.

Half-way through marking, with the children in bed. Clare slipped out of the house, rang the doorbell. After the ringing faded down to silence, she lifted the letter flap. The television was on, nine o'clock news, the promise of worse to come. She rang the bell again, trespassing. Moira's rule was clear; if no-one answers the second time, go away. People have a right to privacy. Even Jo. Clare rang again. This time, there were footsteps, the door opened, on is chain.

'You'd better come in.'

'Are you sure?'

Jo closed the door, fixed the chain again.

'I won't stay long. Too much work, and I shouldn't leave them, even next door. What are you doing for money?'

'Rotten little liar she is. We can manage.'

'On what? Bread, butter and cornflakes?'

'Marge, actually. My giro didn't come. They'll sort it out soon.'

Uninvited, Clare sat down. Jo was wearing a dressing gown, dark-green cord, faded, coming apart at a shoulder seam. The gas fire was not lit. Humped on the sofa, there was a duvet.

'I'll put the fire on, if you're cold. I don't bother, not for myself, not once Emma's in bed.'

'I'm alright.'

The room was winter cold, painfully clean, every bar of the

dead fire winking bright. Toys sat in a neat row on a Victorian washstand. Shelves on either side of the fireplace were thick with books, cracked-spine paperbacks, childhood treasures, educational theory, yellow French novels, a stack of German glossy magazines, nothing that could have belonged to the absent husband. On the mantelpiece, there was a chain-store dried flower arrangement, and two clothes peg rocking chairs, cushioned in red felt.

'Lucy has two, just the same.'

'Christmas fair, at the church.'

'So were ours.'

'That explains it then.'

The afternoon's interview had been a school-gate chat, compared to this, every question predictable, every answer a clever formula, clear round, Kelly wins, congratulations.

'If you must know. . . .'

'I must. . . .'

'We're living on family allowance. You know those funny little lists they print in history books? They work. They really work. Potatoes, bread, marge, skim milk powder. One jar of coffee, one bag of sugar. Cheap vitamins from the clinic, so we don't die of scurvy. One bar of chocolate for Emma. They'll sort something out next week, when the visiting officer calls. Doesn't happen, does it? Why don't you get out that fancy toy of yours and take it all down. Write a piece about me for the Sunday papers.'

'Why didn't you tell me?'

Clare tried to see the screen, repeated luxury; how you'll never live.

'Before you ask, that's paid for. The licence ran out. I sold the set, and there was enough for that thing, and a black-and white licence.'

She was very still, the tears falling silently, splashing the faded green, so the colour became dark again.

'But the hospital . . .'

'Lies. They did send out for my family allowance. And they did fix up an appointment. And I did go . . . walked there, with Emma. There was a meths drinker, slumped on one of the benches, peeing on the floor. We waited for two hours, and I asked how much longer. They couldn't say. Emma was hungry, so we came home. It was raining, and someone pulled up beside us, one of those women from up the road. I told her a lovely story, all about leaving my purse in a phone box, and we chatted brightly all the way home about how dreadful everything is these days. And so silly of me, I'd only to get on a bus, explain, give them my name and address. Or take a taxi, settle up when I got in the house. All the time, I was thinking, any moment, Emma's going to give me away. But she didn't, not till tonight.'

'You're lucky. My two would.'

'Emma's used to keeping quiet. She's never told you about it, has she?'

Clare lied. 'No.'

'Now you know. Hadn't you better go home?'

'Not yet. I've got that job.'

'Congratulations.'

'I haven't accepted. Not yet.'

'You mean, will I look after the kids for you?'

'For pay?'

'Of course.'

Jo moved over to the fire, turned it on. She crouched beside it, greedy for the heat. Clare joined her, so they were physically close. The closeness made impossible questions possible.

'I lied, at the interview. They believe in you already.'

'What if I'd said, No? Emma starts school in September. I might find a job.'

Clare stood up.

'I can advertise.'

'Don't be so bloody daft. No, you take the job, and I'll do the wife and mother bit here.'

Sinister? But she was laughing. They could talk money later.

'I'd better go now. I was in the middle of marking.'

'At least I don't have that. I can't imagine it now, all those nights at a desk strewn with paper.'

At the front door Clare hesitated.

'Let me bring a few things round. Just to tide you over.'

'I can manage.'

'Maybe, but what about Emma?'

The laugh was a sneer this time.

'Lady Bountiful is it? Go on, then, I wouldn't dare say no.'

She waited by the open door. A prowling cat flattened itself against the fence. Clare returned with a full carrier-bag.

'It's not very much. See you in the morning.'

Jo took the bag, not looking inside.

'Thank-you.'

Then goodnights, doors closing, lights on and off. Clare found that she had left the fire on, all that time. She turned it off, worked until one in a room that grew quickly cold. Twelve essays, all marked. One thing about Kelly, she gets your stuff back in good time.

'Donatello?'

'Mmmmmmm. The "David".'

'I only know that muscle-bound macho of Michelangelo's. Anyway, who is it fancies me?'

'Chrissie Hallam. She admired you from her window and expressed interest.'

'She's pregnant, isn't she?'

'You seem to know all about it.'

'Rumour has it Jon Ellis is the father.'

'Do you lot spend your time gossiping about us?'

'Definitely not, except when rumour has it. . . . I can't see it though, can you?'

'No.'

'Maybe she wanted a kid, and Ellis did the decent thing. A neighbourly service, like changing a washer. Only, I can't imagine Ellis changing a washer either.'

'Why not? I can.'

'You, my lovely, are not gay. Practical skills would ruin his image and his pretty hands too. By the way, congrats.'

'Oh?'

'Senate notice board. Dr C.P.M. Kelly from part-time to full-time lecturer. So I see more of you?'

'If you do my courses. Less, if you don't, I'll be too busy.'

Garwy pulled her closer.

'That I won't believe. Get your priorities right.'

'I have. The order is this: Kids, job, house. You happen in whatever free time comes my way.'

'It's not enough.'

Clare was sitting by the window, with a clear view across the courtyard, watching a squirrel that dared to spring and dart, quicksilver, in the birches.

'Twenty years from now, this place might be real.'

'Like the architects drawings? I doubt it. Real rubble, you mean.'

'Sculpture . . . no. . . . Relief. Tiles. It's the rusting concrete that looks so sinister.'

Garwy was arranging notes, trying to put them in order, stapled together.

'You work just like me. I sit at the desk for hours, grinding away. Then it takes me half an hour to put the pages in order. I hope that isn't your dissertation?'

'Not likely. You said we could have until after Easter. No, it's my first editorial.'

'I thought you didn't take over till next term?'

'Meredith's decided to stand down early. He's come down rather badly in grades this term, and wants to make sure of his first. We've decided the editor should always be a second-year man in future.'

'Meredith? Is there a Welsh closed shop on this campus?'

'Born and bred Brummy. Stop humouring me, Clare.'

The squirrel had found a discarded roll. Students had a way of wandering out of the refectory like children, still eating. He sat, tail in its squirrel curve, black eyes darting, gnawing the hard crust. In the stillness, she could hear the rasp of teeth. If the children were here, she would have missed this sound; if they were here, there would, like as not, be no squirrel, only shrieks and wails, he's gone, it's not fair!

'I'm not humouring you.'

'Yes you are. Polite chat about the little games we play. What did you do in school today? Wrote a newspaper? . . . Who's mummy's clever boy?'

'Don't be so childish. May I read it?'

'There you go again. And I doubt if you could read it. Can't work it out myself half the time.'

'Try me. Anyway, why don't you type? If you're serious about jouranalism, you'll have to learn.'

'You'll be selling me a word-processor next.'

'If you've got the money, why not? I would.'

'The moving keyboard types, but second thoughts can cancel every word of it? Not for me, thanks. I need the feel of a pen in my hand.'

'Rubbish. Intellectual luddism, that. Academics can't lord it over the artisans any longer. Imagine what you would do with a machine that moves faster than thought. Imagine Mozart with a computer.'

'I don't want to. Stop lecturing, Clare. Right schoolmarmy bitch you are today. Is it the curse?'

Too intimate, that. She remembered David's distaste; women are such messy creatures, oozing blood; they have no control.

Garwy was very still, aware of guilt, childlike, wanting to appease.

'I wonder why you come here at all.'

'Surely not?'

'You could manage without.'

'Without sex?'

'Without a man.'

Clare didn't move. She was seeing him in detail, ink-stained index finger, pressure mark, on the second finger, from long hours of writing, re-writing, essays, notes, editorials, for the very professional campus paper. Lean, almost thin face, unshaven today, making him look older, his clothes decorous, giving nothing away, nothing individual. David's clothes informed; whether they told the truth about him was another matter.

'Of course I could manage without. But that's a rather desolate solution, isn't it? Merely sex, like eating alone. Am I allowed to read this?'

'If you must. You can tell me what you think.'

'I hardly dare. Next thing, you'll be calling me Nanny.'

'That's an idea. Would you dress up in a starched apron? No, seriously, tell me what you think?'

'I'll risk it.'

She read, instinctively turning away from him, concealing. The content was pure revelation, and only part of her ignorance. She had presumed to know, and teach the boy; the article showed her some of the man. It was fluent, well researched, moving, and prescriptive, could have taken its place with credit in the national press, a study of the long-term mentally ill and mentally-handicapped patients in the local hospital. Silence, while she found any words.

'Honest opinion, please, no flannel.'

'It's very, very good. But you know that, don't you? Is it also true?'

'To the best of my knowledge. Some of us work there, one day a week. If anything, I've understated the worst of the pain. The squalor is spot on. People like squalor; it's easy to send in Rentokil for the cockroaches. Can I publish?'

'You know the answer to that.'

Garwy had taken her hands, making her give up the article, pulling her close, warm lips making her silent. The kiss was a new experience with someone she had not known, when she came into this room. Reluctant, she made him release her, gathered up her belongings, three books, from the library, two borrowed records.

'Don't go. . . .'

'I must. There's so much work to get through. . . .'

'Let it wait.'

He had come between her and the door, and she noticed, suddenly, that the catch was up.

'Careless of us. Anyone might have come in.'

'So? We were only talking.'

Clare thought of resisting, then let her bags drop to the ground. Garwy had her by the wrists, pinning her arms back, kissing roughly, pushing her backwards through the door, into the bedroom.

'You're not going anywhere yet.'

He held her breasts, fists kneading and pounding, cruel, like her babies, the same bullying possession . . . scrabbling through the buttons of her thin wool shirt. She resisted all the way, thrilled.

'You like it, don't you? I'll show you. . . .'

They waited, usually, until she was ready. Not now. . . . One hand over her mouth stifled a cry.

'They called it dying. . . .'

'You passed right out. I was afraid . . .'

Garwy lay beside her, still dressed, white shirt only unbuttoned.

'I want to go away with you.'

'Just a weekend. Even one night.'

'It's not possible. There are the children.'

'Same old excuse. Your husband managed well enough, didn't he? Even when you were married. Isn't there someone who looks after them?'

'Only when I'm working. You knew I had children.'

'Not that you live your life around them.'

'I owe them that.'

She sat up, buttoning her blouse, allowed him to begin kissing again, until there was no more risk of thinking. They rested at last.

'This is impossible.'

'And it can't go on. You'll have to marry me.'

'Not likely!'

'I mean it, Clare. I'm not playing games any more.'

'Nice of you to offer, but no.'

She had the advantage, rejecting. The proposer is necessarily weak, all defences down. Even so, the shock made her unreasonable, driven to conventional excuses. But surely they were enough.

'I'm too old for you, you are too young for me. Marriage would tie you down, restrict your career and threaten my children. And, yes, they do come first.'

'Maybe, but you won't come first with them. In ten years. . . .'

'I'll be forty. I want my own life, and I don't want to marry you or anyone else. Now I want a shower, please.'

Leaving, at last, she kissed him.

'The old routine, kids to collect, feed. Essays to mark, and Daniel's bloody school shirts to iron.'

Clare had to bring the children back into town, for new shoes. The previous pairs had been bought before the funeral. She thought of her life now in three stages, before, it would be such a small part of the whole. Already, she had made a new life.

They managed to park in a side street, near the first, biggest shoe shop. Your child is special, your child is different, even if your child is average our shoes are better for your special average child. There were free badges, there was a giant teddy-bear, and a photo-display of shoes, Ancient Egypt to 1970; painful to find her own youth as history.

'Jesus', said Daniel, knowledgeably, 'wore those sandals with lots of straps, and a buckle.'

And did those feet, Clare thought, come in D, E, F, or G fittings? She had, they told her, two very special children. Daniel managed to combine a high instep with a G fitting. Lucy's slender spindle-feet proved that a real woman might wear Charlotte Bronte's slippers, seen at Haworth, last summer.

'Hardly even a "C", Madam,' said the assistant with pleasure. 'Not every "C" fitting will be suitable for your daughter's foot. Quite remarkably delicate.'

'What's delicate?'

'It means we'll spend hours finding the right shoes for you.'

'But I want these!'

They sat waiting for boxes of shoes, last vestige of service without guilt. Odd, that it should be so right, so praiseworthy, to buy your child shoes to fit a fraction of an inch better than chain-store cheapies. In the shoe shop, children are not born equal. Intellectually, artistically, they must be treated alike, but their feet are different. Selection rules, from C to G. Lucy arched one dainty foot, accepting service from the kneeling man. A good reason for buying shoes.

'Now I like this one.'

The little man made professional apologies.

'Sorry, young lady, but it won't do. You know the story of Cinderella, don't you?'

Lucy nodded.

'Well, this is rather like the story. Only, this time, we have to find the right little shoe for your foot.'

He turned to Clare.

'You see how it is, Madam. The shoe is simply too loose just here. And with wear, the leather will stretch, and she'll be slopping over, with the foot in a bad position. No, I couldn't sell you that shoe.'

They tried eight pairs. There was no need to choose; only the last pair fitted perfectly.

'It says my name, "Lucy". Why didn't we try these first?'

Clare exchanged a glance of sympathy, and fetched Daniel. He had been very quiet, for too long, dangerous, after a day at school. Deliberately demanding? Or was it simply the way any boy of seven behaves, with two live and happily married parents.

'This bear has a hole in it.'

Beside the bear, on the red plush carpet, there was a neat pile of shavings, the kind of toy filling no longer allowed, gone the way of wired glass eyes, and Muffin the Mule, Fifties cosh on strings, disguised as a puppet. The bear was slightly taller than Daniel, a great deal fatter. It would take many more bored children to pull out all his innards. Shameless, Clare edged the bear forwards, sat him on his own sawdust.

The assistant knelt to his work.

'So very different. This goes to show, of course, how unwise it is to hand down shoes in a family. I can see that the little girl takes after you, Madam. And I expect this young man has big strong feet like Daddy?

'No, I haven't.' Daniel stared at his feet, one in a grey sock with a hole in the toe, one heavy and strange in the new shoe. 'My Daddy is dead. Can I try the other one?'

'I'm afraid not. You see, this is only an "F". I thought it might possibly do, but you really must have the next fitting.'

They still had to pay for Lucy's shoes. The man whispered to Clare.

'So very sorry, Madam. . . .'

'It's quite alright. You couldn't possibly know. . . .'

In the street, Daniel was ready to be difficult. Lucy had new shoes, he had not, therefore he was deprived, cheated of his birthright.

'Don't do that again. Understand?'

'But it was an accident! For real! Anyway, there was a hole already. Did you tell?'

Clare held his hand.

'I meant, telling people Daddy is dead. It upsets them.'

'But he is dead.'

In the fourth shoe-shop, they found black leather, G-fitting, size thirteen.

'We'll take them.'

She paid again, added up the cost of both pairs, thought of Jo, shopping with Emma, her special child.

'This last shoe-shop was near the bus-stop.

'If only we didn't have the car, we could get that bus now. Rotten walk to horrible car-park.'

'I'll buy you crisps, if we go the short cut.'

Bribed, they ran ahead of her, down scrubby back streets, heading for Marks and Spencer. Stopping to buy crisps would cancel out any time gained in the short-cut, but she bought them all the same, drove them home, with their boxes of new shoes. They did, just, beat the bus.

Ellen rang that evening.

'The Mothering Sunday service, my dear. I know you have your own church, but this year, I thought you might like to come along. A real *family* occasion. It's all very simple, very sweet. Four o'clock, in church, and then tea afterwards. The first of the lighter evenings, too, so nice for everyone. Perhaps that neighbour of yours would like to come along too?—Mrs Sinclair.'

'Jo?'

'And the little girl, of course. Shall I meet you outside church?'

'Ten to four?'

'I thought, perhaps, three-forty-five. We can get nicely settled, before the service starts.'

Mid-Lent, Mothering Sunday, Mother's Day, Rose-pink vestments, relief from penitent purple, a break in the lenten fast. Clare remembered Convent days, what are you giving up? Only sweets? I'm giving up sweets, and sugar in my tea, and my comic, and ice-cream on Friday nights when Carlo rings his bell. Well, I'm going to Mass every day. Convent girls, hot and red with the shame of an accepted sweet. Spit it out and offend the giver? Clare had a special difficulty, in that her birthday was always in Lent. She had, aged eight, put the question to Sister Mary Dominic. Should she put her birthday off, until Easter? Being a moveable feast, this could mean a long wait, nearly six weeks to April 25th. On the other hand, it might be only a week, to March 22nd, which was the earliest possible date, Sister Mary Dominic hadn't said yes, and she hadn't said no. She pointed out that the great feast of the Eucharist is celebrated most gloriously at Corpus Christi, with none of the sadness of the Last Supper. It suited Moira, anyway, to delay Clare's party until the Easter holidays, and so the matter was resolved. Lent? She tried to become that child, with her sense of sin, convent-born. Laetare, Jerusalem. Time to take stock; what have you made of Lent so far?

Clare, waking early, despite the changing clocks, decided that she would go to Mass.

Daniel and Lucy were chosen to carry up the bread and wine, fruit of the foreign vine, machine-aided work of human hands. At Christmas, Daniel had explained this mystery to David.

'It doesn't *mean* bread and wine any more, Daddy. It means God. But it looks just the same.'

'I see. Amazing!'

Clare reported half this exchange to Moira.

'Theologically, that's very good indeed. Where is he being instructed?'

From the First Reading, until the offertory procession, the children were sent out, bricks and rag books for the babies, lego, and, very occasionally, if someone felt so inclined, gentle discussion about the day's Gospel. Clare re-defined this.

'There's a crèche for babies, and instruction for the older children, during the readings and the sermon.'

Jim and Moira were pleased; the grandchildren were safe after all, and Daniel showing the benefit already.

'Re-inforcement of faith comes, in part, as a grace from this collective worship. Out on our own, knowing our weakness, it's so easy to be swayed. 'This was Cofferidge, off-duty as Vice Chancellor, on Sunday duty as a Catholic father and husband.

'You must find it very difficult, Clare, keeping the faith alive, on your own with those children. It must help, coming here, seeing people you know, all worshipping together. I used to think, as a young man, whenever my faith wavered, well, they're a good deal more dignified than all the rest who're still in bed.'

Cofferidge spoke, always, laboriously, as if afraid of an un-edited word betraying him. Odd to think that David, the faithless, must now know, one way or the other, if it was all true. Easier, almost, to believe that he no longer existed, in any dimension, than to imagine him faced with truth.

All this term, she had avoided the place, first hampered by having no car, and lately, of course, by the affair with Garwy. Kneeling in chapel, seeing the bowl of bread pass from one to another, then the heavy, ceramic chalice, she thought again. It was so very little, set apart from all the hard work of her life, mother, teacher, friend, daughter. Is an hour or so with a lover enough to bar me from the Sacraments? Or is my own lack of faith the reason, and this other only an excuse? She got up suddenly, walked out, right out of the chapel, into the morning air and light.

Outside, there was a low wall, at sitting height, built of lichen green Westmorland slate. A hundred yards away, across the car-park, she saw two hurrying figures, heading for Sunday papers, after their dedicated slog around the seven lakes, seven hills. The lake down by the Hall, picture postcard, prospectus lake, was only the first in a made to measure romantic landscape, that wandered over to face the blue hills of Wales. Hard exercise, papers, breakfast; the right and proper way to begin the day.

'Are you feeling better now? We've taken the children down to the bar. you do look white. . . .'

'I'm all right.'

Pat Murphy, of course, the latest Murphy baby in its corduroy pouch, slung from her shoulders, the four bigger little Murphys presumably downstairs with Dad. Five times nine months, and as many fifth month miscarriages, before they diagnosed and stitched her incompetent cervix, five knife cuts instead of giving birth, faced with terrible courage.

'At least knowing exactly *when* helps me organise things.' Part of the last organisation was, presumably, arranging the birth for Candlemas. The Murphy children were all born on great feast days. How many more, now Tom had been promoted to Senior Lecturer?

'Tom and I thrilled to hear the news of your promotion. We were wondering, would you like to join us for lunch? Bring the children, of course. . . .'

'Wouldn't that be rather a strain?'

Pat stroked the baby's downy head.

'Heavens, no. With all our crowd, your two will hardly be noticed. . . .'

The smug fecundity of a hero-mother.

'I put that badly, didn't I? . . . They must be such a comfort to you.'

Clare did not resist. Pat, loving mother of five, with room in her heart, if not in her house, for more. Five little Murphy's, on time for Mass every Sunday of their lives, the Mass in Pictures, My Book of Saints, A First Missal. Murphy children saying grace before meals, God Bless Mummy and Daddy, every night. Murphy children singing that ghastly rhyme on Lucy's record, clap hands, till Daddy comes home, Daddy has money and Mummy has none. The tears were allowed, this time.

'Sorry, Pat. I don't often cry.'

The baby came between them. Kathleen Mary Murphy, born Candlemas, baptism briefly, in the hospital, the full ceremonies planned for the Easter Vigil.

'Would it help to talk to Phil? We'll look after the children. I feel mean for not coming to see you, but K.M. here's been taking up all Mummy's time, haven't you?'

She nuzzled the baby's head. Clare looked away. The last time, giving birth to Lucy, she had been possessed with sadness; this is the last time, it won't happen again, not to me, not in this life. And that had been enough to kill all the joy, knowing that it would not come again. David had said, mid-term, one hand on her belly, to feel Lucy move.

'This is the last, two's enough. And besides, you want to go back to work, don't you?'

Afterwards, with the baby born, one boy, one girl, symmetrical ideal family, he had said,

'I don't want another child with you.'

Pat's arm round her.

'Clare—oh, you poor dear.'

'Poor Clare? That's what they used to call me at school. Could I hold her?'

The baby was in her arms. Murphy babies arrived small, never more than six pounds. Kathleen Mary, seven weeks old, opened slatey eyes and smiled. The sweetness was not a dream, they did smell like this, the weakness of that heavy head did move you to tears, even another woman's, another man's child. Clare gave the baby back to her mother.

'She's beautiful. I used not to think so. I used to say all the fashionable things, babies are ghastly, I only love my own. Self-defence. I wish there could be one more.'

Pat said, brightly,

'You might marry again. There's plenty of time. Look, here's Phil now. I'll go down to the children.'

'The library? We won't be disturbed there.'

Clare allowed herself to be lead, black clericals, well cut, not shiny with age, black shoes, shiny with polish. She let him show her where to sit, deplore, as usual, the vogue for low discomfort when the chairs were bought. She waited for him to speak. Rigby, Philip S.J., M.A., Ph.D., S.T.L. Rigby had specialised in host/parasite relations, furthering the idea of non-toxic natural pest control for food crops. His papers, two of his books, were still in regular undergraduate use. He had a T.V. series to his credit, and still, from time to time, acted in an advisory capacity to the B.B.C. Natural History Unit.

'I'm sorry.'

'No need. I'm a great believer in tears.'

Rigby knew, because Clare had told him, in confession, what her marriage to David had been. No need to go over old ground. Easy, then, to say it.

'As if I willed his death.'

'But it was an accident.'

'Not the will of God?'

Rigby touched her hand.

'What loving father wills the death of his young children? On the other hand, David chose to be out on that road, in those conditions.'

'I don't think I want to talk about David. I think i'd stopped loving him. It's not David.'

'No?'

She stared past him, past beams that were tailored to sweep down, form the flanks of bookshelves, in this young room, under the eaves of a young chapel. You would look in vain, here, for anything intentionally lovely. The sunbeam had got in by itself, through plain glass. The door, though, had a marquetry centre; crown of thorns, five nails.

'I was crying, just now, holding the Murphy baby. It came home to me suddenly, no more babies, no more marriage. All around David, there are beloved wives. Not me, never me. There was no love. . . . But you know all this.'

'I'm having an affair with someone. Someone much younger. One of the students.'

Time for Rigby to say something, surely? But of course, he would not. They would remain here, until it was time to go, but nothing would be said, unless she wanted it said.

'It began as sex, nothing else. Any excuse you like. I was lonely, he was attractive and willing.'

She looked up.

'You're not making this easy, are you? Would it sound better if I were a man?'

Rigby relented.

'God doesn't operate a double-standard.'

'You make God sound so accessible.'

'You exclude, you decide when to come back. Free will decision, yours to make.'

'So you noticed?'

'That you didn't receive communion? Only because you went out. You excluded yourself.'

'Then I'm not a public sinner. Or hurting anyone. I'm not married, nor is he.'

'No. But would you want your children to know about this—affair—?'

'Of course not.'

'So. As for the boy himself?'

'He thinks he loves me.'

Clare met Rigby's eyes, composed, in control of herself now; the meeting had become properly diagnostic.

'It's strangely beautiful, you know. I'd forgotten all the grace . . . idealism . . . quite certain that he can change the world.'

'And you would harness all that, for a few hours in bed?' She said, crisply,

'Did you join up as a virgin? Or is that an unfair question?'

Rigby smiled. Diagnosis shifted over into sympathy, compassion.

'It's not one a woman would have asked me, ten, fifteen years ago. No, I wasn't a virgin.'

'I was, when I met David.'

'So you think God owes you a free kick or two?'

'More or less, yes, I do. I did. Compensation, if you like, for what I've missed.'

'But you haven't quite the courage of your convictions? You declared yourself unworthy, this morning.'

'Conditioning. Taboo. I was even afraid . . . no, don't smile like that . . . I was even afraid that if I did. . . .'

'Receive Communion in a state of sin?'

'Then . . . something else might be taken away.' She faltered, then faced him, confident, direct, discovering the truth.

'It isn't easy. You see, I've begun to love him too.'

Rigby was colder now.

'Then I have to repeat my question, would you like Lucy and Daniel to know? I take it there is no thought of marriage?'

'I don't want to marry him.'

Accept the inevitable: 'Would you like, now, to make your confession.' Then repeating, coldly, unadorned, everything she had said, then absolution. All in secret, under the seal of the confessional. I have forgiven you, go, and sin no more. The classic sin, too, and now she was released, following him down the steps, into the bar.

The Murphy's, together, repeated their offer of lunch. Daniel and Lucy were engrossed in a game with the eldest Murphy boys.

'They're having such fun. We've nothing very special, I'm afraid, but you mustn't be alone.'

Clare explained about Mothering Sunday.

'But that isn't until four. Come on. It's nice for the children. I was one of two, and it isn't enough. You have to find someone else. Marvellous insight of Ransome's, that, with the Blackett girls, one-parent family, running a bit wild, and then, the elder suddenly showing precocious maturity. They rely on friendship with the other four.'

Clare felt extraordinarily happy. Tom Murphy's special subject was children's literature; better than that, it was his consuming passion. He was in love with childhood, with the enchantment of a parallel world living by its own rules, a world in which all things were possible, and nothing was what it seemed. His first, and so far only publication, The Discovered Country, had been a B.B.C. publication, linked to the series, of the same name. Tom was a happy and confident man; therefore his company was pure pleasure, given that one could stand the reek of his chewed pipe.

'Of course, the single-parent theme is very strong in children's literature. And the orphan proper, of course. The Secret Garden'.

'The Bastables.'

'Wuthering Heights'.

'Peter Rabbit', said Clare, giggling.

'Jane Eyre.'

'What Katy Did.'

'And there you have the explanation, of course. One-parent families were the common experience. The Brontës simply took Jane Austen's admirable advice, and wrote about what they knew. If children are encumbered with two happily married parents, they either declare war. . . .'

'William.'

'Get themselves shipped off to school. . . .'

'Jennings, the Chalet school.'

'Or they find some way of escaping the loving clutches. For instance, the Swallows' father is usually at sea. And the parents are blessedly free of the nanny complex. Now, would you let a non-swimming seven-year-old sail across Windermere to camp on an island, without so much as a life-jacket in sight?'

'Depends on whether I wanted him back or not.'

'And when you do get domestic togetherness, the result is the Swiss Family Robinson, No, as a literary form, the nuclear family is definitely a non-starter.'

Clare considered this.

'Orlando The Marmalade Cat? Every woman's wish-fulfilment husband, always there, always loving, gets them out of trouble, takes them on holiday, and even remembers his wife's birthday.'

Pat detached herself from the group around the bar.

'Is this is a private party or may anyone join?'

Tom smiled across at his wife, happy mother of his five happy children.

'Clare and I were discussing the one-parent family in literature. The only entertaining two-parent family either of us can come up with is Orlando's.'

'Orlando? Virginia Woolf?'

'The Marmalade Cat.'

'Let's try you. Name a children's book you liked.'

'Swallows and Amazons?'

'Nancy and Peggy's father was dead. Any more?'

'I had a long and stormy time with the Chalet School. Joey Bettany. But I think she was an orphan.'

'We allow orphans.'

Cofferidge and his wife came over.

'Feeling better?'

Clare reassured them.

'And she's coming back with us for lunch. Come on, Aidan. We're holding a seminar. One parent families and orphans in literature.'

'Frodo Baggins? Weren't his parents drowned? And there's all those parents we must presume dead. Lear must have had a wife, to give him those lovely daughters, but what became of her?'

'Begin at the beginning, though,' said Tom, sucking his pipe. 'Mother Earth and Uranus. Clear case of necessity being the mother of invention, that.'

Pat captured two small Murphy's, as they scampered past.

'You can find Damian and Dominic. And you've lost me as usual. What happened to Swallows and Amazons?'

Cofferidge explained. 'He's just showing off. They're all the same. Great men. Never grow up. Mother Earth emerged from Chaos. Uranus was her son, who got things organised, trees, flowers and so forth. Then he and Mum canoodled and produced twelve little Titans. Six boys, six girls.'

'I see. No, I don't. How did you get here from there, I

mean, where we were a few minutes ago, We were talking about children? Weren't we?'

Clare caught her own children.

'Lunch with Dominic and Damian?'

'Con and Benedict?'

No need to ask. Define another Sunday at home: Jo—elusive, painfully watching as Clare's own life began again. A cold drizzle was falling, so they would not be staying outside. Reading the papers, through to the bucket shop adverts, reviews of films and plays they would never see, the afternoon hours heavy with the sense of waste. She knew, suddenly, that Rigby was right, even if there was no sin. The affair—or whatever it was—with Garwy, must come to an end. They could never spend a Sunday comfortably together. The Sunday papers said to her, week after week, if you haven't made it by now, you never will. I could do it but no-one will ever ask me, not now. I will not dash in at lunchtime to buy two returns to Patmos. I will never even go north with him, over the sea to Skye. All that's left is this furtive secret coupling. A cheat, and in no way good enough, because he is young, and I am not. They would not survive the enforced retreat of Sunday together. David had said, last November, one almost friendly evening,

'You're a very "if only" person.' He had elaborated.

'You won't accept the consequences of what you've done. Choices you've made.'

'Such as?'

'Marrying me, for a start. "If only I hadn't," you whine. I just get on with my life. So could you.'

'I know you do. So why stay married?'

'Why not? You couldn't afford a house like this on your own. There are the children. Daniel likes his school. My job is quite near. It's a pleasant enough place. So why go to all the expense of a divorce? Do you want to get married again?'

'No. Why, do you?'

'Not at present. So there you are. Len and Betty came to this agreement years ago, so you see, it does work.'

'I don't know anyone more unhappy than your mother.'

Then David's anger,

'What the hell do you know about my mother?'

'That you all used her, and now she has nothing left.'

'Drivel. Sometimes I think you believe the drivel you talk.'

Clare had got up, switched on the television, only to see the nine o'clock news. Then David's stinging slap, then his going. She hadn't seen him again until the evening of the next day. The children hadn't asked where he was. Poor, unmourned David.

The Murphy's didn't live in a council house, only a cheap copy of one, cribbed from some city architects' department, undernourished offspring of the Parker-Morris models. Three beds, one and a half recep., narrow, fraught little kitchens, garages in a separate block, small, easily-maintained gardens front and back, just about bearable for young couples on the way to better things. Nightmarish, surely, for seven. Tom had rigged up a light in the garage, which he used as a study, heating it with a smelly paraffin stove. In summer, the boys kicked footballs against the cheap steel up-and-over door. At all times, unkempt bicycles and half-deflated plastic footballs littered the communal green. The campus wives pegged out identical bedding on rotary dryers, Superman for the boys, coy prints for the girls.

'Give it time,' Tom said, opening the cobalt blue flat door, 'Give it time . . . another century or so and these will be quaint . . . workers' cottages. They'll raise money to preserve them, get in the National Trust.'

'Tom lives on his delusions', said Pat, comfortably, chasing the older boys inside.' He planted ivy and clematis, but the clematis died, and the ivy made the wall damp. I wonder if you could move here, now you're coming full time. The MacLeod's are off to New Zealand this summer.'

'I thought that was just a sabbatical?'

'It is, but they won't be back. Siobhan's coming into a bit of money. They don't even need to go out there.'

'How can anyone "need" to go to New Zealand?'

'Geologists go to the strangest places.'

'You'd better apply pretty soon, if you are intending to move here?'

Clare remembered that Pat had never seen her own solid, suburban comfort, had no idea of Clare's other, wifely life. Pat coped with the appalling conditions of her life simply by never considering any better state. Time off from feeding and bearing the young was devoted to Catholic charities for preventing abortion and feeding the Third World. Pat knew perfectly well that she was, by these standards, rich.

Clare was trying to work out why she had suddenly thought of the Science Museum, closing her eyes, to concentrate better. The trick worked; she had just left the distorting mirrors, to walk round the pre-fab. In the Murphy house, there were the same low oppressive ceilings, the same crushingly close walls, and the room which had been small enough when she first stepped in shrank alarmingly as it filled with bodies. But she said, as if after some thought,

'Oh, I think I might as well stay put. It's a long trek for me, but school's just round the corner.'

Asking for trouble, that was.

'Daniel isn't at the Catholic school, is he?'

'David and I thought it was too far.'

'Well, there's that to consider. If you moved up here, you'd be that much nearer. There's a minibus from here anyway.'

Pat had wandered through the milling children to her peeling formica and chipboard kitchen. She had done her best, with healthy bulk-buys, strange pulses in jars, authentic reproduction scales, even a couple of chipped enamelled advertisements, but the veneer still hung in curling strips from the struts of the built-in units. The windows were permanently fogged with condensation, because Pat was always either washing or cooking. That was no excuse for the wet rot pulping the window frames; nevertheless, it was there, like the half inch gap between the back door and its frame. Yet Pat seemed to radiate the spacious busy affection of a traditional farm kitchen, and this was, quite possibly, how she experienced her lot. Beyond the fog, there was a three-star view of prime pasture, mature forest, and purple hills. Besides, Pat had her children, and was content.

That is to say, she was content so far as Clare knew. They had never been intimate before, never shared a meal, unless one counted the bread and wine at Mass. Tom wasn't, except in the broader sense, even a colleague. There were still some who did not consider Education to be a bone fide discipline. Pat was a familiar stranger. As a full-time mother, she had only used the crèche in emergencies. She was believed to be a devoted mother, on no particular grounds, except the number of her children, and the Caesarian births. But entering another woman's kitchen presumes friendship, even intimacy.

Clare sketched a few of her family details. Bernard, five years older, pathologist, disabled, on the way to being distinguished. Then Ruth, two years younger. 'She writes.'

'Ruth Kelly? . . . Have I read her? Ought I to know?'

Clare prompted, with the title of what Ruth called 'my most worthy book'.

'She writes for children. And she's good. Shaming, to have my little sister so successful.'

Pat said, of course Pat would would say,

'But you have the children.'

'People with children write. Look at Margaret Drabble . . . Antonia Fraser. . . .'

'Even so, I'm sure something suffers. They need us. Tom had an article, explaining how damaging it is, even if a mother works at home.'

Complacent, condemning Pat, always available for her children. Clare, a woman, preparing food, spread cheap margarine on high-fibre white bread. 'Little beasts won't eat wholemeal. This is the next best thing.'

Too late, now, for an ill-timed retreat. Daniel and Lucy would eat too much of the Murphy food, stretched to fill ten, if one counted Kathleen Mary's re-routed share. Would they notice if she ate nothing?

'Pot luck, I'm afraid. And we all just help ourselves. Bread, cheese, sausage. Can your two manage on that?'

Clare said, truthfully, 'that it was more than they would get at home'.

Pat slopped soggy lettuce leaves into a faded plastic collander, then into an outcast expensive bowl, wedding relic unaccountably unbroken. She dredged the lettuce with table salt, and brown vinegar. Chrissie, in the same time, would make a dressing bred in France,

'Afraid I'm not very good with salad. Mine aren't really very keen, so it doesn't seem worth the effort. Chrissie's salads are a dream.'

'I was just thinking of Chrissie myself.'

Their eyes met; not now, let's save it for later, after lunch.

In Pat's kitchen, there were three plastic baskets, of the kind found in launderettes, piled high with washed clothes, not yet ironed. She didn't apologise.

'I'll see to that tomorrow afternoon. Afternoon theatre and the Monday ironing, that's me. If you ever feel like dropping in for a chat, this is where to find me. Then there's another batch during the concert, on Thursdays.'

'So you don't have T.V?'

'Well, yes, of course, but you can't iron and watch, can you. Not if you want to make a good job of it. There . . . I think we're ready to dish up.'

Afterwards, washing up, women together, Tom half-minding the children from behind The Observer, Pat launched straight into it.

'About Chrissie . . . I suppose you know?'

'Even the students know. One of them even told me who the father is.'

'But he isn't. Of course, it's very decent of Jon to put up with thc rumour's.'

'I get the impression he thinks it's all a bit of a joke. And if he *knows* it wasn't him. . . .'

Pat's voice was suddenly majestic, echoes of Sybil Thorndike or Edith Evans. Her expression too was regal, maternal, supremely tolerant, all-forgiving.

'It was Tom of course.'

She didn't give time for the enormity of this information to sink in, hadn't even taken the precaution of closing the door, which was still slightly ajar.

'I was in the Royal, in the Princess of Wales wing, with high blood pressure, having K.M. and Chrissie came round here to give Tom a hand. She's always wonderful with the babes. I mean, look at the way she manages in the crèche. And of course. Tom was over the moon, having a girl at last. They were celebrating, and Chrissie took her chance.'

She added, daringly,

'And I'd always thought she . . . well, you know.'

Courage had failed her. Clare nodded sympathy.

Pat had finished stacking dishes in the rack. Now she lifted rack and contents into the sink, ran scalding hot water for a minute, then replaced the lot onto the draining board. The operation had the clinical precision of any professional skill. She had not forgotten her S.R.N. training; both her sluice room and bedside manner were well matched to the duties of a devoted housewife and mother.

Clare was still speechless. Pat—possibly regretting her candour—began to explain all.

'Only natural, really. He was missing me, and we hadn't had sex for months.'

'But weren't you angry?'

'Homicidal', said Pat, calmly. 'Twice over . . . once when he told me, and then again when Chrissie told us all her little secret. All over and done with now.'

'People have divorced for less.'

'Daft, I call that. Anyway, I don't believe it. There's got to be a lot more wrong before. . . . And at least she isn't planning an abortion.'

'Anything but. Did you know she'd begun a christening robe before she even fixed the pregnancy?'

'There you are. It could have been a great deal worse. Tom's child won't end up in an incerator. It'll be baptised, and we'll even be able to see it grow up.'

Clare tried to polish knives and forks on a tea-towel that said 'A Souvenir of Walsingham'. Our Lady of Walsingham had lost her face.

'You can't seriously call it "Tom's child".'

Pat scooped up the pile of cutlery, squeezed another tea-towel round the lot.

'I never bother with all that. They always dry smeary. It's this water.'

'But how can you bear the idea of seeing Tom's . . .'

'Bastard? Why not? People always managed. You ought to know, teaching all that juicy history. It was only the Victorians made such a fuss. Look at the Duke of Monmouth, nearly getting the throne.'

'William the Bastard managed even better.'

'There you are. And there was Leonardo. . . .'

'Ramsay MacDonald. . . .'

'All those Borgia nephews? I give up. I can think of far more famous people born the right side of the blanket. No matter, it's not the child's fault. Daddy used to say, no such thing as an illegitimate child, only illegitimate parents.' Lucky Pat, still content with what Daddy said.

'But this was deliberate.'

Pat began to stack plates in a cupboard.

'I don't know why I bother. It'll be time to get started with tea soon. Tom likes a good old fashioned high tea. You know, that aspect has been bothering me. Chrissie's made a joke of this for so long, saying she wanted children, but couldn't find anyone to marry her. We'd all be laughing, children all round, well, what's the problem. Borrow Iain for a night. Half an hour, even, it doesn't take long. And then we were all fooling around, talking their nonsense.'

'They?' Pat was shifting pronouns, party to all this, not wholly involved, knowing that she was irrevocably different.

'You know what I mean. The all girls together crowd. And if you don't, it's no use me explaining. Well, I could either stay quiet, poor old Pat, bit of a queer fish, or chip in.'

'Tom would oblige, I'm sure', I said. Then they all laughed, said she ought to take me up on that, because Tom had the best stud record. I was the only one actually looking pregnant. Some of the others were too, but early, it didn't show. Then it was Christmas, and I never gave it another thought, until he told me, after K.M.'

'You believed him?'

'Of course. I trust him.'

Clare, eloquently, made no comment.

'I trust him to tell the truth.'

'I preferred the times David was kind enough to lie, but never mind that. But Chrissie swore it was Jon Ellis.'

'She'll be saying it was Aidan Cofferidge next. Or even poor old Pakenham.'

Clare picked up a tray of smeared glasses.

'Where do these go?'

'In that cupboard.'

'I'm not being much help.'

'I could've managed better without you, yes. I wanted to talk.'

'I wouldn't be so forgiving.'

'But I would. Seventy times seven, remember. It was only the once, and even then he was drunk. Not like Tom at all. . . .'

'Getting drunk or laying Chrissie?'

'Neither . . . either . . . I'm no good at grammar.'

'And Chrissie?'

Pat was perched on a badly varnished home assembly stool, crumpling Our Lady of Walsingham, twisting the wet cloth into a rope. Her accent had become more Irish.

'That's the difficult bit. With her it was pre-meditated.'

'I see. Like murder. She wanted a kid, and Tom—or whoever—was simply the means. So is that worse than Tom's drunken bit on the side?'

Pat untied her apron sgrings, inspected two pale inches of her face in a tiny glass, surrounded by sea-shells, above an egg-timer, a present from Morecambe, brought home from a school trip by Damian and Dominic.

'Worse, I think, because it's using the other person as an object.'

'But Tom had a good excuse?'

'An explanation. After all, he was hardly in control.'

'No-one made him get drunk.'

Irish uppermost, Pat lashed back,

'Sure, 'tis only human. . . . Clare, do you truly think it could be someone else after all, not Tom?'

'Easily. No-one's suggesting she was desperate to have Tom's child. In her position, I'd have tried as many men as possible. Or maybe A.I.D.'

'You're very hard. I thought Chrissie was a friend of yours.'

Clare had the door half-open, keeping her voice low.

'I thought so too. Easy-going, everyone's friend, loveable Chrissie.'

The baby was in full cry. She must have been crying moderately for some time. She had now reached that lusty pitch of fury that requires a deep intake of breath, brief silence, then a long roar of agony, repeated until exhaustion or attention ensues. Pat's blouse, prettily dark and floral, showed two wet patches as she hurried towards the baby. Clare unearthed her coat from the pile slung over the back of a stretch-covered armchair, called her children.

'Thanks for a super lunch. We must dash. See you soon.'

Tom saw her to the door, all of two yards. From the car, they waved goodbye.

In the mirror, she could see the bottom half of Tom and his four sons.

Ellen had called on Jo and Emma.

'I thought, in this nasty rain, you might think it was all off. Then I rang, and there was no answer, so I was worried about you, dear. So I popped down, and there was no sign, and then I thought of asking Mrs Sinclair if she'd seen you.'

'We went up to the University. Then friends asked us to stay for lunch. They have a new baby and I hadn't seen her yet.'

'That *is* nice for you, dear. So good for the children, the chance of real family life. My three felt the loss, I know.'

Oh, yes, Mrs Kenyon? Real drudgery, real adultery, we all miss it.

'They did enjoy themselves.'

Walking into church, mother of children, Clare examined her own two, for signs of deprivation, like vitamin deficiency. The eyes of a fatherless child? Already, the congregation were singing.

Jo whispered,

'Silly old bat! But she's kind. I forgive her.'

The adults, mothers, fathers, parishioners, had to kneel at the back. The children filled ten rows of pews in the centre aisle. Tied to the end of every pew, in the slot once used for candles, there were bunches of daffodils, ivy, and primroses. Greville preached to the children for five digitally-timed minutes, on the theme of the Fifth Commandment. Clare, brought up on the Roman Catholic decalogue, in which this is 'Thou Shalt Not Kill', was a little confused. Finding a Book of Common Prayer in the pew, she improved her education by reading the Thirty-Nine Articles. It was quicker not to attempt understanding. The convent catechism had been short on long words, and the only one she could remember was dismissed thus: 'Transubstantiation, or the change of substance of Bread and Wine in the Supper of the Lord, cannot be proved by Holy Writ; but is repugnant to the plain words of Scripture, overthroweth the nature of a Sacrament, and hath given occasion to many supersitions. . . .'

The nuns . . . in panic, when a fragment of bread dropped to the marble floor, the priest, purifying, distressed, but prepared for this calamity.

Clare flipped the pages backwards and forwards, surreptitiously glancing at Ellen. Greville was calling up selected children to read bidding prayers. Did country vicars really instruct confirmation classes on the finer points of works of Supererogation? How many signed up, casualty or armed service C of E's could name even one out of the thirty-nine? David, baptised, married and buried R.C. would have been hard put to name the current pope. Enough wool-gathering. . . . Instead, she let her eyes wander about this alien, English church. The little green alternative series prayer books were dog eared, and the Book of Common Prayer had a jacket of winter dust when she picked it up. In the far aisle, the Lady Chapel was back in service, bright with spring flowers. God the Mother?

Chrissie had tried to play God, deciding that a child should be born, with scant regard for the effect on her necessary accomplice. She, the mother, was in control. Even the law agreed; she would have sole custody. The child so deliberately found a father would be born fatherless. Clare was suddenly conscious of Jim and Moira, as if they had sublime parental access to her thoughts. Jim, as a father, a generation removed from the act of generation. Closing her eyes, she could see Moira's look of chill disgust. Animal lust, degradation of the body. The Articles didn't mince matters.

'Man is very far gone from original righteousness, the flesh lusteth always contrary to the spirit, and therefore, in every person born into this world, it deserveth God's wrath and damnation.'

The classic error, though, was interpreting this crudely as sexual lust, rather than desiring anything to excess, to the exclusion of God. What had David desired? They had talked about this, years ago, in the days when they still talked.

'What do you really want?'

'Happiness of course. The same things as everyone else, basically.'

'But what do you mean by happiness?'

'Peace of mind. Freedom.'

She had thought this very profound, very noble. She had been deceived. David's way to peace of mind was simple enough. He cut out any disturbing thoughts, allowed no fuss, silenced contradiction, estranged himself. So what did he lust after?

The children now processed to the altar, brothers and sisters, hand in hand, while the organ played, 'All things bright and beautiful'. They sang, in accidental canon. Greville had explained, at some length, his desire to sing even the politically-suspect verse,

'The rich man in his castle
The poor man at his gate
God made them high and lowly
And ordered their estate.'

Strictly in the archaic sense, then, God ordered my holy estate of widowhood? And Mrs Greville's useful income? Half the congregation rebelled, did not even adopt the goldfish ruse. They had come to keep the kids quiet, to earn their places at the free tea.

At the altar steps, the churchwardens handed out posies of flowers, freesias, anemones, tendrils of ivy, pussy-willow. Daniel and Lucy came back with freesias, bound with white satin, what old-fashioned haberdashers call 'baby-ribbon'.

Betty had made the wedding bouquet herself, briskly shaping the flowers, tying them together, stabbing hard wire up their tender stems.

'I don't want anything elaborate. Maybe just one white rose, in a prayer-book. Only, I haven't a prayer-book.'

'People like a bouquet. I didn't have one. Len thought. . . .' Then she checked herself; Clare, not even a daughter-in-law yet, had no right to such intimacy.

'White flowers, then, please. Scented . . . lily of the valley, white roses.'

But the season was all wrong, and the shop sold Betty freesias. Nothing else had any scent.

'Sorry, Mum. These were the only ones left.'

Lucy complained.

'It's not fair. Emma's got purple and yellow and pink. It's not fair, only white.'

Ellen shushed them, but kindly, as the organ began to play. Dear Lord and Father of mankind, forgive our foolish ways. Jo had Emma's hand, and her flowers, smiling. Clare let the tears fall.

'Isn't it being a baby, crying?'

She swallowed on the hardness, wiped away more tears.

'I was remembering when I got married.'

'To Daddy?'

'Yes.'

'Are these the same kind of flowers?'

'Yes.'

Ellen, overhearing, didn't hurry them out with the rest, but waited, until Clare was fit for company. Leaving the church, she left off whispering, gave comfort loud enough for Greville in his cope to hear. 'Think of your two beautiful children. You'll always remember him, seeing them.'

She led the way to the church hall, Mothering Sunday tea, self-conscious revival of old customs, iced buns, pink, white, chocolate, hundreds and thousands, paste sandwiches, on paper doyleys, on parish plates. Tea from an urn, dispensed by Ellen herself, weak orange squash for the children. Greville intoned grace.

Jo nibbled a rock-bun, rock hard.

'You know what this is, don't you? It's a time-warp.'

'I had wondered. What year?'

'Coronation, of course.'

'Thirty-Seven, or Fifty-Three?'

'Thirty-Seven. The plates of 'fancies' are cut out from my gran's 1935 Mrs Beeton. And look up.'

Clare obeyed, and there they were, the King and Queen, pinned onto roof beams, Elizabeth doe-eyed, with three rows of pearls, Bertie heavy with medals.

'Don't you dare mock, that's all.'

'I wasn't going to.'

'That's alright, but I never know, with you.'

Never knew what? The statement implied an intimacy they hadn't—yet—achieved.

The children, reared on multi-flavoured crisps, hamburgers, fried onions, curry, and packets of ready-mix sauce, nibbled a cake or two, and wandered off, to press rubber noses against steamed-up windows. Their elders ate up nicely, as was expected. At last, even the solemn rain was no excuse for lingering. Raincoats were put on, children carried to cars, rotas organised for those without transport.

'Damn. I left the car up by church. Look, you stay here, I'll go up and fetch it.'

Before she could leave, Ellen beckoned.

'Don't go without visiting our little book-stall, will you?'

S.P.C.K. pamphlets, stories from the Bible, crude colouring books, nothing they could conceivably want. Clare paid up, bought two books so old they were priced in shillings and pence.

The children were, curiously, delighted. Clare left them sitting on a bench with Jo, reading, while she fetched the car. Greville caught up with her.

'Mrs Carradus. . . . How splended to see you!'

'Mrs Kenyon invited me. I hope that was alright.'

'Absolutely delighted to see you. Splendid. Now, if there's anything we could do to help. . . .'

'I'm fine, now, really.'

Getting over it nicely, she wanted to add, nasty thing, death, but I'm much, much better, hardly know myself. But she was safe enough; Greville excused himself, made for the vicarage, and his own happy family life. Reaching the car, Clare unlocked it with a new sense of ownership, strapped herself in, thought, even after so brief a separation, of her children. Moira was still possessive, still wanted to mark out the boundaries of experience; don't take this risk, because you are mine.

Jo and the children, seeing the car, ran out to meet her. They brought with them the scent of freesias.

'There's this scene in Popeye . . . I can't remember the story, just this gas-mask, stuck on like a second face. Only, I think, when he pulls it off, there's nothing left. And I was screaming, in the scullery, because I wouldn't have it on, no matter what. Then our Mam said, Hitler'll get you. And it was no use, she couldn't make me. But the teachers managed alright. But you know what was the very worst thing?'

Cue for a murmur of interest and sympathy, a smile for the little man. His age was coded 50–54, but the dark brown eyes belonged to a frightened child. She could see him still.

'It was not knowing. Every blasted day for a week we took off, butties in an Oxo tin, labels on us like blooming suitcases. We'd say goodbye to Mam and our Gran, . . . Dad was in the Border . . . training. . . . And this went on for a week. . . . Every blasted day. . . .'

'And why was this?'

'Well, Hitler. If he'd known, he'd have bombed the train, 'cause we was on it. Anyway, one day I said, no, I'm not giving you's a kiss. I'm sick of kisses. I never saw Gran again. She died, three weeks later. Teacher read the letter out to me. I had to fetch it to school, you see, because the Welsh couple I was with couldn't read English. Talk, yes, but not the reading. You know what, I was at the dentist's a while back, and the girl says, I'll make you an appointment, first of September, and I said, no you won't. Made her change it . . . couldn't explain why.'

The interview went to pattern; where was he billeted, was he at the same school as friends, brothers, sisters, what contact had there been with family, when did he return home. Routine, remembered pain, excised memory. One woman, nine the day she was evacuated had been silent at first, then the halting voice defined this pain, this sickness.

'It's such a little word. A child's word . . . homesick. It's a rich kid, crying under the bedclothes in a prep school dormitory. He'll soon settle down, they say. Children adapt. So I knew the way I felt then wasn't important, an old scar, a thin white line where the pain used to be. My mother came, just for the weekend, when I'd been there six weeks. The next week, she wrote, "it was so nice to see you happy and settled". That's what she'd seen. There I was, safe and happy. Last year, on a long journey, I'd nothing else to read but Bonhoeffer's Letters from Prison. You know what he says? "There is no agony worse than this, this longing for home and for what we love."'

'So I let myself remember, instead of putting the memory away, where it wouldn't hurt. The waking, in that bedroom that wasn't mine, and praying, God, let me wake up at home. They sent me to live in a place where I didn't exist, no-one knew me, or who I had been. The streets were full of faces I didn't know. They said they loved me, but they sent me away. I never saw my mother or any of them again. The house went. There was nothing left.'

Clare switched off the tape. After silence, Garwy said,

'And they would feel all that pain without the words to shape it into something bearable.'

'Finite.'

'It's Marlowe's hell, isn't it? The awful separation from all love.'

'"Hell hath no limits, nor is circumscribed
In one self place, where we are is Hell
And where Hell is, there we must ever be . . ."
Where was she sent?'

'To the Lake District, from a Manchester slum.'

'So beauty is no comfort?'

'No. Would you like to hear some more?'

She began to pick up the labelled tapes, stacking them in order. He was writing already, shoulders hunched, knuckles glistening as he clenched the pen. Clare focussed on a bone, white shadow under skin, lightly etched in down, like the same bone on Daniel. David had been like this when they met, light, exposed, open. In civil service, he had grown massive, gathering weight about the shoulders and neck, a leathery quality in the covering skin, and, in the last year or so, the first paunchy rounding. Without turning, Garwy said,

'You'd better go. I'm sick of being available when you've nothing better to do.'

Clare swung the bag onto her shoulder, snapped the clasp. She was almost at the door.

'I said go. Get out.'

'If that's what you want.'

'It's what you want.'

'No.'

He swung half way round to meet her.

'It's no use, Clare, is it?'

His face was in shadow, eyes averted, shame-faced pupil with teacher. She made no concession. The door could be opened and closed, making an end.

'I mean, there's no point in going on, is there? No future?'

'Does that matter?'

'To you, no.'

'Then I'll go.'

She walked through the door, closed it, without looking back.

At the school gate, she was too early, arriving in time for the mother's meeting, meagre roadside social life, intermezzo, before the day gathered momentum, children's tea, calling them in, bathing them, while cooking a meal for a husband, welcome or not, coming home. Clare stood apart, not a wife, somehow less than a mother. Until Daniel came out, she would be quite alone. Lucy had stayed at home today with Jo, because she had seemed a little feverish. No Jo, and she might have risked taking the child into the crêche as usual, but the day had its blocks of allocated time, no space for a child who might or might not be ill. Nine o'clock lecture, first years, and they would all come, even though it was the last working day of term. Eleven till one, at the studio for a voice test, and a trial run of the first tapes. That had been almost a game, a child's wish fulfilment, playing with studio gadgets, watching the shape made by the sound of her own voice. Bernard had done this once, talking on a programme about the new and virulent flu virus that had struck a few winters ago. Child-like, too, she had pocketed canteen sugar, for her own children. Then end of term prowling about her room, for stray work that must be marked and returned, late essays, delivered sneakily in her absence. Dear Dr Kelly, and long articulate excuses. Garwy . . . and then nothing.

Daniel, tie round his head, anorak a Dracula cloak, cannoned into her, scattering creation. Clare scrambled round the playground, chasing pictures, picking up a nest of glued shavings, sugar eggs, smeared with mud.

'Bugger! That was for Lucy. Do you think she'll mind?'

Clare, mother on display, overheard, explained, less rather than more, why he should not say 'bugger'.

'Mrs Carter does. I heard her, outside the staffroom. She dropped a bottle of milk and it smashed. And you did, the day my gerbil got out.'

'That doesn't mean you should.'

She had found a chick, cotton-wool ball, two tiny felt eyes.

'For you. Isn't he sweet?'

He gave her a card, stiff white paper, no envelope. It was a clever piece of work, travel brochure Jerusalem, skipping lambs, tanks, a Nimrod and crew, a baby at the font, the wrapper from a crème egg, over all, the shadow of a cross. Underneath, in Daniel's heavy print, black felt-tip, 'He is Risen'.

Mrs Carter was heading for them. Time to pretend she had not seen, turn and head for home? Even at this distance, they had eye contact.

'Mrs Carradus!'

Clare had scooped the treasures into her bag, to shuffle down with the tapes and essays.

'So nice to see you, dear. You don't usually manage to get down now, do you?'

Mrs Carradus, then, school gate mother, no sad widow, held her son's hand for safety. She rehearsed explanations. Unless it was raining, Daniel, at seven, was quite capable of walking the mere quarter of a mile home. Mrs Carter, did you know we invented childhood, along with the steam engine, the Bessemer process that meant nothing in an O-level text book? We limit them still more to create work for the likes of you. This is my child. This, incidentally, is my life, and I will not be a problem for you to solve. She smiled at Mrs Carter.

'I usually pick Lucy up on campus and drive straight home.

My neighbour always takes Daniel in if I'm late.'

'So long as the child isn't coming home to an empty house. But Danny does seem to mind about you being here for special occasions. I know it can't be easy, dear, in your situation, but these things mean so much to a child. Perhaps this neighbour . . .?'

Daniel's face was a mask, after the grimace at 'Danny'.

'Special occasions?'

'Only the end of term exhibition, dear. Daniel brought you a note about it. He had done some remarkably good work this term, and he was so upset when you didn't come.'

Still the stony face, not accusing, merely without expression. Clare framed an apology.

'I may have mislaid the note. Of course, I would have come, if I'd known.'

'I'm sure you would, dear. It's so important to a child. Perhaps you'd like a quick look round now? Of course, they've taken some pictures home. . . .'

Clare followed, cowardly, obedient, back into school, participant parent. Daniel followed, three or more paces behind, school tie still around his head, despite Mrs Carter. Because of Mrs Carter? Clare tried a sideways inspection of the woman. Robust, solid, fifty rather than forty, but then, she would be. At forty, Mrs Carter's children had barely stopped needing her full time, forty-one or two she had come back to teaching after the careful years of supply work, nothing that would incommode her essential family. She had a fleshy mole, with one crinkled hair, on the right edge of her upper lip, and her square hands were dappled with age spots. Daniel had slipped past his mother, to take one of these hands, fatherless child, but at least his father was blamelessly dead. Clare imagined the record: Father dead, mother works. One sister (younger). She knew, because Moira had tested her grandson a year ago, that Daniel's reading age was 16—plus, meaning adult, meaning access to whatever adults wanted for themselves. He read indiscriminately, paperback thrillers, Ransome, Kipling, the Beano, New Society, complimentary copies of Ruth's books . . .

'Why don't you write books for me, like Ruth?'

'Because I don't.'

He also, mainly in trains, read the Sun, the News of the World, and in bed at night a torchlit copy of Men Only—filched from a drawer in David's old desk, soon abandoned in favour of instructions for a Lego space station. Her son, and she had access to so very little of him.

Mrs Carter opened the classroom door, where Clare should have been the night before, when she had been writing notes for this morning's studio session.

'This is all Daniel's.'

Clare recognised her son. She comforted herself; at least I know him this well. Without being told, I would have known his work. He had called one painting 'Lord of the Flies'—the book snaffled from her desk, matter for a tutorial on the mythology of childhood. He had understood it quite as well as most adult pretence. But the painting was a shimmering creature, a dragonfly, huge eyed, acrylic and foil, in a nasty landscape peopled with bones—or maggots; shapes without colour.

Then, next to this, 'Tyger!' This was easier to take, less troubled. She knew the origin, a film on television, last Christmas, voice-over of Blake. Afterwards, Daniel had asked to read the poem. He stood now below the glory of his tiger, not quite looking at it, or at his mother, like Garwy, waiting for her to hand back an essay. Did they resent her, for the power she had to praise, or condemn, merely by withholding praise. Daniel's tiger flashed yellow eyes, in a starlit forest, raining spears. Below, he had copied out the Blake in his small, intensely neat handwriting. Mrs Carter smiled briefly at Clare.

'The children were asked to illustrate any poem they liked.' She indicated Puff the Magic Dragon, Popeye the Sailor Man, assorted nursery rhymes.

'Daniel's was quite a surprise. Exceptional, the Head thought. 'Her eyes said to Clare; no more, not praise, not with the child here listening. Daniel's writing book was picked out from a pile, handed to Clare.

'But then, this is in the family, isn't it?'

Daniel, uninvited, agreed.

'When I grow up, I'll send you some of my books.'

The adults smiled across him, let this pass, for once, even if he has overstepped the boundaries of arrogance; who knows what he might do. And they both knew what it was to be jealous of a clever pupil.

Clare paused before the last of Daniel's work, jewel colours, in heavy wax, finely etched, all form and no meaning; at least, no obvious meaning. Then she saw that there were birds, the colours of specific birds, jays, woodpeckers, a kingfisher; the green and blue of leaves and water. As yet, his skill was not quite equal to the concept, immature, imperfect. And, leaving the classroom, she reminded herself that there was nothing original yet in any of this. Daniel had merely re-shaped experience. Even the birds were culled from a book of David's, borrowed last term, taken to school. Mrs Carter waited until Daniel was a little ahead of them, out in the corridor, then lowered her voice.

'Of course, we would understand if his schoolwork suffered now.'

'But it hasn't, has it?'

'Not at all, as you've seen. He's still very young. They don't experience grief as we do, you know.'

Conspiracy, this. Clare knew, was expected to know, that Mrs Carter's husband had died three year's ago, respectably, from an overweight heart-attack. They were widows together, had this grief in common.

'Do you think so?'

She listened to the current wisdom. Daniel was a borderline case, not yet, by chronology, quite able to accept the finality of death, especially the death of his all-powerful father. Mrs Carter had met David once, miraculously free to see the afternoon Christmas concert. She had been charmed, of course, and too welcoming, as if David were the only father present. Apart from a milkman and a postman, the afternoon father were unemployed, embarrassing people, not to be compared with David Carradus, immaculate and impressive, made to measure.

'We're keeping an eye on him of course. If there's the least sign of trouble, we'll let you know. Your other little one starts in September, doesn't she?'

The school gate mothers had gone. A handful of juniors, in shiny training shorts, swung on the playground climbing frame, limbering up for after-school netball, after-school soccer, with dedicated after-school staff. Daniel had reproved her, gently, for the random use of 'football', was learned about league positions, soccer, rugby union, rugby league. Clare walked back to her car with Daniel, turning to wave politely to the teacher, who would now go home, tell her seventeen-year-old youngest daughter that she had been busy, talking to a mother about her child. The daughter was destined for the local university because, youngest child, only girl, she must not risk life away from home, in squalid independence. Clare knew about this daughter from casual S.C.R. gossip, with someone whose wife taught the girl. The school was furious, wanted to enter her for Cambridge. Mrs Carter, did she but know it, had a separate existence, dismembered, analysed, widowed mother, confining her adult child. And would it be worse, or merely different, if this child were a boy? Clare had contributed to this conversation with a line from a Barbara Pym novel, about the kind of man who 'looks as if he has a mother'. Then why should she respect, at all, the view of Mrs Carter, in loco parentis, watching for signs of maladjustment to death?

'There's someone come to see us!'

Clare recognised the doctor's car, remembered with stomach-heaving fear the child she had left at home. The door opened as they reached the house. Jo must have been watching at the window.

'We were kept at school. . . .'

Jo threw the words out.

'He thinks it's meningitis. He's called an ambulance. I've been trying to get you all afternoon.'

She had managed to say this only by holding tightly to Clare, as if to transfer the fear she had adopted, in her role as deputy.

Ten feet by twelve, the cubicle was, the corners rounded, for easier cleaning. It was lit now by one central bulb, dimmed down to fifteen watts, man-made twilight. The partition was probably only plasterboard, little better than curtains. On the other side, a child had been screaming, hour after hour, rattling the bars of a cot. Once, she had gone out into the corridor, peered through the observation window, seen the raging little figure, fists clenched around the bars, nappy-clad, exposed and naked. A nurse patrolling this corridor had sent her back into isolation, the sagging chintz armchair, two Barbara Cartland novels, and twenty-year old copies of the Reader's Digest.

She had been lost, at one point, in a wandering dream, undefined golden woodland, and the children running before her. Through leaves, Virginia Woolf had called that, discovering joy. Now one of those children lay still as death, stripped, but for the disposable nappy they'd fastened round her. Clare tried to see her daughter, and not the drip. Last night, weary, sleepless, she had thought, illogically, this was nemesis, for refusing the drip when Lucy was being born. Ten days overdue, Lucy was, and now they wanted her out quickly. They threatened her with facts; the failing placenta, the baby suffering deprivation, even before it had lived. And she had defied them, because it was her body, her baby, her choice. Lucy had settled the matter by arriving at home, in one half-hour of sublime pain.

All night, she had tried bargaining, refusing to make the only possible prayer. If she stopped to think, there was, over and over again, the wicked needle, plunging deep into Lucy, sucking up spinal fluid. The child, weak as she was, had clung to her mother in terror, clawed into flesh. Very soon, they would come to her with the diagnosis, confirm what they already knew. All night, they had been taking Lucy's temperature, on the hour. Convulsions jerked the sick body into something less than human. Afterwards, the child lay still, burning with fever. They had shown Clare how to do the sponging. Twice, her fever had been brought down, twice it had soared again. Clare didn't bother saying; I have done this before, there have been other convulsions. She remembered the first time with the clarity of three in the morning, the burning baby in her arms, Daniel, curled up in a fleecy sleeping suit, on the sofa, and, when the doctor asked for him, David peacefully asleep in half the double bed.

'Does he know the baby is ill?'

'He says this is my department.'

The doctor had said nothing, merely writing out a prescription. Lucy had been well again the next day, with nothing more than a slight cold, so David was right to sleep. Had been right.

Five past four. This was the watershed. Marking work through the night, when they were babies, she had always known, make it till four, and you've won. Five o'clock was dawn, at six, the BBC woke up and chatted about pigs and heifers, three months wheat prices. At seven, she could finish the last one, drink strong coffee, start the next shift as wife and mother, as the family woke up and claimed her. Today, she had no family, David, Lucy, and if one green bottle. . . . Such things did happen, journalists kept the clichés in their notebooks. Widowed mother's agony. On the bookstalls in churches, there were half a dozen stories of tragic loss, leukaemia, polio, road accidents. Jim's mother had been widowed in 1916, and then all but lost the boys in the 1918 flu. Insurance tables rate the loss of a child less traumatic than divorce, many points below the death of a spouse, but then, they had no tables for loss adjustments on love. No mourning for David, because he, they, had no longer loved. In any case, there had been no prayers or pleading. D.O.A., they had classed him, and she had known nothing until the policeman arrived, when she was already a widow. Lucy would die, or she would live. The antibiotics, and her own little body would decide that. Afterwards, she might be blind, or deaf, or both. Last night, on the phone Clare had spoken first to Jim, then Moira, so there would be enough prayers. The Kelly's granddaughter, make a special effort with this one, God, not just any child, but special. So many prayers, God all of you, if you just let her live. Nothing to lose, either; in the long run, you win, but let me keep her, let us keep her, because we haven't loved her long enough yet.

Clare, without moving, watched the night nurse take her child's temperature, bloodpressure, mark the chart, give the mouth toilet, necessary care of a body past self help. Lucy's lips were cracking, her mouth pinched and dry at the corners. The sick are ugly, pocked, pustulent, fever red, livid or jaundiced. Lucy had been slender, graceful, female. In one day—less than that—she had become gaunt and wasted, hollow eyed, her tongue protruding. Clare watched on, as the nurse lifted limbs that wouldn't move. She knew not to bother with questions. Better to wait now and ask the doctor is my child dying, will my child live?

'Mrs Carradus, there really isn't anything you can do here. Why not go and lie down?'

'I wouldn't sleep.'

'Be sensible, dear. You can't do any good here. We don't want you ill too.'

'If Lucy wakes, she'll want me.'—If Lucy wakes, will she know she has a mother? And if she never wakes again, at least I will have been here, at least with her when she dies.

She kept the indiscreet thoughts hidden, did not move, obeying the advice given to fathers in the labour word; stay calm, don't interfere with routines, your job is simply being there, you and she belong together. But this was her daughter, and the issue not birth, only death, a death measurably less traumatic than the death of a spouse. A curious calculation, that, especially in this age when a spouse could be so temporary.

Twenty-five to five. She remembered a phrase from Marcus Aurelius: 'While you are kissing your child,' Epictetus once said 'murmur under your breath, tomorrow it may be dead.' Yesterday, in all the morning scuffle, she had found time for that precious moment, Lucy's quick passionate lips against hers, small arms tight around her, Lucy, the independent, come to claim her kiss.

The nurse had finished, had left them alone. Clare bent to kiss her daughter, remembered the hot and ridiculous mask.

Surely she and Lucy had cotaminated each other already? She reached for the child's hand, dry and heavy, not moving at all. In the corridor, downstairs, outside, the day was beginning. She sat very still, holding Lucy's hand.

'Mrs Carradus?'

The ward sister was Malaysian, hardly five foot. She touched Lucy's cheek.

'Sleeping. As you should, Mrs Carradus.'

'That isn't my name.'

'No? I'm sorry. I was told you are Mrs Carradus, Lucy's mother.'

'I am her mother. I am not Mrs Carradus.' She began the explanation, ready for patent disapproval.

'So? I understand now. In my country, a woman does not take her husband's name.'

'It's such a difficult name too. I'm really Kelly.'

'Miss Kelly, then.'

'Dr Kelly. I teach at the university.'

'So you feel insulted when we call you Mrs?'

Clare smiled. 'No. Only when they say "dear" Is Lucy dying?'

'She's very sick. Very ill indeed.'

'Thank-you.'

She slumped suddenly, saw nothing. The little woman pushed her back into the chair.

'You need sleep. I promise, we will call you if there is any change. As soon as there is a change.'

'No.'

'Then you must at least have a drink. I'll send for tea.'

'Coffee, please. I don't like tea.' So even in this state, such foibles mattered.

'And something to eat?'

'No.'

At six fifteen, the houseman came to examine Lucy. Clare, banished, went to the telephone. Ring any time, Jo had said. Let me know, please disturb me. In that house next door, there was Daniel too, the son she had left, bewildered, still talking about a film he wanted to watch. Jo answered the phone at once.

'She's very ill. She might die. They've told me.'

Jo, at the end of the line, in a nightdress still, safe with the farming programme and instant coffee, humanly failed to find words. My child is dying—what have you to say?

'Daniel?'

'He was alright. He and Emma had said bedtime prayers. God bless Lucy and make her better soon.'

'And if he doesn't?'

'Daniel said, she'll go to Heaven. But he doesn't want that, because Daddy went and didn't come back.'

Daniel was asleep now, a child, getting on with living, not to be disturbed so early.

'I'll ring again later.'

She hung up, holding on to an image of Jo in her dressing gown, drinking coffee, reading yesterday's paper, setting the table for breakfast for three. Jo, doing the shopping, unprompted, getting in food for all of them. Would Jo have enough money? It must be made up later. Clare dialled again, remembered that the phone was on Moira's side of the bed, remembered the last dawn call, and before that, the news of Lucy's birth. You have a grand-daughter.

Moira must still be asleep. Time, unwanted time, to think, there will be no more babies; I can never have another daughter, if Lucy dies. Moira's morning voice cut in, repeating the number, professional, even when half asleep.

'No change. High fever all night, and they've said, she's very ill, could die.'

'She will not die. We're all praying for her here. She will *not* die.' Moira repeated this as if it were a fact, a truth, as if, like clapping for Tinkerbell, the words had power over death.

'We're going to Mass this morning. And again at mid-day. But she is *not* going to die. Children are very resilient, darling.'

The endearment was awkward and unused, not one of their words. Clare heard the pips, said goodbye. There was no-one else to call now, no-one close enough for this unsocial hour. Die in working hours, Lucy; it will be more convenient.

An auxiliary came at last with coffee, an unasked for glass of chilled orange juice, two unwanted slices of toast. Clare thanked her, drank the orange juice, like spring water, cold and welcome. The hospital tap water was slightly warm, stale.

The auxiliary was ready to talk, a local woman, neatly rounded, plum-tinted hair, pinned under a cap. She was what was needed, a woman who might be Clare's mother, only in her late forties but married young, and matronly since twenty.

'Can't you fancy anything, duck?'

Clare sipped the coffee, bitter, too sweet, welcome.

'No. Thank-you.'

'I could get you an egg? No? Tell you what, how about a bit of chocolate?'

The coffee was finished too soon, not enough in the stubby little cup after twelve hours of thirst.

'Could I possibly have another cup of coffee?'

The phone, chairs, table, and a magazine rack were all in a narrow slice of isolation reserved for watching parents. Four chairs, one stool, one plastic moulded table, child size. Clare identified it as if recognising a face from the past; Mothercare catalogue, the year of Lucy's birth. The magazine rack might just as easily have held dishes, being of covered wire, its contents casual, women's weeklies, monthly glossies, a mail-order brochure for Christmas novelties, a child's comic, a crumpled shopping list, two recent Sunday supplements. This room was where other mothers, other parents had sat, reading a phrase here, a sentence there, concentrating with furrowed intensity on a two-year-old horoscope, while the professionals tested and measured their child; how much life left in this one? And this room was matched by another on the floor below; intensive care. Lucy wasn't on a life-support machine because her condition didn't warrant it, not because she was less close to death then the year old baby brought in last night, hurled through the windscreen from the back seat.

Soon after eight, they came to tell her old news. Meningitis, bacterial.

'What does that mean?'

'She has a good chance. It's easier to treat than viral. She's fighting hard.'

Clare made her way back to Lucy's bedside, watched the still, burning body of her child, moaning now and then, hideous. Lucy was dying. Why not say so, and let her prepare to mourn?

'May I hold her hand?'

'You should get some rest. Go home, see your other child. Your husband could take over.'

'My husband is dead.'

They apologised. But it wasn't their fault. She ought to have a husband, a helpmeet, someone to watch with her. David's calm logic would have been oddly welcome in here. When Daniel had been miserable with mumps, David had looked up the natural course of the infection. He would be ill for a few days, then the swelling would subside, and he would be well again. Nothing to be done about it, except give medicine, and let time pass. David would talk, reasonably, about the efficacy of antibiotics, the white blood cells, called into action, fighting the disease in their child's body. David would find a date on the calendar and say, look, by this time, she will be well again, all this will be forgotten. And he would be right, or not. She would be either well, or dead. David was not a mother, living, childlike, one day at a time.

The consultant began his rounds at nine. Clare was not wanted or welcome. She would be told all she needed to know later. And she could either trust them to tell the truth, or not. The result would be the same. She rang Jo again, made practical arrangements about money, about Daniel, the milkman, a dental appointment that must be cancelled. Without Jo, she would have been forced to turn to Moira again, a child herself, less than adult, hardly a mother.

'Are you coming home tonight?'

'No. I can't. Is that alright?'

'Someone rang. A friend of yours. I told him.'

Him? She left it at that. They talked a little more, curious everyday details. Clare spoke, briefly, to Daniel. On the phone, he sounded younger, sweet-voiced. Love to Lucy, and tell her to get better. Then goodbye. She walked down the shiny corridor with the deliberation of a drunk, trying a straight line. Ten years ago one lost night didn't leave her like this; ten years ago, she didn't lose sleep with a dying child. The corridor was marked out with coloured lines. She followed the green and white track to the chapel. It was like a board game, green for theatre, red for casualty, yellow for X-ray, blue for the wards, follow the yellow brick road.

Green and white, then, for the chapel, for no good reason, except that it was somewhere to go, where they would let her in without question.

Rigby had just finished saying his office, closing the breviary, slipping the book almost furtively out of sight. University vacation, of course, and his relief duty as hospital chaplain. She knelt, briefly, expected to pray, living up to expectation. The right, approved observance might just achieve the desired result, the only bearable result. Let her live, God, if there is a God, let her live.

Rigby knelt down beside her, very still, in the anonymous room, bare, with only a cross, altar table, sacristy lamp. Ten benches, kneelers worked in gross point, with the hospital coat of arms. Chrissie would make such things. Chrissie at this minute, might be making things for her baby. Then one deliberate, wicked thought excluded prayer: I can have another child. If this one dies, I need not be left with just one. Ovum meets sperm, and there you are, another child, any child, my child. Only yesterday morning she had posted off the insurance renewal, new for old, nothing irreplaceable. I can contain a child again. It would be such a little thing.

Rigby crossed himself, touched Clare's shoulder, and it was done, she was allowed to stop, the time for prayer squandered. Nine, ten, eleven years old, at Mass on Sunday, she would struggle with hunger and morning weariness, to find everyone shuffling up to the communion rail; should she receive, when she had been absent in mind from the sacrifice?

'One of the children?'

'My daughter. The younger one. Meningitis.'

'I'm very sorry. She's in good hands, you know.'

Did he mean the Almighty, or merely the hospital? She walked out with the priest, copying his genuflexion to the altar, the crossing with holy water, hypocrite, because, alone, she would have done neither. Rigby came back with her to the ward, a scientist again, friend, and contemporary of the doctors here.

'Jarrett's first-rate, Clare. You couldn't have anyone better.'

Clare thought, he would hardly tell her they were second rate, which they must be, taking posts here.

'It wasn't Jarrett who saw her. Robeiru.'
'Robeiru is brilliant. Gold medallist, two years ago.'
'You know damn well they can do nothing now.'
'Only their best.'
Outside Lucy's cubicle, Rigby turned to her.
'Do you believe in prayer?'
'Do you? Dear God, please make Lucy better soon, please make the sun shine today, because we're going to the seaside, please make me pass that exam. No, I don't. Not that kind.'
'But you came to the chapel?'
'It's the only place I'm allowed. There, and the parents' room. There are two other sets of parents now, a fourteen-year-old overdose, and the remains of a baby. I wanted. . . .'
Rigby didn't end her silence.
'I wanted to see if I could really pray. *Fiat voluntas tua, sicut in coelo et in terra*. Daddy, may I have, and Daddy is free to say yes or no.'
'And could you?'
She stared, intently, at a Health Education Council poster, a scruffy, tumbled after-school child, freckles, grin, concertina socks. She's home. Talk about her day, tell her about yours. And this, God, is all I want. My child, Is it so very much to ask?
'Clare?'
Licensed to touch, Rigby held her close, guided her into the barren room, closed the door, sat down beside her.
'Go on then. Do your job.'
She was allowing him to hold her hand, the left one, still wearing David's ring.
'Do you think it's an easy job?'
'No, but then, you chose it. What are you going to say? The Lord gives, and the Lord takes away, blessed be the name of the Lord?'
'I won't insult you by saying I understand.'
She sneered at him, rudely aggressive.
'Likely, isn't it. You never had a child.'
Rigby didn't move. Clare looked carefully past his face, eyes.
'I was a good little girl at school, you know. Top of the class in religious knowledge. I know all the right answers. It was

still an exact science in our day, with all the answers printed in a book, like log tables. Find the right page, and there you are. God suffers with us, after all, didn't he allow his only son a horrible death, God made the organisms that are making Lucy die. Nice of him, wasn't it? God made the snow and ice that caused David's death. Nice one, God, can you do it again? I've one more left. Firstborn son, too, you can't leave him out, surely. Oh, for Christ's sake, Phil, get out and leave me alone.'

She began to giggle.

'Slip of the tongue. Of course, that's why you're staying, isn't it. I remember the lesson well. We analysed the Sermon on the Mount, by instalment in the fourth year.'

Speaking more slowly, she turned to face him.

'Last night, all night, I was dying with her, sick and parched, burning with fever. And I can't say it . . . not that.'

'Thy will be done?'

'A lie.'

'Or accepting the inevitable?'

'Would that be enough?'

'Have you anything to lose?'

She risked a glance through the window, at the outside world. It was still there, would be waiting for her if. . . .

'So you think I might as well pray, even without faith?'

'I'm not giving you any glib answers.'

Rigby was still holding her, touch filling the space between words. Clare could see only his hands, long fingers, long palms, square clipped nails, finely ridged, dark hair, in some places up to the second finger joint. Nothing sexless about Rigby's celibacy, nothing barren in his childlessness.

'Ever read Marcus Aurelius?'

She nodded.

'I know what you're going to say. Kissing a child, and thinking, tomorrow it may be dead. Too late for that, now. She can't bear to be touched.'

'That will pass, I promise. No, I meant the ninth book, on the direction of prayer. Not "spare my precious child", but "deliver me from the terror of losing him". What are you afraid of?'

'Lucy dying.'

'But she would feel no pain. If the treatment is unsuccessful, she'll die gently, slipping into a coma, then dying quickly. So what is there to fear for her, except eternal life? She's been baptised.'

'You believe all that? No—don't bother. . . . It's your job, believing, isn't it? I hate every word you say. I'd rather see her racked with pain, rather than sit while she drifts away from me. And you believe in this God who cares whether someone slopped water over her, like some petty official moaning because a form isn't filled in properly.'

'I believe in God, yes.'

'And the rest?'

'No, not that he wants your daughter to die.'

'Cronos, eating his own children. I feel sick.'

'When did you last eat?'

'Yesterday . . . no . . . I skipped breakfast.'

She let him take over, propping her feet on the stool, covering her with his jacket.

'Starving won't cure Lucy. Promise to stay put?'

While he was away, a nurse came to report on Lucy.

'Her temperature is steady, Mrs Carradus. Still above normal, but only 100. No more convulsions.'

'Is she awake?'

'Sedated. We want to conserve her strength. Look, why don't you get some sleep? There's a guest room free in the nurses' home. Parents often use it.'

Then she lived in a world peopled with death and grief, knew that children could die. No wonder nurses make neurotic mothers. So would she tell the truth?

'Can you tell me how Lucy is? What chance has she got?'

'I really can't tell you anything. If Sister finds out. . . .'

'Bugger Sister. Is Lucy dying? Have you seen children die of this.'

'They die sometimes.'

Clare let her go, guilty. She let her heavy body weigh into the chair, shivered a little, the shiver of extreme fatigue. Unaccountably, it was already five to three, mother's new shift, time to collect children, clap hands till Daddy comes home. She slept.

When she woke, the sky outside had turned dark blue,

pricked with early stars. Hobbling, stiff-legged to the window, she opened it, leaned out, smelling acrid sweetness of azaleas, and damp tarmac, urban flowerbeds, with marching hyacinths. It had only rained a little, enough to spangle the new grass, damp down the dust. Aprille, with her shoures soote . . . the cruellest month. April 1st? But what day was it? The red calendar on the wall gave no more away, bought in a job lot by the administrators, who didn't want the expense of days and years. Tucked in above this date there was a folded sheet of paper, ripped from a pocket diary.

> You needed that sleep. I've been in to see Lucy. She's very ill, very weak, but the fever is under control. Bacterial meningitis responds quickly, you know. Everything is normal, things are taking their course. At present, she can't bear to be touched.
>
> Don't forget poor old Daniel. Ring him up. Send him a letter. If there's anything I can get for you, call me on this number. I'll bring you some books tomorrow.

Another nurse. This one was older, briskly efficient.

'Feeling better now?'

'Yes.'

'Your friend brought a case in. Would you like a bath in the staff wing? It's not usual, but there's only you here now.'

'I thought there was that baby's family? The car crash?'

'Died, this morning. The overdose is on the main ward now.'

Clare picked up her case, and walked down the corridor, left, into the staff wing. They had given her a staff issue towel, that was the rule. She tried to define what power, if any, the nurses had over her. Secret information about Lucy? Secret understanding of the charts pinned to her bed? If that was all, then they had no power; it didn't take much intelligence to follow a fever chart, read Lucy, reduced to pulse rate, blood pressure, urination, vomiting. The vomiting had stopped; now she had nothing left to vomit, they had prescribed an anti-emetic drug, given intravenously, like the drugs that were fighting her disease. Even if Lucy won now, there would be so little of her left. Once, in the afternoon, she had opened her eyes, stared dully at Clare, as if at the wall. Clare had asked, is she blind, but they could not, or would not answer.

The bath, surprisingly, in a regulation building, was coloured, sour lemon, crusted about the taps with the deposits left by hard water. The water, heated without economy, came scalding and spitting from the taps. Clare opened the case Jo had packed, wondering at the details, two bathcubes, three unused lawn handkerchiefs. Had Daniel helped to choose the clothes, tell her what Clare usually wore, off duty, in private? Tampax . . . that certainly wasn't Daniel. Two bras—how long did Jo think she was staying? A polythene bag, filled with soap flakes, sealed with tape. Clare unhooked her bra, surprised and disgusted by the dark stains of her own sweat. Unclean, she slipped into the scented water.

Afterwards, in a cotton nightdress, she stood at the sink, using the soap flakes, as Jo had intended. The sweat and dirt slipped out, making the water dirty instead. She rinsed the clothes, bra, tights, knickers, three times over, then set to work on the shirt, too ashamed to send it back for a near stranger to see. But David had done just that, hadn't he? Shot back in time, she stood somewhere else, lifting David's shirts and socks out of a washing machine, hanging them up to dry on slatted wood. David, presuming on two weeks friendship, two nights of incomplete sex, had given her his dirty laundry. But that had been man to woman, and, to be fair, he was living in digs, twenty minutes on the bus from the nearest laundrette. David had trusted her with his sweaty socks, stiff underfoot, his shirts, with their grubby collar line and stained armpits, and his briefs, stained yellow where a week of pee had dripped. No secrets, nothing hidden, this is my body, you might as well know it all. She had been surprised, later, to meet Betty, so pitifully clean, in tears over a stain on a kitchen worktop; Betty, who had given her sons and daughter clean clothes every day. Only away from home had David discovered the pleasure of his own dirt.

'Women are messy creatures. I don't bleed and ooze all over the place like you. I don't need to go in for all this washing.'

And then, wordless, he had come to expect, silently insist on the daily shirt, with its knife crease down each sleeve, and another, if he was going out in the evening. All part of the service, dear. So that was why she resented the word. It was nothing to do with the nurses, only David's old contempt.

Leading off this bathroom, there was a drying room, even a few empty hangers. She buttoned her wet shirt, smoothed the collar, hung up the dripping tights, the small, barely-needed bra, conscious of being once more secure in an institution, protected by rules. Time, bidden, has returned, only I have changed; I have a child, can't go back, because I am not who I was. Whatever else, I am a mother.

She went back to the bathroom, only to check that it was clean, just as she had found it. Left, and then back along a corridor of dimmed lights, because it was past ten o'clock. All the way back, she was ten, twelve years in the past, communal, with no grief entirely private. There had always been someone above, below, next door, for talking the thing through; I'm not cheap, am I, screwing with him just one night, I won't fail, will, I, not just for one bad paper. Was I really that drunk? Now the women were safe behind front doors. Rich privacy, that was what they had now, husbands, children, old address books for lost friends. Clare turned another corner, remembered that she had not, yet, told Betty about her granddaughter's illness. She began to run, because she had left Lucy alone so long with these strangers who were used to children dying, wouldn't fight death hard, because it was familiar.

The night shift had just taken over, last night's faces, almost old friends now. Last night there had still been doubt; PUO . . . pyrexia of unknown origin. (Why did doctors have to make the fear worse, making such a mystery of everything?), so a lumbar puncture, blood tests. Suspected meningitis, but don't think too much, or you won't be able to bear it. In the morning, confirmation more than give fear a name, like the time she had insisted, lying in bed, I will lose this baby, and had been right. Clare smiled at the nurse; this is the best I can do, look, a brave smile.

'How is she?'

'Still very poorly, I'm afraid. I've just taken another blood sample and she's crying.'

'May I go to her?'

'Presently, dear. Doctor wants to take another lumbar

puncture. He won't want you in just now.'

'I'm going to her.'

'No dear. Not just now. A few more minutes, and then you'll see her.'

They were all so small, these women. This was another Asian, porcelain, obediently giving orders. Clare bullied her way past.

'I'm sorry, but I have to see my daughter.'

If there had been a fight, she would have won. Did the doctors demand small nurses, to reinforce their own power? The door to Lucy's room was still three yards away.

'No, Dr Kelly. . . . Not yet . . . Doctor hasn't finished.'

Edinburgh, at a guess, metropolitan crispness, Scottish style, lean and tall. Clare had to look up.

'I'm going in. She's my daughter, and I intend to be with her.'

'You can do nothing for her now. You will be allowed to see her later.'

Clare felt five tight fingers, pressure on her arm, remembered David—mind your own business, bitch. . . . Where I go is none of your business. She shook the woman off, strode into Lucy's room.

The animal moaning had words in it . . . 'oh, dear, dear, dear, oh, dear, . . .', the old chant Lucy had made in her cot, a crying one-year-old, when David was trying out his theory of discipline, inheritance from Len.

'You're too soft. They've got to know who's boss. I'm not having my life ruled by children.'

David's way worked, after a fashion, with Daniel. Self-contained, afraid of his big father, Daniel had kept in his room, living in a child's anguish, unspoken, gnawing the sheets into holes. Lucy had cried like this, hour upon hour, up to a crescendo of terror. She had screamed until she was sick, and Clare had had to clear up the mess.

'Filthy little brat. She only did it for attention.'

But David had been so proud of his children, taking them to visit Betty and Len, stopping the car if he happened to spot his family in the town, introducing them all to colleagues. 'My wife, Clare, my son, Daniel, and this is my daughter, Lucy. Daddy's little girl, aren't you?' Then Lucy would be in his arms, a baby, a girl, with the first man in her life.

'Oh, dear, dear, dear . . .'

Had they cropped her hair? Clare looked again, and saw that it was only a cotton cap, like a surgeon's. The thick needle was ready now, plunging into her child's sick body. Clare reached for one dry hand.

'Mum, mum, mum. . . .'

'I'm here, darling. . . .'

Nails scratched and stabbed into her own hands, so there was some strength left. The needle filled up with spinal fluid. Now the doctor had what he wanted; one more sample, to be sent, promptly, to the path. lab. across the courtyard. Lucy's back was swabbed and dressed. Another day of fever and she had shrunk, withered into her sickness. She lay on the sheet naked, foetal but tense, as if she had never seen more than this. The nurses moved carefully past Clare, silently questioning her intrusion. Lucy opened dull eyes.

'Mummy?'

'Recognition', said the doctor. 'That's good. Stay with her until she sleeps, will you.'

Then he was gone. The ward sister marked up the charts herself, hung them—deliberately?—out of Clare's sight. After Daniel's birth, the midwife had done this with a chart for recording involution of the uterus. Clare had asked to see it, had been told it was nothing she need worry about.

'But it's my body.'

One day, the midwife had accidentally left her notes behind, for Clare to discover her absolute normality, blood pressure, lactation, bowel movements, the scarcely normal absence of stitches, uterus shrunken out of the reach of probing fingers. There was no mystery at all, except what had been contrived by recording all this. Five minutes after the ward sister had left them alone, Clare saw that Lucy was asleep, and went to reach the chart. Lucy's temperature was down, her pulse only a little above normal. They had given her an enema, that afternoon. Had that been as painful as the one forced on her before Daniel's birth? The last entry said: Recognised mother. But she must not, would not dare to think, yet, my child will get better; the disease will run its abbreviated course, and she will live.

At eleven, it was safe to leave Lucy for a while, too late to ring Moira, or even Jo, only to give indifferent good news. She dialled Bernard's number.

'I tried to call you yesterday. You know Lucy has meningitis?'

'Dad told me. How is she?'

'Weak. They've just done another lumbar puncture.'

'That's usual. They'll want to check that the drugs are taking effect. Have they told you what kind it is? I mean, is it viral or bacterial?'

'The doctor told me this morning. Meningococcus.'

'Bacterial, then. That's not so bad, you know. How is she in herself?'

'She knew me tonight.'

'It's only the third day, isn't it? Another couple of days, and she should be improving.'

'Easily said.'

'Would you like me to come up, tomorrow?'

Clare thought of the encounter. Bernard, clever, aloof, crippled, and so very public. The hospital staff, even the consultant, even the ward sister, would defer to him, big brother, in command, claiming and getting his privileges, a substitute for the husband she no longer had. Better than David, because he belonged to this mysterious profession, seeing the unseen, baptising nameless fears. Unclean spirit, my little daughter lies at the point of death, what can you do about it?

'No, don't come. Not yet, anyway. Couldn't you just phone, and then tell me what they say?'

'There's no reason why they shouldn't tell you everything.'

'But they don't.'

'Jarrett, isn't it? I'll give him a ring.'

Clare heard her brother's voice blotted out by the pips. Why didn't she want Bernard here, stranger, brother, proof, in this place, that she was not without connection. She allowed herself one impertinent question: why no children? Nothing had ever been said. It was not a subject Jim and Moira would have discussed, even with an adult sister. Shattered pelvis, that was all they said. Or was it Anna, with her wide mother's hips, and all her good works, for the homeless, for the unborn, the starving, the simply unwanted. Anna, deputy head of a primary school, with her regular slot in one of the Catholic papers. Didn't Anna and Bernard deserve children, then? Anna was two years older than Bernard. They were leaving it a bit late, if this childlessness was merely a postponement.

She went back to Lucy, and sat, fully awake, all night, with her sick child. Twice. Lucy woke and stared at her without recognition. Then:

'Mummy—don't go. Don't leave me.'

'I won't leave you.'

Lucy's eyes remained open, unseeing, and Clare knew that her daughter was dead. She called no-one, only kissed the child, and sat there in near darkness holding the little hand.

Lucy was crying, hoarse and parched, because they had given her nothing to drink.

'I thought she was dead. She stared at me, and her eyes were quite dull, like a dead fish.'

Rigby had come with a jar of coffee, milk, and sugar, so she could make her own. Clare, punctilious, first replaced what she had taken from the nurses' small store.

'I don't know much about these things, but it's quite usual. Exhaustion.'

'Nothing more?'

'She's simply too weak just now to close her eyes. But don't take my word for it.'

'They tell me nothing. My brother's promised to ring Jarrett today. Bernard that is.'

'Bernard *Kelly*?'

'You might have heard of his wife too; Anna. So she hardly needs my unbelieving prayers. Better leave it to the experts.'

'Cut that out, Clare.'

'Don't you like honesty? Admitting my unbelief, when you had me down as a good little Catholic mother?'

The nurses kettle switched itself off. Clare spooned coffee into cups stamped with the hospital crest.

'Black or white?'

'Black, one sugar. Perhaps I had you down as whingeing child who didn't want to play any more.'

There was only one stool in the galley sized kitchen. Rigby

heaved himself up to sit on the worktop, long legs dangling.

'Play?'

'The game of being grown up you started with David.'

'I was in love with David.'

'Naturally.'

'No-one should marry when they're in love. I lived only for David and. . . .'

'And he turned out to be an ordinary man, with ordinary wants. That wasn't good enough. Right?'

'That's a nasty way of putting it. David wanted so . . . little.'

'And you are such an exceptional woman.'

Clare slashed out, drew back inches from Ribgy's face.

'Respect for the cloth? I wouldn't let that worry you.'

'No. Respect for you. You have a nasty habit of getting too near the truth. David was no worse than most men, I suppose; lazy in the house, and unfaithful out of it, but I let him get away with both. It was so much easier to settle for that. If I'd wanted him to, he would have tried harder. He knew I didn't love him enough to bother. Now he's dead, and I don't know who I am anymore. I feel like Alice in the wood. I don't even know what day it is.'

'Good Friday. I meant to bring you a couple of hot-cross buns, but the queue was half-way round the block. Well, I must be off now.'

Clare put down the empty cup. Her stomach clenched with hunger, and she longed, suddenly, to slick a finger round the sugar she'd forgotten to stir.

'Can't you stay? I'm so afraid, on my own.'

Rigby was putting on his jacket.

'Sorry, but I'm due on campus. Good Friday service.'

'Of course. I'd forgotten.'

'Why not come with me? I could run you back.'

She had taken her place, seen, conspicuous, *mater dolorosa*, by the bronze pieta, because there was nowhere else. The Virgin was ugly in her grief, middle-aged and gaunt, her face crumpled like a crying child's, the dead Christ, heavy in her arms, was without beauty, beyond anything so petty as human dignity. It was the gift of a Nigerian graduate, work of a modern Benin sculptor. Clare opened her service sheet, made herself act, say the printed words, respond and behave like everyone else, because she was like everyone else.

Afterwards, there were questions, good wishes, reported prayers. Pat Murphy invited Daniel for Easter Sunday. Clare accepted, then remembererd Jo.

'She's on her own, with just one little girl.'

'Then they must come too.'

Soon she was alone in the chapel, watching the Anglican scene changers take over. She tried to pray, but they had used up all the words in the service: the Reproaches, *popule meus, quid feci tibi*; my people, what have I done to thee? Dear God, let my child live. Long ago, when a child had died, in the Admission class, Sister Marie Therese had told them how Martin had gone straight to heaven; four years old, he was too young for sin. But Lucy was not all good, surely? Sullen and defiant at times, whining, even biting, if Daniel would not let her play with his toys. Sin? Lucy was innocent. Clare called her slipshod thoughts to order, opened a prayerbook, read words, kept herself occupied until Rigby was ready at last, five minutes before the Church of England took over from Rome.

Driving back, she thought: we look like a couple. A good-looking couple too; the priest was tall, dark, sturdy, with a neatly cropped beard, open-necked shirt, tweed jacket. A waste, Ruth would say, as if only the undesirable should become priests. She had discouraged the idea, when Daniel suggested it.

'I wouldn't like that.'

'Why not?'

'Because you wouldn't get married and have children!' . . . the simplest of her objections, the one he would understand.

'But Mr Greville is married.'

'I know, but Catholic priests don't.'

'Why not?'

'They just don't.'

The roads were quiet. It was sunny, but very cold, a day to watch spring through glass. They overtook other cars, other couples.

'Not so fast, Phil.'

'I thought you wanted to be back with Lucy.'

'I do, but there's a police car behind. And you were over the limit.'

'Thanks.'

The police car, seen, knowing it had been seen, left them alone. Clare craved for speed again, nothing funereal. And they were back at the hospital too soon.

'Can I drop you off at the lodge?'

'You're not coming in?'

'No. I'll be back this evening.'

He reversed, crossed back into the opposite lane, and was gone. The scarlet Fiat parked, badly, right by the porter's lodge was Ruth's, the least likely, least wanted comforter, come here, unbidden.

'But if she wakes?'

'I'll be here. Get in.'

Clare picked up a Harrods carrier bag, travelling on the front seat.

'Where can this go?'

'In the back, of course. And be careful. It's your Easter eggs. Look, when we get to the house, I won't even come in. Fifteen minutes, and I'll be back here. Satisfied?'

'I still think I should stay.'

Ruth changed gear for the long low hill down from the hospital.

'This is what I can't stand, this mystique of motherhood. I mean, why should it be you, not me, or even one of these perfectly competent nurses? And if I were Lucy, I'd want to see something that looked human.'

'Bitch.'

'Of course I'm a bitch. Have I ever pretended to be nice?'

'Never.'

'On the other hand, I'm the only person who knows how to deal with you. They wanted to sedate you. Did you know?'

'No.'

'They also have quite enough to do, nursing sick children, without the bother of hysterical parents. By the way, Anna sent this for Lucy. I don't know what she'll make of it.'

They had to stop at traffic lights, close to the towns surviving cinema. Clare untied thin gold braid, rich layers of tissue-paper.

'Polish custom, I think, especially that colour. Only, Lucy might not appreciate inedible symbolism. I bought her a chocolate bunny affair, with a wheelbarrow full of eggs.'

'That's more like it.'

'Anna, of course, is praying for you.'

'Of course.'

Amber . . . green. Passing close, Clare took in the cinema, blinked hard, forced herself to speak with sisterly detachment.

'I want to wake up. Find myself standing on the pavement in a holiday queue, with all the other families. We get to the box office at last, and I pay for three seats. We buy over-priced ice-cream, because it's been advertised, and Lucy wants to go to the loo so I miss the end.'

'I'll take Daniel then. No reason why he should miss out. And aren't I supposed to be his godmother, or something?'

One and a half, no, nearly two hours now of Ruth. Unnatural, this; so many years too close, in a shared room, then the years apart, now this forced intimacy. They had sisterhood under control until now, the letters and cards on occasion, casual mention: my sister, Ruth; my sister, Clare

'I didn't mean seeing that film. I meant normality.'

'I know, but really, I'd rather like to go, and taking a child gives me an excuse.'

'Left, here, then first on the right.'

'Thanks. You know what it is? You can't bear the idea of me with your precious children. Spoiled brat, no, it's mine, you can't play. . . . This greedy, obsessive motherhood.'

Clare said, and knew at once how pathetic it was:

'They are all I have now.'

'Then you have nothing.'

Ruth drove on in carefully timed silence, then, with the house in sight said,

'I suppose I'm allowed to kiss your son?'

'That depends on Daniel, doesn't it?'

Clare could see Daniel's nose, pink rubber, flattened and piggish in the front window, the glass steamed up with his breath. She didn't ring, opening the door with her own key. Jo accepted introduction. Emma hid.

Daniel was in Ruth's arms.

'Stay! You can have my room. Or Lucy's . . . she doesn't need it now. *Please* stay!'

Long, playful kisses. Clare, seeing them together thought, he is not like me after all, he could be Ruth herself.

'You will stay, won't you? You never do.'

Ruth sat him down on the stairs, still hugging him.

'No. It's time for me to go. I'm staying with Lucy, so Clare . . . so your mother can come home with you for a bit.'

'I'd rather have you.'

Daniel didn't look at his mother, saying this. Ruth detached herself firmly.

'Later. I promise.'

Another kiss and she was gone, out of the house, into her car, back to the hospital. Daniel lay across the stairs, howling, crying noisily, ugly, not lovable. Jo made her excuses.

'Do you mind if I go? There's a lot to catch up on.'

Clare thought there could hardly be much, not in Jo's life, maybe a little washing, dusting, vacuuming, nothing that couldn't wait. It would be kind, surely, to urge her to stay, pretend it was necessary. She tried, and failed.

'I'll come round tomorrow. The truth is, I need an early night.'

That too was unconvincing; an early night to prepare for what? Still she wanted to be gone, away from a family crisis that was not hers. Daniel stopped his howling at once.

'Is Lucy dead?'

'Of course not.'

'Lots of people die of it. I know. Jo took us out shopping, and they told us. When will she die?'

'She's getting better. She isn't going to die.'

Saying the words, Clare thought, do I believe it? Dare I believe it?

Daniel thought she did not.

'Then why do you look so sad?'

That was easy enough to answer, this time truthfully.

'I was afraid she might die. But the doctor's say she's a little better.'

'Why has Ruth come?'

Why indeed?

'Because she knew Lucy was ill. She came to help us.'

Tired of awkward words, awkward questions, Clare led him into the sitting room, found it almost as she had left it, only, because that was Jo's way, better polished. Evidently, the children had just finished picking up Lego when she arrived. The pieces were all back in the old ice-cream boxes, not yet in the toy chest. Daniel, without being told, lifted the lid, stacked the boxes inside; cue for praise that already sounded patronising, infantile.

'Good boy.'

She sounded like Moira, who could never remember that the child had turned seven, first grandchild for both families.

'Can I have the telly on now? There's a film.'

Telly? . . . was that Jo? No matter, it couldn't be allowed.

'TELEVISION.'

Daniel didn't repeat obediently as he used to when corrected. Leave it at that, then. She picked up the Radio Times from its usual place, was reminded, in heavy print, that this was still Good Friday. The film wasn't due to start till seven, wouldn't end till ten fifteen, Easter entertainment for all the family, and *Stabat Mater* on Radio Three. Time to negotiate.

'If you have a bath straight after tea.'

Once a week, she still supervised his bath, relying, otherwise, on the detergent quality of bubble-bath, clean underwear, and a mother-cat scrub of his face before leaving for school. Later, he would be too big to hold down, too young to be clean. The unwashed years, from ten or so, to whenever he would rediscover girls. Currently, he had a girlfriend, an older woman too, eight and a half, the pair of them caught, once, lying on the sofa, kissing. David had laughed.

'Good for Daniel. . . .'

'But isn't he too young?'

'Didn't you ever let the boys see your knickers in the playground?'

Clare had said, prim, cold:

'No. The boys had to leave as soon as they were seven. And there were nuns on duty.'

'So you missed out. Poor old you.'

Then, perhaps because it was near Christmas, and he had come home a little drunk, office party fashion, that last sad coupling. She had accepted him, passive, surprised that it should hurt so much, as if forced abstinence had made her a virgin again. David seemed to notice nothing, apparently enjoying himself, more drunk than he had seemed. He would never know, and she would never tell him, that merely holding a child close was richer than this, nearer to joy.

'Daniel, your bath's ready.'

He didn't come. She went to fetch him, found him in his room, still dressed, reading a book of Oscar Wilde stories. David again:

'Better not let Grandma see that.'

'Why not? We bought it with her book-token.'

'Then tell her you bought the kid a Bible.'

That time, David had been right, careful not to offend by telling unnecessary truths. His grandmother, born on Diamond Jubilee day, and still living would die decently distrusting queers, along with Jews, Roman Catholics and the Irish.

No-one had yet prescribed a ritual for meeting what remained of David's family; they had been excluded from this crisis, and had nothing to offer.

In the bath, Daniel seemed clean enough. Clare went to fetch his pyjamas, came back to find him out already, and towelling himself dry with his own bathtowel, heated on the radiator.

'Emma only has a bath once a week. Her mummy boils water in a kettle to wash the dishes, and they only put the water heater on on a Friday, because of the bills.'

'Lots of people do that.'

'They don't have the fire on, unless we come.'

'W~ll, it's April.'

'It's still cold though. They watch telly . . . vision under a duvet. Can we do that?'

'If you like.'

'Emma's mummy has a bath straight after Emma, so she can use the same water!'

'If you like, we'll do that. I'll be ready in time for the film.'

When she came down, warm and scented, a towel around her wet hair, Daniel's face peeped out from under the spare duvet.

'I'm hungry still.'

Five minutes to spare. The idea of watching this film had taken hold. Good Friday evening, the cold day ending in relentless rain, what else was there to do? Jim and Moira would go to church again, as they always did, this time to say more prayers, for a sick child.

'I'll make us cheese on toast.'

'No . . . I know what . . . bacon butties. With vinegar. Richard made them when we went to Cambridge.'

'It's Good Friday. You can't have meat.'

'Why not?'

He rejected the explanation. Jim and Moira had a list, weighed quantities, food permitted for the fasting. Her own compliance, tonight, was nothing but superstition; that, and entire lack of appetite, but look, God, I'm keeping all the rules you didn't make.

'You haven't eaten anything, Mum.'

'I'll have half a slice.'

Daniel fed her a cheese sandwich, hand to mouth. They watched the film well enough for the first two hours, falling asleep together before the climax. At one-thirty, she woke to a blank screen, an angry noise, the television, shouting to be switched off. She carried Daniel upstairs and lay awake all night, unable to think. About four, she opened a book, and stared at the printed letters until it was six, within reason, a time to get up, and do ordinary morning things.

Moira's letter fell out when Daniel opened the card. Eight, no, ten Easter cards, masses and prayers for Lucy, organised by Moira, a holy conspiracy. The letter would have to be read; Moira would expect that.

Maundy Thursday

Dear Clare, (there is a letter for Daniel inside his own card)

I have written many letters to you, never one as difficult as this. Almost, I can hear you say, how can she understand my despair, my desolation? It's true, I can't put myself in your shoes, but do believe that Daddy and I share your sorrow. You are our beloved daughter, and your happiness, the well-being of your children, affects us profoundly. We can't leave the house now without being asked for news of Lucy. As I write, Daddy is in church, praying for her. We will keep up this vigil of prayer until she recovers.

Would you believe I have sat here half an hour or more, trying to find words for what I want to say? There are times when I rage against the cruel blows you have suffered this year, first the tragic death of David, now Lucy's grave illness. But other people endure devastating loss, and come through, with their faith strengthened. If the worst happens, and Lucy dies, you know, beyond doubt, that her little soul will go straight to Heaven. *If* she dies, you will still have a loving son, who will need you more than he needs anyone else in the world.

They would be fools who say that they understand the problem of pain and illness. Please take this seriously—have you read the Book of Job? You are not the first, nor will you be the last to know grief and despair.

All I am sure of is that without a firm belief in an all-loving God who will make good out of pain and misery, I could not bear to contemplate your suffering. We will hope and pray with you until this crisis has passed.

All my love,

Mother.

Below, in Jim's unexpected copper-plate,

I can add nothing, except my love. We will be with you soon.

Only Moira could have written anything so stiffly pious, an essay rehearsed and deliberate. Clare stood the cards up on the piano, nine vaguely religious, and a rabbit for Daniel.

'Grandma didn't put 'and Lucy'.

'I expect she sent Lucy's card to the hospital.'

'Perhaps she thought Lucy would be dead. But she isn't, is she?'

He heard the phone first.

'I'll get it.'

Clare almost snatched it from him, heard words that were not meant for her.

'. . . and we won't come home until it's dark, dark night, and the bats are flying.'

'It's Ruth. She wants to talk to you.'

Clare shoved him aside, cruel; she had only one child that mattered now.

'Ruth?'

'What happened to Daniel? We were talking.'

She lied: 'Saturday morning television happened. Lucy?'

'No worse. They call it "stable". No better, no worse.'

'I want to be with her.'

'So you will, this afternoon. Go and do your shopping now.'

'Shopping?'

'Easter weekend, sister dear. People to feed. Me, for one. The parents, I shouldn't wonder. The whole loving family, rallying round. So you'd better get down to town quick, hadn't you. Don't forget the mint sauce.'

'Ruth, are you sure she's better?'

'Of course she isn't better.'

'Ruth. . . .'

'Don't interrupt this time. She isn't better yet. But she isn't dying either.'

Holiday crowds, hunting for food, winter's end, officially. The winter is past, the rain is over and gone. It was, too, lurking only in kerb-side puddles, for the unwary to splash white socks, light-coloured tights. Hurrying crowds, men with their women and children, fathers of families. Clare thought of another theme for a programme: shopping. It would have to wait for another series, depending on success this time round, but it wouldn't hurt, would it, to jot down a few ideas? Across the class spectrum, ideally; the difficulty would be the differential mortality rate among disadvantaged groups. The lower orders. Lower income groups? They would tell her the right current euphemism for poverty. She could even do mail-order, bring in the old Army and Navy catalogues.

'I said, can I buy a present for Lucy?'

One small hand, loosely held. Weeks, months ago, someone—Ellen Kenyon, saying, don't make him your companion. Let him be a child. Clare, walking with her son, across the crowd, remembered herself, still a child, sometimes in the sixties. I wanna hold your hand. Well, for a little while longer, there was someone she could be sure of, Daniel, son, not lover. Closeness allowed for how many more years?

'Have you bought her an Easter egg?'

The sweetshops were bare; Easter was all but over, on this day Moira and Jim refused to call Easter Saturday.

'Let's try this shop. It's big enough, anyway.'

Clare came to herself, crisply awake. They had arrived, drifting with the crowd, if not at the best shop in town, then at least the most expensive, rich and comforting. Painted ladies bore down on them, and passed on, without resentment. The smiles, the social promise to return, if the scent pleased, both women knowing it was hardly likely. Wasted from lack of food, lack of sleep, led by a small child, Clare did not look like a customer.

'I'll buy that for you when Grandad gives me some money.'

'But that money will be for you.'

'I like you to smell nice. And there isn't a Daddy to buy perfume, so I'd better.'

'It's sweet of you to offer, darling. . . .'

She stopped, disgusted with her own banality, publicly bent low, and faced her son.

'I really mean that. I'd love to have some scent.'
'I would buy it, if only I had the money.'
'Well, I haven't given you your Easter money yet.'
Clare trod thick carpet, saw her face again, in rose-tinted glass, the weariness coloured into haggard beauty. Her face? It would be more than easy to slip out her credit card for a lavish plastic treat; essence of spring fragrance of your choice, in a beautifully crafted jewel casket. In the beginning, God crafted the heavens and the earth. Sign here for what you don't need. Daniel had only real money, the price of comics and crisps. Easter money wasn't quite a fiction; she had given him extra at Christmas too.
'Isn't there anyone else in the world to buy you scent?'
Clare, seductive, whispered back,
'No-one.'
Better not to say, buying it for myself wouldn't be the same. Grown-ups pay their way, children and ladies are treated. Last week, she had squabbled with Pakenham, of all people, about a taxi fare. She remembered, acutely, the leather smell of the first pair of boots bought with earned money.
'Go away. You're not to look.'
Clare walked right away, examined gloves, made her retreat as the black-gowned figure could speak. Daniel, with his fat pocket, came shining towards her.
'There was change. Is it mine? What can I spend it on?'
'It's yours.'
He was holding her hand again, her companion in this place.
'Can I buy Lucy an Easter egg now?'
She let him lead the way, past unseen luxuries, left, right, down the subway to the food hall. Daniel would always be good at this kind of thing, confident master of continental time-tables, never, ever going the wrong way round the Circle line. Chrissie had an explanation for this.
'Five senses is just the beginning. In fact, barely above the level medicine was at with the four humours.'
'Really?'
There had been studies proving all manner of comfortable facts, even not knowing left from right was no more a sin than colour blindness.

'So that's it. I've always wondered.'

Chrissie, now, was merely counting the days to quickening.

'You had your eyes shut.'

'Did I?'

'It's a good job I'm looking after you, isn't it?'

'A very good job.'

Her son, newborn such a short time ago, lolling head, spider legs, living on what David nastily called her secretions, and now in charge, but what she wanted was another child. David had cheated her. How simple it was, being Chrissie, calmly choosing to give birth, and never mind the father of it. Daniel was holding her hand again.

'I've been crying, missing you. Jo doesn't mind if I cry.'

He said this walking past trays of tit-bits, olives, black, green, stuffed gherkins, silverskin onions, cream cheese with chives, with pineapple possibly all the cheeses of France. The hunger cramps were real, so was the greedy longing to fill her mouth, cram her stomach with food. So, even if Lucy died, she would survive, the body can only be denied so long. Small and hungry because Religious Knowledge was the last lesson of the day, she had been told by a nun,

'There is no food in Heaven.'

'Then I don't want to go. I like food.'

She must have been very young, because there had been a gentle explanation, so gentle that she had dared another question.

'But what about Jesus? He ate fish and things after being dead.'

Then the bell, and no more idle questions.

Butter, cream, margarine, polyunsaturated, sunflower oil, cream cakes, thus the shift from savoury to sweet was achieved. In bulk, too much cheese smells like vomit. Daniel was gloating at cream meringues. Clare gave her order quickly, before she could think better of it. The child at her side watched hungrily as the Easter cake, fluffy chicks, sugar shells, was packed into stiff cardboard. She ordered the largest size of egg, with Lucy's name to be written on it. A young man made sugar into words; Happy Easter Lucy. Was this his vocation? And now there would have to be another.

'Daniel, go over there.'

He obeyed, delighted, peeping over his shoulder. The sugar pen was busy again. She was buying him an Easter hare, carved and moulded chocolate, pushing his cart, loaded with jewel-bright eggs. Daniel's name was written on the cart.

Never again an Easter like this. David had disapproved; it came too soon after the orgy of Christmas. The chocolate celebration was evil on three counts; commercial exploitation, with equal parts of fat and sugar, loaded with guilt. Watching the young man make fantasies in sugar, hearts, flowers, lambs for the Easter young, David would say; what a pathetic way to earn a living. Clare, as David's wife, used to echo him, and only now thought, as herself. It is his job, he does it well, he gives pleasure. How arrogant to think time spent another way was better. David no longer kept any accounts.

Daniel watched as the flowered boxes were loaded into carrier bags, springtime bright and beautiful. There had been no beauty in David's family Easter, only hard-boiled eggs, worthily dyed with onion skins, and one small hollow chocolate egg each, broken into small pieces, and given out, daily, by Betty, so they would no overeat, and be sick.

'I'm hungry.'

Clare sat with Daniel in a corner seat, lamp-lit, because they were underground. The colours were all soft, sepia tints, shades of peace, the walls hung with Victorian engravings. Highland cattle, sure-footed, stepping down a cliff path, by a rocky coast, moonlight, no emotive detail spared. She put her head down on the table, shameless, crying, just as the girl came with their order.

Daniel's voice, explaining:

'My little sister's in hospital. She might be going to die.'

Moira would call this a 'scene'. Attention-seeking; look at me, I'm hurt. An open invitation to interfere. Voices, overheard, discussing what should be done with her. Send for the manageress? The first-aid office? A doctor? Daniel's voice again:

'No, my daddy can't come for us.'

'Why not, dear? Even if he's busy. . . .'

'He's not busy. He died, in a car-crash.'

Murmured sympathy. They would certainly send for someone now.

'Are you taking any tablets, dear?'

Three times a day, until it doesn't hurt. . . . Clare lifted her head, heavy with tears.

'I'm sorry.'

She could, and did, pull herself together. The brightly prosperous bags helped. Customer, they said, someone who has spent well, no-one really in need. Another cup of coffee was brought, and a gift of ice-cream, for Daniel. She told the manageress, quietly, that her daughter had meningitis, that she seemed to be recovering.

'And your husband?'

As if that were Daniel's fantasy, as if a child's word could not be trusted. Children will say anything: True, they will say, 'There's a wolf under my bed', meaning fear, meaning, there is a wolf. They will also say, if it happens to be true, my daddy is dead, you smell. They are crudely, comfortably open about natural functions.

'I need to go.' Lucy would say.

'You can't, not here, you'll have to wait.'

'But I need to go now. I can't save it. See, it comes out. Told you I couldn't save it.'

Lately, she had become more discreet, whispering her needs to Clare. But they were both cruelly frank, commenting, loudly, about bad smells, the fat, the ugly. Lucy, seeing menstrual blood, disapproved.

'Can't you stop it?'

'No.'

'Why not?'

'Because it comes, every month, until I'm too old to have babies. It would stop only if I had another baby.'

'Then why not have another baby?'

Why not? The insurance companies must live, still, in the days of life-long marriage, when a dying child might be one less mouth to feed. Someone on the next table had an early copy of the evening paper. Fairground death fall, a boy of nine had fallen from the big wheel. Another child, a girl of six, was missing. No need to guess how that would end, grieving parents, new demands for the death penalty. If Lucy lives, I will not let her out of my sight. I won't take the job. I'll take her to school myself, then sit at home, waiting until it's time to bring them back again, safe.

Daniel scraped the ice-cream bowl, lifted the spoon, pink tongue already flickering. She loved his mouth, soft, pink, milky, remembering a poem by Sylvia Plath.

'Your mouth opens

Clean as a cat. . . .'

'No **Not** in here.'

That was enough. He didn't protest. There were limits, and besides, he had had quite a good day so far. No need to invite trouble.

Clare finished her coffee, physically pleased that it was good.

'Come on, sunshine.'

'Don't. . . . Daddy used to call me that. Daddy was silly. He called hands "pandies" and feet "tootsies". That's for babies.'

Queuing to pay her bill, she fought back old tears; David, cautious, calculating, helpless, holding his newborn son's hands and feet. David, using silly, baby, family words, giving too much away.

'Lots of people use special words for babies.'

'I know, but Daddy was silly, wasn't he?'

She handed over her bill, paid, deliberately, with a ten pound note.

'All right now, madam?'

She had disturbed customers, but this time, they were letting her off.

'Thank-you, yes.'

'I hope the little girl gets better soon.'

'Thank-you.'

Outside, the rain was back. The crowds were wrapped in plastic, like sweets. There had better be good television, this cruel Easter. 'Scotland at a standstill', said the street-corner placards. 'Threat of worse to come'. The weather, or merely another strike? Daniel read out another. 'White Easter Nightmare.'

She raced him across at the lights, down into the warmth of Marks and Spencer, last stop before the bus-station. Clever, practical, London Ruth, telling her not to take the car, not into town, not before a Bank Holiday.

'You don't want to be trekking to some godforsaken car-park. And you're too late for a meter.'

Daniel objected:

'We could've bought food in the other shop.'

'Too expensive.'

She didn't know whether that was true or not, mechanically loading the basket with things to be eaten.

'Lucy likes chicken flavour crisps.'

'Then we'll get some.'

There was a covered bridge, from here, right into the bus station. Daniel found the right number, showed her how to pay the fare into a machine. Home. Back to real life, and Lucy, no better, no worse?

The knock was an invasion only of unwanted privacy.

'Your sister said you would be here. I've just come off duty.'

Only then did she see the orderly's white coat, remember, as if it had been a conversation with a stranger, that he chose to work in this place.

'Devious, you see. They're always short-handed, especially on the long stay wards. A paid job, every vac, and lots of lovely copy. . . .'

He sat down, uninvited, beside her, taking off the coat, becoming, with her, out of place.

'I would have come sooner, but that neighbour, the one looking after your children, said no, leave you alone.'

'Child, not children. I have only two.'

She stood up, removing herself a little. Ruth had equipped the place well, a bottle of wine, tea, coffee, food. No other child was especially ill this weekend. Blame Ruth for this; Ruth, who had destroyed so much, laughing at their shared bedroom window, so no man would take her home a second time, intercepting and reading letters, wickedly, wisely predicting what David would become. And now this.

Garwy reached for a biscuit, knobbly, uneven, expensive. Trust Ruth to buy what would pass for home-made. Clare, wife and mother drilled by her children bought things wrapped in shiny paper.

'These are good. Did you bake them?'

'My sister bought them. Probably in Harrods.'

'I haven't eaten all day. Could you come out for a meal?'

'I don't want to eat.'

That was a mistake. He was too concerned now, unwilling to leave her. Three days since she had told the boy, no more, it cannot be. But that had been someone else, *in statu pupillari*, definitely inferior, no question about it.

'I came only because Lucy is so ill. Clare, she really is better. I read the notes just now. Your sister said you wouldn't take it from her. Will you believe me? Look, I came along this corridor, and asked the agency nurse they've got in for the holiday. "Much better, doctor." That's what she said, Clare. . . .'

She clung to him, wet face against a day's growth of beard . . . a child kissing Daddy, home from work, laughing, because it scratched.

'Sorry. I forgot to shave this morning.'

'Sorry to cry all over you. I wasn't crying, until you came.'

The offered handkerchief was clean, but crumpled, had never been ironed. Imagine this man with starched points crusting a breast pocket like . . . like icing.

'What's so funny?'

Clare tried to explain . . . sugar-writing, David's sugar white, never-used pocket handkerchiefs.

'It's no use. It wasn't really very funny.' She gulped back a sob, like a child that has cried too long. Like Lucy, when she had screamed herself hysterical.

'Better?'

He was any age now, someone else, at this moment, necessarily stronger, in command, the giver.

'Better, thanks. Relief, I suppose. Do you know what I'd like to do?'

'Sleep, I should think. Why not change places with that sister of yours.'

Clare remembered, suddenly, why not.

'I can't. She's taking Daniel out to watch bats. And I couldn't, not tonight, I couldn't leave Lucy.'

'I know her, don't I?'

So he had been to the house, and Ruth had known exactly what she was doing.

'She writes in the Guardian sometimes, and they print a funny old picture of her.'

'That's it, then.'

Garwy opened a cupboard, pulled out a hospital blanket, then, without permission, tucked it round her, lifted her feet up onto the stool.

'Go to sleep.'

Did every woman's body feel like this, if a man was simply kind? Rigby had been kind, too, but Rigby was taboo, *verboten*.

'Rigby told me about Lucy, yesterday.'

'Yesterday?'

'Good Friday.'

Clare stopped falling, found herself, warm and peaceful, alone with Garwy, but quite safe.

'I've lost track of time, Was it only yesterday? I remember now. He drove me up to campus, for the service, then back here. How do you come to know Phil?'

It occurred to her, only then, that religion was the one thing they had never discussed, would never, there being no need.

'I know everyone.'

'Of course.'

She was drifting again, talking, only to define memory. Hold on to the memory of Lucy, little white face, sleeping.

'No . . . let me go. I must see her.'

He gave in, supporting her, like an invalid, back into Lucy's room.

The agency nurse had just finished writing up the charts.

'Dr Kelly wanted to see her daughter, before getting some sleep.' Dr? But he would say that.

'Sleeping peacefully, as you see. Temperature normal . . . well, only a little above.'

'You'll call me if she wakes?'

'Of course.'

He folded the blanket round her again. When he had gone,

she would have to get up again, to pee, wash, clean teeth, take off some clothes, but it was nice, this kindness.

'When they were little babies, and I was feeding round the clock, I used to go up to bed in the evening. Not always, of course, especially with Lucy, but when I was too tired to stand. I used to lie on the bed, with a little nestling baby, sucking me, and listen to radio plays.'

'Such as?'

'A nice murder . . . domestic drama . . . ghosts.'

'I would have said, the Third. Weird plays, and atonal music.'

'Now, yes, but then I needed someone talking. Mothers with babies are different. As if I was someone else.'

She said, suddenly hard, disengaging his hand.

'I'm glad you came, but you did understand, didn't you?'

'Perhaps.'

'You'd better go now.' . . . now, before it's too late, before too much more is said.

After he had gone, she reflected that the bargain was no longer necessary; Lucy's life did not depend on it. If the choice had to be made, there must be some other reason. But Ruth would have no part in it. She had done quite enough already.

'Catch me!'

Then a shadow across the sun, the running child seeming to come from the sun itself. Tumble of arms and legs, kisses, mouth on mouth, scent of warm body. Clare held the child close, both hearts pounding.

'I love you.'

'Best of all?'

Blue eyes, questioning. The truth, then:

'I love my best girl.'

Then more kisses, lovers' kisses, this is how we learn, parent and child, but I am only learning now; never kisses like this from Moira, nor would Jim have dared a kiss on the lips. Short measure, then, for David?

Lucy flopped onto the close-cropped grass, bald, from its first April cut. The rotary mower had left, clotted drifts, and a scent of broken grass still strong enough to overcome the urban smells beyond the hospital gates. Another hour, and they would be free to go, suitcases packed, driving out to liberty; one child duly restored to health. Thank-you, God. Mass of Thanksgiving, last night, in the chapel, and more than enough of Lucy's family, offering their prayers of thanks. Bacteria gave up the fight, overpowered by drugs, by Lucy's own body, leucocytes, in armed combat. By Easter Monday, they had known, for certain, that she would recover. An episode, then, merely a word to put on inquisitive forms: Have you suffered from any serious illness? She was not blind, or deaf, or in any other way damaged. True, she had lost weight, but she was eating well. Complete recovery then, victory for modern medicine, answer to prayer, Clare, fastidious, even slightly disgusted, had made a parcel of the offerings, five gaudy plastic bottles of Lourdes water, and one, native cure, from Walsingham, three miraculous medals, one copy of the guaranteed effective St Bridget prayers, two pastel and gilt pictures of St Rita, two of St Jude, and half a dozen of St Bernardette of Lourdes. But she had not been able to put the brown paper parcel in the hospital green tin rubbish bin. Taboo, or, maybe pity for the senders intervened. Better, kinder, to say, Lucy didn't need them anymore, so I have sent them to the Missions. She found an address in a yellowed copy of The Universe and sent the parcel sealed in a cardboard box that had held disposable syringes. The Irish nurse who had provided this offered to take the parcel out to the post herself, beaming approval. Clare watched her go, guilty, because she was allowing this pardoner's pack to be sent where it could do most harm. Lucy was alive, and was not going to die, not from meningitis. Thanks be to God? And what did He want in return?

Ruth had gone. Once Lucy was no longer anywhere near death, once the drama had become merely a matter for review, Ruth's part was over. It would be silence, now, until the Christmas cards, and no plan to meet again until next time, Ruth, who had shown Daniel a horseshoe bat, going back to be my sister Ruth, who lives in London. Did Ruth even live alone? Daniel, after waving goodbye, betrayed her.

'Can I really go and stay with them?'

'With whom?'

'Ruth and Nick.'

'Nick?'

'Her boyfriend. At least, I suppose he must be. You don't get girls called Nick, do you?'

'Not usually.'

'But are you allowed to live with someone? Even if you're not married?'

'If you're grown up, yes.'

Then easily changing the subject, taking him into town, shopping, for nothing necessary. In Smith's, she gave him a pound, to spend on anything he liked, cheap imitation of lavish Ruth. Or simply an excuse to waste money herself, on papers she wouldn't read, on magazines, on a childish bar of chocolate cream, to share with Daniel.

'Why did you give me money?'

'To spend. Because I'm happy.'

'Because Lucy's better?'

'Yes.'

'So am I. I asked God to make her better.'

Small hand in hers, lovely, precious, trusting Daniel, abandoned almost too long. Did he really believe his prayers made any difference? Clare remembered herself at seven, 'Please, God, make it snow', and her mother, nastily reminding her to think of the old people, who would shiver and fall. When the snow came, Clare felt guilty. Grown up, she knew that the prayers were irrelevant, and that if the old shivered and fell, that was, possibly, God's fault, certainly not hers. But it was too late; the child had learned guilt, instead of the joy of waking to snow.

Walking through the town, hand in hand, she tried to find out how he had lived, all this time without her, Ruth's child, her mother's child. Difficult to find words that would not do too much harm. Moira must be responsible for the haircut, brutally short.

'Grandma's very fussy, isn't she?'

'Fussy?'

'You know, do this, do that, time for Mass, eat up everything. She made me, and it was horrible.'

'Eating up?'

'Everything. I wanted you to come home. And Grandad wouldn't let me read in bed, like you do.'

Echoes of childhood, these, clean plates, switch that light out now. The long stillness of Sunday, with the day shaped by Mass, and a late, late breakfast, her stomach still heavy with food when it was time for tea, with tinned ham, syrupy fruit salad, tinned cream. Moira had even turned Daniel into something like her own sons. The hair made him look even more uncannily like Richard, grubby small brother. Three weeks, at least, before he would have his own face back. Clare thought, cold, cruel, I will not let her have him again. This is *mine*. She's had her chance of being a mother. As for Ruth, why didn't she have her own child, instead of buying Daniel's adoration for a few hours, days? Thinking like this, Clare was even reluctant to part with Daniel on the day Lucy was discharged. But Jo had been firm.

'No, you should leave him with me.'

'Why?'

'Do I need to tell you?'

'I suppose not.'

Jo was right. Lucy deserved, they both deserved these last few exclusive minutes together, mother and child that had been so close to death. The paediatrician had admitted how close it had been, yesterday, all danger past.

'We nearly lost her, but you can stop worrying now. Feed her up, mind.'

Clare dressing the child, covering the picked chicken ribs thought, give her something to eat. Never mind the Mass, take her home, feed her, have a party, even, celebrate, because she's alive. It was all safe now. No one would avoid her in the street, as they had for weeks after David's death. No Victorian addition to the stone; also Lucy, daughter of the above, aged four years, four months. And it had all been good experience. She knew, now, with what despairing acceptance one faced a child's death. It was men, male historians, who said that the love for a child was modern . . . but Rachel, weeping for her children, would not be comforted. The only lasting mark, it seemed, was that Lucy had become more precious, as if twice-born. Leaving the ward, she remembered a lost detail; Lucy had been born in a caul. And that was supposed to signify good luck.

Chrissie, complacent, stroked her round belly, five months of deliberate bastard. She had become beautiful with this child, the months of sickness and new life reshaping her lumpish body. Clare thought, sitting nearby, in the S.C.R., that Chrissie must have lost two stones, despite the bump. Glossy hair, full breasts, a child's skin, the unfair wages of sin paying dividends. Wicked, gentle Chrissie, fallen woman, ripely swelling. Clare, supposedly marking third year dissertations, felt barren. It was as well all papers were double-checked. In this mood, she marked spitefully. She had spent the morning invigilating, pitiless. Someone had been sick, three others had been seized with diarrhoea, even, revoltingly, soiled pants. Because the sufferers were all male, she had been spared the worst of that, only, the vomiter had been a girl, then, frightened, unseen all term, locked in her room, revising. She had come back, purged, to answer all questions fluently, as if the act of vomiting had released some mental block.

'Chrissie, how did you get through Finals?'

Half forgotten, this dreaming stillness of the pregnant. Chrissie was somewhere with her child, which was moving. Clare returned to her work, tried to make sense of ten lines with no main verb, five interdependent clauses. She repeated the question. Chrissie could see the students now, the first half-dozen spilling out into an ordinary, early June afternoon, candles on the chestnuts, daisies on the lawns, ragged tulips dying in the flower beds.

'Let me think. . . . I don't remember working. We played Mah-Jong every night. But it's all such rubbish, telling the poor things it's no use revising at the last minute. I wrote my very best paper from a Penguin that came out the day before. Short-term memory, you see.'

'What was it about?'

Chrissie was alive now, the baby distant. It was so easy to forget, to undervalue cleverness in soft covers.

'Interpersonal behaviour. Now, if he'd only called it body language, his bank balance would look very different today. Sad, isn't it, the way some people fold so much away. My gran did it with scarves, and handbags.'

'Lights under bushels?'

'Something like that. Has it ever struck you, that hard commercial streak there is in Christ. Gentle Jesus; what a waste of a good business brain. Parable of the talents, and all that.'

'That's your own nasty commercial reading. Anyway, why bring Christ into it?'

'Research. I wanted to be sure what this christening business involves.'

Clare shuffled papers. A student had efficiently stapled his sheets together, but in the wrong order.

'You're a prime example of why the ignorant layman shouldn't be trusted with the Bible.'

The baby moved again, this time hard enough for the ripple of flesh to show, like a trout in dappled water, not quite seen, but perceived.

'I was forgetting. Catholics aren't supposed to, are they?'

'They may, now, since Vatican II. My dear late godmother spent the month before her death reading the Authorised Version. It was something she'd always wanted to do, and the Catholic translations were dismal.'

'Sounds like my kind of lady.'

Clare considered this. Megan, small, bony, unmarried, obedient household daughter in a family that made priests and nuns. Megan, who was allowed to raise her contralto voice in the church choir, and nowhere else. And so passionately maternal that she was no ordinary font and birthdays godmother, but filled the house where her parents had at last died with borrowed children, the only children she was allowed.

'I suppose she was, in a way. When she was sixty-two, she sold up, and bought a cottage, in the Lake District, because she'd always wanted to and there was no one left to stop her.'

'Definitely my kind of lady. But now did we get to your godmama?'

'I was tired of nineteenth century urban migration and you

were discussing Christ's potential for chairing the C.B.I.'

'Women's conversation, then, so undisciplined. No wonder the men would rather keep us out.'

'It all seemed to flow evenly enough. We responded to each other.'

'Women, you see. It's when the men come that we get left out. And I was quite serious about Christ. If anything would win me over to your crazy religion, it's that man's blessed sanity. Life's for living and loving, to hell with convention. But you let the bloody priests screw it up.'

Clare, uneasy, found herself another script. Classic Chrissie, this, natural outsider, casually discussing Christ as if he were a mutual friend. Chrissie was embarrassing because, childlike, she had stayed intensely curious, had never defined any mental no-go areas. She now spoke about Christ with exactly that note of excitement Lucy had, saying, did you know, spiders have *eight* legs, the roses have turned into red berries. The only defence would be changing the subject, as one did with children who go to far. And from the window, Clare could see Garwy, walking alone, books under one arm, plastic bag of groceries in the other. White shirt, open at the neck, sunburnt skin, hair in need of cutting.

There were cracks in the leather of the heavy armchair in which she sat. It had been patched, once, in darker, coarser leather. The dissertations were piled high on the table beside her, matter for sleepless nights, and days snarling at the children, because she had not slept. Outside, the beeches had just lost the acid sharpness of new leaf, shading into dull summer green. The bluebells had been trodden underfoot, picked by campus children, to wilt indoors. The grass concealed fecund green seed heads, where the flowers had been. Garwy passed out of sight. So what? The world, especially this nursery corner of it, was full of beautiful young men, with long lean bodies and shaggy hair. Forget, then, just as she deliberately forgot, ever, even touching David. She could remember, acutely, the two distinct dramas of birth, but not David's part. There seemed to be no connection.

Chrissie stopped even pretending to read New Society.

'How's the B.B.C. thing going?'

'Well enough.'

'Are you writing a book?'

'Of course.'

'T.V. would be better.'

'I haven't been asked . . . yet.'

Something that was not Chrissie moved. Another month, and this roundness would spread, the uterus become oval, the fundus rising almost to the swollen breasts. Late September, early October, Chrissie would have to stop playing this game, go through the pain barrier, scream her child out into a hospital room, wake up, flattened, a mother. And she had done all this deliberately, without love, without even marriage, because she wanted a child. Already now, the thing was obviously not mere gossip. People were rehearsing their attitudes. It had been established that she would not be sacked; her publication record was too good for that. So far, so good. And there was provision for the occasional student babies.

The stables clock struck the half hour. Five-thirty, time to go home, long past time. She had only stayed so long because Jo had taken all three children to the new sports centre. She excused herself now by telling her nit-picking conscience that Jo was happy enough. And if the scripts had to be marked at midnight, what of it? She deserved this idle time, gentle gossip, with loving, amoral, peaceful Chrissie. Lucy's illness had drained her small stock of devotion; she would love them better for letting them go a little.

Questions again. Gratifying, this curiosity about her broadcasts. Clare, indulgent, a little conceited, talked eagerly about the studios, the reluctant censoring of one man's ribald account of sharing a bed with his parents, three years old, hand around his father's massive erection.

'I did wonder about that. How they managed, if they all really slept in the same beds. Once, nearly asked, in an O-level history class. Did everyone else watch? Or pretend not to see, like when someone stops for a pee, out in the country?'

Clare shivered suddenly, aware, once more, of Chrissie's superb pregnancy. Time indeed to go, drive back to her other life, claim her children, mother them. She gathered up the pile of work to be done, crammed it all into her briefcase, left Chrissie alone, dreamily half asleep, idle question unanswered.

'No . . . I must go. I'm late already.'

He had intercepted her in the Long Walk, short cut, by way of an arching sandstone folly, up to the staff car park. The leaves, dappled in golden light, made dancing shadows. Students brought parents here, touring the grounds, brief lovers came, from the summer ball, from winter parties, surprised to find this kind of beauty. In the campus shop, they were always running out of this postcard that said, look, it isn't so very bad, this is nearly as lovely as the Backs, almost as good.

'Not even a quick drink?'

Shafting sunlight, through green leaves, young voices, somewhere in the distance, the dry burden of paper under her arm, only the children at home safe enough, with Jo.

'How quick?'

Driving behind him, Clare reflected that men still hadn't learned how to manage this one; what if the lady had her own car? There had been so many ridiculous possibilities, walking to the nearest pub, his car, her car, complicated arrangements to pick each other up in the morning all the way to exasperation. Almost a quarrel, in fact. And so much more stimulating than his usual tepid good manners. In the end, he had snapped:

'Meet you there, then.'

The agreed place was on the way home for both of them, of no interest to students, especially now, after an exam, when they were too dazed to move further than the Union bar. Clare found Lewis waiting in the car park, ready to escort her in.

'But I mustn't stay.'

The landlord had just opened up. Clare found herself staring, as she had stared too many times before, at the toupee, which was ginger, and didn't come within inches of the grey tonsure. What kind of woman loved him enough to let that pass, when she could sit here, peevishly notching up Lewis's imperfections? Grey woollen socks, in sandals. Crumpled trousers, slightly stained. Dirt, under his finger-nails. A dismal tie . . . badly ironed shirt . . . (was that why he wanted her?) Garlic, still on his breath from lunchtime. She heard the almost feminine nervous giggle, saw, with distaste, the drops of liquid, beading his moustache after the first greedy drink. I couldn't live with that, not any of it. And that, surely, was a ridiculous attitude; the man was merely a colleague, sharing a drink after work.

Not ridiculous at all. Clare was not deceived, not deceiving herself; she had been too long on the other side not to recognise how hopeless it was. She was pitiless, too, for accepting this one drink. Lewis was here with someone else, a woman he wanted to love, already desired, enough to try again. He had though, got one thing right. Indecisive on these occasions, she felt safe with the gin and tonic he had ordered, disliking the taste enough to sit there, occasionally taking a dose. There was no risk, none whatsoever, of losing control. Poor Lewis. Would it be so very wrong to go on like this, for a few weeks, maybe months, simply to be a woman with a man in her life?

Try again. Not a bad height . . . five foot ten? Thick, fairish hair, in a floppy fringe. Grey eyes, thick lashes, enough lines. A tiny white scar on one cheek, shadow of stubble, neck, chin, sideburns. No . . . don't get confused. That response was merely sex, a craving, nothing more. Even so, she tried to see Lewis with a full beard. David could never have grown more than a puny goatee. No hair had ever grown anywhere except the fleshy centre of his chin, and the stubble had been dingy, almost grey, like his pubic hair. David had never looked agreeably unshaven. Would she like Lewis better, as the evening wore on?

Nasty, nasty taste. She nibbled a cashew nut.

'Time to go, I'm afraid. Thanks for the drink.'

'Must you?'

'I must. Jo will be wondering where I am as it is. And the children.'

'Joe?'

Suspicion, jealousy?

'Jo. J . . . o . . . My next door neighbour. She looks after the kids for me.' She hadn't been mistaken.

'But surely you could give her a ring, say you'll be late back?'

Clare laughed.

'She's not my wife, you know. She's had my screaming kids quite long enough.'

'Some other time?'

He was too eager; she still felt contempt, rather than pity. A woman wouldn't expose herself like this. Would she?

'I'll be marking all day tomorrow.'

'So will I. We deserve a break. Dinner tomorrow night?'

Clare stood up, moved away.

'Sorry. We've got something else on.'

She was sorry for him now, turned back to explain.

'I'm going to work all night, finish this lot tomorrow, and take the kids out for a picnic.'

Lewis said, suddenly bitter.

'I envy you.'

She sat down again, said, bleakly:

'You've no need.' And then deliberately let him misunderstand. That was contemptible, poaching pity, for David's death. Time to say, surely, it's a lie, I'm not sorry; he quite deserved to die.

'What I meant was . . . the children. Having a family life.'

'It isn't all like the commercials, you know.'

He had found a way of just missing eye to eye, as if by accident, as if long practised. Brave, anyway, to set a value on family life, and in public.

'Tell me what you'll do, when you get home.'

'Do you really want to know?'

'Only the details.'

She considered.

'Everything?'

'If you don't mind.'

It would be painless enough. Very well then . . .

'Kick my shoes off, slip into clogs. . . .'

'Why clogs?'

'Because I'll be getting supper, and I inherited my kitchen units from a giantess. It has to be clogs or stilts, and I need both hands for cooking. Clogs, then, and calling the children. It's fine, so they could be in our garden, or next door. Hug them, if Daniel will let me, if no-one else is watching.'

'I remember that age, kissing my mother when no-one else was looking. How old is he?'

'Seven . . . seven and a half.'

'That's right. I was fascinated with her breasts. I poked at them through her Maidenform bra. It was years before I found out they were really soft.'

Why was this place so empty, too intimate? Clare was grateful, briefly, for her own breasts, small, flat, embarrassing neither. And grateful, also, for the reassurance that Daniel was normal, as normal as the small Lewis had been.'

'Are all small boys like that?'

'Well, naturally. Didn't you wonder about men?'

'I don't remember. There was my older brother. When he was seven, we stopped bathing together. But I never touched my mother.'

'Never?'

'Not even hardly ever. I did see her breasts, when she was feeding the little ones, but they weren't things to touch.'

'Surely the first things you ever touched?'

'I suppose so. I've been almost worried about Daniel, this summer.'

'Because he's noticed you're a woman?'

'If you like.'

Her turn, now, to intrude.

'Your mother . . .'

'She's dead.'

'I'm sorry.'

'No need. It was a long time ago. The September after my first degree. Dad remarried, a year later. Rachel's only my age. So . . . after you kick off your clogs?'

She glanced, deliberately, at the Parliament clock on the wall. Twenty-past six.

'Look, James, I really must go. Some other time.' She added, nastily, 'I've got a home to go to, even if you haven't.' And walked out on the deliberate insult.

At the supper table, Clare felt newly proud of them all. They smelt of chlorine, but Jo, Emma and Lucy smelt also of cologne, something lightly floral. Jo managed wet hair better than most women, tying a scarf with gipsy dash. Clare, furtive, inspected her. A little more weight, and the haggard look would be gone forever. More than that, she glowed with unaccountable happiness, as if she had been given something precious. She didn't look, in the least, the deserted wife, despairing enough for suicide. A man? Hardly. Then it must be the absence of one particular man, and the presence of these children. She had managed the swimming without hitch, even shampooing their hair afterwards.

'Ask Daniel how far he swam tonight!'

'A length. . . . A whole length. And two on my back. And Lucy did three strokes. What did you do all day?'

'Work.'

When the children were asleep, this lie had to become truth. Jo was at the door, unwelcome.

'Emma's asleep. Can I make you some coffee?'

She had changed, stood there, on the doorstep, in a white embroidered blouse, black jeans, an enamel butterfly pinned above one ankle.

'No, thank you. I really must work.'

Close the door, disappear upstairs, out of sight, pile the desk with papers, shut out all intruders. She worked, mechanical, steady, until almost midnight, getting through more than she'd expected.

The phone was really ringing. Pound downstairs, then, race to it, as if anyone ringing at this time had a right to be answered. Pip . . . pip . . . pip . . . and then they got the money in at last.

'Clare. . . .'

Well, he deserved invective.

'Five to midnight, I know. Have I disturbed you? I mean, were you working?'

'Both.'

'Sorry.'

'You could have woken the children. . . .'

Easy enough to slam the receiver down, no point in prolonging this except to erase guilt.

'Are you alright? I mean, are you ill?'

'I was sick . . . over now.'

Food poisoning? She imagined a seamy kitchen, stinking dishcloths, male squalor. He said, half laughing,

'Drunk . . . serve me right.'

'Where are you?'

She knew perfectly well what was coming. Time to hang up, let him walk home, get back to work. And what about the children, likely as not to wake up with wolves under the bed, wandering into her empty room. Daniel sometimes still walked in his sleep, peeing, perversely, on the same bit of landing carpet, every time. Jo had said, why not put a pot there. Victorian, if you must.

'I should let you walk home.'

'I know.'

'But it's raining, and I was rather a bitch, wasn't I? Alright, get out of the phone box, and sit in your car waiting.'

'Drunk in charge?'

She heard the whispering rain, heavier than it seemed, muffled by summer leaves, summer grass. Wet roads, and the Bristol needed new tyres. Nag him about that tomorrow. Whereas David, who prefered a company Volvo had the tread measured at the garage, long before it could be necessary.

Jo's light was still on. She came down at once, willingly, not even leaning out of an upstairs window.

'I have to rescue a friend.'

'Mad axe-man? Alright, I'll be in charge. I'll fetch Emma round to Lucy's bed.'

She deserved an explanation, especially as she hadn't asked.

'Very drunk, and he's been sick, outside the pub. He wants me to drive him home.'

'The police would do that. They often brought Mike back. For a consideration of course. Worth it, because he needed the car in the morning. Why pick on you? I mean, what would he do if David were still around?'

Clare was in the car already; no need to answer. So Sinclair had had an excuse, of sorts, for beating his wife. Kind of them to bring him home to her; small wonder she had never complained. And what if we had reported anything, tears, blows, Emma's screams. They would have been forced to investigate.

David, indifferent: 'It's their business. Some women like violence. Gets them nicely worked up for a fuck.' Then, eloquent, stripping off his clothes, throwing them at a chair, closing the door on her.

She had to pull up, dazed by this living memory of David,

every inch of him, even the puckered scar, where a tuberculosis jab had become infected, David's body, familiar even after love, broad shoulders, hairless chest, the hips surprisingly wide, for a man, the legs, once elegant, becoming thick.

'Are you alright, madam?'

Check hysterical laughter. Would they really get out the kit, take her to the station?

'Fine, thank-you. I was trying to remember how to get to the Woolpack. I'm on my way to rescue friends having trouble with their car.' She listened, obediently, to unneeded directions. They let her go. No, officer, I am not under the influence; on the contrary, this night rain is my antidote to the water of Lethe. I stopped because I suddenly remembered my dead husband. They would have been kind, naturally, writing a report about her. Young widow, found in her car, 12.20 a.m. Questions, at the station, about the children, about Jo, and all the time, poor drunken James, in his phone box. There isn't actually a law against tears; just don't do it in public, even at midnight. It seemed safest to take their way to the pub, though she knew a better one. They were still watching.

Poor huddled figure, damp and dejected, on the wall. This evening, the same wall would have been bright with summer evening drinkers, barefoot girls in filmy cotton, young men in shirt sleeves. And the poor creature had sat here, paying to vomit and shiver in the darkness, when everyone else had gone home to one bed or another.

'I thought you weren't coming.'

'Well, I did. Have you locked her up?'

She could smell the vomit now, nasty, much worse than a child's.

'You can get in the back. Lie down. And here. . . .'

'Thanks.'

Another stab. This time, it was David, with a sprained ankle, grateful for a sacrificed silk scarf, and the use of her shoulder, hobbling down to Derwentwater, and rowing back across the lake in an April sunset. They should have know it wasn't reality.

Lewis accepted the sachet, mother's handbag emergency

kit, for blood, vomit, or mere chocolate, kept like spare knickers, travel sickness pills, safety pins, Christmas cracker whistle, plasters. She tucked a rug around him, went to check the Bristol herself, returned with the keys he had left in the lock. Next?

'Where's your doorkey?'

Shake less gently. . . .

'Key, James. . . .'

'Key?'

She had to grope in his pockets, found, with relief, the neat leather clip; labelled, front door, back door, garage. No need, thank God, to give in, take him home . . . something the cat brought in. Pulling up outside the cottage she let herself in first, switched lights on.

The tears hurt him, obviously; hurt her too, because she should not have seen, or heard, should not have been there at all. Words being inadequate, she led the man into his own house, onto his own sofa, removed clothes. Motherhood is a good basic training for all emergencies, everyone should take the course. The suit into a polythene bag, to be dropped off at the dry-cleaners tomorrow. Shirt, tie, socks, into the washing machine; lucky that he had bought this house full of left-overs, including a rusty old Indesit. One naked friend, sleeping it off on his own sofa; mission accomplished, duty done, debt settled. Relenting, she went upstairs, discovered pyjamas, fastidiously folded, in a bedroom old maid neat. Even in early June, dawn came cold. Might as well drag the duvet downstairs, spare him the cold waking, alone. How often had Jo managed this routine, neatly restoring order for the outside world. And what if he were sick again?

That was the last detail. She fetched the plastic bowl from the kitchen, fashionably deep green. So often, a man on his own would live with balding brushes, aged, pale yellow bowls, the polythene peeling like dead skin. Cover him gently now, tucked up like a child. Glass of water on the table, where he could reach it. David had disliked the idea of being out of control had never been drunk. She remembered an incident, a girl, drunk, and locked in the lavatory. Clare had been sent to the rescue, because she was small, and a good climber. It was the first time she had seen anyone, man or woman, incapable; impossible to imagine Jim drunk. They had, in female conspiracy, bathed the girl, put her to bed, silently seeing the dark bruised vulva, thighs, the teeth marks. The matter had never been mentioned again.

'Clare?'

'I must go. Will you be alright now?'

The hand reaching out had to be taken. A nicely staged scene, soft lights, exposed beams, oak bookcases, richly filled. Escher prints, a Ben Nicholson, one of the unexpected Lowry landscapes, one painful ikon, bottles on a wine table, sherry, whisky, bright glasses. I could live here. I could, really. It might not be at all bad.

She could drive back, alone, lock the car, let herself in, not waking Jo and the children, and either sit up all night with those dreary scripts, or wake up to them. Saturday of children, interruptions, lawnmowers, taking the children somewhere, with or without Jo. Every day had become so heavily the same that she had forgotten this was Friday night. Better to go now, see Lewis again on Monday, after a decent sober interval, see him again in the expected place. It wasn't fair, to take advantage now. Last time, the mere furtiveness had simplified things. That, and wanting Garwy anyway.

But it was done, hand in hand. He struggled a little to sit up.

'So tired . . .'

'So drunk, you mean. Go to sleep. I couldn't get you upstairs.'

He reached for the water, sipped it cautiously.

'Better now. Don't go yet.'

That was her last chance. The pyjamas should have been ridiculous, but they were black, without even a pretentious monogram. He was walking steadily enough now, so it would be perfectly safe to leave him; no sordid choking on his own vomit.

He came back, smelling freshly of mouthwash, cologne, something astringent.

'I'm a louse, aren't I?'

'Not very sensible, anyway. Why pay good money, just to make yourself ill? And could I have my hand back, please?'

Lazy line of least resistance, giving in, hands, lips, tongues.

Time to remember that he had to be driven home, incapable.

'Sorry. . . .'

'Don't keep apologising.'

'Will you stay? If I get some sleep. . . .'

Poor men, such frail, complex creatures. And what harm would it do to anyone, sleeping children, sleeping friend. They would still be there at daybreak. And it was raining, blowing hard, a summer storm, with thunder and lightning.

'What time is it?'

'Twenty to four.'

No more rain, and a thrush, clocking in. Honeysuckle and roses around the open window. Lewis got up, drew the curtains, which had been left open last night, came back. Not bad, not unpleasant. She had, naively, supposed that love, or at least fascination, was necessary. Evidently not. Or, maybe, the night's events conspired against her. Make it easy for him, then. . . .

Wash in the alien bathroom, leave no trace of him. Safer not to prolong it, no matter how much her easily deceived body wanted to stay. Busy day ahead, breakfast, children, fruit to be picked in the garden, and those damned scripts to mark. An entirely busy life, with no need for any man, definitely not this man, even though he was in love with her, even though, amazingly, he was such an accomplished lover.

'Where shall we go?'

Jo had made breakfast a ceremony for five, the table spread with white, and flowers in a vase, and no trouble at all, because the children had enjoyed the work. Daniel had washed up; even the little girls had done no damage, removing cornflakes, honey, eggshells. The presence of another adult allowed one, at least, behind the paper privacy, no weary need to shout, badger, hurry, get a move on, time for school. Even so, it was an intrusion . . . imagine, if she were here all the time. . . .

'Go? You know I can't go anywhere.'

'You were so late back. . . . Give yourself a break . . .'

Tactful, that. Late had been early, five o'clock, black coffee, then nearly three hours at her desk, until the children and Jo woke up, the milkman clattered at the door, wanting money.

'And anyway, you promised.' Daniel, my word is my bond.

'Seaside!'

'Or the zoo?'

'No, the seaside!'

The children shrieked, excited, as if this were their one Victorian treat for all the year. Two for the seaside, one for the zoo. . . .

'If you behave. . . .'

Three desperate small faces; were children always so venal, so easily bought?

'We could always go to both.'

Clare was in charge now, her car, her time, her money.

'Everyone ready to leave then, in half an hour. Buckets and spades, swimsuits.'

'And if Daniel's sick, he can be sick in a bucket.'

Lucy, never sick in cars, was smug, superior.

'Nobody is going to be sick.'

They were ready to leave when the phone rang, and should have been ignored.

'Last night . . .'

'Sorry. We're on our way out.'

Replace the receiver; so it was that simple.

Final check, water heater on, for baths, for removing crusted sand. Bags of fruit, crisps, a loaf, butter, cheese, ham, the week's stale bread for ducks and seagulls. She had even retrieved, from a kitchen drawer, a magazine voucher, two children admitted free with two adults. In the magazine world, every child is equipped with two free adults.

'Can you navigate?'

Jo said:

'I can drive.'

'You're taking lessons?'

'Passed my test, last week. And don't look so stunned. It isn't very flattering. If we come off the motorway here, we can pick up the A54 and take the ring road to get to the zoo. That way we'd miss all the Chester snarl.'

The Cheshire plain, indecently lush, buttercup meadows, vast acid yellow fields.

'Is that mustard?'

'Rape.'

'Of course. I was wondering why I felt twelve years old. The summer we went to Normandy. . . .'

'Why the driving?'

'Bound to be useful. You paid for my lessons, in a way. Two a week, while Emma was at playgroup. They had a special offer.'

'How many?'

'Ten.'

'And you passed first time?'

'Failing would be a waste of money.'

Clare was impressed.

'It took me thirty, and hours of extra practice with my father.'

She had nearly added 'and I was much younger then', but stopped, because neither of them was very young, not any more. She was possessed with the memory of James' too much lined face. And how old was he? Thirty-five, six, seven?

'I like the blue bum best!'

That was Lucy, delighted with the mandrill, masturbating for, or despite his audience. Clare remembered being hurried past, by Moira and an aunt. On to the wretched cat house, and the biggest lion had stood up against the bars to spray all over the small girl in smocked fifties gingham. Daniel had heard the story before, from Ruth, who had been a baby, left outside in her pram.

'Lions piss, like a million tom cats! Pooh!'

'Why on earth did we come to the zoo?'

They were drinking tea, at a splintery rustic table, willow-pattern cups, blue plastic cloths, a cherry tree above that had been pretty a month ago. The children, eating lurid ice-lollies, would not sit down, had found a clutter of pigeons, last resort now every cage snapped: DO NOT FEED. A sparrow muscled in, then a cock chaffinch.

'For the children?'

'But look at them. . . . Perfectly happy feeding pigeons. And the pigeons are free.'

'It's not even educational. Television does it better. There's no excuse for the cages.'

'Not even breeding things that would die out?'

'A.I.D. for pandas? No . . . who are we to interfere?'

'I know why we came.'

'Then tell me. . . .'

'Remembering our own zoos. . . .'

'Riding in a howdah on an elephant. . . .'

'Feeding them buns. . . .'

'A giant tortoise. . . .'

'Seeing a real Guinness bird. . . .'

'Flea circuses.'

'The stench, and the hippos dreadful dirty teeth.'

'Daniel and Lucy like stories about animals escaping from zoos.'

'So does Emma.'

'And we'd hardly take them to the Scrubs or Strangeways for a day out.'

'Let's go.'

The children didn't object. Clare bought them all toys, a trio of bathtub alligators.

'Welsh coast?'

'All those caravans?'

'I know. Birkenhead, New Brighton, the Mersey tunnel, and home on the motorway.'

'Fish and chips . . . mugs of tea.'

'Dirty old Mersey. Mind if I drive?'

Impossible to say, yes, I mind very much, this is mine, and the children, or two of them, are mine also, too precious to risk. It was more than that; a disturbing change, undefined. Jo knew the roads, even the new ones, nippy short cuts, back streets, one-way systems. She had them, all alone, in cobbled dockland, perilously near the quayside, out, and back into noisy Mersey traffic. Another question never asked; where do you come from, where were you born?

'Rain tomorrow.'

She was pointing to high cloud, grey and white, crossing the Irish Sea with Sunday rain.

'But you've no accent. . . .'

Patronising, silly, better left unsaid.

'Shall I take you home?'

Clare glanced round, briefly, at the children, happy as they should be, feeding gulls, Emma hard at work, with a row of fifteen perfect sandcastles. Daniel and Lucy were digging a hole.

'You mean, visit your family? Now?'

'Why not?'

It was easy enough to gather up the children, with the rain clouds scudding across, ill tempered, a wicked gust of wind, the scummy tide coming in fast. Offer them the tunnel, and it would be easy enough. How did children think, taken out by adults . . . would they really mind if they never went anywhere, merely played close to home, in countries of their own, the way children used to?

Emma knew where she was.

'We're going to see Gran and Grandad. This is the way the bus comes.'

Jo pulled up by a coin box, dialled, spoke, came out more relaxed.

'They're in.'

'So why all the mystery?'

'No mystery. You never asked. You had me nicely classified, didn't you . . . poor Jo . . . nameless waif.'

'Nothing of the kind. . . .'

'Liar. . . .'

Daniel was too quiet, white-faced. Clare cursed herself, for not noticing sooner. He was sick soon after they stopped, then crying in her arms. Clare hated the two girls, scornfully staring out of the window. She had been Daniel, the sick one, despised, miserably wishing the miles away; Moira; so sure it was imagined, wilful. He drank water, retching even on that.

'I'm going to take him for a walk.'

Away from the car, Daniel looked better.

'It's very horrible, being sick, isn't it? Why did I cry?'

'Grown-ups cry, when they're sick.'

'Do they? Do they really? Even men?'

'Even men. And being car sick isn't your fault.'

They sat down in long grass, uncut, lady's smock, red

clover, moon daisies, vetches, young shoots of willowherb, all uninvited. Daniel pulled a long blade of grass, whistled.

'Guess who taught me that?'

'Grandma.'

'How did you know?'

'She tried to teach me, but I can't do it.'

'But it's easy.'

After three lessons, he gave up.

'Perhaps your mouth isn't the right shape. Like an oboe mouthpiece is different from a flute. I'm better now.'

She made him take the tablets, too late, but at least he should be alright on the way home. Why not sell the car, travel by train, use taxis? It isn't as if I enjoy driving. Apply cost benefit analysis, and the answer would be: sell. One strange benefactor had given her this car; the snow covered branch that had killed David.

Walking back to the others, Daniel still held her hand.

'It was morning when you came in. I heard you go, and I heard you come back. I was scared.'

'But Jo was there. . . .'

'Lucy wanted you too. She came in my bed, and cried. Where did you go?'

'Someone . . . a friend of mine, was ill, and I had to take him home.'

'But you should of come back.'

'Should HAVE. Yes . . . I should have come back, straight away.'

'Promise not to go away again? Ever, ever?'

Frightened, she promised. Better to leave it at that, better not to think; my life is my own what right has he to make such demands?

'Liverpool posh', said Jo, cheerfully. 'Dad was head of the school. My mother' (she very nearly said "Mummy") '. . . was the secretary. Only since we all left home, of course.'

Leafy suburb, solid red brick, plane trees, a few late flowering laburnums, lilacs, in neat gardens, beginning their summer season; lupins, hopeful staked delphiniums, the leaves of spring bulbs bound with raffia. A comforting place to live, if that was what you wanted out of life. Clare felt crazily envious, seeing a couple, about her own age, hand in hand, children skipping along beside them, a new baby in a new pram. Jo waved.

'Next door but one. The boy goes to Daddy's school.'

'Then you must know. . . .'

Of course she knew, or rather, could find faces to match the offered names. Friends of Jim, and Moira . . . to be claimed. Jo had escaped somewhere with her father, and the girls. Daniel had fallen asleep on the sofa, had been given a clean shirt.

'So long as we can have it back sometime. Poor little boy. . . .'

They knew who she was, next door neighbour, friend, mother of Emma's playmate.

'Josephine told us how wonderful you were, when she was ill. We were in Australia, you know, Adelaide, visiting our eldest girl, Kay.'

Ill? Was that what they had been told, all they would ever know? Lucy, Daniel, when will the lies begin?

'Anyone would have done the same.'

Not entirely true, that. Anyone might just as easily have panicked, and there would be no daughter Josephine, to walk on striped grass with her father, dead-heading early roses.

'And how wonderful that you should both be Catholics. . . .'

Mrs Fitzpatrick paused.

'You don't mind my saying that, do you?'

'Why should I?'

'It could be so difficult for her, on her own, so far from everybody. Michael wasn't Catholic, you know . . . silly, of course you would know.'

Clare's expression veiled tactless memories of so many Sundays, aware of faint scorn, as she took the children and her unbelieving self to the chapel on campus. or even the Catholic church. Time for a change of subject, brothers and sisters. Kay, who had been to Strawberry Hill, and now had ten hectares of garden, west of Adelaide.

'I can never remember which way round it is—acres and hectares.'

'Well, I voted against going in. It's all to do with the Common Market, isn't it?'

Sisters and brothers. . . .

'Ruth Kelly. . . . Wait till I tell Des. . . .'

Shameless, Clare played the game:

'And my sister-in-law, Anna.'

'You must be very proud of her. Of both of them. The unborn child . . .'

Imagine thickset, immaculate Anna, with a real, grubby small child, a child wetting its bed, screaming in temper, defying saintly, barren Anna, who spent her life doing good. Spin the game out, try for a common ancestor. Time to produce the trump-card, the real, bone fide historic family archbishop. How easy it would be to despise this nice little woman, happily imagining a new life for her daughter, no longer in the wilderness with her unbelieving mate; two good Catholic mothers together, bringing up their children. Daniel's playground taunt fitted the bill. 'Liar, liar, your bum's on fire . . .'

Go on lying. It's so easy, it's what she wants to hear, anything else would be cruel; she deserves this fate, nor would I lie at lower rate. Desmond Fitzpatrick, grandad, adopted grandad, retired headmaster came back with two little girls, and an armful of roses. Time to make tea, then time to be on their way.

'Brilliant. I know you were a liar, but that was brilliant.'

Clare had reclaimed her car. The children were all asleep.

'What lies? And you might have warned me.'

'About my mother, or Mother Church? I liked the archbishop story.'

'Genuine. Great great something uncle.'

'An English Martyr would be even better.'

'Idiot.'

Motorway junction. Now the home stretch:

'Seriously, though, don't you think it's kinder to deceive? Especially when the truth would hurt so much.'

'And if you'd succeeded?'

'You know . . . I'd almost forgotten. I can't imagine wanting to die now.'

'Better that they should never know, then?'

'Much better. You wouldn't tell yours about life as a merry widow, now, would you?'

Clare didn't take her eyes off the road, answered, evenly.

'I don't follow . . .'

'Last night . . .'

'Last night won't happen again.'

'Until the next time.'

'Bitch!'

'I won't give you away, if that's what's worrying you.'

'You won't get a chance.'

After that, nothing but silence, untl they had to help each other, carrying tired children in to bed. In the morning, Clare drove up to campus, with her children, for Mass, on the last Sunday of term. Afterwards, she sought out the Murphys, made sure they would come to tea, bring all the children. Then, expecting him to decline, she invited Rigby for supper.

'As if there were only one sin?'

But Rigby had come to play chess, to eat supper cooked by someone else.

'Plague someone else, Clare. Check . . . Get out of that if you can.'

Another bad move.

'Checkmate. You don't usually play so badly.'

'Daniel beats me so often I'm demoralised.'

'Not concentrating. You were somewhere else half the time. And you look tired.'

'No time to sleep, marking these blasted papers night and day.'

'Then why invite me round?'

'Unfair to the students, marking in this state. And I needed company.'

'And I suppose I'm safe?'

'You play a good game of chess. Another game, or shall we put them away?'

The chessmen had been David's, yew and ebony, pawns, bishops, rooks, knights, kings, queens, eight squares by eight, play the game forever and never win.

'It would be too easy to win. Anything on the box?'

'Depends on your standards. Judging by the number of repeats, it must be summer.'

'They switched on, watched news, read the promise of rain, and further rain, spreading from the west.

'Then it must be Wimbledon. . . .'

'Almost. I will be very, very lazy, and lie on this sofa, all afternoon, watching until the children make me switch over.'

'All alone?'

'Of course.'

'I wasn't fishing.'

'Don't worry, I wasn't going to confess.'

The shift back into consciousness wasn't quite quick enough.

'Time for me to go. Thanks for the meal.'

She saw him to the door, then had to pull herself upstairs, clutching the rail.

Tear days from the calendar, breathe with relief when June passes double figures, meet solemnly to decide temporary fates. What happens, then, if every summer is spent like this? The answer was all too clear; become like Murphy, like Lewis, like Pakenham, realise, by forty-five or so that you are unlikely, now, ever to get a chair, become Vice Chancellor. It was supposed to be scholarship, but what were undergraduates? Only clever children, delaying work for a few more years, too young to be equals. And what kind of man or woman chooses to spend a lifetime drilling inferiors?

'No high fliers in this lot.' Pakenham dumped a pile of marked scripts on the table beside him.

Clare said:

'Well, of course not. They wouldn't come here, would they?'

'Not willingly, no. We've had a few . . .'

'They don't stay.'

'They get firsts, which is better than anyone hoped when they settled for this place. Then they go on to better things.'

'And is that what you're doing? Settling for here?'

Impertinent, that, and not what she would have dared six months ago. But he was younger than she had supposed, with, too, this year's stirring paper in the Economic History Review.

So you've heard rumours?'

'Nothing . . . Not a word. . . .'

'Have it from the horse's mouth, then. I'm taking a year's sabbatical, starting in January. Going back to my old college . . .'

Surprising that it should be Magdalen. She would have guessed at Worcester, or Keble. David's college. Imagine Pakenham, young, a watcher, from his room, not part of anything.

'I remember going to a party there once, and we had to climb out. The last year of climbing . . .'

He had been a watcher . . .

'And what happened?'

'A fat girl got stuck, between the parapets, in Longwall Street. David and the other men arranged a diversion for the bulldogs, while we undressed her.'

'She must have been very fat.'

'She was. I used to look up at those parapets and think, she can't have been that size. But she was, honestly.'

He fingered the scripts, decided not to pick one out.

'Better material next year. That young Jones, for one. Very sound work, in spite of the writing.'

Don't flicker, give nothing away.

Jones?

'Gary . . . no . . . Garwy. Yesterday's Guardian. People were impressed.'

'I hadn't heard.'

'Of course, you've been taking this marking so seriously. One learns to cut down. Well. I must be off . . . viva voce this afternoon. Viva voce indeed. . . . Lucky if there's any sign of life, let alone voice. They sit there like cold suet.'

Two dusty milk bottles in the crate, on the half landing. A powerful smell . . . Rentokil? Another classy reason to live in the Stables, dry rot, woodworm . . . infinitely superior to rusting reinforced concrete.

Time to retreat, because he was definitely in, unless he made a habit of leaving the radio on. Lunchtime concert from St Martin's, just ending, soothing female voice ready with the news headlines. And switched off, so he *must* be in . . .

No . . . not necessarily. It could be the radio switching itself off, after recording the concert. Detective fiction must be so much harder to write now; no wonder the emphasis has shifted to studying obsession, perversion. One dry leaf from last winter rattled down the stairs. Knock at the door, be prepared for whatever there is behind it.

'Come in.'

No pleasure, but no open hostility either. Exactly the same face, and body seen in classes. The first week of this term, she had thought it couldn't be done; some excuse would have to be made. And then it had been surprisingly easy. Go on as if nothing has happened.

She was in the room now, a season too late. Green light, from the creeper outside. Young voices below, crossing the courtyard, giddy with relief. His generation. One step further, sit down, bag still slung over her sholder, proof that she didn't intend to stay. Without looking up from the work spread over the desk, he said:

'In thc hospital. I thought we agreed, in the hospital. . . .'

'Agreed what?'

'Wasn't that the bargain? Giving me up, if Lucy lived?'

He added, gentler.

'How is she now?'

'Absolutely fine. We saw the paediatrician last week. Complete recovery, he said.'

'But more precious now?'

How did he know that, never having a child?

'No. . . . It was before I knew she was ill. No connection.'

Find an excuse to hurry away . . .

'I'm disturbing you. I shouldn't have come.'

'Clare . . .'

No use struggling, not with his arms round her, because she could have only one reason for being here.

'Surely Lewis would be more suitable?'

'You're well informed.'

'So it's true?'

'Nothing is true, nothing you hear in this place.'

'Even I can see the advantages. Nicely settled, never going very far, but no matter, he's doing well enough. He'll make a devoted husband. Someone to fix the fuses while you iron shirts.'

'I can fix my own fuses.'

'Is that all? Alright, give him the ironing.'

'I don't love him.'

Why the two rooms, making this shift from study to bed so unequivocal admitting, silent consent; I don't love him . . . and instead, impossibly, I love you.

'Marry me.'

'I couldn't.'

'Why not?'

'You know damn well why not. Nineteen . . . thirty. . . .'

'Twenty. It was my birthday last week, and you didn't even send me a card. What happened to equality? Switch the ages round, and the faces split open with approval. Look at . . .'

'That's different. Ten years, and I'll be forty.'

'So what? Look, how many of your friends are still married? The ones who got married when you did?'

'Not many.'

'Assortative mating, same age band. The program looks right, but the results are coming out wrong, aren't they? We could hardly do worse. You were heading for divorce too . . .'

'I shouldn't have told you that.'

Three, four, five . . . She undid the last button. . . .

'Look, if it's sex you want, why all the fuss? Why marriage?'

She turned face down on the bed, crying silently, allowed the gentle stroking of her hair.

'What time is it?'

'Relax. Only five. I sent a message . . . unavoidable delay. I said you might be back after six.'

And what am I supposed to be doing?'

'Sorting out a student problem. The truth, you see, and nothing but. It's always safest.'

'You spoke to Jo?'

He had a kettle on. already boiling.

'Chrissie rang for me. And there's no need to look like that. She won't blab.'

'You don't know Chrissie.'

'Don't I?'

Clare sat up suddenly.

'It's yours, isn't it?'

'Chrissie's kid? Good God, no. I like my women skinny. But it could be any of half a dozen others. She planned the whole thing at a party last Christmas. I thought it was all a joke, especially when Ellis agreed to be the putative father. He was the only one there sober enough to say it.'

'I give up.'

'Lemon, jasmine, or lapsang souchong?'

'Serve you right if I said P.G. Tips. Lapsang, since you're showing off.'

She accepted the cup, market stall seconds, but fine, delicate, unexpected grace.

'You Catholics ought to approve, surely? Sex for a new life. . . . The trinity of conception?'

'Fornication, though . . . Adultery, too. I don't suppose all the men were single.'

'That does rather complicate things. Chrissie thought of asking Rigby for his opinion, but we persuaded her to let him off.'

'We?'

'Nothing sinister. I told you, it was a crazy party in Chrissie's flat. That's why I thought it was all a joke. Didn't take her long, did it?'

'So you approve?'

'She might be a good mother.'

'The end justifies the means? I wonder why the Jesuits get the blame for that one . . .'

Time to stop talking, simply sit, drinking tea, watching the breeze lift the leaves of a whitebeam in the courtyard. No doubt about it now.

She put down the empty cup.

'I'll ring you tonight.'

'Make it late then. I must work.'

Then walking out, into sunlight, going home, where Jo had a cold supper ready, and the children had moved into a tent in the garden, allegedly for the night. At nine, she stopped for a rest, and to join Jo, mothers carrying one sleeping child each. Daniel, protesting, was brought in too.

'You promised. You mean old cat.'

'I said, when we've bought a new groundsheet.'

'But it isn't raining.'

'Honestly, Daniel, I can't let you. Daddy and I once slept out without a groundsheet, at the end of a long hot day, in a long hot summer. And we woke up, soaked to the skin, from the dew.'

'You and Daddy? Camping?' Then: 'Tell me all about it. Everything.'

Six months, nearly, and not a willing word about David, unless they went to the grave. Now Daniel extracted the whole of that unremembered day; extraordinary, the dam—burst of details, the forest above Pitlochry, hot skin cooling in green darkness, the smell of sweat, of pines, bracken. David, saying, as he bent to pick up a cone that a squirrel had gnawed, one day we'll bring our children here.

'Why?'

'Because it's a child's fairytale forest. Anything might happen. At the very least, a white stag.'

Then the white stag itself, a roebuck, but unusually pale; bleached white in a sunbeam.

David had talked like that?

Later, when Jo had gone home, she sat at her desk, haunted. Surely there had been some warning? She toured the past unkindly, like a surveyor, picking out every fault in a house, and identified a flaw. No . . . more than a flaw. A major structural fault; the lies they had told each other about children. David's children in the forest were a fantasy, no more than the other trappings he expected to have some day. Clare, knowing this, had lied:

'I'm not sure that I want children.'

'Then we won't have any!'

'But you do. . . .'

After that, she had let everything go ahead, the wedding date was already ringed in red, a decision already final, expected. She married because she wanted children, wanted them so badly that she had tried again, after the third miscarriage, and long after David's temporary love.

She pushed the papers away, left the desk, went in first to Lucy, then Daniel, kissing each small perspiring face. Sometimes, Daniel would look exactly like his father, asleep, then she would look again, and find the resemblance gone, not physical, probably more enduring. They would always be David's children. For the first time in months, she tried to say a prayer for David, but couldn't get past his name, couldn't remember what should be said. Ellen Kenyon had suggested, cautiously, a weekly prayer meeting, and had accepted, without rebuke, the polite refusal.

Without death, how would it have ended? Undoubtedly, a petty and wretched divorce . . . better not to think, much better to get back to work instead, direct the hired part of her brain to consider nineteenth-century census evidence, cholera, sewage schemes, family size. She worked, clever, automatic, justly awarding what was deserved, coming back to life when the phone rang at last.

'Quarter to midnight. I'm sorry.'

'It doesn't matter. I was working.'

'People came. I couldn't throw them out any sooner. Clare, could I come round?'

'Now?'

'There's a car I could use. I could be with you in ten minutes.'

'Make it twenty. I don't want you done for speeding.'

'Any minute now, one of them will come down. Daniel always did. I used to wonder how people ever had a second child.'

'Well, children never really want the baby, do they. My sister stuck a nappy pin in my brother.'

'Brother?'

'One of several, but only one girl I suppose she objected to the fuss about a new baby.'

'My mother was very organised about it. Two of each. . . .'

Overhead there were footsteps, the creak of a door.

'Daniel. At least he gets up now. I couldn't face all that again. . . . On call round the clock for no reward. No. . . . I don't mean it. . . . Before you rang, I went up, just to see them asleep.'

'Lullaby . . .'

Closer now. She had offered him, as a guest, the sofa, then knelt beside him, on the rug. Close enough, now, to let her head droop and find support, the way Moira, past sixty, would still lean against Jim.

'Shall we go to bed now?'

He was so sure of her, but then, she had given him reason. . . .

'Not yet. Give Daniel time to go back to sleep.'

'I'm very tired. That's all I want, to sleep with you.'

Memories again; the beginning, when to be apart had been an insult. She had forgotten though, this content, loving stillness. . . . Had never known it, with David?

They had moved, to lie, side by side on the sofa, cuddled together like children. A letter from David:

'Only a single bed, but just about room for two, if they hold on tight.'

All the way from that to separate rooms. She sat up slowly.

'No, we can't sleep here. Come to bed.'

In the bathroom, carelessly together,

'Lend me some toothpaste?'

'Of course. You'll need a brush too.'

Multi-pack, three for the price of two . . . coming in useful. The fourth brush, slotted into the rack, should have been thrown out. David had good teeth, only two fillings, a credit to Betty.

'I think I'll have a shower. . . .'

David, when they first bathed together, had made it horseplay, tickling, squeezing her breasts. She remembered, without pleasure, feeling used, a plaything a toy. Be grateful, though, for the mortice lock he had fitted to their bedroom door.

'Keeps the little buggers out. I don't like the way they mess with things.'

Garwy asked:

'Could I see the children?'

He stayed longest by Lucy's bed, watching the small sleeping figure.

'She's beautiful.'

'So is Daniel.'

'Which one. . . .'

'Don't ask! They ask all the time, who do you love the best? . . . is it me . . . it's not fair. . . .'

In bed, she began to say, remember last time. But that had been utterly different, furtive, almost guilty, in bed with a near stranger. Garwy moved his arm around her.

'Not tonight. I'm bleeding.'

'I wouldn't mind.'

'But I would. Beside, I've got cramps.'

'Is that bad?'

'It isn't good. Not unlike gut-rot. Or early labour.'

'Should you take something?'

'It will be better tomorrow.'

'My mother drank raspberry leaf tea. That's how I knew about periods.'

'My mother could never bring herself to mention the subject. We were instructed by books, left all over the place. "The Virgin Mary had a body just like yours." Ruth wrote, in the margin, "Want a bet?" Then at least there were no more books.'

'It wasn't her fault.'

'Of course not.'

She lay in his arms, thinking, I have no right to this. When she was woken, at seven, by the children, he had already gone.

Summer was taking a day off. Clare, ringing Chrissie's bell, shivered in thin white shirt and jeans, bare feet in sandals.

'Can you spare half an hour?'

The wind chased Chrissie's nightdress up thick legs, only, they were no longer columns of flesh, the floppy thighs surely harder, the folds around her knees diminished, nor was there any trace of varicose veins. Chrissie held the fine lawn down, a spinsterish gesture from the days of routine suspenders, which had lasted so much longer for her, until the advent of tights for the fat.

'Lazy cow, aren't I? Let me go and get dressed.'

More Chrissie this, dressing in secret. Ruth, Jo, most women, would dress indifferently in the presence of other women. But they had nothing to hide, firm breasts, trim waists, everything in control. Ruth, after Daniel's birth, had been curious about stretch marks.

'You're out of luck. I didn't get any.'

Nor with Lucy; a wasted blessing. By then, David would not even touch her, not so much as to hold her hand in labour. Loading the carry-cot into the car, he had once accidentally brushed against her, apologising with deadly courtesy, a stranger, and such contact an offence.

'You disgust me.'

'Why? What have I done?'

'Nothing. . . . Nothing at all.'

Then, coldly,

'I don't feel any affection for you any more.'

Poor David, Clare reflected, sitting on Chrissie's velvet chaise longue . . . re-upholstered, recovered, naturally, by those crafty hands. Poor David, falling out of love so badly. He had a very simple mind, could never be faulted, mastering any technique, doggedly learning formulae, theorems, scales, chords, rules of harmony, passing his Grade VIII at thirteen, staggering under prizes at school, and then, the falling-off, the sad inability to discover just one, original, unlearned truth. After his death, tearless, pitying, she had found his divorce schedule; formal separation, joint custody of the children, the house hers to occupy until Lucy reached sixteen, then to be sold and divided. An allowance, for the children, no mention of herself. Then—pathetic? pathological?—the inventory of everything in the house, down to the children's toys, and 1930's Kilner jars in the garden shed. Even her typewriter was included, because a repair had been paid for out of the joint account, making it now one eighth part his. He had remembered, exactly, the source of each wedding present; bad planning, that, all the sheets coming from her side, and all the towels from his. She pictured him, solemnly packing cases with worn towels, half a tea-set, half the initialled cutlery. And half the electric whisk? Half the washing machine? David had missed nothing, checking the second hand value of all these chattels. She was to be allowed the washing-machine and the fridge-freezer, set against everything small and time-saving. No use then, to mourn for him. She had locked this list away, in a writing case given by Megan for her twenty-first, a reminder, if she were ever tempted to grieve. Later, she had remembered one mistake. The washing-machine was entirely hers. David had not judged it necessary; moreover, it would be her own time she was saving. She had bought it herself, instead of any clothes that year, and had paid all the repair bills too.

Chrissie came back just as her clock struck eleven, and the white mouse, on its chain, ran down. She was dressed as the radiant mother-to-be, Liberty print and fine velvet, entirely beautiful. And this without any of the essentials, knitting grandmas, or even the catalogue expectant father.

'Coffee?'

Clare nodded, watched the familiar preparations. There was something new, a Georgian silver pot, found, black and dented, on a white elephant stall, for thirty pence.

'But, if you knew what it was . . .'

'I paid the asking price.'

'Even so . . .'

Clare looked for her own face, saw only moonlit colour; a pity mirror glass is now so cheap with the instant truth. She watched Chrissie's loving hands lift the pot. This was another detail; the stubby nails had been allowed to grow, the ragged cuticles shaped, nor had these hands suffered marriage. And why was the wretched woman laughing?

'Did you hear about my special delivery?'

She lead the way to the spare bedroom, half ready for a child.

'I worked it all out. Six or seven nappies a day, call it fifty a week. Five thousand should see me through the first couple of years, don't you think? This isn't the lot, of course. The rest are down in the garage. But just imagine, washing five thousand shitty nappies.'

'You forget, I don't need to.'

Chrissie closed the door on her treasure.

'I'm being boring, aren't I?'

'All mothers are.'

'And you didn't come to talk about disposable nappies.'

'Not exactly. David disapproved of them. If I wanted any, for emergencies, I had to buy them myself.'

'I don't believe in David.'

'Just as well. He doesn't exist. David is the contents of a wooden box, the statutory six feet under. David stinks.'

Chrissie poured coffee into pewter mugs, something else old and new.

'One day I intend to have silver.'

'Saves breakages, I suppose. Are you putting me down for a silver christening mug?'

'Possibly. Suppose she wanted to get married in church; I mean I wouldn't want her getting baptised at that age.'

'Baptise, immunise?'

'Twenty, or thereabouts might take it seriously.'

'Twenty takes everything seriously.'

'Garwy?'

'Yes.'

'Do you want to talk?'

'No one else seemed to suit.'

Chrissie finished her coffee, lifted the pot as if to pour a second cup, thought better of it.

'Fair exchange, I suppose. I pestered you with this, didn't I?'

She cradled her belly, proud, secretive. Clare could describe, now, the child's position, sixth months, already head down, though there was still a chance of it shifting back to breech. The swollen uterus was just on the point of change, apple roundness drooping into a pear, as Chrissie entered the third trimester. July, August September, every step of the journey recorded in textbooks, photographed, invaded by ultrasound and laser light, no mystery left. And she had, herself, finished with all that, carrying strange passengers. It was ridiculous to sit here, jealous of Chrissie because she contained a child. Chrissie wouldn't look like the Arnolfini bride when this roundness had become gross, nor, on the delivery table would she smile like this.

'Pull faces like that, and the wind might change.'

'Did I look very bad?'

'Not nice to know.'

'I'm jealous.'

'Well, if it's a baby you want . . .'

She was instantly contrite.

'Sorry, kid. Really, really. . . . I forget . . . we all forget.' Then, changing key, becoming, once more, the main subject, she said:

'I wish, now, that I knew whose it was. Ellis is about the only one it can't be.'

'You're incredible.'

Chrissie became suddenly coy, shifty, innocent.

'Do you really like all that?'

'Didn't you?'

'Not in the least. Is that all there is to it? I came every time, they said, but it didn't seem anything special.'

Clare found herself a cup of lukewarm coffee.

'I had no breakfast. Any food to spare?'

Chrissie pushed the fruitbowl over, richly filled with peaches, apricots, grapes, nectarines, bananas. Clare broke off a cluster of grapes, and discovered she couldn't eat.

'You have got it badly, haven't you?'

'A hopeless case, yes. I love him, he says he loves me.'

'Then why all the fuss? . . . No . . . don't tell me. . . . The stuff the women's weeklies are made of . . . My love for a younger man.'

'More like the smutty Sundays.'

Always, with Chrissie, this easy, gentle silence, sitting together, not even waiting for words. Then:

'Look, kid, what have you got to lose? You've tried marriage, Mr and Mrs, two by two in your nice little house. What was that like?'

Clare was staring straight ahead, out of the window, across the lake. Then she faced Chrissie.

'In the end, nearer to hell than I ever want to be again.'

'So, you've nothing to lose . . .'

'But . . .'

'Shit to that. Shit to whatever you were going to say. And don't look so po-faced. I don't have your fancy touch with words. What are you scared of?'

'Hurting him, losing him. Being hurt myself.'

'Checklist: you're both free, you love, he loves; love-all. So what's the problem?'

'He wants to marry me.'

Chrissie ready, at twelve, for the day's action, was clearing the table, carrying a lacquer tray to the kitchen.

'Are you pregnant?'

'Of course not.'

'Then I really don't see the problem. I suppose I'm not being much help?'

Clare, dismissed, said:

'No. . . . You have helped. But there are still two answers, and they could both be right.'

'I don't see the point. Wasn't the first time bad enough?'

They were in Jo's shiny kitchen, strigging blackcurrants; a heavy crop.

'This is different.'

'Screwing someone half your age? I suppose it must be.'

'That was uncalled for.'

No apology, no comment. They had managed, at last, to suspend a muslin parcel of fruit above Jo's preserving pan, and now watched, satisfied, the slow purple-brown drip of juice.

'I don't see what can go wrong now. Those knots should last forever.'

'Fermentation?'

'Then we call it wine and drink it ourselves. Better than making jam they won't eat. Whatever happened to the sweet tooth?'

'N.H.S. plastic choppers happened. My mother can't understand when Emma won't eat jelly and iced cake.'

'My mother is the same. Maybe it was all that poverty and rationing. I think we can leave this in peace now, don't you.'

Jo closed the kitchen door, flopped into a chair. Out of sight, the children shouted with summer abandon, set free in the garden.

'I once had a vac job in a canning factory in Norfolk.'

'Exciting?'

'Strawberries, peas, plums, in that order, for ten weeks.'

'I spent nearly every vac digging.'

'Archaeology? Yes, of course you would. Factory work pays better.'

'Well, what did you do with the money?'

'I don't know . . . clothes . . . ciggies . . . I could afford forty a day.'

'There you are, then.'

'What a prig you are, Clare. People spend their lives in canning factories.'

'No need. Machines can do those jobs. You should know that.'

'But people need work. . . .'

Clare picked up a neatly folded paper, the Guardian, four days old.

'What a piece of work is man, to spend his life putting peas in a can. Why buy this if you aren't going to read it?'

'I did.'

'Doesn't look like it.'

'I don't mangle everything the way you do.'

'Who's a prig now? And it's time to round up those kids.'

'Where are we going today?'

'I thought the Peak District. They'll like the caves.'

Long vacation, parliament in recess, wasted time, time to waste. Pointless, now, long since all hands to the harvest, but the habit was now statutory, a right. In October, she would become a real, full-time worker again. Meanwhile, there was this gift of three months, for research, for preparing work, one week set aside for recording programmes. Not long, now, before the schools would break up. Time, not before time, for a business deal with Jo, time to bully her into signing a contract. In the end, cunning achieved it, the sly presentation of Government forms to be filled.

'But Lucy will be in school. You can't possibly need me all those hours.'

'No, but this way, you get paid well for what you do. And they pay the difference. And you get free prescriptions. . . .'

'Sharp, aren't you. . . . Alright, give me the pen. Where does lover boy fit in? Do I iron his shirts? No . . . sorry . . .

my mistake. Servants don't ask questions.'

'I could always hire someone else. By the way, I was planning to set up a bankers order.'

'Can't you face handing over grubby notes?'

After that, Clare gave up, knowing that it was too late, that the damage was done, and Jo already out of reach. Moira had managed all this so much better. Her cleaning lady had been Ancoats Irish, scrubbing, sweeping, shining, until the house smelled of lavender and she stank of sweat; the money left, always, in an envelope, behind the statue of the Sacred Heart. Moira had taught the Doherty children, and was paid by the Education Committee, directly into the joint account.

Safely, underground, the children touched stalagmites, stalactites, heard the thunder of underground rivers. Jo said, into the darkness:

'By the way, I forgot to tell you. They've found him. At least, there was a message. Emigrated, would you believe it? Living happily ever after in Sydney. I'm supposed to sue for maintenance.'

'Do you want him back?'

'God . . . no. . . . They can keep him. What I can't understand is you wanting all that again. I wouldn't even *live* with another man.'

Later, Clare suggested tea at a café in Eyam. Jo refused.

'I packed a picnic for the children. You go. . . .'

'I can't sit there on my own.'

'Looks as if you'll have to, doesn't it.'

Clare walked away, but not into the café. Outside a gift shop, a small girl was asking questions.

'Did everybody die? Even the children?'

'Nearly everyone.'

The adults with her were bored, and not teachers, paid to inform.

'Were they very sad, the ones that didn't die?'

The child got no answer, as they headed back to the car, on to some other obligatory stopping place. Daniel had begun to talk about death insistently, anxiously following her, even to the kitchen sink, into the bathroom, like a two year old. Anxiety, the Carter woman had warned; a child who has lost one parent is reasonably afraid of losing the other. Will you die, when will you die, why don't you know? Then:

'Did you know Daddy was going to die?'

'No. How could I? It was an accident.'

'If you die, I'll be all by myself.'

And there the conversation had ended, because there were no more answers. David had been decent enough to die, not survive, crippled and dependent. Jo's husband, Emma's father, had left them deliberately; the cruelty of it was hard to define. Of course Jo was bitter. Merely abandoned, she had to be given money to live on, to keep herself and Emma fed and clothed so they wouldn't be a public disgrace, money allotted from behind a grille, counted out pounds and pence. Clare had seen the Supplementary Benefit budget, remarkable only for what it left out, the space between living and existence.

'Don't you mean subsistence?'

'A much abused word. The subsister grows his own living.'

'And I don't. On the other hand, I can't be allowed to starve.'

It would be better, Clare thought, going into the shop, if Jo could find a way to go home, back to that loving place where she had an identity, and dignity. The price of staying away, on her own, was almost certainly too high.

Ring-a-ring of roses, a pocket full of posies. She bought bunches of dried flowers, a herb pillow, peg dolls, that must all be put away, for Christmas, because Jo would reject any unofficial, ill-timed presents. Then, because she couldn't go back to them empty-handed, she bought a postcard, and five identical ice-lollies, the cheapest they had.

'LIAF? What does that mean?'

'Live in, all found. Shift work, six days on, three off.'

'I'll miss you. I'd thought of spending the summer together.'

'Say that again . . .'

'Why?'

'Because, sometimes, I think you merely tolerate me.'

'You know that isn't true.'

But was it? Lying in bed, alone, Clare tried to remember the first heady months with David. They had fallen in love in the expected way, classic case, acute onset, a crowded room with one face in it. She had known, then, that marriage was likely. By degrees, then, from infatuation to desire, delighted, both, with the other's young body. Impossible, soon, to bear being apart at all, from the first fumbling touch, kiss, the first night together. A perfect couple, said the camera, taking them hand in hand, against walls heavy with wisteria and ivy, on the river, at balls, concerts, London, Venice, Salzburg. A game played in public, lovely Clare, handsome David.

Garwy was no virgin; she wasn't guilty of that. If anything, he had more experience. Definitely not first love, for either of them. Lying alone, she tried to analyse what was going on. Physical pleasure, yes, no doubt about that. She ran her hands lightly over her own naked body, small and slender, white skin, with no scars, small breasts, narrow waist, slim hips, not noticeably the body of an older woman. She would shrivel with age, not grow fat. So far, so good. As for Garwy. . . . He was beautiful; the Donatello body lean and seductive, not innocent. She remembered briefly, the one night with Lewis. No regrets, but for her part, there had never been any question of marriage. To her relief, he had let himself be discarded, had not troubled her again.

David could never stand the way she would play the same record over and over—the B minor Sanctus, the Bach Partita in D for violin solo, Bridge over troubled water, Sergeant Pepper . . . Orfeo. . . . That was the real test . . . *que faro* . . . what is left without him? A great deal . . . the children, for as long as the three of them lived . . . friends, work. . . . As for her family, there was scarcely any need to think about or need it. She wouldn't choose Ruth as a friend, her brothers were strangers, Jim too dear, Moira for ever inaccessible, but all essential, being the source of all identity. And then, this unexpected love.

Unexpected, or simply unnecessary?

Five o'clock, time to get up, the sun already busy, the best time to work on a summer's day. Just as well, then, that Garwy wasn't here. He wasn't ready, yet, to allow her peace. Give it time, and would he come, like Daniel, only when he needed her, they needed each other. She settled down to work, correcting proofs, for her book. The phone rang at ten to eight.

'Did I wake you?'

'Of course not. I've been working since five. Why are you ringing?'

'Only to talk. What are you doing today?'

'Proof reading, cutting the grass, school sports day, then back to work. And you?'

'Work.'

'You didn't even tell me what the job is.'

'Didn't I? Clare attendant, temporary, in a home. Feeding them, changing them, playing a baby games with forty-, fifty-, sixty-year-old babies. No lightweights either, some of them.'

She could see him, slight, strained, in difficulty, exhausted.

'I don't think I could do it.'

'Of course you could. They need so little, like babies.'

'Babies need everything.'

'Exactly. Isn't it much easier to be everything, rather than accept a bit part in someone's life? See you Friday night.'

She went back to her desk, chastened.

Jetsam from the past; no chance of forgetting that life with David. Letters came, still, from distant friends, who didn't expect him to be dead. Bills arrived, for Mr D.C. Carradus. The building society, with less excuse, sent a letter for Mr and Mrs. Clare reminded them, politely enough, that the mortgage had been repaid with the insurance money, after David's death. David was invited to a college dinner in Oxford, to an old boys' reunion at his school, offered a huge discount for ordering encyclopaedias within ten days. So the morning was typical, TV licence reminder, addressed to him, AA membership renewal, two postcards, David, Clare, kids, one letter all her very own, to be opened as a small private treat, because there was no way of guessing the contents, nor did it look in the least sinister. She put it aside, unopened, until the house was clear of children, and the resentful presence of Jo. When, at last, she did allow herself to open it, a different past became her present.

Jo, returning from somewhere, with the children, found Clare still bent over her desk.

'At least stop for some lunch. . . .'

Clare looked up, begrudging the stolen time. Five more lectures, and she would be done. Next year, there would only be revision, minor updating. She remembered a tip from Pakenham—get a few photocopies made, then the yellowing bundle isn't a giveaway.

'In fact, it's nearly four. . . . Why do you never eat when you're working?'

'Because I'm so lazy. If I stopped, I'd never start again. Here, look at this. It came this morning.'

She handed the stiff paper over, knew, before Jo had read half, that this was one mistake she would not be forgiven. Megan had died the week before Christmas, and after posting her card. The law's delay accounted for the rest, except, of course, the extraordinary last gift; extraordinary because Megan might have given it to so many others. But Jo would not see it as mere good fortune, a happy transfer of something Megan herself no longer needed, not a reward, not the mark of any special grace in herself. She read Jo's expression of envy, resentment, and then, disgust with herself, who had inherited nothing, and tried, too late, to salvage something.

'She was my godmother. I used to stay with her, walk on the fells in all weathers. I cried, the first time, because I didn't know there could be anywhere so beautiful. We can take the children . . .'

'I can't afford a holiday, not this year.'

'Oh, for God's sake, Jo! Must we have all this again? Do you want to come or don't you? It's mine . . . there isn't even any rent to pay.'

'Why not take lover boy?'

Let that pass. Clare said, quietly,

'He's working. He might want to come for a few days.'

'Happy families. The children will know what's going on.'

'What is going on?'

'You know very well. This—affair. Nice example for the girls, isn't it. Nice for Daniel, so soon after his father. . . .'

Clare deliberately began to write again. Garwy was coming every weekend now; weekend being a moveable feast, whenever he had three days off. Jo always withdrew until he had gone.

'When does he arrive this time?'

'Friday. Look, do you want a time-table?'

'Emma and I will go to Liverpool then. She's started to ask questions already . . . you know what children are like.'

'Go. . . . I'm not stopping you.'

'Is she afraid it might be catching?'

Garwy had bathed the children, sat, now, with Lucy on his knee, one arm around Daniel, reading Asterix.

'I don't think so. More like jealousy. She's so angry. . . .'

Daniel looked up. 'Who's angry?'

'No-one . . . no-one you know.'

'I do. It's Emma's Mummy. She doesn't like you kissing.'

Clare sat down with them, one tactful cushion a barrier between them, herself, children, lover. There was already quite enough trouble. So far, the children had explored him with interest, discovering whatever they chose.

'It's true, though, isn't it.'

'Perhaps.'

'She's a dumbo. Loony.'

Garwy held the small boy close. 'Do you mind if I kiss your mother?'

'Do you think she's pretty?'

'I'm not going to answer that.'

'Well, she is, so there. Daddy didn't use to kiss her though. Will you get married?'

Clare stiffened, measured the silence, before Garwy answered,

'Would you let me marry her?'

Daniel, assuming, naturally, that it was in his gift replied,

'Of course, if you love her.'

Lucy sat through all this silent, at last whispering,

'And I can be a bridesmaid.'

Then, mercifully, back to Asterix in Britain, and carrying a sleepy Lucy up to bed. Clare thought, making supper for three, that they were getting lost in the script of a soap opera.

Eating Camembert, biting into a roll, Daniel said,

'Emma's mummy says eating cheese at night gives you dreams.'

'She would. Don't you like dreams?'

'Some . . . not ones about going to school with no trousers on. Or the falling dream. But why cheese?'

Garwy explained. 'But you haven't eaten much, and I bet you never get indigestion.'

Clare switched on the nine o'clock news.

'Rotten old news. Is it my bedtime?'

'Yes.'

'Will you read me a story . . .?'

Clare was ready to say no, snap angrily at him, point out that he had already had a story, and thought better of it.

'No, she won't, because she's very tired. I will.'

'Carry me up, over your shoulder, like Daddy.'

Half an hour later, he came down, yawning.

'That child has too many books.'

'Your own fault. Anyway, he can read perfectly well by himself.'

'It's not the same, though, is it. I remember Mam, reading at bedtime, winter nights. It was her best time. . . .'

'Was? Is she dead?'

'Five years ago, the day before my O-level results.'

Clare could hear every filed-sharp word; her own analysis, Chrissie deliberating; mother-figure, naturally, it would be that. She couldn't speak without touching him first, then the inarticulate, helpless, 'I'm sorry'.

'I wanted her to die. It was cancer, and she was right inside the pain. They kept cutting bits of her out, until Dad made them stop.'

Move from pity, compassion, to passion; easily done. Clare shook her head, stood up, locked the door with a key hung above it on a nail.

'David fitted that, of course. He used to practice in here.'

'Thoughtful of him, anyway. Is it dark enough to draw those curtains?'

Clare had withdrawn, sat, now, very tense, hands knotted, staring at her own white knuckles.

'Tell me . . .'

'Nothing to tell.'

'Of course there is.'

'Jo. I feel as if she's watching. Hating. It's odd . . . she never goes near a church, and suddenly she's raging at me, for being with you. As if she owned me. . . . As if she were my conscience.'

'But she isn't here.'

She relaxed, became deliberately wanton.

'Undress me. . . .'

'Asking for it, are you . . .?'

Afterwards, when he was asleep in her arms, she thought, puzzled; but that wasn't love. If I forget everything, how can it be? I loved him reading to Daniel, washing the supper dishes, telling me about his dead mother. That's the love.

Then Garwy was awake again, pulling her close.

'You're insatiable . . .'

'Not complaining, are you?'

'No, but I must get some sleep, and preferably in bed. The children . . .'

'You live for those children.'

He said it without rancour, only amusement, a quick kiss.

'Clare . . . could we have a child?'

She saw, acutely, Megan's body, small and thin on the high hospital bed, Megan, dying childless at eighty-four, and then Chrissie, nearly eight months pregnant now, heavy with life, Daniel, Lucy, newborn, a six-inch foetus, floating in blood.

'Don't cry, my love . . .'

'She was having his child. . . . We told no one. The police helped. They were very discreet. No one knows, not even my family.'

'We?'

'Me, the lawyers, the police. Even his parents didn't know. I buried David the good husband and father, you see.

Requiem aeternam dona ei. . . . Yes, I would like to have your child.'

'I was so afraid you would say no.'

Family life, domesticity, Saturday morning whirl round the town, changing books, buying school uniform for Lucy, pushing a cart around Sainsbury's, this is life, detail on detail, man, woman and children. She had tried to leave him behind.

'The shops are hell on Saturdays.'

'All the more reason for me to come and help.'

'The grass needs cutting.'

'And how many inches will it grow this morning? You don't want to be seen with me, do you?'

'It isn't that.'

'Then what is it?'

'All right, suppose we are seen?'

'Christ!'

Pre-departure check, handbag, purse, car keys, dry-cleaner's ticket, crabbed age and youth should not make an exhibition of themselves.

She said, peevishly,

'I wish you wouldn't say that.'

'Thou shalt not take the name of the Lord thy God in vain.'

'Precisely . . . at least, not in front of the children.'

'Original, this morning, aren't you. Besides, they're out in the garden.'

'I've tried to stop swearing since Daniel was about ten months old.'

'Why?'

He knocked over a beaker of milk and said, Oh, shit.'

Arms around her now, laughter, impossible to resist.

'No more swearing then. But I refuse to stay hidden. Do you love me?'

'Yes.'

'Say it. . . .'

'I love you, I love you, I love you . . .'

She let him drive to town. The children, in the back, squabbled, because they always did, from habit, without lasting malice.

'Stop that row, or I'll hang you by the feet from the town hall clock.'

'You wouldn't, would you?'

Lucy squealed with delight.

'If you do I'll bite you.'

'She bit mum's tit when she was a baby.'

Multi-storey car park, again, the man driving, the woman, as she should, handing money from the passenger seat, and up to the top, because everywhere else was full, and not merely to please the children.

'I never did that before.'

'What?'

'Climb right to the top, like a helter-skelter.'

'I'll drive down.'

'You still don't trust me, do you.'

The children studied bright, misshapen fruit, as if the mangoes, yams, plantains and nameless things were reptiles, that would suddenly declare themselves alive. Purse-lipped women scrabbled in carts full of dented cans, split flour bags, broken packets, bruised fruit, life's leftovers. David always wanted to get things cheap. Someone had broken a bottle of sweet sherry, the scent of it combined with the reek of antiseptic, detergent, as the matter was dealt with, sticking plaster, sympathy, and a replacement bottle.

Indulgent, she let the children choose. Moira wouldn't approve, still less Jim, but what use was it, buying what they would never eat? Remember the way food would lie, leaden, undigested, remember heaving up the boiled egg they had forced her to eat, shivering in the outside loo, rather than the disgrace of being sick in the house. In the worst nightmares I am a child again.

Lucy had become very quiet, a new development, this. Fear of starting school next month? She gripped Clare hard.

'Tighter.'

'Isn't this tight enough?'

'No, *tighter*. I might lose you.'

Lucy was right, better not to risk what had nearly been lost. Locked in the queue, she bent down swiftly, to kiss the child. Imagine being old, alone, never touching lips. But it shoud have been done out of Daniel's sight.

'Kiss, kiss, kiss. Kiss anyone, never me.'

'Don't be so stupid. For Heaven's sake, Daniel, you're nearly eight.'

'How old's he, then? He isn't as old as you, is he? I thought the lady had to be the youngest.'

'Younger, not youngest. And you thought wrong.'

Wicked little summer wind, chasing plane-leaves across the precinct. Lucy gathered them.

'Autumn. It's autumn, isn't it?'

Garwy took her on his knee, sitting on a bench, someone's memorial.

'Not quite. Next month, autumn begins. I like it best of all.'

Daniel spoke through a mouthful of crisps.

'So do I. Conkers, and blackberries, and fireworks. Jumping into leaves . . . throwing them at Lucy.'

'Rose-hips, and silver frosts.'

Clare joined in:

'Halloween, treacle toffee, duck-apple, chestnut sellers, the clocks going back.'

'Our birthdays. We were both born on Fridays.'

'So was I.'

'Friday's child is loving and giving. It said that on Lucy's bib. Are you?'

'I don't know.'

Did every family live like this? Had she and David been the odd ones out, all the time? She was full of distrust, and sick fear, the invisible worm, eating away from within. Sitting with them, apart, she told herself, coldly, this won't last, I will not be happy for long, because my life is not like that. A little girl in convent serge repeated:

'God made me to know Him, love Him and serve Him in this world, and to be happy with Him forever in the next.' Rigby had snapped, one angry sermon, 'That I simply can't accept; what kind of a father breeds children to serve him, dangling a carrot of happiness, sometime, never?' Too late, the damage had been done, mind-scarred, like a twisted sapling, the child had grown up knowing better: don't trust happiness, it isn't for you.

But if she abdicated, let someone else take control, she

couldn't be entirely responsible for the consequences. Walking back, an observer would have seen the male in command, directing them. Clare carried the bright orange bag, full of next term's clothes.

'Grey children. Why grey, of all the unchildlike colours?'

'Because it's the one colour they wouldn't choose? And tradition, bastard tradition. The English grey flannel prep school child handed down in state polyester. Uniforms frighten me.'

'And yet you bought all this stuff for your rainbow daughter?'

'Lucy in the sky?'

'Don't. . . . No mourning. She's alive. It didn't happen.'

But David's death was real. What price that life of married contempt? The body that said, don't touch, you are not wanted, not any more. Driving home, she said,

'About the cottage . . . Jo refuses to come. You're free all September, aren't you?'

'Yes, but . . .'

She studied his face, hunting for a lie, but there was nothing, nothing rehearsed.

'Only, I was already going up there, climbing in the Langdalcs.'

Hide the resentment, forget, no . . . *remember*, because it needs to be remembered, cancelling all plans, cutting out all former friends, because of David.

'Jo's being completely unreasonable. Says she can't afford it.'

'Depends what she can't afford. We don't want to be your property, you know.'

Clare parked, badly, a foot from the kerb, tried to right herself, fighting tears.

'Let me.'

She carried shopping up to the porch, hating the car for obeying him so neatly. Lucy staggered along, half-dragging the bag that held blouses, grey pinafore, cardigan, socks, and a pullover for Daniel. They both stared at her, full of pity.

He was drawing the curtains on a blue velvet sky.

'Why didn't you wake me?'

'Didn't seem a good idea, the mood you were in. You've been working too hard.'

'Where are the children?'

'Asleep . . . in bed anyway, what more do you want?'

'You meant all that, didn't you?'

The quarrel had been vicious, armed with all the weapons designed to assault every weak point.

'I hated you, this afternoon.'

'For defending Jo? Clare, I know—a little—what happens to women like Jo. Would you like to sit with a stranger, showing her your bank statements, your unpaid bills, your child's piggy bank savings? Prowling round your house, looking for signs of a man, reclaiming your benefit book, questioning neighbours . . .'

'I'd hang pyjamas out for the neighbours to see, and leave a razor in the bathroom.'

'And see your children go hungry? Clare, where I come from, they took a woman's book away for a month, while they made enquiries. Some bloody neighbour reported a car outside the door every day. The doctor's car—because the kids were ill.'

'You don't understand. She can be free of all that.'

'As your servant? Fine, go ahead, but don't pretend you can have her as a friend.'

The casual rebuke, that evening with Lewis;

'She's not my wife, you know.'

'You're right, of course.'

And knowing it, too, lying on his back with the confidence, the appalling arrogance of youth. Once, she had been this young, and had known everything.

'If I were Jo, I'd get right away from this place, go and find out who I really am, before turning into a piece in someone else's game. you women, you must have someone to pity. You should be glad she has enough fight left to be angry.'

Right again? She threw a cushion at him.

'Brat! You've no right to know so much.'

The cushion came back, and in the scuffle she was once more in his arms, not wanting to be anywhere else. The solution might not exist, nor any answers at all.

'Why do you know so much?'

'I don't. . . .'

Clare, at peace, for once, wanted to stop fighting or questioning. It occurred to her, almost as if she hadn't noticed before, that Garwy might have reasons of his own. She had acquired too much of the teacher's habit; always making the running, starting every conversation. It ws time to be still, and listen more.

'Dad had a bad time, when my mother died. Five kids, and the social services asking, "Manage on this, can you?" I stopped being young. . . . There wasn't really any option. It was the summer after O-levels.'

'I wondered, just how you knew all that. . . .'

She was stroking his hair, seeing, for the first time, grey, where it should only be black. Garwy smiled up at her.

'Found my five grey hairs? Ancestry, my love, not anguish. We survived. . . . And Da's found himself a new wife. The kids don't need big brother anymore. Clare no longer wanted explanations. They would come, perhaps.

'So you're free. . . .'

'If I choose to be, yes.'

Define happiness—easier to write the whole dictionary. Define beauty? Clare stood by the deepest window, slowly unpacking clothes for summer's end, old shirts, light sweaters. The children were somewhere near, laughter under gold and silver birches, by the waterfall. Take the scene apart, give each a name and a number; why should the sum be beauty? Lichens on grey stone, and crusted on dead branches, the bronze of dying bracken, the season's alchemy of green into gold. Why look up to those particular jagged peaks, and call them beautiful, one below the other, steps on a kitchen stool? No point, then, in trying definitions; this is beauty, and we are part of it; better to accept with grace.

Daniel lay flat, not moving, one hand alive in the water. Don't move, don't break this spell, and never be forgiven.

'Got him!'

Clare knelt, with Lucy, to admire the poor thrashing body, the flapping gills red and raw.

'Why is he brown on top, and spotted, and then silver?'

'Shall I kill him? Bang him on the head?'

She saw the child reach for a stone, then the arching leap to freedom.

'Anyway, I didn't really want to kill him. I don't like making things dead.'

'But you eat meat. Things have to be killed for you to eat meat.'

'Then I won't, not any more. I don't even like meat.'

'Not even sausages?'

The confidence of childhood, able to reject, absolutely.

'No.'

They helped her gather sticks for the log fire, stood with her to watch the sun fall. The bats were only an echo of movement, sight too slow to see all of it.

'Why do they move so fast?'

Lucy clung to her, terrified,

'Will they suck our blood?'

'No, not this kind. Come on, time to go in. Time for bed, really.'

'But we're on holiday! You promised!'

They did, at last, agree to be led upstairs, to sleep in a shared room, though the cottage had three bedrooms.

'Someone else could come too. Why didn't Emma and her mummy want to come?'

'They've gone on holiday with Emma's grandma.'

'Oh . . . I thought maybe they didn't want to be friends.'

'Go to sleep.'

She left them, almost afraid to walk back through the cottage alone. But it was only darkness, banished with one flick of a switch, nothing to fear; Megan had bought modern comfort to the four-hundred-years-old cottage.

'When you come next holidays, all this mess will be over. No ghosts, I promise. All that business of lights going out and strange stains on the walls was just old fuses and rising damp.'

That year when Lucy was a baby, Megan had lent Clare the cottage, for the space of her own eightieth birthday holiday,

Rome, Venice, Naples, Ravenna. David had said:

'Go—take the kids, do what you like. Look, do you want me to spell it out?'

David's ghost was hardly likely to come here, of all places. She watched the old and flickering television until closedown, and went up to bed, unafraid.

'When I grow up,' Daniel said, breaking the image of mountains with one skimming pebble, 'I'll come back and stay here for ever and ever.'

'But you'll have to have a job.'

'No, I'll think of something else to be. I'll only be alive once, won't I? I don't count going to heaven. Anyway, this is better than heaven. It's the most beautiful place in the world.'

Lucy, purple to the elbow, ate blackberries. She joined Daniel on the shore, tried, and failed to make a pebble dance, watched with envy as a water-skier ripped past.

'But I like boats best, and swans. If I were a bird, I'd be a swan.'

'Fat and greedy, gobbling bread. And they have ugly feet. I'd be an eagle, high up in the mountains.'

Clare surprised herself, the flat pebble skipping four times before sinking.

'You'd have to eat meat then.'

'Of course I would. And I'd grab baby lambs in my fierce . . . fierce . . .'

'Talons?'

'Yes. Tear off their skin, and feed my babies, and my wife . . . like on that programme.'

The third day, there was a postcard, perversely, a view of the Pavilion, at Brighton.

'Never again. Climbing, that is. I'd like to die in my bed after all. See you Thursday.'

That gave her two more days, an idyll for three, first and last summer alone with her children. One, given entirely to the lake, in a hired boat.

'When's Garwy coming?'

'Tomorrow.'

'Good. He promised to take me over the crags. You can come too if you like. Not Lucy, she's a baby.'

'Rubbish. You climbed Scafell when you weren't even four . . .'

One more day. Postcard photographers must load their cameras at dawn, on days like this, the sky unnaturally blue, above and behind carved mountains. They bought a new loaf simply to feed ducks. A day of waiting, a day to be entirely sure of this life. In the afternoon, they climbed the smallest, laziest mountain, so slowly that dusk overtook them. Daniel, trusted with the torch, led the way, a shadow, sure-footed. The descent was a textbook classic, from heather and bare limestone, then birch, blackthorn, stunted oak, down into planted larches, lined up like children in a school yard. The children slowed down, made sure she was close.

Lucy stopped, listening.

'There might be a fox . . .'

'Of course . . . there are foxes. And snakes.'

The fox itself was quick, handsome, unexpected, elegant, in black stockings, then lost in darkness.

'Was it a real one?'

'Of course, stupid.'

'Was it the one in my story?'

Daniel was scornful. 'Isn't she stupid, thinking a story's real.'

Clare loathed him. It was all David, this petty insistence on truth.

'I thought it would be red, all over, but it had black socks, like a Siamese cat. And I thought they were bigger.'

She held them both by the hand, not before time. Daniel was already excluding himself, wrenching away, racked with jealousy.

Half a mile more, and they were back on the road, walking through the evening village, across the bridge, past a pub already empty of summer visitors.

'Which way shall we go? Along the road, or by the old railway?'

'Railway!'

Daniel was a dreaming child again, a train, hooting as he took the bends. Lucy was all his coaches, the passengers, the guard. In the forest, it was the children who were afraid of shadows. Clare had known there was nothing to hurt them.

So why was she haunted, walking along this track? David was at her side, walking along a steep banked Devon lane, their son on his back, six months old, nibbling his father's ear.

'I want to resign. We'll sell the house, buy a smallholding, rent something.'

'But you can't.'

'I can. I refuse to spend the rest of my life counting up other people's money.'

She had taken his hand, loving wife, reasoning, wait, not now. No-one in their right mind gives up a secure job now. And it had been all right, he had seen sense. A year or two later even he had, shrewdly put his job first, set his sights on the next step, and then another, living an entirely separate life, being someone else.

No light from the cottage window meant that he hadn't arrived. Perhaps, now, he wouldn't come till morning.

'Race you . . .'

'First the worst . . .'

Opening the cottage door, letting the children in, she thought, this is all I want, this is my life. On the mat, there was another postcard.

> We caught a pike. Ate it, too. I wonder if it was a good idea, consuming all that malevolence. Sorry, won't see you till Friday.
>
> P.S. Tell Daniel I saved some pike's teeth for him.

After supper, she cleared the table, washed up. Five minutes, and it was all done. Why had David made such an issue of this? Refusing ever to wash so much as a tea-cup? David had thought in straight lines, making decisions, X should pay Y in tax, I do not love my wife. Wiping down the draining board, well-trained housewife, she remembered one decision of his, overiding her doubts.

'I want to marry you.' And, in a letter: 'You need looking after. I intend to devote my life to it.'

My fault, then, for being someone else, not who he thought I was at all. Mistake of person, and grounds for annulment. I was never David's wife.

In the morning, all her anger had gone. They would have one last day together, and she would know exactly who she was;

their mother, her unlikely lover out of view. She remembered a rare conversation with Ruth, about one of her books. The publishers had asked her to eliminate one character. Ruth had written, deliberately, about twins; they demanded one child. In the re-writing Ruth—it being only her second book—had done exactly as they asked, but the child was still there.

'She wouldn't go away. I did my best, and it seemed to satisfy them, but she simply refused to go.'

Self-deceit, then, pretending he could so easily be forgotten, impossible to know who she might be now, only as David's widow. Walking out of the cottage, she thought the day had, already, a clear precision about it, a hint of chill, all the better for thinking.

Halfway to the village, they stopped to lean over a wall, watching red hens scratch in muddy grass, gaggles of womenfolk, talking about nothing. There were two cocks, one evidently very young, comb and wattle bright, every feather glossy. The older bird, high on his real dunghill, crowed feebly as the young one darted forward, jabbing hard with his yellow beak, shouting in triumph.

Daniel was impatient to move on.

'They're only playing "I'm the king of the castle".'

Lucy had remembered a promise made the day they arrived; she could buy, at the newsagents, a tiny doll in a matchwood bed, with money Moira and Jim had given, for this holiday.

The shop had already sold out of both *The Times* and *Guardian*. Clare settled for the local paper, began to read it as they left the shop. Students in death fall.

'I thought you were dead. I rang the hospital, and they said yes, Jones, can you come to identify? I drove there with the children, and it was someone else.'

She had to crush his hand, inflict pain, to prove he was there, alive, not the broken body from the mortuary.

'Poor love. I should have come sooner. I didn't even see the paper. When you weren't here, I thought you were furious with me.'

'I was, on the way back. He could almost have been you.'

'Someone else's son.'

The cottage was the right place to be now, inside walls two and three feet thick, away from falling rain, and the first screaming gales of autumn.

'Pathetic fallacy.' He tossed a damp log onto the fire. It hissed, and presently wheezed out blue smoke. 'Isn't that what it's called, the weather acting up in sympathy? Kids asleep?'

She was kneeling before the fire, drugged a little by the smoke, fixed by the shifting flames, and entirely willing now to yield to emotion and instinct.

'Asleep, yes.'

'I won't leave you alone again.'

The fireback had buckled and re-formed in the heat of unnumbered fires, but the date of its making, 1581, was still legible. Another four centuries, and who would care about here and now; the actions of one woman, or man. . . . She stood up, gathering plates, mugs, bowls, the litter of their supper, and walked as if on eggshells, to the kitchen. He followed, stood beside her at the sink, hands on her shoulders. He watched as the water splayed across the back of a spoon, watched the swish of detergent bubbles. She handed him things to be dried.

'Did you know Chrissie Hallam and Lewis are getting married?'

'No . . . I'm glad, though.'

'I saw them when I picked up some books, on my way here. Christmas, they said, give her time to get over the birth.'

Chrissie and James? She considered, remembered. Yes, that seemed right, even if James was not the father of this one. They'd be good together.

The job was done, the kitchen, that was still so much Megan's, restored to order, and very cold. They returned to the fireside. In their absence, the flames had been greedy, the fire being little more than embers. Garwy picked up another log, dry, silvered with lichen.

'As the man said . . . better to marry . . .'

Clare corrected him.

'Wouldn't it be easier not to marry?'

He wasn't touching her. The answer was unhampered by contact, distracting touch.

'All the more reason, surely, Clare? I knew, really, that day in the hospital. Leaving you then was one of the hardest things I've ever done. Does it really matter to us what anyone else thinks?'

Clare, very deliberately, took his right hand. It was the right hand you took, she remembered.

'It matters, but not enough. Finally . . . not enough.'

Dear Reader,

You have been reading a Piatkus Paperback, one of a new range of novels which we hope will offer you what you want – an enjoyable, well-written story with realistic characters which leaves you feeling good at the end (though we don't promise that it will always be a happy one).

If you have enjoyed this book, please recommend it to your friends and look out for our distinctive pink, grey and cream covers in your local bookshop. If you don't see them, please ask the bookseller to order them for you.

Among other novels we are publishing at the moment are *Sisters* by Debby Mayer, the story of an independent young woman who unexpectedly finds herself guardian to her eight year old half-sister, *To the Tenth Generation* by Rita Kashner, a powerful novel about a mother and son set in Israel, and *An Honest Woman* by Anne Christie, about the breakdown of a modern marriage.

We would love to hear from you with comments about our new series and if you would like to be put on our mailing list please send a large stamped addressed envelope to

Piatkus Paperbacks
5 Windmill Street
London W1P 1HF

Thank you for reading us.

Judy Piatkus